Wizar

The Five King

Toby Neighbors

Published by Mythic Adventure Publishing
2483 Partridge Loop, Post Falls, ID, 83854 USA

Wizard Rising

ISBN-13: 978-0615642864 (Mythic Adventure Publishers)
ISBN-10: 0615642861

For more information contact Mythic Adventure Publishing at:
MythicPublisher@yahoo.com

Cover design by Camille Denae

Copy Editing by Esther Bernstein

Other Books By Toby Neighbors

Third Prince
Royal Destiny
The Other Side
Magic Awakening

Dedication:
To my sons, Samuel, Andrew, and Thomas.
I love going on great adventures with you guys,
And I can't wait to see what you do with your incredible lives.

Prologue

"I sense a blossom opening," said the Wizard.

He wasn't talking about a flower.

"We have felt it," said another Wizard. This man was younger, although still well along in years.

"The power is rare," declared the first Wizard, whose face was hidden beneath the dark hood of his robe.

"Yes, much like your own."

"We must begin our search," said the first Wizard, who was obviously the master.

"The child was probably only just born," said the younger Wizard.

"Yes, but it would be best to find this child before he discovers his power. We need to train him in his early years to ensure he will never betray us."

"It could be a girl," said the second Wizard.

"Yes, and if so we must destroy her."

The second Wizard bowed his head. Wars had been fought over women, kingdoms brought to utter ruin. A woman with power could destroy the Torr, and so if this new sense of magic was found in a girl, she would be killed.

The first Wizard noticed his companion's hesitation and said, "Do not forget your own loyalty, Branock. The Torr must not be divided over senseless moral concerns."

"Yes, Master."

"In time we will rule the Five Kingdoms of Emporia and our power will be unstoppable."

"You are right, of course," said Branock.

"Now, begin your search. This new one must be found and dealt with or we may have to wait another lifetime to secure our hold on Emporia."

The Wizard Branock bowed and left the room. The first Wizard moved to the window and looked out over the city far below. He could see the King's palace and the garrison which represented the kingdom's power. Osla was the largest and most influential of the Five Kingdoms. The Wizard looking down from the Torr stronghold could have reached out and destroyed the garrison. He controlled such power and could have caused the roof to cave in or the walls to topple, but such a feat would turn the populace against him. He had spent years convincing the people that the Wizards of the Torr served to protect the Five Kingdoms. In reality, he had merely consolidated his power and destroyed any Wizard who would oppose him. And he knew that the people scurrying about their lives like ants in the dust below needed their illusions of power, so if he destroyed their army they would have no security and the other kingdoms would turn against him. He could defeat them, he was confident of that. His power, along with the power of the other three Wizards of the Torr, could destroy the combined might of the Five Kingdoms, but he had no wish to rule over a land of anarchy. When he took his place as High King of Emporia, he wanted peace and stability. And now, when they were so close, the only thing that stood on the horizon between him and his destiny was the strange bloom of power.

Wizards could sense the magic in other people. If the person was close enough, they could isolate that power, feel it approach or move away. When the members of the Torr were together their power overlapped and allowed them to sense magic at great distances. This new spark of magic was rare in its brightness. The Wizards couldn't locate the bloom of power, but they could feel it, as if the clouds had parted, and although they couldn't see the sun, the light would shine through. At first that warmth and brightness was pleasant, even exciting, but the Master Wizard knew that before long, just like the sunlight, that feeling would turn to discomfort and eventually to pain. The Master knew that if this powerful person, whoever it was, continued to grow in strength, he or she could eventually challenge the power of the Torr. He would not let that happen. On the other hand, if this new bloom of magic, this flower in a field of grass, could be added to the Torr, then the Master would have his executioner, a Wizard loyal only to him with the power to keep the other Wizards in line and perhaps even allow the Torr to extend their power.

The Master Wizard turned from the window and sat down at the desk which occupied the center of the room. The walls were lined with thick books on everything from anatomy to astronomy. There were treasures from each of the Five Kingdoms and from across the oceans. Some of the books were so old that only the Master's magic held them together. They represented his power which was vast, and as he looked at them, he saw his dream, his destiny, to line up the people of the Five Kingdoms around him like the books, all in their proper place, all serving him, the Master of the Torr.

Chapter 1

Zollin sat on the post that was to be the corner support for the new Inn that was being built in Tranaugh Shire. He wasn't very good at carpentry and being so high up in the air made him dizzy. The Inn was to be a two-story building, one of the biggest in town. Quinn, Zollin's father, rarely asked Zollin for help, but a two-story building needed multiple hands, and so Zollin sat atop the post, waiting for his father's apprentice, Mansel, to hand up the connecting beam.

"Here you go," said Mansel as he hefted a stout oak log that had been cut and shaped into a square beam.

"I just hold it?" Zollin asked.

"That's right, son," came his father's gruff voice, and Zollin thought he detected a note of frustration in it. Zollin had been his father's apprentice for five years, but he just wasn't skilled with his hands. Nor was he strong enough to lift the heavy beams, which would have made the job pass more quickly. Instead, he would hold the beam while Mansel lifted and raised the far end up to his father.

"It's going to be heavy, but whatever you do, don't drop it," his father instructed. "If it splits, it'll have to be milled again and we can't afford to waste good timber."

Zollin nodded. He hated the pressure of being put in such a position. He had stopped wondering why he had to work with his father. Every man in the village had to earn a living. Most sons learned their father's trade, and at 16 years old Zollin should have been able to work on his own, but as hard as he tried, Zollin just wasn't a good carpenter. Mansel was two years older than Zollin, and he had been Quinn's apprentice for three years. He was the youngest of a large family and although his father was a master tanner, Mansel's four older brothers were already working in the tannery and so his father had found another profession for him.

"I've got it," Zollin said as he gripped the rough timber beam.

"Brace yourself," his father said.

Zollin wrapped his legs around the post he was sitting on and strained to hold the beam as Mansel lifted it.

"Uuhhhggg," Zollin grunted, straining to hold the unruly beam.

"Steady, Zollin!" his father barked.

Zollin felt a stab of resentment but ignored it. He was determined not to drop the beam.

Mansel was helping to hold the beam steady and Quinn, with a rope around the beam, was pulling it up. Once the beam was high enough, Quinn stepped on a long iron spike he had hammered into the post he was sitting on opposite Zollin. He set the beam on the post and looked at his son.

This was the moment Zollin had been dreading. He would have to stand on his own spike and place his end of the beam on the post. Then, once the log was in place, he would need to swing around and sit on the beam so that he could secure it by nailing it to the post with two of the long iron spikes. It was a difficult maneuver for Zollin, who preferred to keep both feet on the ground. But the beam's weight helped to steady him and he managed to set the big oak timber on the post without much fuss. He then sat on the beam and threw his leg over, turning as he did so that he faced away from his father, who was already hammering at his own spike with steady blows that vibrated through the beam and up Zollin's rigid spine.

Now that he was in place, all he needed to do was to nail in the spikes. He looked for his hammer and nail bag. It was hanging from the spike by his foot. He should have retrieved it before situating himself on the beam but it was too late now. As he leaned down for it he could see Mansel smiling up at him, smirking actually. And after a joint-stretching second he knew why – the bag was too low to pull off the spike. He would have to turn back around and get on the spike again to get it. He was so angry he wanted to scream. It wasn't his fault he wasn't any good at carpentry. He assumed he was more like his mother than his father, although he had never known her. She had died while giving birth and Zollin didn't even know what she looked like.

He reached one more time, straining with all his might. The strap was so close, but he couldn't get his finger under it. In his mind he could see his finger wiggling beneath the strap but the bag was too heavy and only tore at his fingernail. Come on, he thought to himself as he willed the bag to move. And suddenly it did.

The strap lifted about a finger's breadth off the spike. For an instant Zollin didn't move. He just sat there staring at the nail bag. Then, something heavy was pulling at his mind and the strap started to quiver. The movement propelled Zollin into action and he slipped his fingers under the strap as the bag's weight pulled his arm. And then, with a gentle sway he felt himself starting to fall. His heart leapt in his chest as his left arm wrapped around the roughly hewn beam to steady himself. He lifted the bag and waited a moment to let his heart settle back into a normal rhythm. He still hadn't moved when his father shouted at him.

"Zollin, get those spikes nailed down, we haven't got all day."

"Yes sir!" Zollin called back over his shoulder. He was glad that his father couldn't see his face and he deliberately avoided looking at Mansel. He wiped the sweat that had suddenly sprung out on his forehead and began nailing the spike through the wood. Yet even as his arm and shoulder moved, even as he felt the wood shake as if in pain from the spike smashing through its flesh, all he could think about was how he had moved the nail bag. It was magic, there was no doubt, and in that moment something connected within him, something strong that was at the core of his being, as if it had always been there and now suddenly it had come into alignment. And the magic began to flow out.

The rest of the day progressed more easily, and they had just finished the heavy framing as the sun began to set. The Inn was on the edge of town, just down the hard-packed street from a stable where several of the more wealthy citizens kept horses. Zollin's home, the house his father had built for his mother, was just outside of town. Quinn was giving Mansel instructions for the morning as Zollin started for home. He usually had a fire going by the time his father arrived. Quinn was on the town Council and habitually stopped at several houses at the end of the day to visit with friends and people who wanted to talk. Zollin made his way up the small hill that their house was built on and looked at the wood pile. It was getting low and his father would want him to cut more soon. He gathered enough for a cooking fire and headed inside.

The house had a low ceiling and was hot inside. There were big windows that were shuttered with thick pine wood planks set on leather hinges. Zollin pushed them open to let the rapidly cooling evening air in. The fireplace was getting thick with ash and Zollin knew his father would want him to clean that too. He hated the little chores his father gave him, even though he knew they were necessary. He felt resentment rising up in his chest like a river overflowing its banks during flood season.

Blast the stupid ash, he thought vehemently to himself. And suddenly, the ash burst into flame. The heat and light rose up so quickly before him that Zollin fell back onto the sturdy wooden table his father had built in the middle of the small kitchen. The flames flashed and crackled and then just as suddenly as they had appeared, they winked out.

Zollin looked at the fireplace, but it was too dark to see anything, especially after his eyes had been dazzled by the light of the fire. He lit a candle and looked into the hearth. It was empty, and not even a trace of ash remained. Zollin was so surprised by what had happened that he took no notice of his heart racing and the stifling sense of fatigue that settled in on him like a heavy quilt around his shoulders.

How did I do that? he thought to himself. There was no doubt that he had caused the flames to burn up the ash, just as he had somehow summoned the nail bag to rise up off the spike. He decided to try an experiment. He placed the candle on the counter and then placed an apple beside it. He reached his hand out toward the apple but nothing happened. He concentrated, visualizing the apple moving into his hand. Suddenly there was a rush of something hot inside his body like wind on a summer day, and the apple leapt into his hand. This time he felt the sag of spent energy, felt the heaviness of his arms and the rapid beating of his heart. He was suddenly very thirsty and sat on a stool to eat the apple. It was cool and sweet and he sucked the juice from the meat as he chomped into the fruit.

After a few minutes he began to feel better. He made supper and wondered if he should risk telling his father. Quinn was a good man. He was kind and a very hard worker. Zollin had never seen his father shirk a task, and he had scolded his son for such behavior often. Still, Zollin didn't feel that this was something his father would approve of. He decided to keep his newfound ability a secret.

Chapter 2

The construction of the new Inn kept Quinn and his apprentices busy all week, and it wasn't until week's end that Zollin really had a chance to be alone. He slipped off into the woods to a place with a large, mossy boulder where he had often played as a child and began to experiment. All week in the back of his mind he had wondered more about the fireplace and the ash that caught fire. Moving things was very helpful, but if he could conjure fire, could he conjure other things?

It was early summer and the ground was clear of leaves, but there were plenty of dry twigs, and after arranging them for a small fire, Zollin pictured the twigs ablaze in his mind. Nothing happened, and he focused harder. "Blast the twigs!" he said out loud, mimicking what he had said about the ash. The twigs flew apart, burning so brightly and hot that they were consumed before they touched the ground where they crumbled into cinders. Zollin watched in surprise and sudden fatigue as the little bits of glowing red ash slowly faded.

After a bit of rest, he gathered another pile of dry wood together. He focused his mind on a small tongue of flame and thin wisp of smoke rising from the pile. "Burn!" he ordered the wood and saw a yellow flame spring to life. The dry wood and straw caught immediately and smoke began to rise. After a moment, the small pile of wood was a brightly glowing fire. Zollin smiled and sat back. He was tired, but the small controlled fire was not nearly as exhausting as blasting the wood apart. He had packed fruit, dried meat and bread into his satchel, enough for several meals. He had felt better after eating that first night, and so he took some of the bread and tore a piece off and stuffed it into his mouth. The bread was dry and soon he was thirsty. He stood and walked down toward a stream that ran through the woods nearby. The water was clear and cold. He cupped his hands together, scooped up some water and then slurped the cool, refreshing liquid. Then a thought occurred to him and he pictured a small wooden cup in his hand and said, "Cup!"

Nothing happened. He tried several more times in different ways, and although he could not conjure a cup from thin air, he could feel a swirl of heat inside his chest as he tried. After a while he decided to move objects again, and spent the rest of the afternoon making leaves dance in the air before him. He could not sustain the magic long, only for a few minutes at a time before exhaustion overcame him. It reminded him of hammering. At first driving iron into wood with a hammer seemed like fun, but soon the swinging of the heavy tool and the jarring impact over and over became exhausting.

Over the next several weeks, he was able to move small objects and control fire proficiently. He practiced as often as he could get alone, and although he was still skinny and not as strong as Mansel, he felt the magic growing within him. Each day the small tricks he performed took less and less toll on him physically.

It was midsummer when he discovered the willow tree in a clearing near the little stream where he had rested that first day. He had been walking through the woods and decided to follow the stream in hopes of finding a fish to see if he could lift it from the water. But as he grew closer to the tree, he felt a sense of something, the way a large bonfire will glow into the night sky to be seen from far away. Zollin moved forward, curious as to what could make him feel this way. It wasn't a bad feeling; in fact he was drawn to whatever it was, the same way a person's eyes are drawn to light in a dark room. Zollin moved into the clearing and saw the tree but assumed the feeling was still further ahead. The tree was on the opposite side of the stream from him and he walked past it, but as he did, he felt the sense lessening. He turned back and crossed the stream. The sense grew as he approached the tree and he started to look into the woods beyond but realized that the feeling was coming from the tree.

The willow was large, its branches full of leaves were hanging down, concealing the trunk of the tree. Zollin realized that anything could be hiding under the hanging limbs. Still, he didn't feel a sense of dread or reservation, so he reached out to pull back the slender boughs. As soon as his hand touched the first leaf he felt a thrill. He jerked his hand back surprised, but realized the feeling that had shot through his arm had connected with the swirling sense of magic – at least Zollin considered the feeling inside him to be magic. He touched the leaf again and felt the tingle as the magic once again connected. This tree, Zollin thought, like himself, was full of magic. He pulled the tree limbs to one side and went under the canopy toward the trunk of the tree. He placed his hands on the tree and felt a hum of power that made him giddy. There were rocks on the bare ground inside the canopy of the willow tree. Zollin had never been able to lift rocks very well – the heavier the object, the less he could move it. At first he hadn't been able to lift rocks at all. Then, as his power grew, he could move them slightly. He had continued to practice lifting them and could now lift a rock the size of his fist and move the stone with some speed, but not for long and the effort exhausted him quickly.

He looked at one of the stones that lay at his feet now. It was the size of a small melon. He projected a mental image of the stone rising into the air and said, "Rise!" The stone shot up, as did several others, some even half buried, broke free from the soil and jumped into the air. Zollin was amazed and laughed with delight. Soon he had the stones dancing and swirling around him. He could feel the power in his chest swirling too, and he wasn't tired. The magic flowed into him from the tree, giving him strength. He moved the stones for a long time and finally arranged them neatly on the ground in a ring around the trunk of the willow. He sat down on one of the stones to eat but found he wasn't really tired or hungry.

For the next several weeks, he visited the willow often. His power grew steadily and he even discovered that after a storm had shaken several limbs from the tree, magic still resonated in the slender boughs. He stripped the limbs of leaves and twigs and wove them into a belt which he wrapped around his waist under his shirt. He reveled in the power that the limbs imbued in him. He could now sense traces of magic in all kinds of things. In plants there was often magic that felt strong but small at the same time. It was different than the raw power he felt within himself – it was concentrated and not as broad. There was power in certain minerals and stones. And there was magic even in people, although most had none, and the ones that Zollin noticed were so faint that they seemed like echoes. Zollin was so fascinated that he had completely forgotten about the Harvest Festival that was fast approaching. His best friend Todrek reminded him one afternoon as he complained that Zollin never spent time in town anymore.

"Are you becoming a hermit out in the woods all the time?" his friend teased.

Zollin took the ribbing with good humor, but he also felt the resentment in his friend's words. They had been friends a long time even though Todrek was three years older than Zollin.. They had been in essentials school together where they learned to read and write. Neither was athletic like most of the other boys who spent their free time wrestling and competing in mock battles. Todrek was almost the opposite of Zollin. He was short and thick with muscle and fat that blended together. His father was a butcher and his family never went without meat. Todrek was strong too – he spent most of his time pulling the thick hides from the animals they butchered and moving the heavy carcasses for his father, whose back was bad. His hands, too, were strong and his forearms powerful, but he carried his strength lightly, and having killed more docile animals than he cared to remember, he had no desire to play at war.

And so Zollin, thin as a whip, and Todrek, thick as a boar, were close friends. They often spent their free time debating the qualities of food or games, although most recently their talk had seemed to center around girls. Todrek was beginning to catch the eye of several young ladies. His size was impressive as was the quality of life a village butcher could provide. Zollin, on the other hand, was almost invisible, not only to the young ladies of Tranaugh Shire, but to the adults as well. His father was well known and liked, so Zollin was known simply as Quinn's son. If he carried no message from his father, he was ignored.

"I've got something to show you," Zollin told his friend. "Can you get away for a while?"

"Get away where, out into the lonely woods?" Todrek asked. "Why can't you just show me whatever it is here?"

18

"I just can't, okay?"

"It's really hot," Todrek complained. "Do we have to go far?"

"No, now come on."

Zollin dragged his friend into the forest and when he was confident that they were far enough away from town, he stopped.

"What is it?" Todrek asked. "Have you met a forest Imp who's beguiled you and wants to make you into a tree?"

"No," Zollin said with a smile, and then he took a leaf from the forest floor and held it in his palm. Todrek was just about to complain again when the leaf rose from his friend's hand.

"Blast," Zollin said softly, and the leaf burned away in a flash. The ash fell back into Zollin's hand and blew away on the breeze.

"How… I mean… what did you just do?" Todrek stammered.

"Magic," Zollin said. He was amused by his friend who still looked bewildered.

"You mean like a trick," Todrek said. He looked relieved as if he had just realized that Zollin was playing a game or showing him an illusion.

"No, I mean like real magic. I can feel it, inside me, in those plants," he said, pointing at some small weeds growing near the roots of a tree. "I've been learning to use it all summer. I even found a willow tree that's full of magical power. I've got some of the branches and they increase my abilities."

"Increase your abilities?" Todrek asked incredulously. "What are you saying, that you're some kind of Sorcerer or something?"

"No, of course not," Zollin said, aghast.

"Are you crazy?" Todrek's voice was rising, his eyes wide in his round face. "Zollin, Sorcerers are evil. You really want to be some crazy old man in a tower casting spells and summoning demons?"

"Of course not," Zollin said, a little shocked by his friend's reaction.

"Well, that's where you're headed."

"It is not."

"That power that you're talking about, it's going to twist you into someone I don't know, someone I don't want to know. Perhaps it already has."

"Don't be crazy," Zollin pleaded. He was shocked by his friend's reaction, and while he didn't mind being alone, he had thought that of all the people who would understand, Todrek would.

"I'm not being crazy, you are. You're spending all your time out here by yourself experimenting with who knows what. How many rabbits and birds have you sacrificed to your demi-god for more power?"

"Todrek, you know me better than that. I'm not sacrificing animals."

"Then where did this power come from?" Todrek challenged.

"I don't know."

"Oh, it just sort of happened. You've just sort of learned to make things levitate and burn up on command?"

"No, it wasn't like that. See I was helping my dad –"

Todrek cut him off.

"Does Quinn know about this too?"

"No," Zollin said, raising his voice for the first time.

"Why not, don't you want your daddy to be proud of you?"

Zollin wanted to double over. Todrek's words had been like a punch in his stomach. His big friend had been the only person Zollin had ever confided in. He had told the Butcher's son how he hated carpentry and how much he feared his father's rejection. He had even cried once, shortly after Quinn had taken on Mansel as an apprentice. Zollin had felt betrayed, replaced, especially when he saw the camaraderie that his father had with his new student.

"I thought you were my friend," Zollin said.

"Yeah, well, I thought you were a person, not a freak. I've got a life now, Zollin. Dad's giving me more responsibility in the shop. We've even talked about negotiating for Brianna's hand in marriage. If this is who you are, I can't be your friend."

Zollin was so shocked by all the revelations he had just heard that he stood mute and watched Todrek walk away. Part of him wanted to lift his friend into the air and spin him around or shake some sense into him. He felt the magic surging within him, and there was no question that he could do it, but it felt wrong somehow. He didn't want to be the kind of person who used his power to hurt others.

It was also hard to believe that his friend had really considered marriage to Brianna. She was by far the most beautiful girl in the village, but she knew it and Zollin couldn't imagine that she would make a good wife. He had never known his mother, and his father had lost all interest in women after she died giving birth to Zollin. He couldn't really imagine having a girl in the house with them and had only really been interested in girls for the last year or so. Still, his best friend, his only friend really, was walking away and it felt to Zollin like the world was coming to an end.

He went home after that. He took off his willow belt and tried to push out all of the magic that swirled within him. He couldn't, of course, but it felt good to try. He would have given it all up at that moment if could have. All the wonder and excitement was gone, replaced by a nagging feeling that Todrek was right. Was the magic changing him? Would he end up an evil, twisted, shell of a man, always grasping for more and more power? He had never considered that possibility before. In fact, he had never given magic much thought. His father was not a speculative man, not about philosophy or religion, and certainly not about such mysterious topics as magic. He fixed his mind on the solid things he could touch or build with, and there was never room in his mind for anything that wasn't rational. And yet Zollin knew magic, not much about it, but he had experienced it, channeled it, used it even to help him with the more practical things his father had him doing. He hadn't used flint and steel to start a fire in over a month. He could conjure a flame by merely thinking about it with the willow belt on. And it had seemed like he was finally coming to know himself. Going to school and making friends with the other kids from the village and even apprenticing with his father felt somehow like he was imitating life. Magic was who he was, not something he did. And, he thought to himself, if I am good, then the magic in me must be good. But still, he didn't want to leave the village, and if other people felt the way

Todrek did about magic, if they jumped to the conclusion that all magic was evil, he would have to be careful. An icy chill of fear ran up his spine then as he wondered if his friend would tell people what he had seen. What if Todrek turned the town against him?

Chapter 3

Zollin didn't sleep much that night, but at some point he did make a decision. It was only a matter of time before he was discovered, so it only made sense to prepare now for the inevitable. In the days that followed, he moved things to the willow tree by the stream. His father had been a soldier in the King's Army before he had married Zollin's mother, but he never talked about it. There were weapons in their house, but Quinn had never taught Zollin to use any of them. So after storing away warm blankets, cooking utensils and a bit of dried fruit and meat, Zollin began to look for a staff. The forest was full of broken branches and sticks, but none that suited him. He did learn to peal the bark from the wood on command, but without his willow belt, it was exhausting work. He had managed to fashion himself a travel pack, and he put all his most prized possessions in it. He used his power to lift it high into the willow tree where no human could get to it.

The days passed swiftly, either full of work finishing the Inn, which the owner hoped to have ready in time for the Harvest Festival, or searching for a staff. He wasn't quite sure what he was looking for, but some deep sense within him propelled him to search. He was soon exploring the woods and hills farther and farther from his home, wild places that he had never ventured to before. He saw woodland creatures and plants that he had never seen or noticed before. And then one day, on his way home from the village, Zollin decided to take a new path through the woods on the north side of town. He was wandering along when he came to a tree that had been struck by lightning. The branches above were black from the fire that had consumed the tree, and nearby on the ground was a section of branches that had been split off of the tree by the lightning bolt. Most of it was burned too, but oddly enough one branch looked full of life. It was a rich brown color, and bright green leaves were sprouting from it. As Zollin came closer, he began to feel the branch's power radiating lightly. He bent down over the branch and touched it with a finger. He felt the tingling power rush through his body and he went rigid for a moment from the pain. He didn't know how he knew, but somehow he could sense that the lightning had imparted this power. The tingling had ceased and was replaced now by a warm flow of magic that moved into him and from him. He immediately pulled out his small knife and began stripping the leaves from the branch. They fell away easily, and when he put his foot on the larger limb the branch grew from, it snapped off cleanly with hardly any effort. The branch was as tall as Zollin, sturdy but lightweight. It was as straight as a tree branch ever gets and did not taper but was equally thick its entire length, except for the head, which ended in a stubby knob. Zollin's hand wrapped almost all the way around the bough, leaving his fingers nearly touching his palm. With the branch in his hand, Zollin felt incredibly powerful. He had intended to find a weapon to fend off animals or perhaps a brigand, but the limb's magic mingled with his own. They seemed to feed off of each other. While the power of the willow tree had been strong, it had also been a life power, like the involuntary strength of a heart pumping without being willed or even remembered, and carrying the necessary essentials of life. But the power of the branch was greater than the willow. It was more focused, more willful and direct. Whereas the willow tree radiated its power, the branch contained it, like a raging torrent waiting to be unleashed or a powerful stallion ready to stretch its legs and run.

Zollin looked at the branch for a moment and then, with a shout of joy, thrust it into the air. Lightning crackled around the branch and ran up and down Zollin's arm. There was no pain from the energy, only exhilaration. The bark burst off in tiny bits, and the wood was bright white underneath. The lightning pulled back into the staff, for it was no longer a branch of any tree, but rather the staff of a Wizard. And although Zollin didn't know it, that was what he was, the Wizard of Tranaugh Shire.

* * *

Branock felt a ripple, like being in a still pool of water when a rock is thrown in. The ripple passed silently, and the men and women in the Inn were oblivious to it. But to Branock and the other two Wizards with him, the ripple caught and held their attention. The bloom of magic they felt seemed to brighten and grow stronger. They were searching for the source of the magic, just as they had been for the last year, and they were currently in the Kingdom of Falxis. They had traveled up and down the Five Kingdoms, spending time in taverns and festivals just to be near people. It was the only way to find the person they were searching for. Branock knew that his Master was not pleased. They had hoped to find their quarry while he or she was oblivious of their power, but it was like trying to find a needle in the middle of a forest, in the middle of the night, when clouds blocked even the moon and starlight. They moved among the people in the hopes of accidentally bumping into the person with bright magic power, but it had not happened.

It was obvious now that the person had discovered their power, and while they still could not track the person, the ripple itself gave them a clue.

"To the north?" said Branock.

"Yes," said one companion.

"Let's move," said Branock. He was in charge of the small band of Wizards, and they followed him without comment.

Outside, as they waited for the stable man to prepare their horses, they formed a plan. Branock and Wytlethane, the two older Wizards, both elderly by normal standards, would ride on to Orrock, the capital of Yelsia, the northern kingdom. Cassis would return to the Torr and report to their Master and then meet them in the capital.

Their task had become easier and harder at the same time. As the young Wizard used his power, he became more definable, taking on a shape and personality that the other Wizards could sense and recognize. On the other hand, if he was learning to use his power, then he could also use that power against them.

As they rode, Wytlethane spoke, which was unusual for the Wizard dressed in simple brown robes. He was usually quiet and reserved, a very patient and diligent Wizard.

"At last things seem to be moving forward," he said.

"Yes, it has been a wearying search," Branock replied. "It shouldn't be long now."

"It will be nice to return to the Torr."

"I agree. I've experienced as much of the Five Kingdoms as I can stand."

They rode on in silence for a bit before Branock spoke up.

"How do you think Cassis will deal with the novice Wizard?" he said.

"Not well…" said Wytlethane, leaving the thought hanging and unfinished.

After a moment Branock continued, "But do you think he can co-exist with a younger, brighter Wizard?"

Branock was confident that Wytlethane felt the same as he did, but this was their first chance to discuss the subject. He waited patiently while Wytlethane measured his words before speaking them aloud.

"I do not think that is possible."

"Nor do I. We must keep our eyes on him."

"Cassis is a strong young Wizard," said Wytlethane after a short pause. "The Master would not be pleased if Cassis' pride disrupts our mission."

"No, nor would I," said Branock. He disliked the way Wytlethane always made sure to bring up the fact that Branock's authority was merely temporary. There was no hierarchy among the Wizards of the Torr, there was only the Master and everyone else. "Especially if we end up fighting each other."

"That would be unfortunate," said Wytlethane.

Branock was confident that he was the stronger Wizard, but magical battles were unpredictable. Strength flowed and ebbed. Knowledge was the power of the Torr and it was often horded like a treasure guarded by a dragon. He looked at his companion. The Wizard in his plain brown robes hid his prowess well. Branock was well aware of the ambitions of the other Wizards. There were only four in the Torr, including the Master. Branock had helped the Master eliminate the other Wizards that resisted the Torr. He had a few scars from those encounters, constant reminders that magical battles could be deadly. Fortunately he had always come out on top, but Wytlethane would be a formidable opponent when the day of that battle came. Branock knew he would face the other members of his order someday – he was ambitious himself, but he could wait. He would need an edge when that day came, and in the back of his mind, he toyed with the idea that this bright young Wizard might somehow become his ally.

They rode late into the night, using their power to light torches and riding along the gloomy path. Each man held his thoughts until at last they came to a small farm with a barn. They did not wake the occupants of the small farmhouse, but quietly entered the barn, saw to their horses and found a dry place to rest. As dawn broke they rose and started out again. If the farmer or his family saw them, they made no attempt to either greet them or challenge them. Wizards and Sorcerers had a cruel reputation, although that was not Branock's way. He knew however that Wytlethane would have killed the farmer without cause or an inkling of regret and he was glad they had managed to avoid that.

Around noon they came to a small town. There was no Inn, and their supplies were beginning to dwindle so they stopped and Branock asked if there was a place they might buy supplies. The townsman who answered eyed them both nervously, but pointed to a small shop where they could buy food. They ate, paying for their fare with copper coins from their bulging purses. They had no fear of being robbed, as even outlaws avoided Wizards.

The days passed like soldiers in a parade, each one nearly identical to the last. When they finally reached Orrock, they settled into one of the nicer Inns and began their wait for Cassis. Branock spent most of his time in the main hall of the Inn, watching and listening to the local gossip and snatches of news from the other kingdoms. Wytlethane preferred the solitude of his room.

Cassis arrived two weeks after Branock and Wytlethane had settled. The young Wizard was now escorted by a band of mercenaries. The warriors carried swords and shields, and some even had longbows. They wore chain mail under their black cloaks. They were large men who soon drove the locals from the Inn and terrorized the young bar maids.

"We are to approach King Felix," said Cassis to the other Wizards once they had gathered to eat and make plans. "The Master requires it."

"King Felix is worthless," said Branock, who was himself from Yelsia. He made it his business to keep abreast of the happenings in what would one day be his kingdom.

"Nevertheless, we will go," said Wytlethane.

Branock knew the other Wizard was only agreeing because it annoyed Branock, but like it or not, if the Master had ordered it, they would do it.

"And what are we to say?" Branock asked.

"We are to request information," said Cassis. He was arrogant and he dangled his news from the Torr over them because it was the only time he could be superior to the senior Wizards. "The Master is ready for his new pupil."

"Perhaps he tires of the last," Branock said.

"What?" Cassis thundered, his anger flaring in an instant, showing his immaturity and lack of control.

"I merely implied that perhaps you have reached the limit of your ability," Branock said smugly.

"Old man," Cassis snarled. "I'll show you the limits of my power."

He was rising from his seat when Wytlethane put a hand on the young man's arm.

"Peace, Cassis," said Wytlethane. "Branock is only baiting you. He is jealous that the Master confided in you."

Branock was well aware that Wytlethane had allied himself with Cassis, but the boy was pompous and slow to learn. Of course, most young men were, in Branock's opinion, simply too full of themselves for their own good. He did not fear the younger Wizard, who thought more highly of his skills than he should have, but Wytlethane and Cassis together could possibly overpower him.

"The Master is not pleased with your progress," Cassis said imperiously as he sat back down.

"I doubt the Master is very pleased with any of us," Branock retorted, "but he will be happy enough when we return with his new prize. Now, what else did he say?"

They talked late into the night. The Master had felt the surge of magic just as Branock and the others had. Their quarry was powerful, perhaps even as strong as the Master himself. Of course, that strength had to be harnessed and developed, but if the raw potential was there, this new Wizard was incredibly valuable. In fact, it occurred to Branock that perhaps the Master didn't plan to train this new Wizard, but merely to kill him and ensure that he remained the supreme power in the Five Kingdoms. If that were the case, then perhaps Branock's best course of action would not be finding this young Wizard after all. As they talked, a plan began to form in the Branock's mind, a plan that would establish his own power, or perhaps get him killed.

Chapter 4

A few days before the Harvest Festival began, days filled with work from daylight till dusk, a strange sense began to develop in the back of Zollin's mind. He felt something approaching. He could not see it or tell what it was, but it was getting closer, the mysterious sense growing day by day. They completed the work on the Inn the day before the festival, although it was nearly half-full with patrons already, and the long tables were merely planks of wood set on frames. It was enough for the owner, who paid Quinn the final sum owed and promised him free drinks throughout the festival.

The atmosphere in Tranaugh Shire was contagious, and after being given a bonus by his father from their payment for the Inn, Zollin was beginning to feel cheerful despite the strange feeling he was experiencing. Zollin had not spoken to Todrek since he revealed his secret in the forest, and his friend had told no one. So the morning of the festival Zollin sought his friend out. He rose early and climbed the stairs to the Butcher's home above his shop. There was a sickly sweet smell of blood that often blew into the home from the shed nearby where the animals were slaughtered. Todrek opened the door and smiled, which Zollin was hoping for but not expecting.

"I'm glad you're here early," said Todrek, pulling his friend into the home. "I've made Brianna's father an offer and he's going to make his decision today. I knew this was going to be the best year ever."

Zollin sat stunned for a moment; he wasn't sure what to say. "Brianna, the daughter of Horace the Tailor?"

"Of course, silly, can you imagine it? Brianna and me, it was actually father's idea, and he said if Horace accepts the bride price that he would loan me the money to have Quinn build us a house."

Brianna was beautiful, thin and graceful, always smiling and jolly. She was 15 years old and of marrying age, but she had never shown any interest in either Todrek or Zollin.

"Do you think she'll accept?" Zollin asked.

"Father does, we made a handsome offer. I know that one of the Tanner boys did too but who would want to marry them, they all stink of the tannery. Plus, none of the farm boys could match our offer and I doubt she would want to move out of the Shire to work a farm."

"Well, then, congratulations," Zollin said.

"We'll be married after the first winter snows," Todrek said happily. "By then the house should be finished. We only need a small place to start. You'll stand with me right?"

"Of course, I'd be honored."

Todrek grabbed Zollin up in a fierce embrace that made the smaller boy gasp. They rushed out after that to see what was happening in town. Several traveling merchants were setting up shops and a troupe of entertainers was pulling into town. The Inn Keeper spotted the boys as they ambled past the large building, and he called for them to come inside and have some cider.

And so the day passed quickly, filled with contests and food and laughter and more food. The women had all baked pies and treats which they shared from colorful tents they set up around the town square. There was a merchant from Orrock selling weapons of all sizes, from small daggers to long, two-handed broad swords. There were cloths from Janzia and an array of pottery and finely crafted house goods from all over the kingdom. Craftsmen traded their goods with the merchants and the haggling was as entertaining as the contests. There were wrestling matches and foot races, feats of strength and duels with wooden staves. Finally, shortly before the evening feast, was the announcement of town news. It was traditional that babies would be presented, achievements recognized and marriages announced. People had been gathering all afternoon in the town square. Zollin stood beside a very nervous Todrek, each nursing a tall mug of cider that was cool and crisp.

Most of Zollin's coins had gone to treats of various kinds, pies and cookies and candies, but there were also a few trinkets in his pocket. He had been looking through the various goods of the traveling merchants when a small silver ring with a white stone caught his attention. He wasn't wearing the willow belt or carrying his staff, but he could sense the magic in the ring. It seemed to push against him as his hand drew near to it. It was a woman's ring and too small for him to wear, but he asked the merchant how much he wanted for it. They haggled for a bit and Zollin even began to walk away at one point but finally a deal was struck. He had also found an amulet that the merchant said would bring good luck, but there was something strange about the small object. It was a shiny black stone on a leather thong and it felt anything but lucky to Zollin. Still, the man had nearly given it away, so it too was in Zollin's small money pouch. He had no intention of wearing it, but he was interested to see if he could discern the strange magic that it held.

From the small platform boomed the voice of the village mayor. It was time to announce betrothals and Todrek was shaking with excitement beside Zollin.

"Nervous, Butcherboy?" Quinn asked from behind them. They hadn't noticed he was there before.

Todrek managed to nod.

"Well, good luck. Your father told me about your offer. If she accepts, Zollin and I will build you a place by the first snows, you can count on it. Right, Zollin?"

"Yes sir, absolutely."

Zollin tried to smile, tried to be excited about the announcements, but he was also confused. Brianna was beautiful, but could she ever love Todrek? Zollin didn't want to see his friend hurt. He also didn't want to be excluded, and if Todrek married, he would devote all his time to his new wife. And, even though he hated to admit it, there was also a twinge of jealously. He didn't feel he could ever be as lucky as Todrek.

When Brianna and her father approached the small platform, Quinn placed a hand on Zollin's shoulder. Beside him Todrek was shifting from foot to foot, and as Zollin turned to look at his friend, he saw his father watching him. There was a reassuring look in the older man's eyes, a glimmer of understanding, and for the first time since he was a small boy he felt his father's love. It was a fleeting moment, for Brianna's father announced that she would marry Todrek, and Todrek raced through the crowd that parted before him.

There was clapping and cheering, and a few quick-witted men made suggestions to Todrek as he approached the small stage so that the crowd was laughing good-naturedly by the time he arrived. He climbed up to stand next to the girl who had long black hair that hung like a shimmering curtain around her face. Her skin was pale, her lips full and red. She had large, brown eyes and long lashes. She looked at Todrek with neither excitement nor dread. Todrek took her hand and led her away to his family while the next young girl was led up on the stage.

"We should maybe make an offer soon too," Quinn said quietly to Zollin.

"I doubt anyone would have me," Zollin said as he watched his friend. Todrek had not mentioned their time in the forest and had acted as jovial as always, but Zollin knew that things would never be the same. They had been friends a long time, but now their lives were on diverging paths. Todrek's was here in Tranaugh Shire, but the little town suddenly felt stifling to Zollin.

"Father," he said suddenly. "You served in the King's Army when you were young. What made you leave your home?" Zollin knew his grandfather had been a carpenter and had taught Quinn the trade. It was something they never discussed, but suddenly Zollin felt he needed to know.

"Can you guess?" his father asked.

"A girl," Zollin said after only a second's thought.

Quinn nodded, and they walked away from the crowd. The feast was followed by entertainment. Musicians played and singers sang tales of war and of love and of glory. Zollin sat with his father while Todrek and Brianna sat together. It was traditional for a betrothed couple to share the feast meal, but afterward the groom would make arrangements for their home while the bride prepared herself for marriage. They would not spend time together again until their wedding day.

Normally Zollin would have delighted in the food and in the entertainment, but he had lost his appetite. He was on the verge of returning home early when a new member of the troupe took center stage. There was a flare from the hot wind of magic within Zollin.

33

He could not detect magic in the man, but he instinctively knew that the man had power. It was the feeling of the approaching magic – Zollin recognized it at once. The magic in this man was different. It felt playful and fun. Zollin watched as the man performed illusions, making seemingly solid rings connect and separate. He pulled scarves from his fist and made doves appear in mid air. He made coins disappear and pulled a very fat rabbit from a small box that he held in his hand.

It was all very entertaining, but Zollin knew that the tricks were simply illusion. He did not catch how the man was doing most of the tricks, but he sensed the magic was of a mocking nature. There was no strength to it, only the feel of laughter. It was trickery in the truest sense. Zollin thought that this man could have used his power to con people out of their possessions, but his strength was only illusion, and he could not move or hurt or heal.

Zollin stayed through the last of the show and then went to find the illusionist. The man was tall with a head full of thick wavy hair. He had a long mustache which he curled using beeswax. As Zollin approached, the man suddenly looked straight at him.

"Do I know you?" the man asked.

"I don't think so. I'm Zollin, son of Quinn the carpenter."

"Have you ever been to Orrock?"

"No, sir."

"Strange, you seem oddly familiar. But no matter, I am Lotair the Great. How may I be of service?"

"I have questions," Zollin said.

"Ah, another fan I see. Well, a Wizard never reveals his secrets my lad, never. I dare not even think them lest my enemies read my mind and know my powers."

"I know your power," said Zollin sincerely. He wasn't trying to be rude, but he needed answers and he thought perhaps this man might have some.

"I'm sorry," said Lotair. "You know my powers?" His voice had lost the performer's boisterous volume and diction. He spoke like any farmer in the kingdom then.

"I sensed it; I have for several days now. Can you tell me more about it?"

"About what?"

"About magic."

"Ah," cried the performer again. "I'm afraid not my boy, I learned my secrets in the Tower of Elgarath from Topin the Wise himself. Magic is an ability that comes at great sacrifice, and only a few have the fortitude to look into the mysterious realms."

Zollin knew then that he would have to show Lotair what he could do before the man would take him seriously. He reached into his small coin pouch and found the ring. He held it in his palm and pictured it rising up into mid air. The ring didn't move. "Rise," Zollin commanded, but the ring sat perfectly still. He felt it pulse with power, but he did not recognize what it meant.

"Perhaps a few more years of study, my young apprentice," Lotair said loftily and began to turn away.

Zollin grabbed his arm and turned the man to face him again. He pulled a silver coin from his pocket and placed it in his palm. He pictured the coin rising and it did, straight up in front of the illusionist's eyes, which grew round at the sight.

"Hold out your hand," Zollin told him.

Then a flame appeared around the coin. The flame flickered and the people walking past thought the magician was showing Zollin a new trick. Then the coin dropped into the man's palm and he yelled in surprise.

"Holy Maker, that's hot!" cried Lotair.

"Now," said Zollin. "I sensed your power. I need to know where it comes from."

The man grabbed Zollin and pulled him into a colorful tent where he collapsed onto a three legged stool. He rubbed his face with a towel and then looked up angrily.

"Who taught you to do that?" the magician demand. "Are you trying to make me look like a fool?"

"No," Zollin said. He was surprised at the man's hostility.

"Then show me how you do it."

"I just imagine it or speak it and it happens."

"Don't lie to me boy! I've been in this trade for more years than you've been alive. There is no such thing as magic. It's all sleight of hand and illusion. I'm a master at it."

"You're wrong," Zollin said.

"Are you going to tell me how to do that trick?"

"It's not a trick!" Zollin said, his voice loud.

"Not a trick, huh? Prove it."

Zollin wished he had his willow belt – he would have made the illusionist's mustache burst into flame. Instead, he looked around the tent, found a pair of the magician's boots under the bed, and made them walk out and then perform a little dance.

"When did you get in here," the man asked vehemently. "I want to know how you're doing those things. What have you got, invisible strings? Is there someone under my bed?"

Zollin's head was swimming from the exertion of moving the man's boots. He placed his hand on the table to steady himself.

"Don't you know any real magic?" he asked tiredly.

The man scowled and then looked away. Zollin left the tent disappointed. He was hungry and made his way over to where the remnants of the feast were sitting. The meat was gone and he regretted that, but there were still vegetables and bread and cheese. He ate and drank a cup of watered wine. When he felt better, he returned home and fell exhausted into bed.

The next morning there was a knock on the door. When Zollin and his father looked through the window, they saw Lotair the Great holding the reins of a skinny looking brown mare.

"What's he want," Quinn said, irritable from being awakened after a night when he had obviously drunk too much wine or ale. His face was red and his breath still smelled of drink.

"I don't know, but I'll take care of it, Dad. Get some rest."

Quinn nodded and shuffled back to bed. The air outside was crisp with a hint of autumn when Zollin opened the door. The illusionist eyed him warily.

"I've come to make you an offer," said the man.

"Let's talk outside, my father's sleeping."

"As you wish," said Lotair.

They walked out into a patch of warm sunlight before the magician spoke.

"I'd like you to come with me. You can levitate objects in the crowd, warm them up for me. We'll make a killing and you'll get out of this little town," Lotair said brightly, as if the suggestion were the best news a young man could get.

"Ah," said Zollin softly. "I don't think that's a good idea."

"I knew it," said Lotair triumphantly. "I knew you were only tricking me, but I must admit it was good. Better than good, really. I tell you what, tell me how you did it and I'll give you this fine horse." He held out the reins.

"It's not a trick," Zollin said.

The man laughed. "Oh, no trick, huh? Then do it again. Do it in the daylight with my coin. If you can, I'll give you the horse."

Zollin looked at the horse. She wasn't the flower of youth, but they could use a good horse and so he told the man to wait for him. He opened the door of the house and retrieved his staff. He looked to make sure his father was asleep and, seeing that he was, returned to the man.

"I wasn't lying," he said confidently.

The illusionist smirked and started to say something when he rose suddenly in the air.

"Aaahhhhh!" the man shouted.

"Keep your voice down!" Zollin warned him, "or I'll drop you on your head."

He gently lowered the man back down to the ground and the man backed away from him.

"What are you, a devil?" he asked, his voice suddenly high and squeaking.

"No," Zollin replied bitterly, "but I'm no poser either. Now give me the horse."

"I refuse," said Lotair.

"You what?" Zollin demanded.

"I won't give you the horse."

"Yes you will, you challenged me and I accepted. You lost, so pay up."

"I won't."

"Okay," said Zollin. "That's fine. Flame."

The magician's long cloak ignited and the man screamed as he scrambled to get it off. Zollin laughed. It was the first hearty laugh he had had since he revealed his power to Todrek.

"Take the horse!" Lotair shouted. "Take the horse!"

Zollin waited until the man had given him the reins before extinguishing the flames. The magician, still smoking, ran away. Zollin looked at the horse and smiled.

"Welcome to your new home," he said. "Let's see if we can find a place for you."

He spent the morning clearing out the little lean-to shed to make a place for the horse. When his father finally roused himself, he asked about the shouting he had heard.

"Oh," said Zollin. "I sort of made a bet with that magician last night because I saw how he was doing some of his tricks. I won a horse but he tried to cheat me out of it. I told him I would tell everyone he was a fake and he got mad. But I got the horse."

"You gambled for a horse?" Quinn asked. "What did you bet, the house?"

"No, he was just overly confident. I bet him all the money I had left and he bet the horse. I won and now we have a horse."

Quinn went out to look at the horse while Zollin made breakfast. After they had eaten and seen to the chores, they made their way down the hill to town to meet with Todrek and his father.

Later that afternoon, after plans had been made for Todrek's house and Quinn had returned to the Inn for a meeting of the village Council, Zollin went to examine the two trinkets he had purchased the day before. He was especially interested in the ring, which seemed to resist his magic. He wondered if it was a fluke or if there was something about the ring's power that kept him from moving it. After checking on the horse, Zollin made his way to the willow tree. He had both the willow belt and the staff. He was determined to learn as much as he could about magic and was bitterly disappointed that the illusionist was so ignorant.

In his mind, he outlined what he knew so far, that magic came from within him, that it wasn't a learned skill. People who did not have the magic in them could not just make it happen. Magic also resided in various things, such as plants and trees, rocks, and perhaps even metals. He had heard stories, fairy tales really, of enchanted swords or magic crystals. It seemed that these stories had at least some basis of truth. Finally, not all magic was the same; the power of the willow tree was different from the power in his staff. This final thought brought to mind the medallion he had bought that was supposed to bring good luck. Zollin laid the medallion on the ground in front of him. He knew the power within it was different; it seemed shady somehow, malevolent. He thought briefly about putting the medallion around his neck, supposing that like the willow belt or the staff, it might increase his power. But he dismissed the thought outright and determined never to use the medallion until he understood it.

The ring, which was small and looked to be silver, seemed on its own to be nothing more than a bit of metal. But the stone, a small, white stone that was round rather than angled like many gemstones, resonated with power, but only when touched. It was almost as if the magic inside it were veiled or hidden. Zollin placed it in his palm again and concentrated. The staff was beside him but he wasn't holding it yet. The willow belt around his waist seemed to charge with power as he pictured the ring rising into the air, but the small band didn't move.

"Rise!" he commanded, concentrating fiercely, but still nothing happened. He reached out with his right hand and grasped the staff beside him. There was a shock of power as he let the magic flow into him, his hair began to stand up, and little blue sparks began running up and down the staff. "Rise!" he commanded again, and he could feel the power surging through him, rushing toward the ring. He could almost see the magic peeling away from the ring as if an invisible bubble surrounded it. Rocks and twigs began to shoot up off the ground as Zollin focused all his concentration on seeing the ring rise, but the little band of silver never moved.

Finally he stopped and the fatigue settled in. All around him rocks and twigs and even clumps of dirt rained down around him. He lay back on the dirt and let his heart slow back down to normal. He had lifted the illusionist into the air without much effort at all, but this ring was unmovable. He wondered if perhaps the ring's power repelled magic. It was an interesting thought, and one that made sense. If some objects resonated power, perhaps some objects deflected it. The only thing Zollin knew for sure was that there was much more to this world than he had known. There was a sphere or realm that was just as real as the ground he lay on, yet he could not see it, could not touch it or contain it. It was there, hidden just beyond sight, and he was determined to know it. But he could not learn what he needed to know in Tranaugh Shire. He would have to leave, to search for the answers in other parts of the kingdom. But he would wait until he had Todrek's home finished. He had given his word that he would stand with his friend when the vows were taken, and he owed Todrek that much.

Autumn seemed to race by at a gallop. The leaves turned rich colors and then fell from the trees as cold northern winds raced through the village. The work on the new house went smoothly, but there was much to be done before the first snows, which seemed to threaten to fall at anytime. Zollin also had the chore of getting their own home ready for the winter. He plastered mud into every gap or crack in the walls. It would be a cold winter if the winds could find their way into the house. He spent one day scrubbing the chimney so that they would not have to choke on smoke all winter long. Even though the work did not come easily to Zollin's hands, he felt better about his work that fall than at any other time in his life. He supposed it was because he was taking care of the people he loved, his father and his best friend, and a small part of him felt guilty for knowing that he would soon be leaving them. He hadn't told anyone his plans, but he planned to tell his father shortly before the wedding.

It won't be long, he told himself as he drifted off to sleep and even though the world beyond the village was wide and unknown, it was also exciting. He focused on thoughts of adventure and tried not to let his mind drift to Brianna, whose face had been troubling his dreams of late. As he felt sleep washing over him, he saw himself seated on large horse, with his staff in one hand and a sword in the other. The dream made him smile until he saw that beside him was another horse, a smaller horse, and Brianna sat on it.

Chapter 5

"No! No! Don't do it!" she screamed.

Brianna sat up abruptly and looked around the dark room. Her sisters had not stirred, but the curtain that separated her sleeping chamber from the main room was pulled aside, and her mother came in.

"Another nightmare, dear?" her mother asked.

Brianna nodded and lay back down. She had been having the nightmares for nearly a month. Every night without fail, she dreamed that Todrek was being slain by a dark warrior on a great horse. She watched with terrified fascination as the assailant's blade swept down and ended her betrothed's life. But that wasn't the worst part of the dream – in fact, she was indifferent to Todrek's death. She barely knew him, after all. She could remember him from the school house, but he was older than she was, and he didn't seem interested in her at all then. Now they were going to be married and it felt like it was happening to someone else. She was neither excited nor scared of marrying the Butcher's son, but her parents thought otherwise.

"I know this is hard, dear," her mother was saying. "But marriage is a part of life. And Todrek is a good match. He works hard and will provide well. A Butcher never goes hungry, dear."

"Yes, I know," Brianna said absently.

Lately, as she woke up screaming, her mother had taken on the task of settling Brianna down. She didn't need to be reassured about the wedding; it was the other part of her dream that terrified her. She saw Todrek's friend, the Carpenter's son, riding off, and for some reason that she could not understand, the sight filled her with dread. She thought that she would rather face the dark attacker who had killed Todrek than watch Zollin leave her. She felt extremely guilty for dreaming about another boy rather than her betrothed, but she couldn't help it. She had no control over her dreams, after all. She wasn't in love with Zollin; in fact she knew him even less than she knew Todrek. He had been in school too, before they began their apprenticeships, but he was nearly invisible. She had no real memory of him and didn't even see his face in her dream, but somehow she knew it was him.

She hadn't told her parents the truth about her dreams. They assumed it was pre-wedding jitters, and she was happy to let them go on thinking that. As her mother prattled on, Brianna lay back and smoothed her hair from her face. She needed to relax, relax and sleep.

***

In Orrock, the Wizards were entrenched at the Inn, rehashing what they had just learned from the traveling illusionist. The man was raving about a boy in a village who had made him levitate. It was just the sort of break they had been hoping for. They had bought the man drinks and heard the whole story, although they were sure most of it was not true. Still, they could move on now, which was good since the mercenaries seemed to find new ways to provoke the King's Guard daily. They searched the maps for the small village of Tranaugh Shire and plotted their course.

"We can leave at first light," said Branock.

"Why not leave now?" said Cassis defiantly.

"Because, dear child," Branock explained. "While you may not need much in the way of sleep, your military guard does. They will be hard pressed to keep up with us as it is. They are drunk, and on their best day they require twice as much time as we do to prepare."

"You should go and tell them now," added Wytlethane. "And make sure the matron wakes them before dawn."

"With buckets of icy water if need be," Branock added. He felt no real animosity for the soldiers, but they had come with Cassis and reported directly to him. Branock assumed that respect came at a high price, but since Cassis had hired and paid them, they were loyal to him, at least as loyal as a mercenary can be. Cassis had used the threat of their force against Branock a time or two, and in reply, Branock merely made the young Wizard keep up with the soldiers. Cassis gave them their weekly stipend but also had to deal with the destruction the men caused in their bar fights and the local trouble their carousing caused among the families of the city. He was constantly looking for them, bribing the King's Guard to let them out of the stocks where their fighting had landed them and arranging payment to Inn Keepers and fathers all over the capital.

"How long do you think?" Branock asked, tapping his finger on the small dot that represented Tranaugh Shire on the map.

"At least two weeks," Wytlethane said, "maybe more. We'll have to go slowly at first to let the soldiers keep up with us."

"If they don't get lost trying," Branock remarked.

"They are fighters, not trackers."

"And all together they don't have as much wit as one bright child."

Wytlethane did not argue. He merely nodded.

"Well, let Cassis lead them to us," Branock said. "That way we won't have to worry about them."

"I'll make a list of supplies and ensure that we have all that we need," said Wytlethane.

"Good, I'm ready to end this wild pig hunt."

Branock rose and left the room. He acted exasperated, but in fact he was excited. He was glad to finally be on the move again. He didn't mind spending long periods of time in contemplation and study, but the Inn, although the nicest in town, was not to his standards. Besides, he had planned his moves, and he hoped to soon be rid of the brat Cassis and perhaps Wytlethane as well.

***

When Todrek's new house was nearly finished, on a night when the wind was howling through the hills and trees, as Zollin lay sleeping under warm quilts, the feeling began. It was a strange sensation, much like the feeling he had had before the Harvest Festival, but this time it was different. It was stronger and more distinct. There was more than one person with magic power approaching, and it made Zollin nervous. The feeling was dark and ominous, the people, if that's what really was approaching, felt malevolent, as if their errand or purpose was not a cheerful one. Zollin worked hard in those days, always wearing his willow belt and carrying his staff. He stocked his pack in the willow tree and made sure he had plenty of supplies to get him started on his journey.

When the first snows fell, there was three days' work left on the small house, and then it would need to be decorated and the cupboards stocked. The people of Tranaugh Shire were in a mood to celebrate, and plans were made. The wedding would take place in one week, with a pounding and feast the day before to prepare and supply the young couple's home. It was traditional for gifts to be given to the young couple, and as the feeling of the approaching figures grew stronger Zollin decided to give them the ring he had gotten at the Harvest Festival. He had nothing more valuable to share and if the ring really did offer protection, he wanted Todrek to have it.

When the house was finished, Zollin was sent to fetch Brianna so she could inspect it. Todrek was paying for the house, but a home was a woman's domain and Quinn wanted to insure that the young bride would be happy. Girls normally made Zollin uncomfortable, especially beautiful ones, but he was too preoccupied with the sense of approaching power to be nervous about Brianna. He could almost make out figures in his mind, and it felt as if three distinct magical presences were approaching, en masse with a larger group. It occurred to Zollin that it could be another troupe of entertainers, but somehow he doubted it. These figures weren't traveling showmen – they had real power.

"So, it's finally complete?" Brianna asked.

"Yes," Zollin said.

"You know, you've changed," she said, and the look on her face as Zollin glanced at her made a lump form in his throat. "You seem older," she continued, "more like an elder than a boy."

"Is that right," he murmured. I feel like a child now, he thought to himself.

"I guess we're all growing up. I can't believe I'm getting married."

"Scared?" Zollin suggested. He knew he would be.

"Excited, silly. I'll finally be out of my mother's house and that will be so wonderful."

"Oh," Zollin said, unsure what to say. The remark had seared like a red-hot poker to a boy who had never known his mother. He couldn't imagine having one and wanting to leave. He loved his father and didn't want to leave him, even though he knew they were worlds apart.

"To have my own home and do as I please," she said, almost talking to herself. "It will be wonderful. And then of course babies. I plan to have a house full of them."

She struck Zollin as incredibly naïve although he knew nothing of marriage or children, but she sounded much more like she would be playing house, rather than starting a family. He wondered what would happen to his best friend and this beautiful but young girl when they realized life was not what they expected.

They arrived at the home and Zollin stood with Quinn just outside while Brianna inspected every inch of it. She made several suggestions, which Quinn praised her for noticing and promised to fix. And when she was done, she declared herself overjoyed, before asking if Zollin would escort her home. Mansel was there and he shot Zollin a jealous look, which he took to be utterly foolish since the girl was betrothed. Still, he did feel a small bit of satisfaction that she had asked for him to walk her home rather than the strong and older Tanner's son who apparently had no trouble catching the interest of most girls.

"You and Todrek are good friends?" she asked, as if she didn't already know the answer.

"Yes, best friends."

"What is he really like?"

"What do you mean?" Zollin asked.

"Well, you know, he's incredibly polite but that's just to woo me. He seems sweet enough, strong and handsome in a way, but I want to know the real man before I marry him."

To Zollin, this seemed the wisest thing he had heard from either of the happy couple and was glad for it. Apparently there was more to Brianna than good looks and dreams of the perfect life.

"He's smart," Zollin said. "He is strong but he doesn't feel that he must prove it to anyone. He loves to laugh, is very opinionated, works hard and never complains. Well, almost never."

"Do you think he'll be a good husband and a good father?"

"I think you must be careful," Zollin said, stopping to look at her. "I think he is overwhelmed by your beauty and would do anything to make you happy. For his sake, please treat him fairly."

"Zollin, you speak as if I'm a selfish and cruel girl," she said, pouting.

"I just want my friend to be happy."

"And you think I would make him unhappy?"

"I don't know. It's just that life can be hard. I'm really happy for him, but I hope that you will love him."

"What do you know of love," she said, turning and beginning to walk back toward her father's house.

"Nothing. All I mean is that he will need a good friend and I hope that you will be one for him."

"Why does he need a friend? Doesn't he have you?"

"No," said Zollin softly. "I'm... I'm leaving after the wedding."

"Why?" asked Brianna, her voice rising. Zollin knew she would be surprised. People rarely left Tranaugh Shire.

"I will tell you if you promise not to share it with anyone until after I'm gone."

She looked at him sternly for a moment, and Zollin felt his heart flutter and his hands begin to sweat. Until that moment he had been able to see her only as Todrek's betrothed, but now he saw the beautiful girl before him. She was thin, with long arms and fingers. Her dark hair fell on her shoulders and her brown eyes looked deeply into his. She had a long graceful neck and a noble demeanor that gave her an elegant presence that was hard to resist.

"You may not believe me, but you can ask Todrek when I'm gone. I have power, magic power, and I'm going to learn how to use it."

She eyed him critically for a moment and then burst out laughing. Zollin felt his face grow red with embarrassment, and his fury blossomed inside him. He felt like he was a small boy again being teased by the other children. He grabbed her arm and pulled her from the street between two houses. He looked around to see that no one was looking and then pulled a coin from his small pouch.

"Hold out your hand!" he ordered her.

"Why, are you going to make a rabbit appear?" she mocked.

"Just hold out your hand!" he said, emphasizing each word.

She did, and he placed the coin in it. She was starting to say something when the coin flew up and began to dance in front of her eyes. Zollin felt the crackle of power from the staff but held it in check. He didn't want his anger causing things to go flying around the town.

Brianna's eyes widened in wonder and she waved her hands around the coin, looking for a string or some other trick.

"How are you doing that?" she asked him, and there was wonder in her voice.

"It doesn't matter, but that's why I'm leaving. And let me warn you about something else – there are people coming here and I don't think they've got good intentions."

"What do you mean?"

"I mean there are powerful magicians coming here, to Tranaugh Shire. I can feel them approaching."

"Will they be here before the wedding?" she asked.

"I don't know, but I want you to take this." He held out the ring.

"What is it?"

"It's my wedding gift. It isn't much, but it might protect you."

"Protect me from what?"

"From magic. In fact, let me try something."

He slid the ring on her finger and ignored the strange look in her eyes as she watched him. He snatched the coin from the air and set it on her palm again, ignoring the tingle of excitement he felt as he touched her skin. He stepped back and tried to make the coin rise, but it did not move.

"Rise!" he commanded, but again the coin remained motionless. He decided to try and lift Brianna herself. "Rise!" he commanded again, picturing the girl rising several inches into the air. He was ready to lower her back to the ground and reassure her that all was well if she panicked, but she didn't move. He concentrated all his strength and felt the crackle of power from his staff racing through him, but he could do nothing to her. The ring offered its wearer some form of protection from his power at least.

"Don't take the ring off," he told her, "not until the strangers leave. Do you understand?"

She nodded and Zollin ignored the beautiful brown eyes that stared up into his with wonder. He motioned for her to go ahead of him back out toward the street.

"I knew you had changed," she said quietly.

"You were right."

"When did you…" she asked, not wanting to speak of magic out loud.

"At the first of summer," he said.

She nodded and was silent until they reached her father's home.

"Thank you, Zollin son of Quinn, for your fine work on Todrek's home and for the wedding gift. I shall think of you whenever I see it."

He smiled and felt his knees go weak under him. He decided to beat a hasty retreat and said goodbye.

Chapter 6

The day of the wedding dawned bright and clear. The first snows had melted, but the temperature was cold, and Zollin threw too many logs into the fireplace and then set them ablaze with a thought. The heat from the fire soon filled the little kitchen, and Quinn rose from his bunk with a quilt about his shoulders and went to stand next to it.

"Father," Zollin said. "Can we talk?"

"I figured we would need to sooner or later," Quinn said wearily, and for the first time Zollin realized that his father was not anxious to have his son leave, even the son who always seemed a disappointment. So much had changed so fast – Zollin had changed, Brianna was right. He could see things from his father's point of view now, and it filled him with sadness. He wanted to tell Quinn everything, the magic, the willow tree, his staff, even the ring he had given to Brianna. But he felt like it was too much and he honestly didn't think he could handle it if his father reacted the way Todrek had.

"I'm leaving Tranaugh Shire," Zollin said sadly.

"I expected something like that," his father said. "What's your plan?"

"Head south, perhaps visit Orrock. Maybe even go as far as Osla."

"How do you expect to make a living?" Quinn asked skeptically.

Zollin wanted to say that he could do a few magic tricks to make ends meet, but he knew his father wouldn't understand. In so many ways, Zollin knew his father would never understand him, and the realization of that fact felt like a deep, dark pit in his soul. "I'll manage," he said quietly.

"That's just like you," Quinn said sharply. "You think you'll be fine. You've probably got a little money saved and you think it'll last forever. It won't. You don't know a trade, Zollin. You've no friends, no family to lean on. You'll be destitute in a month, if not robbed and left for dead before then."

"I can take care of myself, Dad," Zollin said, his anger rising.

"There's no doubt you're a resourceful lad, but you need a trade. Stay here a few more years. Then you'll be an adult with a trade. You can go anywhere and find work. I know it seems like your world is ending. I've seen the way you look at Brianna-"

"This has nothing to do with her," Zollin shouted. The magic inside him swirled angrily.

"I know your best friend is marrying a beautiful young girl, but when the time is right you'll marry too. That's why you need a trade."

"Dad, I don't care about getting married."

"It's normal, son, all young boys your age feel that way."

"This has nothing to do with Todrek or girls, I just need to leave. And I'm not waiting. I'm taking Lilly, unless you need her."

The horse, which Zollin had named Lilly, had taken new life with plenty of rest and good oats each night. She regained her strength and had a cheerful demeanor. She didn't look nearly as old and would be a good horse.

"We'll talk about it tomorrow."

"There's nothing to talk about," Zollin said, turning away.

"We'll see, son, we'll see." Quinn moved away from the fire. "Well, it's a big day, lots to do. I guess we better get moving."

"Sure," Zollin said, turning back to the fireplace. He began to fix breakfast for the two of them, and the task seemed somehow bittersweet.

Quinn paused for a moment before going to get dressed. "This is your home, Zollin," he said softly.

Zollin had his back to his father and could not turn around. Tears were springing to his eyes and he couldn't stop them. Most of his life, he had felt that he wasn't welcome, that his father somehow blamed him for his mother's death. He never felt quite at home in the house Quinn had built for Zollin's mother, had never felt like he measured up or made his dad proud.

"Thanks, Dad," he managed to say.

Quinn went to his small bedroom to change, and Zollin wiped the tears away from his cheeks and finished preparing the oatmeal for breakfast.

***

The wedding was a beautiful ceremony. Todrek was so excited he was shaking. Brianna looked beautiful in a long gown of green that matched the winter decorations. They were married in the town square, and then everyone moved into the Inn to celebrate. There was dancing and singing, lots of ale and wine, and congratulating. Zollin noticed that Brianna wore the ring and occasionally glanced at him. Todrek was in the midst of his happiest moment, the center of attention. Soon the happy couple left to spend their first night together in the new house Quinn had build for them. As Todrek's best man, it was Zollin's job to make sure they had everything they needed before he left them for the night. He stood outside in the cold as night fell, moving constantly to try and stay warm. His apprehension about the approaching figures was stronger than ever, and his jealousy of Todrek was also rearing its ugly head. It was a long thirty minutes before Todrek stuck his head out of the door to say everything was fine.

Zollin ran back up to the Inn and announced the good news, and there was cheering and toasting, the ale and wine flowing like a swollen river in springtime. Zollin found a warm spot by the fire and drank mulled wine until he could feel his fingers and toes again. He thought about waiting till spring to begin his journey, but the dread of the approaching figures drove that thought from his mind. He realized some time during that night of revelry that he would have to toughen up physically if he were to survive on his own. Long, cold nights awaited him, nights without a warm bed and perhaps not even enough food. But he would make it. He determined in his mind that no matter what happened in the days ahead, he would endure, he would survive. He had no idea at the time he made that decision that it would mean the difference between life and death.

***

In the hills south of Tranaugh Shire, the Wizards waited. Cassis and the mercenaries had finally caught up to the senior

52

Wizards, but the snows had slowed them down considerably. They had decided to wait until dawn to enter the town proper. With everyone celebrating the marriage, no one had noticed the smoke rising from the trees. The Wizards were anxious, each for his own reasons, but mostly because they felt their task drawing to a close. They would soon be back in their tower, surrounded by the physical symbols of their power.

It could happen none too soon for the elder two Wizards, because although they could prolong their lives with magic, they could not keep the bitter winter winds from chilling them deep down into their bones. In the hour before sunrise, the Wizards met one last time to ensure that their plan of action was clear. Branock knew that Wytlethane did not need to be reminded, but he didn't trust Cassis. He knew that this initial confrontation would be the young Wizard's best opportunity to attack his rival, and Branock was determined not to let that happen.

"When we identify the boy," Branock explained again, "you will let me do the talking."

"If you insist," said Cassis.

Branock bristled and wanted to crush the life from the young man's body, but he was too well controlled. Besides, the time to challenge Cassis and Wytlethane was not yet right. Perhaps with the boy, perhaps... He let his own ambitions drain away his temper and he settled for merely nodding at Cassis.

"Keep the soldiers in check," he continued. "We don't want them destroying the town."

"It isn't much of a town, is it?" Cassis smirked.

"That is irrelevant," said Wytlethane in his creaking voice.

"They are your responsibility," Branock said to the young Wizard. "Make sure they understand that the Master wants this boy alive."

Cassis nodded and moved away. Branock eyed Wytlethane but could see nothing in the other Wizard's face that gave away his intentions. If Cassis were to attack the boy, would that please Wytlethane, Branock wondered? Or was the old Wizard too afraid of disappointing the Master? It was a risk he would have to take.

"They are ready," Cassis said as he returned.

"Good, the dawn is breaking," Branock said. "Let us go down and claim our prize."

***

Quinn and Zollin, along with most of the town, spent the night on the floor of the Inn's large hall. When the roosters began to crow, they stirred with heads heavy and pounding from the excess of the night before. But it was the start of winter, which was a slow time in Tranaugh Shire. Little work was done during the heavy snows that would soon be coming. When the group of riders came into the town, they were met with bewildered looks by rumpled and tired people. Most people in Tranaugh Shire had never seen so many armed riders before, and none so finely armored. The guards were warriors with chain mail coats under their dark cloaks and heavy shields that hung from their saddles. Their horses, too, were draped with armor and were large beasts with powerful bodies that could carry a man into war. The guards carried long swords and short, double edged swords, and some even long bows strung and slung over their shoulders.

The townspeople who weren't already at the Inn now hurried there, including Todrek and Brianna, who came and stood next to Zollin. Quinn had moved beside his son, too, and had somehow managed to find a sword.

Zollin's dread was full-grown into fear. He could feel the magic radiating from the three Wizards – it was dark and as full of death as the willow tree's magic was full of life. He held his staff tightly and looked at Brianna's hands to see if the ring was still there. It was, and he breathed easier. She looked at him and he nodded slightly as if to say, yes, these are the men I told you about.

One of the Wizards spoke to the crowd. He was old, his face lined with so many wrinkles it was hard to see his eyes. He had a long, white beard that was trimmed into a point. In his hand he carried what looked like a small scepter or cane.

"We are looking for Zollin, son of Quinn the Carpenter," said the Wizard, his voice loud in the cold winter morning.

"Who are you?" said Brianna's father, who was also on the

Council and often spoke for the Council in town meetings.

"My name is Branock, and my companions are Wytlethane and Cassis. We are looking for a young man named Zollin."

"Yes, we know Zollin," shouted Quinn. "What do you want with him?"

Zollin saw the warriors look at his father with baleful expressions. He felt anger flare in his chest at the thought of these armed men attacking his father.

"He is wanted in Osla," said Branock. "We are here to see that he reaches the city safely."

"And what if he doesn't want to go to Osla?" Quinn asked, and there was hostility in his voice.

"That is a matter between the boy and us," said the Wizard named Cassis. "There is no need for the town to be involved in this matter. Let Zollin come forward and the rest of you may return to your homes."

Zollin started to move forward – he felt that people would be hurt if he didn't – but his father stopped him. Brianna looked at Zollin with concern, but Todrek seemed angry. As Zollin looked at his friend, it was as if the larger boy was saying, I told you this would happen.

Brianna's father spoke again. "Gentlemen, please come inside. We would hear news of Osla and you can speak with the boy where it is warm. We have mulled-"

He was cut off by Branock. "You misunderstand me," he said bitterly. "Produce the boy now, or we shall kill you one by one until you do."

There was a sudden rush of noise as people began talking, some loudly with voices pitched high by fear. Some of the people started to leave the crowd, but the guards on their chargers fanned out and surrounded the group.

Around Zollin, people were suddenly pointing and talking. Most had pulled back, moving away from him, but Quinn stepped in front of his son and lay the naked sword he carried on his shoulder. Todrek stared to move away too, but Brianna stepped forward to stand beside Zollin. A look of disgust crossed Todrek's face, but he stepped up beside his wife.

"I am Quinn, Zollin's father. I will not let him go with you. Tranaugh Sire is a village of Yelsia, not Osla. You have no authority here."

"You are foolish," said Branock. "But I understand the tie of a father and son. Unfortunately it is a tie that must be broken." He waved a hand, and one of the warriors urged his mount forward. The crowd had already parted before Zollin and his father, allowing the warrior to ride within a few feet of Quinn. He had a nasty-looking mace with a handle as long as a man's forearm connected to a chain that ended with a spiked ball. The warrior swung the mace around and around before suddenly swinging it down toward Quinn's head. Zollin sucked in a breath to shout for his father but Quinn was already in motion. He spun out of the path of the mace and brought his sword around in a full circle that slashed through the warrior's leg just above the greave he wore to protect his lower leg and ankle. The sword also cut into the charger's side and blood sprayed out over Quinn as the horse reared and screamed before turning away. The warrior toppled back out of the saddle in a sickening crunch of metal and flesh. He did not move but lay still in the dirt, his leg bleeding onto the ground hardened by winter's cold. The horse bucked and kicked and ran from the crowd shrieking. Quinn merely stood easy with the sword back on his shoulder.

"I see you are a man of skill, Quinn, in trades beyond carpentry," said Branock. "I respect that. Unfortunately, I cannot allow you to keep young Zollin here, and I too am a man of skill." He said the last words with a deep-seated hatred that narrowed his eyes and made his lips curl back from his teeth like a wild dog.

Without a moment's hesitation, as the Wizard raised his scepter, Zollin reacted. He thrust his staff out toward the Wizards and shouted "Blast!"

The power of the staff erupted with such force that it momentarily blinded those who saw it. Bolts of white light shot from the staff and Zollin felt the power of the willow belt and his own magic feeding into the blast. There was a flash of heat that made people fall back, and when the light hit the Wizards, they toppled from their horses. The warriors' horses bucked and reared and people began running in all directions. Quinn grabbed his son's arm and they ran past the warriors struggling to control their chargers, who were bucking and kicking in circles. They ran hard and fast, away from the Inn, away from their friends and neighbors who were screaming and running.

Zollin heard men shouting to get weapons and defend their homes. Women were wailing and children crying. He felt a sick lump in his stomach and wondered if he had killed the old Wizards. He could still feel their power, but that did not necessarily meant they had survived – the willow branches, for instance, still had power even though they were severed from the tree. They ran out of the village and up the nearby hill before turning back to see what was happening. It was only then that Zollin realized that Todrek and Brianna had followed them.

"What are you doing here?" he asked them.

"We're here to help," said Brianna. "We won't let them take you, Zollin."

"You should go home," Quinn said, but there was no conviction in his voice.

"I agree. Sorry, Zollin, but I warned you nothing good would come from magic," said Todrek. He grabbed Brianna's hand and started to pull her back down the hill, but she wrenched her arm free.

"What is wrong with you, Todrek, you're his best friend," she said angrily. "Would you leave him now in his hour of need?"

"Well, no, but there is nothing I can do!"

"You can fight, can't you?"

"I have no weapon," he cried.

"We do at home," Zollin said. "Brianna can ready Lilly while we hold back anyone who comes near. Then I'll leave and hopefully you'll all be safe."

"You're not going alone, son," said Quinn. "I'll not leave you to fend for yourself."

"This is your home, Dad, you should stay."

"No, my home is with my family, and that's you. We go together."

Zollin looked at his father and both had tears in their eyes. Zollin could see the questions, the wonder of why his son had kept the truth of his power from him, and even pride at the way he had reacted in that desperate moment.

"There are three riders coming," said Todrek, and his voice squeaked a little as he said it.

They turned and ran for the house that sat not far away on the crest of the hill. Brianna went immediately to the lean-to and began saddling the horse. Quinn handed Todrek his sword and ran inside to get his own weapons. Todrek swung the blade around to get a feel for the weapon. By the time the horses were drawing near, Quinn had reappeared. He too had a mail coat that he was pulling over his head. He had a large round shield and a sword, but he wasn't quite ready to fight. The warriors would be on them before his father could be ready, so Zollin thrust his staff forward again, this time shouting, "Move!" He felt a large wall of invisible power leap out toward the riders, expanding as it went.

Two of the warriors were thrown backward, clear of their horses who continued forward. Quinn and Zollin leapt to one side while Todrek raised his sword. The third warrior raised his own sword but at the last minute nudged his horse into Todrek. Then the sword flashed and there was an arc of blood.

"Todrek!" Zollin screamed. He blasted the warrior with lightning from his staff while Quinn ran to slay the other two warriors. The power burned out of Zollin like an erupting volcano. Thick bolts of blue-white lightning wrapped around the warrior, who shook so hard that his armor, blackened by Zollin's magic, flew off in different directions. The man was flung from the horse, which bolted away, and landed in a smoldering, twitching heap.

Zollin ran to his friend, who had fallen onto his back. His throat was cut, and his life's blood was spilling out. He gurgled and cried, tears flowing down his cheeks. There was look of absolute horror on his face as he struggled.

Zollin placed his hand on his friend's throat and cried out, "Heal!" He felt power flow from him, but there was still a warm gush of blood on his hand. "Heal!" he wailed over and over, but the

58

damage was too great. At one point the skin sealed together, but the arteries were still severed and his neck bulged as he bled to death. "No," Zollin cried as his friend's eyes glazed and his body when limp.

Brianna raced from the lean-to on Lilly's back, and Zollin thought that she was fleeing. Her abandonment reinforced his feelings of guilt and shame. He wanted to die but he also wanted to kill every last one of the men who had come to town.

"I will avenge you!" he shouted. "I'll kill them all."

"No, son," Quinn said. He had slain the other two warriors and was now pulling his son away from his best friend. "He died defending you; he would want you to live. Now we must go."

"No, he hated me," Zollin cried. "He was here for her, and now he's dead and it's my fault. I should have blasted those warriors like I did the Wizards."

"It wouldn't have made a difference," his father said forcefully. "It was his time and it was a good death."

Zollin looked at his father as if he were crazy, but Quinn merely said, "Trust me, son. Now let's go."

They heard horses approaching and prepared to fight, but then Brianna appeared with the chargers of the three warriors they had just killed. She rode up to them and looked down at Todrek's body. There were tears in her eyes, but she did not hesitate. She tossed Quinn the reins and said, "We should go."

Zollin and Quinn climbed up into the saddles of the horses and were about to ride off when they heard someone else shouting.

"Wait, wait!" they heard. Then Mansel came running up the hill, his bow in his hand, a quiver of arrows slung over his shoulder. "I'm coming with you!" he shouted.

Zollin looked at his father and saw doubt flicker across his face for the first time that morning.

"No," shouted Zollin. "Go home."

"No," Mansel shouted back, and he came running up, making the horses shuffle back nervously. "I'm coming and if you don't let me ride, I'll follow you."

"Why?" Zollin asked.

"For Quinn," said the older boy, his broad chest rising and falling quickly as he tried to catch his breath.

Zollin did not want Mansel to come, but his father waved a hand at the boy, who climbed up into the empty saddle of the third charger. That should have been Todrek, Zollin thought with a twinge of regret. He took one last look at his friend's body, but it was already bloated with internal bleeding, the face pale, the lips blue, the eyes waxy and lifeless. His friend was gone.

They rode into the forest, well aware that there were still eight warriors out searching for them. Zollin could feel the Wizards moving and knew that they somehow lived. He led the small group to the willow tree, where he retrieved his pack.

"You've been planning this?" his father asked.

"I knew I might need to leave suddenly, and this has been a place of refuge for me. I didn't know there would be people coming for me, I just thought people in the village wouldn't want me around and I didn't want to make things hard on you."

"We should go," said Quinn, a pained look on his face.

"There are only supplies in here for one," Zollin said.

"It will have to do," his father replied.

"Brianna and Mansel could go home. They don't have to do this."

"No," said Brianna. "I have to come. I don't know why but I knew. Ever since you told me, I knew I couldn't stay here in Tranaugh Shire. I'm coming."

"Me, too," said Mansel. "I'm more at home with Quinn than with my own family. I'm just a mouth to feed there, but I can help you. Quinn can teach me to fight and I can hunt with my bow. I'll pull my weight."

"I'm sure you will," Quinn said, smiling.

Jealously shot through Zollin like molten fire and he wanted to blast Mansel to dust and let the wind carry him far away, but he wrestled down the emotion even as his staff crackled with energy.

"Let's go, Zollin," said Brianna soothingly.

Zollin looked at her, and even though her face was darkened with pain, whether from leaving her family or losing her husband,

Zollin was not sure, but there was compassion in her eyes. He felt something in him stir for her, and then guilt over the thought brought tears to his eyes. His best friend had died for him, and Zollin was thinking about his wife. Perhaps it could not be helped, but he hated himself for it.

"The Wizards are still alive, and moving closer," said Zollin.

"Yes, I wish you had told me of your gift. Those Wizards were members of the Torr, powerful men that will abide no threat to their rule."

"But King Felix rules the kingdom," said Brianna.

"Yes, and the Torr have ruled the Kings of this kingdom and others for many generations. They will not stop until they have what they want."

"Then what do we do?" Mansel asked.

"We ride, stay ahead of them until we figure things out," said Quinn. "This is the last chance you'll have to turn back."

"No, I'm coming," said Mansel.

Brianna nodded too, and they rode off into the forest.

Chapter 7

Branock lay on the ground. He felt... cold. He had successfully blocked the lightning spell Zollin had cast at him, but his defense had not prepared him for the force of the young Wizard's strike, nor had he managed to soften his landing. He slowly moved each of his limbs and was pleased to discover that nothing was broken or out of joint, but he was sore and would be worse in the morning, he knew.

Slowly he stirred. He could hear the frightened shouts of the townspeople. The horses were bucking and snorting with fear. His own mount and those of his fellow Wizards had fled. Branock looked over at Wytlethane. He too was moving, making a slow, careful effort to sit up.

Branock turned to see about their young companion, but Cassis wasn't moving. The elder Wizard had half expected to see the younger man already on his feet and smirking, but Cassis lay completely still, his blood red robes blackened all along his left shoulder.

"Wytlethane," Branock said as he turned quickly back to the other Wizard.

"Is he dead?" Wytlethane asked, his voice as even as a frozen pond. Branock knew his rival was worried but he would never let it show.

"I don't know," Branock groaned as he got to his feet. He moved quickly to the younger Wizard and peered down at him. The lightning spell had broken through Cassis' defenses and burned a ragged hole in his shoulder. The flesh was scorched, as was the fabric of his robe, but the younger man was breathing – he wasn't dead.

"He lives," Branock said. "But his blocking spell wasn't strong enough."

"Perhaps now he will stop complaining about having to practice," Wytlethane said. "He knows the spell, it just isn't second nature to him yet."

"I'll find the horses while you look after him," Branock said.

He shuffled away as Wytlethane bent over the younger Wizard. Branock could have healed him, but healing was a delicate art that required patience, and at that moment Branock's mind was reeling. He couldn't believe the sheer power that Zollin had unleashed. To be sure, it was raw, totally unrefined. In fact Branock doubted the boy had even cast a spell at all – it was simply unrestrained power. That was why the blow had sent them flying, and the thought made the elder Wizard giddy. Truly, he thought, this boy was a power to rival the Master.

"Sir," shouted one of the mercenaries as he came charging forward on a horse that was still fighting to break away from its rider. "The boy and his father fled in that direction."

He pointed away from the village proper toward a small hill.

"Three of our best are after him now, sir," the soldier said. "We'll have him soon."

Branock merely nodded and calculated his plan of action. He knew the mercenaries would be slain, and the thought caused him no ill feelings. Nothing mattered except getting Zollin under his control. He didn't care how many people had to die, as long as he got to the young Wizard first, and without his companions.

"Gather your remaining men, Captain," Branock said to the solider. "Have them meet us here. And retrieve our horses."

"Yes, lord," the man said as he hauled on the reins of the frantic animal. He dug his heels into the horse's flanks and the charger leapt away, kicking up dust with its thick hooves.

It took nearly an hour to heal Cassis. The young Wizard was up and moving, but he too was sore from the fall and weak from the wound. Although the injury had been completely healed, his body had suffered from the trauma and was still in shock. The mercenaries had found the Wizard's horses, and together they made their way up toward the Carpenter's house on the outskirts of town.

"My back is killing me," Cassis complained. "Why didn't you heal that too?"

"Stop whining," Branock said, trying to keep his amusement

at the younger Wizard's misfortune hidden. "You are lucky to be alive. Besides, healing every little ache and pain would take hours. Meanwhile, our quarry is fleeing into the woods."

"How do you know that?" Cassis asked.

"Well, it's merely a guess, but it makes sense. Besides, I have felt the draw of his power receding, haven't you?"

"Of course I have. I merely asked how you knew he was fleeing into the forest."

"Simple logic," Branock said smugly. "I know because I think. You should try it some time."

Cassis glared at the elder Wizard, but before he could respond, Wytlethane spoke.

"Patience, Cassis. Branock is only trying to bait you."

"It's working," Cassis said under his breath.

Just then, they spotted the two slain mercenaries lying in the shadow of the house. One of the other soldiers rode ahead and inspected the bodies. Another searched the house and two others scouted ahead to ensure that their company wasn't riding into an ambush.

"Are they dead?" asked Branock.

"Yes, my lord," said the soldier.

"I thought you said that three of your men rode up here, Captain?"

"They did," said the soldier, looking at the man who ducked back out of the house.

"No one in there, sir," said the mercenary, jerking his thumb toward the house.

From the far side, a horse came galloping up.

"Tank's over there, sir," the recent arrival said to the captain of the mercenaries. "He looks burned."

"And who is that?" Branock said, pointing to another body that was lying just inside the small lean-to on the far end of the house.

One of the soldier's walked over, "He's a local, my lord. He's dead too."

Branock slowly dismounted and walked toward where

Todrek's body lay.

"Why are you wasting time?" Cassis grumbled. "Shouldn't we be pursing the boy?"

"Yes," Branock replied as he bent forward over the swollen body. "But it helps to know your quarry."

"What do you plan to learn from a dead boy?" Cassis smirked.

Branock straightened slowly, his back stiffer already, which wasn't a good sign. He was dreading the long, cold night ahead.

"Well, not much," the elder Wizard said. "But I know that this boy was important to Zollin. And I know he hasn't yet learned to heal."

"What?" Cassis remarked, surprised. He nudged his horse forward to see Todrek's body.

"He took the time to try and heal this boy," Branock explained. "See the blood all over the boy's tunic. And the swollen neck, but no visible wound? He healed him, but his focus was only skin deep."

Branock left the group and went into the small home. He took his time, studying anything that seemed interesting. There was much to learn. The home was neat and efficient with two small bedrooms leading off the main room. There were typical fixtures around the home, cooking utensils, beds, well-crafted wooden furniture. But what Branock found most interesting wasn't what he found, it was what seemed to be absent from the home. There was no sign of anything feminine in the entire house, no flowers, no hair brushes or aprons or dresses of any kind. Branock made his way back out into the cold winter sunlight.

"The Captain's men have found the boy's trail," Cassis sneered. "Now that you are finally finished inspecting the house, we can go after him."

"Yes, well, perhaps we should split up," Branock suggested.

"What? Why?" Cassis asked.

"You can obviously ride much faster than we can," Branock said, indicating Wytlethane and himself. "Take your soldiers and range ahead. We will follow as quickly as our decrepit bodies will allow."

"Just get on your horse," Wytlethane said.

"Tell me you aren't sore," Branock replied. "Tell me you can ride through the night and all day long tomorrow."

Wytlethane looked at Branock for a moment and there was the barest hint of indecision. He wasn't sure if he could trust his colleague, but he had no desire to sit on his skittish horse a moment longer than he had to.

"Alright," Wytlethane said. "Ride on, Cassis, and pursue the boy. But do not engage him without us."

"That's right, Cassis, you'd just get yourself killed," Branock added, his voice grave as if he cared only for the younger Wizard's safety.

"We'll see about that," Cassis sneered. "Come on, Captain, you heard them. Let's ride."

The younger Wizard kicked his horse and galloped away, the mercenaries following along behind.

"Why did you do that?" Wytlethane asked.

"I didn't want to listen to him complaining constantly."

"Surely you don't think Cassis could control himself. He'll kill the Master's prize."

"I doubt that."

"Why, because he caught us by surprise? Cassis is impatient and impetuous, but he is no fool. He'll be ready the next time they meet."

"I've no doubt about that," Branock agreed. "But I doubt he'll find the boy. His mercenaries are not woodsmen. They'll lose the trail and wander aimlessly through the night. Zollin and his father will head north, into the mountains."

"And you think we'll find them?"

"Yes, eventually, but not tonight and not tomorrow, not even if we could ride without rest. They are hunted and scared. They won't stop moving, and in the end our patience will win out. They'll be exhausted and beaten down when we find them. Perhaps the boy will simply agree to come with us without a fight."

"Perhaps," said Wytlethane, his deep voice unconvinced.

"Perhaps not."

Chapter 8

They rode single file, urging their horses to move as fast as possible through the trees and over the rough, uneven ground. They did not speak. Quinn rode in the lead, followed by Mansel, Brianna, and finally Zollin. It was a bright and beautiful winter day. The sky was clear and the sunlight would have been welcome, but stark branches over their heads seemed to filter any heat that might have warmed them. The forest floor was covered in leaves, but they were packed down and stuck together from the snow that had fallen on them from the branches above. The horses moved almost silently, their normally heavy steps muffled by the decaying leaves.

Zollin noticed all these things, the way the wind seemed to find every opening in his cloak, the way the leather saddles creaked as they rode, the smell of damp foliage all around them. He tried to think of anything except the events of the morning in Tranaugh Shire, but his mind kept reliving the awful moment that Todrek had died. He saw the sword flashing as it swung down. He saw his friend's clumsy attempt to block the stroke, then the blood, dark crimson as it arced up after the sword. Todrek had seemed to fall in slow motion, dropping his sword and grabbing his throat in a useless attempt to stop the blood. He had dropped to his knees and then toppled backward on the brown winter grass.

It was worse than a nightmare, it both terrified him and filled him with grief. He had cried, trying desperately to do so without making a sound. Fortunately his horse, a veteran of countless journeys, knew to follow the animals in front of him without any direction from its rider. Zollin spent most of the day hunched over his saddle, his head close to or even resting on the big horse's neck. He watched the ground, numb to the sparks of magic that represented the three Wizards of the Torr who were surely following him. He wished he had just stepped up and gone with them. What would it have hurt, he argued to himself. He was planning on leaving anyway; if he had gone with the other Wizards no one would have been hurt. Now his best friend was dead and it was Zollin's fault.

The truth of it was so bitter in his mouth that he felt he would retch.

Just a few yards ahead of him was Todrek's widow. He wondered how he would ever be able to look at her again. Why had she come with them? he wondered. He had sat up once, trying to shake off the black mood that possessed him, but Brianna's lingering perfume had wafted to him, standing out from the damp earth and rotting vegetation of the forest around him. It stirred feelings within him, natural feelings, but feelings he hated all the same. He hated himself and wished he could die. When they stopped for a very brief rest to share the food from his pack, he couldn't bring himself to eat. And at some point during the day he had dozed off. He was lucky he hadn't fallen from the saddle. But when he finally opened his eyes, night was falling.

Quinn finally reined his horse to a stop. There was a small clearing near a noisy stream, and the riders all came together and dismounted, letting the horses drink. Quinn moved quietly to Zollin and took him aside.

"You need to tell me everything," his father whispered.

"About what?" Zollin asked.

"About you, about this magic, how long you've been practicing it, everything."

Zollin stammered for a moment. He felt so awful, the weight of his guilt was overwhelming. He told his father about the day they were framing the Inn, about the tool bag and later the fireplace. He told him how he had discovered the willow tree and his staff. He told the truth about the traveling illusionist and how he had gotten their horse, Lilly.

"Who else did you tell about this?" Quinn asked.

"I told Todrek," Zollin admitted, feeling ashamed for even speaking his friend's name aloud. "He panicked and said all magic was evil sorcery. So I didn't tell anyone else. After he was engaged to Brianna I was going to leave, but he asked me to stand with him. I've told no one else, except Brianna."

"Brianna," Quinn called to the girl.

She moved toward them, her slim form moving carefully. She was obviously very saddle sore.

"Alright," Quinn said as she arrived. "We have to know how these Wizards knew about us. Zollin said he told you he could use magic. Did you tell anyone?"

"No," she said, her large eyes looking directly into Quinn's as she spoke. "I doubt anyone would have believed me if I had."

"Didn't you and Todrek talk about it?" Quinn asked.

"No," she said, her eyes dropping for an instant when Quinn mentioned her husband's name.

Zollin felt a lump rising in his throat, and although he didn't think he could cry anymore, his eyes burned and blurred with tears. He wanted to run away, to lose himself in oblivion, to find a hole, crawl inside and die.

"I mentioned it once, but Todrek would not speak of it," Brianna said.

"And you don't know if he told anyone either?" Quinn asked.

"I don't know, but I doubt it. He acted like he didn't want to acknowledge it."

"Alright, so then the only other person who could have told them about you was the illusionist."

Zollin nodded. He wished he hadn't revealed himself to the traveling entertainer, but he could have thought of no other way to get the man to take him seriously. Now they were all paying for his mistakes.

"Well, there's no way to know if they're following us but-"

"They are," Zollin interrupted. "I can feel them."

"You can what?"

"I can feel them. It's like a sense of dread, or like when someone is watching you."

"That's just paranoia," Quinn said matter-of-factly.

"No, it's different. I can sense magic within people and things, like the willow tree or my staff. I can tell if someone has magic in them. I've been feeling the Wizards approaching for the last few weeks. I can feel them getting closer – the feeling is growing stronger."

"How close are they?"

"I don't know. I can't tell how close or where exactly, just

70

that they're getting closer."

Zollin could tell his father was frustrated, but he didn't know what else to say. There was a long, awkward silence before Brianna finally spoke.

"Can we make camp here for the night? There's fresh water and plenty of wood for a fire."

"No, we need to press on," Quinn said sadly. "If Zollin can feel the other Wizards it's a safe bet they can feel him too. They can probably track us by it, so we need to put as much distance as we can between us. Go ahead and get out some food. We'll eat, then move on."

Brianna nodded then shuffled away. Quinn stood looking at his son; Zollin looked down at the ground. He couldn't imagine what his father was feeling, and even though he was sure it wasn't good, at that moment he really didn't care. He was numb, and his grief raged like a stormy ocean in his soul. He was overcome by it, unable to cope with it, much less control it.

"I know it's hard," Quinn said softly.

Zollin looked up, surprised at hearing his father speak. Quinn was only a little taller than his son, his hair going grey at the temples, his face lined with age and too much time spent in the sun, but his body was still solid. There wasn't much excess fat on him, and his arms and shoulders were well rounded with muscle. He looked as comfortable in armor with a sword at his waist as he did with a tool bag over his shoulder and a sturdy piece of timber in his hands.

"I lost my best friend, too, you know," he said.

Zollin looked up, surprised and hopeful, until he realized that his father was talking about his mother. It was almost more than he could stand. He knew his mother had died giving birth to him, and the guilt pushed his emotions over the edge.

"I'm sorry," Zollin said, his voice cracking as tears flowed down his checks. He sobbed, his knees buckling beneath him. His father caught him and they both ended up on the damp ground. "I didn't mean to kill her," Zollin managed to say between gasps for breath.

"Her?" Quinn asked. "You mean your mother?"

Zollin nodded.

"Son, I don't blame you for your mother's death."

But Zollin couldn't take any more. He didn't want to hear anyone rationalize about how this wasn't his fault, or that he wasn't to blame. It was his fault. People were dead and it was because of him. If he stayed with his father and Brianna, they would probably be killed too. In fact, if his father was right and the Wizards from the Torr could track him, then his presence was putting them in danger.

He pushed away from his father and rose to his feet on shaking legs. "I'm leaving. You're better off without me."

"No son – "

But Zollin wouldn't let him finish. "If they're after me, then you should go as far from me as possible. Take Brianna with you and keep her safe."

"No, I'm not leaving you. Not now, not like this."

"Go back to Tranaugh Shire, tell everyone I'm sorry. Tell Todrek's parents that I'm sorry."

He was crying uncontrollably. He started to turn away, but his father grabbed his arm. Before Zollin knew what was happening, his father had spun him back around and slapped his gloved hand across his son's face. The impact was jarring and made Zollin gasp at the pain. After a moment of surprise, a white hot anger sprang up. His father hadn't struck him in years and never like that. His face throbbed from the impact.

"What the hell do you think you're doing?" he shouted.

"You mad?" his father shouted back.

"You're lucky I don't…" he let the thought trail off.

"You listen to me, boy," Quinn said stepping close, his face mere inches from his son's. "I know you're hurting but we need you. I know you feel guilty and you blame yourself but you didn't kill Todrek. A mercenary killed your friend. Do you know what that means? It means cold blooded killers are chasing us. It means that those Wizards who want to carry you away are still out there right now. You want to blame someone, blame them. We need you. If you run off on your own, you'll be playing right into their hands."

"But I don't know what to do!" Zollin said, his frustration making his voice harsh.

"We'll learn as we go," his father assured him. "Right now we need to get to safety. The winter snows will be here soon, and then we'll have time to plot our next move. But for now we need to keep moving, stay ahead of those mercenaries, keep Mansel and Brianna safe."

"Keep moving where?" Zollin asked.

"We move north. Hopefully we can make it into the mountains before the snows hit. That way we'll be safe for a while. We can find shelter and sit out the worst of the winter storms. And hopefully in that time we'll come up with a plan."

"Have you ever been in the mountains?" Zollin asked, his anger and grief receding.

"Yes, once, before you were born. I worked for a while in a small village called Brighton's Gate. It's on Telford's Pass through the mountains, and if we can get there I'm sure some of the townsfolk will give us shelter."

"Can we make it? How far is it?"

"It will be close, but I don't want to go south. Too many people, and we won't know who to trust."

"Can we trust the people at Brighton's Gate?"

"It won't matter. We'll all be snowed in for the season. The passes fill up with snow so there's no way to leave. When the passes reopen, we'll move on."

"I hope you're right," Zollin said.

"Have you got any better ideas?" his father asked.

At first Zollin thought that Quinn was simply asking a rhetorical question, but his father waited, obviously expecting an answer. There was a strange look of respect on Quinn's face. Zollin had expected the question to simply end the argument, but it seemed as if his father genuinely wanted to know if he had any ideas.

"No, sir, that sounds like a good plan."

"Alright then," Quinn said, "we press on. Let's get something to eat."

Zollin started to protest, but then his stomach growled. He

couldn't imagine enjoying a meal, but he could at least fill his stomach. They walked back to where Mansel and Brianna were sitting on a fallen log. Mansel was chatting amiably, seemingly oblivious to the danger that was pursuing them. Brianna, Zollin noticed, didn't seem distraught. He had avoided her all day, expecting to see anger and grief over Todrek's death, but she seemed fine. In fact, she had prepared food for him and motioned for him to sit beside her.

It was physically painful to see how beautiful she was. Even though she had been riding all day long, her face and hands pale from the cold, her eyes drooping slightly from exhaustion, she was still captivating. Zollin remembered how thrilled Todrek had been to have won her hand in marriage. She had inspired his friend to greatness, to achieving all that he could, and Zollin could see why. But her beauty was like an open wound to him. He wouldn't let himself feel the giddy sweetness of being close to her. He willed himself at that moment to never love her, no matter what. She was Todrek's and he could not betray his friend's memory.

"So what's the plan?" Mansel asked.

"We head north," Quinn said and then took a huge bite of bread.

"Well, we won't last long on these rations. We'll have to find more food. I would have laid out some of the dried meat but there just isn't much left."

"I can provide some more food," Zollin said. He walked over to the stream, which was shallow but wide. The icy water was clear, and after a moment, he spotted a big trout resting behind a large stone from the swift current. Zollin took a firm grip on his staff and concentrated on the fish. He had done this at home, but now he had an audience. He closed his eyes and directed the flow of magic. The power from his staff mingled with the magic of the willow belt and flowed through him. He felt it move out into the water until he could feel the smooth skin of the fish through the connection. Then he lifted it up out of the water. It took all his concentration to hold onto the wiggling fish. In the small stream near the magic willow tree, Zollin had dropped more fish than he had caught, and none of them had been the size of this trout. But he had this one, and he was determined not to lose it. It wiggled madly, flipping back and forth, trying to escape and return to the safety of the stream. Zollin moved it over to the bank and laid it gently on the rocks. It jumped but was too far from the water to return on its own.

"That's a handy trick!" Mansel called out excitedly.

"True, but I don't think we can risk a fire," Quinn said, his voice heavy with frustration. "We're going to need to move on soon, and the smoke from a fire would lead them right to us."

"I can take care of that, too," Zollin said. "Mansel, would you clean it?"

The older boy, normally taunting Zollin and making life miserable, responded happily, as if he wasn't running for his life from powerful Wizards but rather was on a family picnic. Quinn frowned and pulled Zollin aside again.

"We really don't have time for this."

"We have to eat, Dad."

"No one wants to eat raw fish."

"I'll cook it, trust me."

"I know you think you're helping, but our first priority is to put distance between us and those Wizards. We got the best of them in Tranaugh Shire because they weren't expecting us to resist. But they'll be ready this time."

"Look, Dad, I'm not asking you to do anything different than what you had planned. If you're ready to go, let's go."

Quinn smiled, glad that Zollin had complied without a confrontation. He turned and called out to the others, "Alright, everyone, grab your horse and let's cross the stream. Then we'll walk them for a while."

"What about the trout?" Mansel asked.

"Just toss it back into the stream," Quinn said.

"No, keep cleaning it," Zollin interjected.

"Zollin, he can't lead his horse and clean the fish at the same time."

"I'll lead his horse until he's finished."

Quinn sighed in exasperation. "He'll freeze if he walks

across the stream."

"He won't wade," Zollin said. He concentrated on Mansel and lifted him several inches off the ground. The young apprentice froze, his face flushing with embarrassment as he floated smoothly to the other side of the stream. Zollin sagged as he set the boy down. Normally with his staff and willow belt he could have levitated Mansel across the stream a dozen times without getting tired. But after the shock of the morning's events and his lack of food, he felt as if he had just run a long race. His heart was pounding in his ears and he was breathing heavily.

"What exactly do you have planned?" his father asked, clearly angry now.

"I can cook the fish, Dad, as we walk and without a fire. It may not be just right, but it'll be edible and hot. It won't slow us down and we'll all feel better."

"I'm not sure how I feel about all this," Quinn said, his voice a little shaky. Zollin couldn't tell if it was from anger or fear, but he didn't know what to say.

"I think it's okay," Brianna said quietly from behind them.

"I'm just a little out of my element," Quinn said softly.

"We all are," she said, laying her hand gently on his shoulder. "But I don't think Zollin's power is bad."

"I don't…" Quinn hesitated. "I just wish you had shared your gift with me sooner, son."

"I'm sorry, but I didn't think you'd be okay with it."

"I'm not sure I would have been, but everything is happening so fast. You're growing up and I thought I had accepted that. You wanted to leave and I was planning on convincing you to stay in the village a few more years, but when those Wizards arrived today, I just… well, I just couldn't let you go."

It was an awkward moment. Zollin wanted to say something, to reassure his father, but he didn't know what he could say. He loved his dad, and he was really glad that Quinn had come with him, but he didn't want to be coddled. He needed his father to trust him, to let him contribute. His whole life he had felt out of place, like someone who needed to be helped rather than a productive part of their little family. He had always thought his father tolerated him, but now he was able to bring more than an equal share to their group and he resented being held back and second guessed.

"A lot has changed, but one thing is common among us all," Brianna said. She was young, but she seemed older somehow, more mature. "We all knew that we had to go with Zollin. Maybe we all had our own reasons, but we all came." She looked into Zollin's eyes, and although he wanted to, he couldn't look away. "We came because we wanted to, not because we had to."

***

"I propose we split up," Branock said.

"Why?" asked Wytlethane.

"We can cover more ground, of course. I don't know about you, but I'm tired of chasing this boy. I'm tired of tramping around in the wilderness and would like to return to the Torr."

Branock smiled inwardly at his own suggestion. He knew Cassis didn't have the patience to take his time finding the boy. It was a calculated risk, since there was a good chance that Cassis would find the boy and kill him. He didn't worry about Wytlethane – the elderly Wizard moved so slowly, the odds that he would find the boy were miniscule. Cassis, on the other hand, would blunder about and hopefully be easy to avoid. If Branock could find the boy and influence him, away from the others, he would have a much better chance of making him an ally.

"I don't like the idea," Wytlethane said.

"Oh, come now," said Branock, "Cassis has split the soldiers among us. We'll spread out, find the boy quickly, and be back in Osla before you know it."

"Well, if you insist," Wytlethane said wearily.

"Yes, well, I think it's only prudent," Branock said, sounding very high-handed.

Wytlethane frowned but didn't object. Cassis had divided the soldiers into three small groups. Branock thought he would enjoy destroying Cassis when the time was right. He would make it last as long as possible... when the time was right. There were now six men-at-arms with each Wizard. They knew the boy Zollin and his companions were heading northeast, toward the forest of Peddinggar. There was little chance the boy would be able to change directions and slip past them. And there was only so far to go before they ran into the mountains or the sea.

"When you have the boy, send out a pulse and we will come to you," Branock said.

Cassis and his soldiers, the youngest of the group of mercenaries, had alread set out at a brisk trot and were soon well away from the others. Branock now moved past Wytlethane quickly, anxious to carry out the second part of his plan. After an hour of steady travel, he reined his horse in and said he needed to rest. Suddenly, he pretended to have an idea and suggested the soldiers ride ahead in search of the boy. He gave them strict orders not to engage the group if they found them, but he knew the mercenaries would ignore him. They didn't know why the boy was valuable, although they had certainly seen his power. But they would undoubtedly decide they could make a better deal for the boy if they had him in their custody. He considered it a test. The boy should be able to defeat the soldiers, and if he couldn't then Branock would not waste his time mentoring Zollin. Plus, he would seem much less threatening alone than riding with armed guards. It was another risk, but he needed to be alone when he found Zollin, to gain the boy's trust. It was essential that he have time alone – besides, to him the soldiers were little more than servants. He could protect himself much more adequately than they could. And so the soldiers rode away, and the aging Wizard was alone. He waited a few moments before following after the soldiers. He had no intention of letting them get too far ahead. When the time came, he wanted to see how the boy handled himself.

Chapter 9

Zollin, Quinn, and Brianna joined Mansel on the other side of the stream and began walking, leading their weary horses to give them a break. Once Mansel had cleaned the trout, he took the horses and gave Zollin the fish. The young Wizard was tired. All he wanted was to lie down and sleep, but he kept plodding along, putting one foot in front of the other. It was getting dark fast, and he knew they would have a long, cold night ahead of them. He knew he needed to eat if he was going to make it, but the thought of eating was difficult to bear. He lifted the fish into the air and concentrated on heating the meat. He imagined the fish cooking as if it were in a pan. Soon the fish was sizzling and Zollin's head was swimming. He knew he would need to ride if he was going to make it much longer. They stopped and divided the trout. The food was good, if a bit bland, but they were all hungry and cold, so having something warm in their hands and in their stomachs was comforting.

The night grew cold, bitterly cold, so that they sat on their horses shivering in the ragged blankets they had gathered before fleeing Tranaugh Shire. The horses blew clouds of moist air from their nostrils, their heads hanging low. They traveled by moonlight until the moon set. Then Quinn finally let them stop in a stand of cedar trees to rest for a few hours until the sun came up. They talked briefly about standing watch, but it was so dark they knew they wouldn't be able to see if anyone approached. Their best chance was stay near the horses, whose keen ears would hear anyone who came near. So they tied the horses to some low-hanging branches and lay down on the cold ground together. Despite the frigid night, they fell asleep almost immediately, and it seemed to Zollin as if he had just closed his eyes when he was roused by his cold, aching body.

Quinn was already awake, rubbing his chest with his hands to increase the blood flow. The sun was rising and Zollin knew they needed to press on. He rose slowly and gathered some more food from his pack. There would be enough for two more small meals, and then they would be completely out of rations. He bit off a chunk of dried beef and let the salty meat soften up in his mouth. He handed some of the meat to his father, who nodded gratefully.

"Been a long time since I camped cold," Quinn said.

"You've done this before?"

"Sure, with the army. We spent lots of nights out in the open, drilling and scouting."

"That's where you learned to fight?"

"Yes."

"How come you never taught me?" Zollin asked.

"I didn't want you to fight," Quinn said sadly. "I wanted you to become a carpenter. I wanted you to marry a nice girl like Brianna and settle down, have a family. Just like my father wanted, only I didn't want that life. Or at least I thought I didn't when I was your age."

Zollin felt an eruption of pain when his father mentioned Brianna. He felt so guilty because he had been jealous of Todrek. He had wanted to be with Brianna, had day-dreamed of her running away with him, and now here she was. Only he couldn't be with her, he couldn't even let himself imagine it.

"Why did you leave home?" he asked, hoping to get his mind off the girl who was sleeping not far away.

"Over a girl," his father said, smirking. "I was young and infatuated, but her father wanted her to marry an older boy. I couldn't stand by and watch her marry another so I left. I joined the Royal Army and decided to live a life of adventure. Only being a soldier is a lot of hard work, constant discipline, and disappointment. I thought it would be exciting, even though my father warned me it wouldn't. But we mostly drilled and marched and made inspections."

"But you fought the Shirtac raiders?"

"Yes, but mostly we chased them back into their boats. It was a tedious life punctuated with brief moments of terror. Waging war is not exciting or glorious. It is pain and fear and luck and incredible sadness, as you now know."

Zollin thought about what his father had said. He agreed with the description, but at least his one skirmish had been over so fast, he only really knew the terror of it and the loss of his best friend.

"So how did you end up in Tranaugh Shire?" Zollin asked.

"Your mother wanted to live in the valley. When we married, we set off to find a home and Tranaugh Shire was in need of a carpenter. So we made our home and soon you were on the way. It was the happiest time of my life."

Zollin wanted to hear more. His father rarely ever spoke of his mother. Zollin had no memory of her, only a deep wound in his soul, a missing piece that she should have filled. Still, he knew his father wouldn't say more. His own pain over the loss of Zollin's mother was too painful to linger on.

Quinn stood up. "Better wake the others," he said. "We should be moving soon."

Zollin thought the need for constant travel was a bit extreme, but by that afternoon he would realize how wrong he was.

***

Branock's soldiers had stumbled across their quarry's trail and had caught up with Zollin's group not long after dawn. They took their time trailing along quietly, studying the group. Around midday, they broke off their pursuit and circled around the group, all of whom were riding their horses again but still moving at a very slow pace.

Branock watched them, guessing correctly that they planned to move ahead and ambush the young Wizard and his companions. It was a good plan, Branock conceded. The small band of refugees was expecting an attack from the rear, pushing themselves and their mounts almost to exhaustion. But even though the strategy was sound, it was the tactics themselves which really mattered. If the soldiers were not able to subdue Zollin very quickly, and Branock doubted that they could, there was little chance of success. Still, if they could manage to wound or kill some or all of the young Wizard's friends, that would make Branock's job that much easier. He smiled as he rode along, wondering why the soldiers hadn't noticed that their horses seemed so fresh. Branock had been close enough to rejuvenate their mounts. He carried Zipple Weed for that very purpose. The plant was poisonous if ingested, but had a strengthening magic that could be transferred rather easily to man or beast. It always boggled his mind how non-magical people could be affected so easily with magic and never know it.

He rode on, drawing as close to the small band as he could without risking detection. He was anxious to see what would happen. He could sense Zollin ahead of him, or perhaps it was knowing that the boy was ahead that made if feel as if he could feel the magic's location. He could sense Cassis and Wytlethane as well, but he had no idea where the other Wizards were. Soon enough though, they would know where Zollin was. Wizards could sense magic in others, could feel a powerful Wizard approaching, but if that Wizard used his power, it would send out a pulse, much like a rock thrown into a quiet pond would make ripples. That pulse could be felt, its direction perceived. And if the Wizard cast multiple spells, the exact location could be ascertained. Branock would have to deal with that, too. He needed to take advantage of Cassis being alone. This was his chance to cripple Wytlethane and create a controlling interest in the Torr. If he could dispose of Cassis and make it appear that the headstrong Wizard had bitten off more than he could chew, this prolonged search would be very valuable. He smiled at the thought of being his own master, with Zollin carrying out his every whim. It was a very pleasant fantasy, one that he needed to bring to life.

***

The day passed slowly for Zollin. They walked the horses as much as they could, but the small band was extremely tired. Their short nap on the frozen ground hadn't done much to refresh them. Mansel alone seemed energetic. Quinn was lost deep in his own thoughts, and Brianna was suffering from saddle soreness that the cold night had only made worse. She was moving slowly and limping when she walked. Zollin wished he could help her, but he had no idea how. He could still feel the Wizards approaching, although they seemed closer and farther away at the same time; closer, yet not as strong. Still, he was sorely tempted to force his father to stop and let Brianna rest. He was bone-weary himself, his eyes felt full of sand, and his stomach was aching from too little food and too little sleep.

It was late afternoon when the attack came. The group was making their way into a clearing when they heard a shout, and suddenly horses were galloping toward them. There were three attackers on their left and three more riding in on their right. At first the group froze, watching as the mercenaries, those who had been sent ahead by Branock, raced toward them, waving their long swords in the air.

"Ride!" Quinn shouted, kicking his horse into motion. He spun his horse and began galloping back the way they had come. The others followed as the soldiers charged after them.

"What are we doing?" Zollin shouted.

"We've got to find a place to make a stand."

Zollin looked at the terrain, but it was the same in every direction, gently rolling hills lightly wooded, no one place more defensible than another. His horse was heaving, with foam flying from its mouth. He knew they couldn't keep up their pace much longer without killing the horses. He looked at Brianna, who was wide eyed with fear, but seeing her in that state steeled his resolve. He pulled back on the reins and his horse slid to a stop. He jumped down, his staff in his hand. The horse, still heaving with exertion, its sides slick with sweat, trotted several paces away. Zollin didn't notice as he turned back to face the oncoming riders.

He wondered at what distance his magic would be effective. He could feel the power within him raging, worked into a frenzy by his emotions like storm winds churning the sea. He was scared mostly of failing. He could see Todrek falling, his ruined throat covered in his life's blood. He couldn't let that happen to his father, or worse yet Brianna. Even Mansel, whom he had despised for so long, deserved better than to be cut down by these murderers.

***

Branock had almost been exposed as the group raced back to escape the soldiers. He moved silently among the trees, keeping his eyes on Zollin. When the young Wizard reined in his horse and prepared to take a stand, the old Wizard smiled. The boy had courage, but separating himself from his companions was a mistake.

But perhaps he did not care for them, perhaps as the Master had said Branock thought too much about mortal concerns and now he was projecting them onto Zollin. He held his breath and waited to see what the boy would do as the soldiers came within range of his attacks.

***

Zollin felt the magic coursing through him like a river, swollen by spring rains, threatening to overflow its banks. The soldiers were almost close enough. He had to hold himself in check as they drew closer. Just a little closer, he thought to himself, I have to make this count.

But before he could unleash the raging torrent of power building up within him, the riders split apart again. They circled him, staying out of long bow range. Zollin wasn't an archer, but he didn't think his magic would be very effective at this distance. He realized their tactic, avoiding him to pursue the others. His heart dropped into his stomach as he saw his father in the distance realizing that Zollin had stopped. The group was now turning back to help him.

"No!" shouted Zollin. He ran to his horse but the exhausted animal trotted just out of reach. He looked up and saw the soldiers flanking his father and friends. The soldiers, three on each side, were now turning in toward their prey. Zollin sprinted toward them.

Fear felt like a noose around his neck, his arms and legs felt heavy, his movements seemed so slow. But he ran on, intent on helping, even though it was obvious he could only focus his attention on one group of riders. Instinctively he turned toward the soldiers riding toward Brianna. They were closing in on her when he reacted, almost without thought. The range was still extreme, but he couldn't wait any longer.

"Blast!" he shouted, pointing his staff at the riders. Lightning shot out, bright and crackling in the afternoon sunlight. The energy hit the horse closest to Zollin and knocked it into the others. All three riders were knocked into the air, two tumbling and rolling along the ground, the third crashing with bone-shattering force into a tree. The third soldier fell in heap and lay still.

Brianna hesitated then, unsure what to do. Meanwhile there

was a clashing of blades as the other riders closed in on Quinn and Mansel. Quinn, with his sword and shield, was struggling against two of the attackers. Mansel and the third soldier were circling each other. The big man in black armor looked like a cat who was toying with the mouse he had caught. Abruptly, one of the soldiers facing Quinn turned his horse and moved toward Brianna.

"Ride, Brianna!" Zollin shouted. "To me, quickly!"

She urged her horse forward, but the beast was too tired. It moved slowly and the other soldier was gaining ground quickly. Zollin raised his staff but the soldier fell into line with Brianna. There was no way the young Wizard could attack without hurting the girl. He was running as fast as he could, but he was still too far away.

"Faster!" he shouted, but Brianna's mare, the old horse Zollin had won from the illusionist, was just too exhausted.

He saw the soldier raise his sword as he closed in on Brianna. Suddenly the world darkened all around Zollin, and in his sight all he could see was the bright blade flashing in the sunlight that shone through the bare winter branches overhead.

"Rise!" Zollin shouted and he felt a tug, as if the magic had been jerked out of him. But the sword was flying up, spinning through air and finally tumbling back to the ground behind the soldier. The attacker reined his horse in and turned back for his weapon.

Zollin looked back to his father. Quinn was using his legs and knees to keep his horse moving away from his attacker. The soldier had a long cavalry sword while Quinn had a shorter blade and shield. It was obvious that Quinn was on the defensive, the soldier using the longer reach of his weapon to attack without coming close enough for Quinn to strike back.

Mansel was now on the ground, having successfully defended the soldier's first blow, but the force of the two blades colliding had knocked the apprentice carpenter off his horse. Mansel was trying desperately to remain in the defensive stance that Quinn had taught him. It was obviously the only swordsmanship the boy knew.

Quinn's shield was tarnished from disuse, but sparks flew off of it as the soldier attacked, over and over again. Quinn was holding his own, until the cavalry sword bounced from the shield and clipped the horse's neck. Quinn's mount reared in pain, its hooves waving madly at the other rider, whose own horse reared in return. The Master Carpenter tumbled backward off the horse as the soldier struggled to remain in the saddle.

Finally, Brianna's horse reached Zollin. He swung up behind her, his staff extended in his right hand, his left arm curving around her waist and taking the reins. He turned the horse and kicked back into a gallop. The soldier who had been chasing Brianna had retrieved his sword and was now charging toward them again. Without thinking, Zollin raised his staff. It crackled and hissed as magic ran visibly up and down the shaft, dancing around his hand and flickering up his arm. As they approached each other, like knights on a tournament joust, the magic leapt out of Zollin without him even speaking the command. The blast hit the soldier in the chest and blew his chainmail shirt to pieces, knocking him backward off his horse to land in a smoking heap on the ground.

Quinn's attacker had his mount under control now and was charging back toward the Carpenter. Zollin pointed his staff at the soldier but he closed too quickly, swinging his long sword in a wicked arc. Quinn raised his shield in time to block the blow, but the force knocked him backward off his feet. He lay still on the turf, making Zollin's heart race. But as the soldier advanced toward Quinn, Zollin noticed that Mansel was cornered between two trees. The young apprentice had lost his sword, and only his ability to scramble, learned by years of evading four older brothers, had kept him alive this long. The soldier, with a wicked grin on his face, raised his sword for the killing stroke, but Mansel proved to be inventive as well as quick. Without a moment's hesitation, the young apprentice grabbed the horse by the nose and shoved the beast's head between himself and the sword. The soldier was knocked off balance as the horse kicked out, snapping three of Mansel's ribs, and his sword lodged firmly in the trunk of the tree. Mansel dropped to the ground as the soldier fought to stay on his horse, which was bucking and kicking wildly.

Just then, the other soldier reached Quinn, urging his mount to trample his downed opponent. Zollin was just about to blast the soldier, but at that moment Quinn slashed at the horse's front leg, slicing through flesh and bone. The Master Carpenter was barely fast enough to roll out of the way before the horse toppled, rolling right over the soldier on its back. Quinn was back on his feet, but the soldiers Zollin had knocked from their horses in his initial attack were now closing in on him.

Zollin acted quickly, blasting the soldier still on his horse near Mansel before turning his attention to the other two attackers. Both men had slowed, seeing Zollin and Brianna on horseback, Quinn armed and waiting. First one, then the other, turned and began running away. Zollin swung his staff and the nearest soldier was battered by an invisible force into a large oak tree, knocking the man unconscious. Then he focused his thoughts on the other man and thrust his staff at him. Even from a distance of over a hundred paces, they heard the man's spine crack. The soldier's body suddenly went limp and he fell, skidding along the forest floor before coming to stop and lying perfectly still.

For a moment, the only sound was the ragged breathing of Brianna's horse. The group was frozen, looking at the soldier Zollin had just killed. Then they heard Mansel moan. The young apprentice was leaning back onto the tree where the soldier's sword was still stuck. He was having trouble breathing and was obviously in pain. Brianna slipped off the horse, moving with Quinn quickly to the boy's side. Zollin felt a twinge of jealously seeing Brianna hurrying to aid the young apprentice. Then the guilt of such an emotion overwhelmed him.

I'm sorry, Todrek, Zollin thought. Then he turned his attention to the soldier he had knocked into the tree. He made a conscious effort not to look at the men he had killed. In the heat of battle he had acted without reservation and had felt no remorse. He knew the soldiers had no qualms about killing him or his friends, but seeing their lifeless bodies was unnerving. Facing death was hard, facing death he had inflicted was almost debilitating. He swung down from the tired horse, who dropped her head and moved slowly toward Brianna. Zollin walked in the opposite direction and found the man still senseless, his face stained with blood from a small wound in his scalp.

Zollin took hold of the soldier's collar and began slowly dragging him back to where the others had Mansel stretched out on the ground.

"How is he?" Zollin asked as he let go of the soldier near the others.

"Broken ribs, I think," Quinn said.

Mansel's face was wet with sweat and tears, pain distorting his features with each breath. But he was doing his best to not give in to the pain.

"Can you do anything to broken ribs?" Zollin asked his father.

Quinn shook his head. "Let's just hope he's not bleeding inside." The look in the elder man's eyes told Zollin that Mansel could possibly die.

"Zollin, can't you do something?" Brianna pleaded.

"I'm afraid to. I don't really know what I'm doing."

"But he's in so much pain," she said, her voice full of sympathy.

"But I can't help him," Zollin said.

"No, but I can," came a voice from behind them.

Chapter 10

Zollin spun around, his face frozen in shock. Without thinking, he raised his staff across his body for protection, but the spell he was expecting didn't come. Branock, who had seen the entire attack, was simply standing a short distance from the group gathered around Mansel. The air was thick with tension and nobody spoke at first, but finally Zollin found his tongue.

"What do you want?" he asked.

"To help, of course," Branock said, smiling. "Your friend is hurt. I can help him. May I approach?"

"Don't trust him," Quinn whispered.

"Perhaps he really can help," Brianna said, pleading with Zollin.

"Why are you following me?" Zollin asked. "Why did your soldiers attack us?"

"I'm afraid they were supposed to be protecting me," Branock said, trying his best to sound like a friendly old man. "Not that I needed it, but things being what they are in the world, I suppose it makes sense to travel with protection. Of course, these mercenaries," he said the last word with contempt, "only cared about money. They abandoned me and sought to capture you. You see, your talent is a rare thing, and I've come to help you develop it."

Branock intentionally played on Zollin's desire to know about the magic he possessed. He remembered how he had felt when he had discovered his own powers and how his Master had used a similar argument to lure him into joining the Torr.

Zollin's mind whirled. When the Wizards and soldiers had arrived at Tranaugh Shire, he had assumed that it was a bad thing, but now he wasn't so sure. Perhaps all they wanted was to help him, and their aggression was merely a response to his own.

"So you're saying you didn't order the attack?" Quinn said, the distrust in his voice clear to everyone.

"No, I would never do that," Branock lied. "Like I said, I only want to help."

"That's not what you said at Tranaugh Shire," Quinn said loudly, his distrust obvious.

"No, that's not true. I was forced by my companions to take an aggressive posture, but I assure you I meant no harm. You see, I'm not much of a Wizard," Branock lied again. "I'm really more of a teacher than anything else. I'm afraid Wytlethane and Cassis are threatened by your son. That's why I suggested that we split up. I'm only glad that I found you before they did. They would like nothing more than a reason to kill you, Zollin." As he said this, he slowly moved toward the group. His voice was soft and reassuring. "But I want to help you. I know it's hard to believe. I'm sure so much has happened so quickly, but I assure you, I only want to help you. And I can protect you from the others, protect your friends too. I'll prove myself. I'll heal your friend and then you'll see that I'm being honest. May I?"

He had drawn close now. He was merely feet away from Zollin, who had yet to move. Branock smiled as innocently as possible, his robes and beard making him seem powerful yet benign. He reached out a hand, the palm up, the way one might approach a skittish horse, as if to say, look, I'm not going to hurt you.

There was another tense moment, and then Zollin reached behind him with his free arm and moved slowly backward, lightly pushing Brianna and Quinn away from Mansel but careful to keep himself between them and the Wizard.

Branock smiled, then moved quickly to Mansel's side. The boy was still moaning in pain. Branock raised Mansel's shirt, revealing a wicked looking bruise. Branock held his hand close to the boy's skin but did not touch the wound. Zollin felt magic begin to flow. At first he was startled. He could sense the magic in Branock, but he had never been so close to another Wizard. The magic inside of Zollin churned, as did the power in the willow belt and his staff. He could feel it surging like a river at high tide, as if his own power wanted to join that of the other Wizard.

"What's he doing?" Quinn whispered, his voice harsh in Zollin's ear.

"He's helping."

"How do you know?"

"I'm not sure, but the magic doesn't feel evil, it feels good, like sunlight."

"I still don't trust him," Quinn said, his voice a little louder, as if he was daring the Wizard to hear him and take offense.

"I don't think we have a choice," Brianna said, joining the whispered conversation.

"We can at least hear him out," Zollin said. "I'm fairly certain he means no harm."

"Well, I'm not going to stand around and watch him do whatever it is he's trying to do," Quinn said. "I'm going to gather the horses. But don't let your guard down, Zollin."

"I won't."

Quinn walked away, mumbling to himself. Brianna took hold of Zollin's arm just above the elbow. She was close behind him, and although he was watching the Wizard minister to Mansel, he couldn't help but feel a flash of heat from the girl. It was intoxicating to be near her, just knowing she was close, feeling her hands around his arm. It made him happy, and he hated himself for that. He choked down the feelings, refusing to revel in them the way he wanted to. He was miserable at that moment, attracted to Brianna, jealous of her fussing over Mansel, sick at what he thought Todrek would say if he knew that Zollin felt that way.

It took several minutes, but eventually Mansel stopped moaning and lay still. Zollin and Brianna watched as the bruising slowly faded and Mansel's skin became clear. The boy didn't move though, merely lay still, breathing deeply.

"He's resting," Branock said. And Zollin realized that he was looking at his father's apprentice, not the Wizard anymore. "He'll be fine when he wakes. He's just tired, as you are I'm sure. I know I am. You all travel fast."

"Why have you been following us?" Zollin asked again.

"Like I said, I want to help you."

"But you said the other Wizards want to hurt me."

"No, I said they are threatened by you. I'm afraid this is all rather complicated. You'll soon find out just how complicated the world is. Most people are afraid of Wizards, of people who can do what they can't."

Branock had been kneeling beside Mansel, and now he stood up. He was taller than Zollin, his eyes a cold grey color, like winter clouds. There was something inviting about the elder Wizard, something that excited Zollin. He had known there were other Wizards in the world, he had just never thought about what it would be like to meet one. But there was also something else about the Wizard that made Zollin a bit uncomfortable. It was like fire – he was drawn to the warmth of Branock's knowledge and demeanor, but he knew he couldn't get too close or he risked being burned.

"But," Branock continued, "we have a special gift. We have the ability to shape the world around us, rather than being shaped by it. Some Wizards horde that gift, others flaunt it, but some, those with good hearts, can use it to help those they love." He smiled at Zollin. "At the Torr we use our combined talents to help the Five Kingdoms. By staying in one place we can support each other and protect ourselves from being exploited. I've been a Wizard for a long time now, Zollin, and I've seen many talented people fall without the right tutelage. I want to help you reach your potential."

"And the others you mentioned," Zollin asked. "What do they want with me?"

"They only want you to join us, but they are frightened of you. Your spell at the village," he said wistfully, rubbing his chest, "that was so powerful, it nearly caught us off guard. You can understand that they would feel a little resentment. After all, you attacked us first, remember."

"That's because you rode in with a heavily armed guard," Quinn said as he approached the group with their horses and the ones the soldiers had ridden in on, "demanding that Zollin go with you, as if he were an outlaw being brought to justice."

"I said I was sorry-" Branock began, but Quinn cut him off.

"That may be, but we aren't going to let Zollin ride off with you to Osla."

"We can all go," said Branock.

"No," Quinn said firmly, "we are heading north, alone. If you are trustworthy as you say, you'll honor our decision and ride away."

"I'm afraid I can't do that," said Branock. "Please, I know this all sounds strange, but it really is for the best. Zollin needs to be at the Torr. He needs to learn to use his power. If he doesn't, he'll be a hunted man all his life. Kings will send soldiers to find him and bring him into their service. Wars will be fought over him. He'll be forced to use his power to kill, and many, many people will suffer. Believe me, keeping the power of a Wizard like your son at the Torr is the very best thing for everyone."

"According to you," Quinn said, as he swung up into the saddle of one of the mercenaries' horses.

Zollin was torn. He desperately wanted to go with Branock and learn to use his magic, but he sensed that something wasn't as friendly as the Wizard was trying to make it seem. He turned to Brianna and told her to wake Mansel.

"If what you are saying is true, and the Torr is the best place for me," Zollin said, trying to hide the fear that was creeping through him. "Then by the time the summer winds blow, I will come to the Torr."

"You shouldn't travel alone," Branock said.

"He won't be alone," Mansel said. He was awake now and standing, although he looked shaky on his feet.

Branock smirked. His patience had run out. It was unfortunate that he hadn't been able to persuade the boy rationally, but he had other means at his disposal. He focused his magic as he prepared to speak, then pushed slightly at the minds of the group.

"Zollin should come with me," he said. "It's the very best thing."

Confusion clouded Zollin's mind. He couldn't think straight. He sensed the magic being used but didn't know how to stop it. Quinn and Mansel suddenly felt as though they couldn't think for themselves. Quinn tried to resist but an explosion of pain was the only result.

Brianna laughed, "Are you crazy or something?"

"It is for the best," Branock said, pushing a little harder at her mind.

93

"No, it isn't," she said. She stepped up to Zollin and laid her hand on his forearm. "Don't listen to him, Zollin."

The moment Brianna touched Zollin, his mind cleared. Without thinking, the magic in him rebelled, shoving the suggestion that Branock was making back toward the Wizard. Branock snarled as Quinn and Mansel shook their heads to clear the cobwebs.

"Get to the horses!" Zollin said raising his staff.

Branock attacked quickly, aiming his blast at Quinn, but Zollin was ready. He pushed his father from the horse with his own power and cushioned the fall. Branock's attack was a pillar of fire, erupting from the elder Wizard's hand and shooting toward where Quinn had sat on the horse. The fire raced through the air over the horse's head and sent the beast galloping away in panic. The other horses were stomping around as a tree that had taken the brunt of the attack burst into flames.

Branock turned his next attack at Zollin, who ducked to the ground and swung his staff at the Wizard's legs. Branock was in middle of lowering his flaming attack toward Zollin when his legs were swept out from under him, causing his aim to fly wildly into the sky.

The horses were bolting away now, running away from the battle. Zollin shouted at the others to run for the horses. Then he sent a blast of crackling energy at the elder Wizard, who was just getting back to his feet. Branock blocked the blast, although the force of it caused him to step back a few steps.

"Do you really think you can best me?" he screamed.

"Rise!" Zollin cried, hoping to throw the Wizard into the air as he had done the mercenaries.

Branock merely laughed. Zollin shouted his command again, this time concentrating with all his strength. He pointed his staff at Branock, who in turned raised his hand, palm out, toward Zollin. There was what appeared to be a ripple in the air as two invisible blasts collided. Throughout the clearing, rocks, twigs and leaves rose up into the air. Many burst into flames, casting an eerie glow in the fading sunlight.

Zollin was tired, although he had forgotten just how tired he was up until that moment. He felt like he was hanging from a cliff, holding on for dear life. His arms and legs were shaking and he could feel the heat from his power, added with that of the willow belt and staff, racing through him. His heart was pounding and his breathing was coming in gasps.

Mansel had caught up with one of the horses and was now racing toward the elder Wizard, his sword held high over his head. He roared out his battle cry as he rode. But Branock merely raised his other hand and sent the young apprentice flying backward from his horse. In that moment, though, Zollin felt the resistance lessen and he pushed forward, gaining some momentum in the fight.

"Give up now, Zollin," Branock shouted, "or I'll kill them all."

"Never!" Zollin screamed.

Quinn had recovered three of the horses.

"Son, this way," the Master Carpenter shouted.

Zollin knew he couldn't break off his attack now without being caught in Branock's attack. From the corner of his eye, Zollin saw Mansel, holding his chest but making his way toward Quinn. He was worried about Brianna, but he couldn't risk taking his eyes off Branock for fear that his concentration would falter. But suddenly she appeared, riding Lilly, and charging straight at Branock.

"No!" Zollin screamed. He saw Branock's face light up with wicked pleasure as he raised his hand toward the girl. Flames erupted from the Wizard's palm and shot toward her like an arrow from a bow. There was no time for Brianna to dodge, and Zollin was helpless to save her. His heart leapt into his throat, but as the flames reached her something odd happened. The gout of flame suddenly rebounded, just as it should have been ruining Brianna's delicate skin. The flames shot back from the girl and blasted the Wizard. Suddenly the resistance to Zollin's spell was gone and he sent the Wizard, now ablaze, flying backward through the trees. Lilly had slid to a stop as the flames shot toward her, and she was now moving quickly toward Quinn and the others.

"Time to go!" Quinn shouted at Zollin.

The young Wizard felt as though he were in a dream, and he

could hardly force his legs to move. Quinn and Mansel were waiting as he stumbled toward them. He wasn't sure if he could pull himself into the saddle, but Mansel reached out and took hold of Zollin's cloak to help haul him up. Then they were off, moving quickly through the shadowy forest, pushing their horses hard. Only Lilly seemed tired, while the other mounts taken from the defeated mercenaries seemed fresh.

They rode swiftly through the night, their only thought to gain as much distance between themselves and the Wizards behind them as possible.

Chapter 11

They rode for as long as they could see. It was a clear night and the moon shone through the branches of the barren winter trees. At some point, the forest grew thicker, the hardwood trees turning to pine and cedar with needles that poked and roused the dozing Zollin. He didn't know if the others were as exhausted as he was, but he was too tired to care. All he wanted to do was sleep, to get off the smelly horse and lie down. His body was aching and his head was spinning. He was hungry, too, his stomach acid churning. But he ignored all that, focusing only on holding onto the saddle and staying close to his companions.

As the moon began its descent, the hills rose sharply. They were no longer among the rolling hills they had been traveling through the last two days. And as the night wore on, clouds began drifting in. The air was turning colder and a strong wind was blowing in their faces from the north.

"Storm's coming," Quinn said as he reined his horse to a stop. "Zollin, do you think the Wizards can track us once the snow hits?"

"I don't know," Zollin said. "I don't see how."

"Can't you feel them or something? Can they use that?"

"I can still sense them, but I don't know where they are. I guess it's possible that they could find us that way."

"Well, we need to rest," Quinn said after a moment. "We'll just have to take that chance."

"What about food?" Mansel said.

"There's a week's ration in our saddle bags," Quinn said. "I found it when I first rounded up the horses. We'll divide it up, and hopefully it'll get us through the worst of the storm."

"How bad a storm do you think?" Brianna asked. She was so cold her teeth were chattering.

"Impossible to tell. We'll just have to do our best to survive. Right now, we need to find a place we can shelter out of this wind."

"Speaking of survival," Mansel said, riding his horse closely beside Zollin's. "I'm not sure how you did it, but thank you for saving Brianna. When I saw that fire coming at her, my heart almost stopped."

Zollin nodded but didn't say anything. He was as amazed as anyone at the turn of events. Brianna should have been burned to death, but she wasn't. He wondered if it was the ring he had given her, but he was too tired to really think about it.

They pushed on for another half hour or so before they found a suitable place. It was a small clearing about halfway up one of the steep hills. The soil was thin and the rugged hillside rose sharply from the fairly level ground of the clearing. There were large boulders on one side and a thick stand of cedar trees on the other. The valley below them was open, but after tying the horses inside the grove of cedars, Mansel and Quinn found some brush to arrange at the edge of the clearing, giving the space boundaries and at least some cover from prying eyes. Brianna and Zollin gathered firewood as the first of the snow started falling. The mercenaries' horses were much better equipped than the meager provisions Zollin had stashed away, and after piling all their gear near the cliff, Quinn removed a blanket that was waxed on one side. He managed to tie it to the boulders and hillside. Using Zollin's staff, the blanket gave them shelter from the falling snow. They wrapped up in blankets, ate a small bite of hard, dry bread, and then fell asleep.

***

Branock tried to open his eyes. The whole left side of his body felt stiff, almost like it was covered with mud that had dried. There was pain that ached deeply in his neck and chest. His vision was clear, but limited. He realized his left eye must not be open. Instinctively, he tried to raise his left hand to touch his face, but his limb didn't move. For a moment, he thought perhaps something was pinning his body to the ground. He lifted his right hand and touched his left shoulder. The fabric of his robe was gone, and the skin was stiff and rubbery. There was no sensation in his shoulder. It was like touching a piece of meat. He tried to remember what had happened. He remembered battling Zollin – the boy's power was surprisingly strong but unfocused. He had been confident he could beat the boy,

98

but then something had happened.

Fire. He remembered now – the girl, riding toward him. He had meant to blast her with fire, but something had happened. His spell had rebounded back on him. His heart was beating fast now. His own spell had roasted him alive. Half of his body was burned, and his staff was out of reach.

He turned his head, searching for his staff in the dim twilight. The long, dark staff was several feet away, but luckily on his right side. He tried to raise his legs, but pain exploded in his left thigh. The pain was searing, the ache so intense it paralyzed him. He ground his teeth and waited for the pain to subside, but it didn't. It only radiated out through his entire body. The world grew dark as he lay, shuddering now in pain. Finally, the rational part of his brain recognized that the pain wasn't going to stop. His only hope was to get to his staff. He was weak, his breath starting to rattle in his chest.

He lifted his right leg and pushed against the earth. He moved only a few inches before the pain made bursts of light pulse in the vision of his good eye. The ground felt like a torture device. His stomach was heaving, so he forced himself to take deep breaths. A racking cough crippled him again. He had to lie still for several moments. He could feel his lungs slowly filling with liquid. He knew time was short, so he held his breath, raised his right leg again, and pushed. This time he moved farther before the silhouettes of trees above him began to sway and spin. He rested, and a powerful urge to close his eyes came over him. He wanted nothing more in that moment than to let go of the pain and struggle for survival, and just slip away into the darkness. But he pushed the craving away, raised his right leg, and pushed again. Then, reaching out with his right hand, he tried to grab his staff. He could barely touch the ancient piece of wood. It was once an ash sapling, but many years ago he had made it his slave. Now he needed it once again.

He felt the magic swirl into his ravaged body. It spread through the healthy parts of him, and he realized just how near death he was. He closed his eyes and made one more small push. His hand closed over the smooth wood and he immediately concentrated on his lungs. In his weakened state, he was forced to work slowly. But as the moon rose, he was able to breathe easy once more. He lifted the staff and began to force life back into his ruined left side. It was another hour before he stopped to rest. He was so tired, but he could once again move his arm and leg. Both were stiff, the skin pulling when he moved as if it had somehow shrunk. He opened his eyes and he could see again. Snow was falling, drifting in large, soft flakes that fell silently all around him. Once again, the rational part of his mind told him that if he stayed where he was, if he closed his eyes and slept as his body wanted, he would freeze to death.

He forced himself to stand. His body was shuddering from the cold and the pain. He had healed as much of his body as he could for now, but it would still take hours of work before he could walk normally or use his left hand with any strength. He needed to find his horse and find shelter before it was too late. Leaning heavily on his staff, he shuffled off through the dark forest.

***

The morning was dim, the sky thick with clouds, the air filled with falling snow. The shelter grew cold despite their body heat, and so Quinn and Zollin got up to find almost a foot of snow on the ground around them. Their makeshift tent was sagging, threatening to collapse.

"Can you move that snow off the blanket?" Quinn asked.

"Sure," Zollin said. He visualized the snow being brushed off, and it fell with wet thunk into the snow on the two open sides of their shelter.

"Good," Quinn said. "Let's pack this snow into walls and then we can build a fire."

"You think that's safe?" Zollin asked.

"I doubt anyone would see smoke in this weather," Quinn said.

So they packed down the snow, which reminded Zollin of making snow forts with Todrek. His hands ached from the cold, but the task was quickly done and helped to keep stray winds from whipping around the bounders to chill their camp. Quinn had covered the firewood with another of the blankets, and soon Zollin had a bright fire burning just beyond the edge of their shelter. The heat was contained by the snowbank in front and the hillside behind them, warming their camp up so well that Zollin was soon asleep again. When he woke later that day, the snow was still falling heavily, the flakes hissing as the fire melted those that fell too close, causing the water to drop into the flames. Quinn had Zollin push the snow off their shelter again with his magic. He was careful not to let the snow fall into fire.

They set to work again, this time with Mansel's help, packing the snow into walls that rose up as high as the shelter's blanket roof. They were all hungry and divided up the salted beef, cheese, and bread to make a good meal. They packed snow into their water skins and set them by the fire to melt. There was a bottle of wine in one of the saddle bags which they were happy to drink, and then with the light of the day fading and their stomachs full, they were soon asleep again. At some point in the night, Zollin opened his eyes to a sagging blanket, and without even sitting up, he used his magic to levitate the snow to the ground beyond the snow walls of their camp. Then he promptly fell back asleep.

The sun was just rising when he woke up again. The fire had died, and Brianna was struggling to uncover their firewood beyond the small shelter. Zollin stepped beyond the shelter and looked at a clear sky that was just turning pink in the east. The snow was up almost to his mid-thigh but had stopped falling. He moved over and helped Brianna uncover the firewood.

"Thanks," she said, her smile bright in the predawn light.

Zollin couldn't think of anything to say and so he shrugged his shoulders. It was extremely cold, and he was soon shivering as they carried the wood back toward the shelter.

"Do you think we should risk a fire?" she asked.

"Probably not," Zollin said. "But I can handle that." He laid the wood in their fire pit and concentrated. The wood suddenly shone with a brilliant light and then softened to a red glow. It had become embers, radiating a good deal of warmth without any smoke. They sat on blankets and warmed their hands. Brianna broke out more dried rations. They had a bit of cheese left, which they softened over the embers, and they drank the ice-cold melted snow.

"I'll bet you miss home," Zollin said, trying to be polite but feeling extremely awkward. He wished his father or Mansel would wake up and join them so he wouldn't have to be the focus of Brianna's attention. He had never seen her so disheveled. Her hair, which she had tied back into a ponytail the first day they had left Tranaugh Shire, had begun to frizz and escape the leather thong she used to tie it back. Her clothes were rumpled and stained, but her smile was dazzling. Somehow, even as a fugitive far from home, with no decent place to rest, she was stunningly beautiful. Zollin felt his resolve to withhold his feelings wavering. It was like trying to move upstream against a strong current. He was getting tired of trying not to like her. And yet, Todrek's face was always in the back of Zollin's mind.

"Not really. I feel like I'm where I'm supposed to be." Brianna's tone was matter of fact, as if running from Wizards and mercenaries were as normal as gathering eggs in the morning.

"You should be enjoying your life with Todrek," Zollin said, his mood turning dark.

"Should I?" She raised an eyebrow. "Zollin, do you think that Todrek was my choice?"

"Wasn't he?"

"No, I had no desire for him."

"Then why did you marry him?"

"I had no choice. Marriage is expected, and if I hadn't married Todrek I would have had to marry someone else. Todrek made the best offer and promised the best life in Tranaugh Shire, but my father made that decision. Was I happy to be out of my mother's house? Of course, but what I really wanted was to get out of the village and see the world. I'm doing that with you."

"But we're being chased by mercenaries and Wizards, sleeping out in the freezing cold. This can't be how you imagined you'd see the world."

"It's not," she said slowly, as if trying to decide what she would say next. "When you revealed your power to me, I knew that my future was with you. I can't say how I knew, just that it seemed inevitable. You want to know a secret?" she asked, giggling from embarrassment.

"Sure," Zollin said without a second's hesitation. He was enjoying himself despite his resolve to keep Brianna at a distance.

"I'd been having dreams that you were leaving Tranaugh Shire without me." She blushed a little and looked down at her hands. "I would wake up calling out, and my mother thought I was nervous about marrying Todrek. I never told anyone what I was really afraid of."

Zollin's face flushed from shame. Just hearing Brianna say his friend's name was like a slap in the face. He couldn't believe that he had just been chatting casually with his best friend's widow.

"I think I'll check on the horses," he said hastily.

"Would you like some help?" she asked.

"No," he said quickly, charging off through the snow.

He saw through the corner of his eye the look of surprise and pain that clouded Brianna's face. Still, he wouldn't let himself give in. He took the pain, his own and what he imagined Todrek would feel, and stuffed them down deep inside. He accepted Brianna's hurt – it was inevitable, and couldn't be helped. Her lack of remorse only made him feel worse. How could she be so cold and callous? But deep down he knew he couldn't despise her the way he should. She and Todrek had only been married one night and really hadn't known each other before that, but it was the principle of the matter. Todrek had been his best friend, and he deserved to be loved and grieved in death.

The horses were anxious under the limbs of heavy snow, but their body heat in the close confines of the pine and cedar grove made the space warm despite the chilly weather. Zollin spent the next hour rubbing the horses down and talking to them. He spent most of his time with Lilly and tried to convince himself it was because she was his horse, not because she was Brianna's mount.

When he reemerged, Mansel and Quinn were awake. They had eaten, and their camp was warmed by the coals that were only now starting to die. The sun was actually warm and the snow was melting slightly. Quinn said they should push on. They needed to get into the mountains before the passes filled with snow.

"Aren't we in the mountains?" Mansel asked.

"These are merely the foothills," Quinn said. "The mountains are towering cliffs, so tall you can't climb them. The only way in is the Telford's Pass or from the sea. Brighton's Gate is in the Great Valley that runs the entire breadth of the Northern Highlands. If we can get in before the snows fill the passes, we should be safe through the winter."

"And if we can't?" Brianna asked.

"Then we die," Mansel said as if were telling a ghost story.

Quinn merely looked down at the ground between his knees. He was squatting the same way that Zollin had seen him rest around a camp fire hundreds of times, but somehow he seemed older, as if the mention of death had aged him.

"We aren't going to die," Zollin said.

"No," Quinn agreed, his voice firm, "but we can't stay here."

They broke camp an hour later. They were well rested, but the snow was still thick. They were forced to lead their horses and trudge through the snow. They traveled in a single line, moving through a single trail in the snow. They took turns in the lead position, but they didn't cover much distance. That night they made camp in a steep valley that seemed to funnel the northern wind. Their arms and legs ached from the cold. Throwing caution to the wind, they built a big fire and tried to warm themselves. They also tried to dry their clothes but without much success. It was a miserable night, but the next day was bright and sunny. The snows receded quickly and they were able to travel more easily. They spent most of the day on horseback, winding through the hills and drawing closer to the mountains. That night they camped in a cave, and Quinn began drilling Mansel with the sword and shield. Zollin avoided Brianna by keeping watch.

The next day, they came to Telford's Pass that led into the mountains. The trail wasn't quite a road but more than a well worn path. Wagons had rolled that route enough times that the trail was wide enough for them to ride together and talk. The last few days had been cold, but the sunshine had brightened their spirits, and riding along a path made them feel more at ease. Their fears were forgotten as they rode along, occasionally even joking and laughing. Quinn said another two days would see them in Brighton's Gate, but when they turned a curve in the trail around a huge, rugged boulder, they were surprised to see a group of men waiting for them.

The riders directly ahead immediately started toward them, so they quickly turned back the way they had come. Their jovial mood was banished instantly as fear fell over them like a torrential rainstorm. Before they could spur their horses to speed, three more riders appeared down the trail behind them, their horses trotting quickly toward the group. Zollin recognized the center rider as one of the Wizards of the Torr.

"It's one of the Wizards," he said, his voice shrill.

"What do we do?" Brianna asked.

"Go back," Zollin said.

"I don't relish turning my back on a Wizard," Quinn said.

"I say we fight," Mansel said with exuberance. It was obvious that he was anxious to try out his new skills.

"I can handle the riders up the trail," Zollin said. "I'm not so sure about the Wizard."

"Come on then," Quinn ordered. And they turned their horses once again and raced into the mountains.

Chapter 12

They raced around the bend once more, while the group of mercenaries in front of them sat waiting. It was a tense moment for Zollin. He felt the magic churning hot within him, but he did not relish the idea of unleashing his magic on people again. Still, he needed to protect is father and friends. He would not let anyone hurt them. So he raised his staff and pointed it at the group. The riders in turn raised long bows and fired arrows at the oncoming riders. The arrows took all of Zollin's attention.

"They're just trying to distract you," Quinn yelled at his son.

Zollin didn't hear him. He swung his staff so that it was over his head and parallel with his friends. He envisioned an impenetrable screen of magic above them. The arrows hit the screen and bounced in mid air, falling harmlessly to the ground.

The mercenaries had fired more arrows, but Zollin easily blocked those as well. He was about to blast the mercenaries out of his way when his horse bellowed in fear. Quinn's and Mansel's horses, too, were suddenly locking their legs and sliding to a stop. Zollin saw their mounts' eyes wide with fear, their lips drawn back, their manes standing up along their necks.

"What's going on?" Brianna shouted. Lilly had slowed along with the others but didn't seem as affected.

Zollin looked up at the soldiers in front of them – their horses too seemed frightened.

"I don't know," shouted Quinn.

Zollin looked behind them and saw the riders approaching but still at an extreme distance. He didn't understand why his horse was suddenly turning against his protests and trying to flee from the soldiers. At first, he thought the Wizard behind them had somehow cast a spell that was frightening their mounts, but then he heard the screams from the soldiers. Zollin looked over his shoulder and saw lions leaping down on the soldiers. There were several big cats, at least half as big as the horses. Zollin's mount was still twisting in fear, trying to break from his control. The lions had bronze-colored hides and long teeth that curved up from their lower jaws. The soldiers were hacking at the big cats with their long swords, but their horses were dancing with fear, making their attacks almost useless. Two of the horses had fallen as the lions leapt upon them, tearing into their necks with fangs and claws.

"What do we do?" Mansel shouted over the carnage.

"I don't think we have any choice," Quinn yelled. "Get your bow out, Mansel. Brianna, do your best to hold the horses. Zollin, the Wizard's yours. We're fish in a barrel here, but we've no other choice."

Zollin slipped off his horse and ran toward the approaching riders. "Blast," he yelled. Energy crackled from his staff toward the riders. Their horses reared, but the attack was thwarted. Zollin could sense the magic like an invisible wall between them. He knew any attack he made would be repulsed. So he changed his tactic.

"So you're the novice Branock warned me about," Zollin shouted. He saw the look of bewilderment on the other Wizard's face.

"He said you were a coward, and now I sense your fear," Zollin shouted again, hoping his lie was believable. This time he swung his staff theatrically and sent a shower of sparks snapping and popping against the invisible barrier. The attack was all for show with no real power, but he saw that the barrier was pulling back. He took a chance and aimed his next attack at the soldier on the right. This time the spell was not deflected, and the mercenary was sent flying from his horse. The other soldier reined his horse around and galloped away.

Behind Zollin, one of the lions was now slowly stalking toward Mansel and Quinn. They raised their bows and let their arrows fly. The first found its mark and caused the lion to leap back. The other arrow, slightly behind the first, glanced off the lion as it moved. The rest of the pride was busy with the soldiers and their horses, gorging themselves on the fresh meat. Quinn turned and saw that Zollin now faced the Wizard alone, and he chanced an arrow at the rider. But the arrow bounced harmlessly away, and the Wizard never took his eyes off of Zollin.

"I can't stand Wizards!" Quinn spat, then turned his attention back to the lions.

Cassis had now brought his horse to stop. His mind was reeling. He knew that Branock was crafty but the old Wizard had double-crossed them, or so it seemed. He knew better than to take the boy's words at face value, but he also remembered the attack at the village, and he was taking no chances.

Zollin could feel the hair on his arms and neck standing up as the air seemed charged with magic. Every sense came alive, his vision sharp, his mind racing through possibilities. There were rocks on the steep hills to Zollin's right. With his mind, he flung them down and then immediately raised a mental shield between himself and the other Wizard. Just as Zollin expected, the other Wizard attacked at that moment. He felt the blast of power against his defenses like an ax blow against a shield. He tried to keep his features from revealing his shock at the strength of the blow.

The boulders came crashing down and would have crushed Cassis and his horse, but the Wizard deflected the barrage. Zollin took that opportunity to try a new spell. He focused his mind on panic and sent the feelings straight at the Wizard's horse. It was a desperate ploy – he didn't even know if he could do it. But with the Wizard's attention momentarily diverted, his defenses had pulled back, leaving the horse exposed. Zollin saw the whites around the horse's dark irises, and then the beast reared, pawing the air and sending the Wizard toppling backwards. The horse, free of its rider, bolted away.

Cassis was unprepared for the horse's sudden buck, and it sent him crashing to the ground. Fortunately, his defenses softened his landing and the boulders were already diverted from their course. He fell to the ground but quickly gained his feet on the wet turf. He immediately sent a wild blast of fire toward Zollin, as much to distract the young Wizard as to actually harm him.

Zollin was waiting, and he saw that the blast was going wide away from him and toward where Brianna was holding the horses. He was confident the attack would not harm her, but he feared the horses might panic and crush her, so he deflected the blast.

There was still snow on the mountain side and Zollin pulled it down. Only this time it wasn't aimed at the other Wizard, but between them. There was a moment's hesitation as the ice and snow rumbled down the steep hillsides. Zollin was relieved when Cassis raised his defenses to ward off this new attack. He had hoped the distraction would keep the other Wizard from attacking again. The snow and ice, along with dirt and rocks and some scrubby vegetation, fell in a towering heap between them. Zollin spun around to ensure that the lions weren't overwhelming his father. The beasts were mostly engaged with the soldiers and the horses that they had killed, but one was circling around, staying high up on the hillside, crouching low. Zollin pointed at it and yelled for his father, just as the mound of snow and ice blew apart, showering them all and causing them to duck for cover.

Zollin shrouded himself with a magical shield and saw that in that instant the lion had sprung. It was sailing down toward the horses who were dancing with fear from the explosion of snow. Brianna was trying desperately to soothe them as she held tightly to the reins, but she was oblivious to the danger. Zollin knew that he needed to return his attention to the Wizard who was advancing behind him, but he also knew and feared that the lion might find Brianna easier prey than the horses. He shoved with all his power against the lion, but the beast's weight and momentum were such that though he managed to hurl the animal back, he was knocked off his feet by the force of the collision.

Cassis took that opportune moment to attack. He hurled fire at Zollin, who raised his arm instinctively. There was a searing pain, but then Zollin raised his defenses and pushed the fire back. He rolled to his feet in time to block another blast. And then, just like with Branock, both Wizards attacked at the same time, their spells clashing together. Energy snapped and hissed along Zollin's staff and up his arm. He felt the power welling up in him as his emotions fed his effort. He could see Todrek in his mind, could see Brianna and his father, even Mansel and their horses. He knew in that moment that the only way to stop Cassis was to kill him. He sensed the other's intent in the ferocity of this attack. It was like a gambler knowing that it was time to bet his entire fortune on one turn of the cards. So Zollin pushed, pushed his magic against the resistance of his opponent's spell. He felt the muscles in his legs and back straining. He focused his mind and will behind the spell.

"You're finished," he shouted. "I'm going to kill you!"

Cassis didn't answer. He couldn't believe the amount of power that was flooding against him. It was taking all his ability to hold the spell, and fear was beginning to turn his bowels to water. He wanted to escape but knew that if he broke off the spell without first pushing his opponent back, he would be killed. Still, even though his mind was racing to find a way out of his predicament, Zollin's raw power was overwhelming him.

Zollin felt Cassis' spell falter for a moment, and then it surged. But as it did, the Wizard's staff burst into tiny shards. The magic that just moments before had seemed like a raging river suddenly ceased, and in the stillness of the moment, Zollin felt a stab of sympathy for Cassis. The Wizard looked older, tired and weak. He had fallen to his knees, his robes tattered, his black hair disheveled. Zollin was just about to speak when the older Wizard raised both hands and cast his final spell. Zollin had been holding his staff in front of him, and without thought, he blocked the spell, but he doubted if there was enough power in Cassis to have done any real damage. Zollin stood effortlessly before him while Cassis strained, the veins in his neck bulged, his face turned red, his lips peeled back in a snarl of anger and hatred. But the strain was too much, his magic draining him. The Wizard dropped dead in the mud.

Zollin felt the magic suddenly disappear, like light disappearing into darkness when a candle is snuffed out. The sensation left a melancholy echo in Zollin. He turned and saw that his father and Mansel had dispatched the lion. The horses were still straining to break away, but Brianna, despite her small frame, was unyielding. Zollin looked at the horses and imagined calm happiness, then pushed his thoughts toward them. The horses immediately settled down and began nuzzling Brianna.

"We should go," Zollin said.

Quinn turned and saw the dead Wizard lying in the mud. He didn't speak, only nodded and gathered the horses from Brianna. With one last spell, Zollin scattered the lions with panic, and the group rode away from the carnage and into the mountains.

Chapter 13

Branock felt the battle. He was still working to repair the damage his rebounding spell had caused. He had managed to find a fallen log where an animal had dug out a shallow depression. He had wrapped himself in blankets and fallen asleep. When he woke, he was buried in snow, his hunger so fierce he was shaking. He had used his saddle bag as a pillow, and so he ate and slept. Using only as much energy as it took to uncover himself from the snow and chew the dry rations he fed on, he slept as much as possible. On the day the group had set out from their camp, Branock began working to heal more of his left side. He started with his leg, concentrating on each nerve, transforming the scar tissue back to health, even smoothing the skin. It was slow, tedious work that did not suit his power, but he was determined. The magic drained him of energy quickly. But by the time the battle between Zollin and Cassis took place, he was able to walk normally and use his left arm and hand with close to normal strength and dexterity. His face was still a mass of withered skin, his beard and hair burned away, his left eye a milky white.

When the battle took place, far to the north, Branock felt it as slight pulses. He knew what must be happening and cursed his luck. The boy had been in his hands, and now Cassis would either kill or capture him. He would have to return to the Torr empty handed and weakened, without the ally he had hoped to have. Then he felt the churning of Zollin's spell that had shattered Cassis' staff. It was like lightning hidden behind thick clouds whose thunder shakes everything around and resonates deep a person's chest. He knew then that there was hope, although if Zollin continued into the mountains it would be hope deferred. Still, Branock knew that Cassis could never wield that much power – he himself was not that powerful. In fact, Branock had never felt such awesome, raw force. It was proof that if he could control the boy, he would be unstoppable, and if he couldn't, that Zollin would have to die.

His horse had wandered away to survive the snowstorm, so Branock turned south. He would need to return to the Torr and explain to his Master what had happened. He would have to think of a good explanation, but he had plenty of time to do that. First he needed to find a better mode of transport and to heal his disfigured facial features. Then he would worry about his Master in the tower.

***

Wytlethane felt the battle, too. He had turned south soon after splitting up with other two Wizards. He was now comfortably ensconced in small inn. There were two other guests who had left as soon as the sun had begun melting the snow. Wytlethane decided to wait. Cassis would turn south with the boy, and then they could return to the Torr together, ensuring that his reputation with the Master was unspoiled.

When the battle took place, he was resting in his room with a comfortable fire warming the small space nicely. He was dozing in a chair when the wave of power from Zollin's final effort shook him awake. He stood and began pacing. It was obvious that splitting up was a mistake. The boy was more powerful than Wytlethane had anticipated. Now he would have to travel north again, to find Branock and then the boy. He was weary of traveling and wished nothing more than to be left in peace. But he knew the danger of allowing the boy to live. He felt Cassis disappear like a whiff of smoke. His alliance with Cassis had not been as beneficial as he had hoped. And if they returned to the Torr without the boy, the Master would most likely kill one or both of them.

He began packing his things again. He would travel to Isos city before the winter snows made travel impossible. When spring arrived, he would go north by sea and enter the Great Valley before the passes had cleared. With luck, he would have the boy and be home by summer, and then life could return to normal.

***

They were planning to camp just before dark, but snow began falling again, not large flakes and certainly not blizzard-like conditions, but the sight of snow spurred them on. They rode until they came to small tree just after dark. Quinn and Mansel cut

113

branches and then, one by one, Zollin would ignite them to use as torches. In this way they rode through most of the night. The trail rose and fell as it rounded the roots of the mountains around them. The horses were tired, but Quinn was desperate to get them through the pass. The ground slowly became rougher as soil with stunted grass and weeds gave way to bare bedrock. Just before dawn, the last torch burned through. They didn't have pitch, so the branches didn't last very long. In the darkness, they huddled together. Zollin warmed the rocks they huddled on, but he was so tired he couldn't keep them from cooling quickly. He had eaten most of his rations after the battle with Cassis, and now he dozed fitfully.

Mansel and Brianna slept as well, but Quinn stayed awake, trying to keep his senses alert in case more lions appeared. As gray dawn broke over the mountain tops, they rode on. The temperature fell dramatically as they rose in altitude, and the mountains seemed to close in on the pass, keeping the trail veiled in shadow. The snow had stopped sometime during the night, but the farther they rode, the deeper the snow became. They put on all their clothes and wrapped up in blankets, but still they ached with cold until all they could think about was being warm again. When they happened along another stunted tree that was growing out of a crack in the side of a mountain, Mansel volunteered to go and cut it. The others waited while he made the ascent. The small tree was crooked, twisted and leafless. The wood was extremely hard to cut, and the thin air made Mansel's stamina short, but eventually he felled the little tree. It tumbled down the steep slope until it caught on an outcrop of rock. Zollin lifted it free and let it tumble the rest of the way down. They broke the limbs and waited for Mansel. As soon as he arrived, Zollin cast the wood ablaze and they stood as close as they could, letting the heat thaw their frozen bodies. They ate what little food they had left and then rode on. It was another cold dark night, but no snow fell, and exhaustion overtook them. They all slept together, huddled for warmth on the rocky ground. They woke aching and tired but felt better than the day before. They rode on. There was so little vegetation that the horses began to plod along with their heads drooping. But early that morning, they came to a long, upward-winding trek. They walked the horses, their feet aching, their lungs burning from the cold air, their thighs quivering and threatening to cramp from exertion. They stopped to rest several times, and when they were near the top, snow began to softly fall. They were too tired to talk, but when they finally crested the hill, they were shocked by what lay ahead.

***

"You sent for us, Master of the Torr," said the man in white. He was tall and skeletally thin, with milk-white skin and hair. He was so white that his teeth stood out in dark contrast with his lips.

"Yes, I have need of your services once again," the Wizard said.

"You have always been a valued customer."

"This is a delicate matter," said the Wizard. "My own associates have failed. If you are to succeed, it will take all your resources."

"For that right price, that can be arranged."

"Good. This is a Wizard. A young man. He is in the north. He must not come south alive. Is that understood?"

"Yes," said the man in white. "What else can you tell us about him?"

"That is all I know."

"I see. That does complicate things."

"How many Wizards do you think are roaming around the Five Kingdoms?" the Master snapped. He was growing angry, and the man in white recognized that as a bad sign. The Master of the Torr was not a man he cared to have angry with him.

"You have a point."

"Yes, I'm glad you see it my way. If you come across any older Wizards, know that they are mine, but they are also expendable. Do whatever you must to complete this assignment."

"As always, we will not fail. Now, let us discuss the price of this request," the man in white smiled broadly, revealing his filmy yellow teeth.

***

Zollin couldn't believe his eyes. For days they had traveled through snow and dead, grey vegetation which gave way to cold, grey stone. But what lay below them, like a jewel on drab velvet cloth, was breathtaking. There was grass and trees and a sparkling blue river. The Great Valley was wide, and the sun shone so bright that it was brilliant, making Zollin squint. Snow was falling and starting to dust the tall pines and spruce trees. In the distance, they could see a small town with people and animals. It was only a small village, but it was the first sign of civilization the group had seen since they had left Tranaugh Shire.

"Oh my," said Brianna. "It's beautiful."

"It's amazing," said Mansel.

"It's the Great Valley, and that is Brighton's Gate," said Quinn.

They were safe, at least for a season, and so they mounted their horses and rode down into the valley, leaving the death and fear of the last few weeks behind them.

Book II
Brighton's Gate

Chapter 14

Zollin wanted to run, but he was too tired. Instead he climbed on his horse and started down into the valley. They followed the Zimmer Trail as it wound down into the tree lined hillside. Once in the trees, they could no longer see the river or the village beside it, but they were happy just the same. They were still cold, still hungry and exhausted, but hope now burned in their hearts and they felt more alive.

At midday, they ate the rest of their rations. And then, after a long afternoon, they rode out of the trees and into a long stretch of farmland. The Great Valley's soil was rich and dark as it lay fallow. The snow had not quite covered it, and it stood out in contrast against the powdery whiteness of the snow. Clouds had rolled in and a gray pallor had settled in the valley. Heavier snow would fall that night, but for now, it still drifted lazily, like water spilling from a bucket that was too full.

At twilight, they came to the edge of the village. There was smoke rising from the chimneys of the small stone cottages. The animals had been settled into stalls or barns, with lots of fodder so that they would not need tending for several days. The village was quiet – the only sound was that of their own horses' hooves crunching the newly fallen snow.

"It seems so quaint," Brianna said.

"And quiet," Mansel said.

"Looks like everyone is settled in for the night," Quinn said.

"That sounds wonderful," Zollin said.

"That and a good, hot meal," said Mansel.

"I'd not say no to some mulled wine," Quinn agreed.

"Or a hot bath," Brianna said.

All those things that he had taken for granted all his life now sounded like luxuries to Zollin. He couldn't help but smile at the thought of it. There were two Inns, one tall and quiet, the other long and low with bright light spilling out of the frosted windows. There was music and laughter that could be heard in the street. They reined in their horses and climbed down.

"We are a family," Quinn said. "We're looking for a place to settle. Let's not mention what happened in Tranaugh Shire."

"What if word has arrived ahead of us?" Zollin asked.

"We'll deal with that if we have to. Do you have the coins I gave you?"

Zollin nodded while he reached into his pack. There wasn't much, but it was enough to give them shelter for a few days in the Inn. After that, they would have to figure something else out.

As Zollin handed Quinn the coins, a man came bustling out of the Inn. He was heavyset with red checks and a thick handlebar mustache that was well oiled and combed.

"Visitors to Brighton's Gate, I see," he said in a loud, jovial voice. "You've come to the right place. Welcome to the Valley Inn. My name's Buck. I'll take your horses and you can warm yourselves inside by the fire."

They all smiled and handed their reins to the man. He hurried off around the Inn while Zollin and the others ducked inside the low doorway. The common room of the Inn was a long room with rough hewn wooden benches. There were men and women seated along the benches, and the air was permeated with the smell of food, wine, and pipe smoke.

"Look at you," came a voice from a short, pleasant-looking woman. She had bright red hair tied back into a bun and wore a long apron over her woolen dress. "You all look nearly frozen. Come with me," she ordered.

They obeyed as she led them to a place close to the fire. The warmth felt so good to Zollin that he could have lain down on the wooden floor and slept right there. But then his stomach rumbled and reminded him how hungry he was.

"I'm guessing you'll be wanting rooms?" she said expectantly.

"Yes," said Quinn. He held out two silver coins to the woman. "One room for my daughter and me, one for my sons, and we'd like supper."

"And a bath I wouldn't suppose," said the woman. "Well, this will more than cover that. You sit and warm yourselves. I'll send mulled cider over and have Viv start heating water for the bath. Snow's coming and I don't think you'll be wanting to move on too soon. Can you afford a few days?"

"We can work," Quinn said. "I'm a carpenter and the boys are apprentices."

"If you're skilled, you can find work. The Gateway Inn caught fire a few months back. They can certainly use some help getting it back together."

"That would be fine," said Quinn.

"Sit, relax. My name is Ollasam, but everyone calls me Ollie."

"I'm Quinn," he said.

They sat down and soon had cups of warm cider in their hands. The drink was rich, and soon Zollin felt his face flushing, the alcohol hitting his empty stomach and then going right to his head. Then food was brought out, fresh bread, cheese, beans in a thick sauce, and cabbage. The food was delicious, and they all had seconds before they felt satisfied. Brianna took the first turn in the bath, then Zollin, who was having trouble keeping his eyes open now that he was warm and well-fed.

A young girl about Brianna's age led Zollin to a room that was warmed by a wood stove and furnished with two small beds and a tiny table with stools rather than chairs to sit on. The girl offered to wash his clothes, and he promised her a coin if she could wash all their clothes. Then he climbed into one of the beds and fell instantly asleep.

The next morning, Zollin woke to Mansel's snoring. He found his clothes washed and folded just inside the door. He dressed quietly and then took up his staff and headed out to find his father. He knew that Quinn had probably enjoyed too much wine after supper, but he also knew his father would never sleep when there was work to be done. In the common room, he found Quinn talking quietly to another plump man who was wearing a heavy wool coat with fleece showing along the edges. Zollin went to the fire and was met by the serving girl from the night before.

"Thank you for cleaning our clothes," he said to her as she handed him a mug of fresh milk, still warm from the cow.

"It was no trouble at all."

"No, it was," Zollin replied. "Let me just get you a coin."

"Your father paid me well, Zollin," she said smiling.

"You know my name?"

"It's winter and the Gate's a small place. I imagine most everyone knows everything hereabouts."

"I see, but I don't know yours," he said, smiling.

"Ellie. Ollie's my mother. She and father have run the Inn for years. My grandparents built it."

"It's very nice."

"Well, actually the Gateway is a much nicer place, but since the fire, we've had plenty of business. I guess Master Quinn's going to change all that. He's talking to Norwin, who owns the Gateway."

"Oh, I'm sorry," Zollin said.

"No, don't be. The Gateway's a good place, and we'll need both Inns up and running by summer. But here I am prattling on when I should be getting your breakfast."

"No, that's okay," Zollin said, but Ellie was already off toward the kitchen.

"It seems like you're making friends," said a voice behind Zollin.

He turned to see Brianna and his breath caught in his throat. She had combed her hair till it was shinning, her face had color, and her dress was clean. She looked thinner than she had on her wedding day, but just as beautiful. Zollin was suddenly embarrassed. He had been friendly with the girl, but he hadn't really been trying to be.

"Just being polite," he said.

Brianna merely raised an eyebrow and sat down beside Zollin. After a minute, Ellie returned with a tray that had two steaming bowls of oatmeal and another mug of milk. She set it all on the table in front of them, along with a jar of honey. They ate all the oatmeal and drank the milk. Zollin was beginning to feel his energy returning.

Mansel still hadn't shown up when Quinn finally finished talking to Norwin and joined Zollin and Brianna.

"Well, we've got work," he said. "Brighton's got a carpenter, but he's busy making barrels for ale to be sent down river. We can rebuild the Inn, and Norwin's agreed to pay our room and board here with a little extra coin to line our purse when we're through."

"That's good news," Zollin said.

"Great news, actually," Quinn said. "We'll be able to work right away since it's mostly indoor work, and we can push on if we need to as soon as the passes open up."

Brianna smiled. "What shall I do?" she asked.

"I'm not sure. Have you got a trade?"

"I can sew a little, but I've never trained to do anything."

"Well, you can't help us much," Quinn said. He continued thinking out loud but Zollin was no longer listening.

The door had opened and a man quietly entered the room. He was tall and lean, wearing a snow-covered cloak and a large round hat with a drooping brim. His appearance was ordinary, but Zollin noticed immediately that the man radiated magic. He ignored Zollin, but it was obvious that he had come seeking the young Wizard. Zollin knew that even before the Inn Keeper approached him with a look of surprise. He ordered breakfast and paid with a coin, then sat at the far end of the common room and watched Zollin with obvious sidelong glances.

"Excuse me," Zollin said, getting to his feet.

"Well, don't go far," Quinn said. "We'll need to inspect the Gateway Inn soon. Why isn't Mansel up?"

"Probably because he tried to keep up with you in wine cups," Zollin said, smiling. "He was snoring peacefully when I left him."

Zollin stepped away from their table and walked across the room toward the man who was waiting for his breakfast. He deliberately walked past the man, who hadn't looked at him once as he approached, a fact that Zollin recognized as someone trying too hard not to be noticed. He stepped into the hallway just out of sight and waited for Ellie to bring the man his food. When she had served him and was returning to the kitchen, he called out to her.

"Pssst," he whispered.

Ellie was almost at the kitchen door when she hesitated. Zollin hoped the man hadn't noticed. Then she came into the hallway. Her face was glowing with excitement and Zollin noticed that it wasn't an unpleasant face.

"You've become a very popular person," she said with a giggle.

"He asked about me?"

"Yes, Master Kelvich is his name. I can't believe he's here. I've only ever seen him come to the Inn once, when I was a little girl."

Zollin started to say that she was a little girl now, but he stopped himself short of actually saying it out loud. And even as the thought was crossing his mind, he saw that she wasn't as young as he thought. She was probably Brianna's age, marrying age. Zollin flushed and was thankful that the hallway was dimly lit.

"What did he want?" Zollin asked.

"He wanted to know when you arrived and who all was with you."

"Did you tell him?"

"Yes, I didn't see the harm in it," she said, and there was a note of worry in her tone.

"Of course," he said, trying to reassure her. "It's no big deal. What does he do?"

"No one knows," she said softly, moving closer to him. She had to look up, and he couldn't help but look into her large brown eyes. His breath grew shallow and he could hear his heart beating loudly in his ears.

"He lives in a little stone cottage near the forest. He rarely comes into town. He has no family, no real friends. He's sort of the town mystery," she said excitedly.

"Okay, thanks for your help," he said.

She smiled and then hurried away. He felt bad. He didn't want to lead her on, but she was attractive and he liked her attention. There was certainly no crime there, he told himself. Then he forced the thoughts from his mind. The man sitting alone, Master Kelvich she had called him, was a magic user, although his power felt different somehow. It was both strong and at the same time distant. Zollin was determined to find out what it was.

"Ahhhhhh," Mansel yawned, as he walked up behind Zollin. "Good morning."

"Yes," Zollin said a little loudly, having been surprised by Mansel's quiet approach. "Morning," he said in a more normal tone of voice.

"I hope breakfast is as good as dinner," said the young apprentice.

"I hope Quinn lets you eat," Zollin said smirking. "He's been hired to rebuild the Gateway Inn and he's anxious to start. He's been looking for you."

A pained look crossed Mansel's face and he hurried into the common room. Zollin waited several more minutes, unsure of exactly what to do. At last he decided he needed to face this man Kelvich – if he didn't he would have no rest while they were in Brighton's Gate. Still, he didn't want to make a scene in the Inn. He would have to go out to the man's cottage, and he had an idea of just how to do it.

Chapter 15

"Father, I was thinking," Zollin said as Mansel wolfed down his breakfast.

"Yes," Quinn said slowly, suspiciously.

"The passes haven't closed yet, have they?"

"Well, there was some snow last night, but…"

"But not enough to stop someone who was determined to follow us into the Great Valley?"

"That's true enough."

"So, I was thinking I would ride out to keep an eye on the pass today."

"There's a storm coming soon, it'll close the passes soon enough," Quinn said.

"Yes, but let's face it, I won't be much help to you in the Inn."

"That's true," said Mansel with his mouth full.

"I think it's a good idea," Brianna stated thoughtfully.

Zollin smiled at her, but she ignored him.

"Well…" said Quinn.

"And I'll go with him," she said.

"What? No," Zollin said. "It's too dangerous. You should stay here and rest."

"Too dangerous? I survived this long."

"Thanks to Zollin," Mansel said, smirking. "If he hadn't saved you, you'd be cooked well done."

"That's enough," Quinn said sharply.

Brianna looked at Zollin but he looked at the table and spoke softly.

"It's going to be cold. Are you sure you want to do this?"

"If you can do it, so can I."

"Alright, let's get ready."

They all rose from the table except for Mansel.

"Wait, I'm not finished yet," he said, stuffing his mouth with more food.

Quinn rolled his eyes. "Times wasting, let's move."

Zollin returned to his room and pulled on his extra pair of pants and tunic, wrapped his cloak around his shoulders, and headed back to the common room. The Inn Keeper was busy wiping down the tables when Zollin approached.

"My, uh, sister and I will be taking a ride today," he said. "Are the stables out back?"

"I'll get your horses," said the Inn Keeper.

"Oh, no, that's not necessary. I'll be glad to do it."

"Alright. Well, there's more snow coming, so don't stay out too long. Many a folk's been lost in a white out."

"Yes, sir, we'll be careful."

He went to the door and stepped out into the cold. About a foot of snow had fallen in the night and the sky looked heavy and gray, ready to dump even more snow at any moment. He pulled his cloak around him more tightly and followed the tracks someone had already made out toward the stables. The horses looked up, and Zollin thought they looked as if they were disappointed to see him. The stable was warm, there was straw in each animal's stall, and oats hung in a bag beside each animal. He didn't blame them for wanting to stay in the stable – only Lilly looked excited to see him. He walked up to her and rubbed her nose.

"Hey, girl," he said cheerily. "Did you sleep well? You look happy, yes, you do."

The horse stepped forward and nuzzled his shoulder.

"I think maybe you should stay here today. Stay warm and cozy in this nice stall."

Lilly shook her head and blew out her breath as if to say, no way.

He rubbed her nose and turned to one of the other horses, but Lilly strained against the wooden door and neighed.

Zollin turned back to her. "Okay, okay," he said laughing. "I'll get you out."

He saddled Lilly and another of their horses and was about to lead them out when Ellie appeared. She was wrapped around the shoulders in a bright red shawl, and the cold had made her cheeks pink. She was the exact opposite of Brianna, whose high cheek bones and long, slender figure gave her the air of royalty. Ellie on the other hand was rounder, not short but certainly not tall. She wore her long brown hair pulled back into a sensible ponytail. While Brianna's beauty made her stand apart, Ellie's cheerful demeanor and contagious smile made you feel welcome and wanted. Zollin certainly felt wanted. He returned her smile as she called out to him.

"Master Zollin," she said happily. "I heard you were going riding and I thought you might like some bread and cheese."

"Oh," said Zollin surprised. "That's very nice of you."

"It's no trouble at all. I even packed you a bit of apple tart. I made it myself."

"Wow, I don't know what to say! Thank you."

"You could ask if there's enough for me," Brianna said from the stable doorway.

"Oh," Ellie said, "I didn't think of you. I'm so addle-brained. Let me run and fetch some more."

"That's really not necessary," Zollin began but Ellie was already hurrying back to the Inn, her plain woolen dress held up to avoid the snow.

"No trouble," she called out as she disappeared out of the stable.

"I think she has a crush on you," Brianna said sharply.

Zollin was embarrassed and not sure what to say. He didn't like the way he felt guilty for liking Ellie's attention. Of course, he knew there could be no future for an Inn Keeper's daughter and Wizard on the run for his life, but what did a little flirting hurt? He'd never had so much pleasant attention from a girl before. He'd seemed invisible in Tranaugh Shire, and the only time the girls had noticed him was to laugh at his mistakes. Besides, he'd made a vow to himself about Brianna – she was Todrek's wife and he had no intentions of pursuing her. He wished that no one would, that she would remain true to Todrek, but he knew that was childish thinking. They'd been married for less than a day before Todrek was slain, and she said herself she had had no real feelings for him. But Zollin knew that Todrek had been crazy about Brianna – it was all his friend could talk about. So he pushed away the awkward feelings and led the horses out of the stable.

"I saddled Lilly for you," he said, changing the subject and hoping she wouldn't continue to look at him so strangely. She was staring at him, her face completely unreadable. It made him uncomfortable, as if she could see into his soul and she didn't care for what she saw.

"You should have let her rest," Brianna said. "I could have ridden one of the other horses, you know, or even shared one with you."

"That wouldn't be wise," Zollin said, thinking of his real plan for the day. "If we ran into trouble, you'd have to wait for me or leave me. This way, if you need to turn back, you can."

"I won't turn back," she said firmly.

"I didn't say you would."

"You implied that I would."

"No, I didn't."

"You did," she insisted. "You probably don't think I'm as useful as your new girlfriend."

"My new what?"

"Oh, please, Zollin, don't pretend you haven't been flirting with the Inn Keeper's daughter ever since we arrived. I know I'm just a nuisance, someone for you to protect with your amazing powers, but I can stand guard as well as you. I would have thought you'd enjoy the company."

"I never said I wouldn't enjoy having you to keep me company. I was just saying – " But she wouldn't let him finish.

"You were just saying how you wished I hadn't come along."

"I never said that!" he said, his voice getting louder.

"I don't know why I came," she said hotly. "You obviously wish I hadn't."

She climbed on her horse.

"Wait, why are you so angry?" Zollin asked.

"As if you didn't know," she sneered. "Hah!" she yelled, digging her heels into Lilly's flanks, making the horse race away.

Snow flew all over Zollin and the horse he was holding by the reins.

"Wow, you're sister's in a bad mood," said Ellie, who had just reappeared. She was as jolly as ever. "Here's the extra food."

"Thanks," Zollin said as he swung up into the saddle. He reached down and took the food from Ellie, who was smiling up at him. He was a little embarrassed and flustered, but he managed to say, "See you later," before following after Brianna.

The air was cold and the thick clouds made visibility less than ideal. He had intended to ride up to the forest line of trees and search for Kelvich's cottage, but now he would have to follow Brianna. He had hoped, even after she volunteered herself to keep him company, that he could find an excuse to send her back to the village, but her strange behavior made that seem unlikely.

He trotted after her, following her trail through the snow easily enough. She hadn't ridden that far ahead, and he caught up to her shortly. He rode up beside her and looked at her. She in turn looked straight ahead, her face as cold as the snow all around them. He wanted to ask why she was mad, but he didn't want to fight with her anymore. He had a vague notion of jealousy, but he pushed the thought aside as ludicrous. Brianna couldn't be jealous of him, unless she was just used to being the center of attention. He could make a case that he'd been the center of attention since they had left Tranaugh Shire, but it was the attention of powerful Wizards who wanted to abduct him and murder his family and friends. That wasn't exactly the kind of attention he figured Brianna or any sane person wanted. He certainly didn't. He wished he could go back to the way things were before magic entered his life. At that time he was miserable, but miserable seemed a step up from his current position. Being a Wizard was exciting but also incredibly dangerous. He had no idea how he had survived this long.

"Why did you do it?" Brianna asked, breaking the silence.

Her voice startled Zollin out of his reverie and he looked over at her, but she was still staring straight ahead.

"Why did I do what?" he asked tentatively, hoping not to make her angry again.

"Why did you show me your power? Why did you do so much for Todrek when… when it was so obvious that you didn't want him to marry me? Why did you save me from that Wizard when you could have been rid of me forever? Why did you give me this stupid ring? Why?"

"I…" Zollin wasn't sure what to say. He had no idea why she was asking all these questions, but at least he understood one of them. He answered slowly, "That ring saved your life, not me."

"What?"

"I didn't do anything to save you from Branock. I was struggling just to survive myself. And you rode in so fast, I didn't even have time to react. I've thought a lot about what happened. I think the ring, or more exactly the stone in the ring, protected you. Do you remember that in the alley back home I couldn't lift you or the ring? Somehow it repels magic. The ring saved you."

"That's because it's a White Alzerstone," said a voice from behind them.

Zollin and Brianna whirled around, totally taken by surprise. Kelvich had ridden up behind them so silently that they hadn't heard him approach. Zollin was a bit unnerved. He hadn't felt the man approach, and even though he could sense magic in the man, it was strangely subdued, like pebbles in a stream bed hidden by the movement of the water around them. Zollin had to look intently to sense the power that was obviously there.

"Who are you?" Brianna asked suspiciously.

"Just a friend, I assure you. I was hoping to have a word with your friend," Kelvich said. "Do you have a moment?"

"No," Brianna said.

"Yes," Zollin said.

They looked at each other and Brianna sighed. "I'm going to do what we're supposed to be doing. I guess you could join me when you're through," she said, her voice icy. Then she spurred her horse and galloped away through the snow, making Zollin's horse shuffle around in the road.

"Your friend isn't happy," Kelvich said.

Zollin ignored the comment. "Why were you asking about me at the Inn?"

"Ah, I guess Ellianna told you. I need to remember not to trust young girls. They're too easily convinced by handsome young men to tell their secrets."

"You haven't answered my question," Zollin said.

"No, I haven't, but I would wager you could guess the answer yourself."

"I sense power in you."

"Well, that's kind of you, very kind indeed. But I'm merely a candle while you shine as brightly as the sun."

Zollin was confused, unsure of what the man meant.

"How long have you been aware of your gift?" Kelvich asked.

"I'm not sure what you mean."

"Oh, I think you do. I assure you I only want to help. I'm a Sorcerer, Zollin. Do you know what that means?"

Zollin's heart was pounding. Like any young boy, his father and friends had told him stories about Sorcerers. They were said to be evil men who stole children to be sacrificed in wicked ceremonies that bound them with soul-ties to demons or worse creatures. There were stories of Sorcerers who bewitched men into giving away their treasures and their daughters. Zollin had always thought the stories were just bedtime tales to get children to behave. Even after he had discovered his powers, he hadn't given sorcery much thought. Fear crept into his belly as Todrek's words came back to him, "Do you really want to be an old man in a tower, casting spells and summoning demons?"

"I know," said Kelvich. "It's not the best way to start a conversation. Most people are terrified of Sorcerers, but I'm a pretty poor one, and I assure you, I mean no harm."

"Aren't..." Zollin hesitated before speaking his thoughts aloud.

"Aren't Sorcerers evil?" Kelvich finished the question for him. "Well, that's a good question and I would say that depends on the Sorcerer. But before we go into all that, I need to ask that you do me a favor."

Zollin's face flushed. He was afraid of what Kelvich was going to ask him to do. But the Sorcerer ignored Zollin's obvious discomfort and continued. "None of the people of Brighton's Gate know what I am. They assume I'm just an eccentric old man, and I'd like to keep it that way. I'll answer all your questions, but first you must promise to keep my secret."

It seemed like a reasonable request, so Zollin nodded.

"Come on," Kelvich said. "Let's ride after your friend and I'll see if I can explain exactly who, and what, I am."

Chapter 16

"A Sorcerer is not what you think," Kelvich said. "We don't steal babies or mate with demons or anything like the stories you've heard. We're more like teachers."

"I've never heard that before," Zollin said cautiously.

"Indeed, well, most people haven't, but let me continue. Sorcerers are much like Wizards, but we don't really have much power on our own. Our power comes in the abilities of other people."

"What do you mean?"

"Well, I can control the magic in you," he said, grinning. "Observe." He pulled out three small metal balls, polished until they shone like mirrors. He held them in his open palm. Suddenly Zollin felt the magic in his chest and staff and willow belt blend together. The balls rose into the air and danced around in circles. Zollin knew he was causing the balls to levitate, but he hadn't tried to cast a spell, and even when he tried to break the flow of magic, he was unable to. Finally, the balls slowly moved back down into Kelvich's hand, and he quickly hid them away inside his cloak.

"How did you do that?" Zollin asked incredulously.

"That is what a Sorcerer does," Kelvich answered. "That much magic would leave me exhausted, but tapping into your strength is as easy as breathing. Most Sorcerers will either work with Wizards to develop their skills or bend the power of Warlocks to their will for their own purposes."

"Warlocks?" Zollin asked.

"Insane, most of them, but very powerful. Warlocks are a lot like your staff there, perfect reservoirs of power but totally helpless to use it on their own. But under the control of a Sorcerer, a Warlock's power can be tapped and exploited. That's where the stories come from."

"But you don't do that kind of thing?"

"No, like I said, whether a Sorcerer is evil or good depends on the man. Just like Wizards, for that matter. It all comes down to character, just like everything else in life. Give a poor man money, and if he was generous while he was poor, he'll be generous when he's rich. If he was miserly without money, he'll be a greedy wretch with it."

"You said that some Sorcerers teach? What do you mean?"

"I mean I can help you develop your gifts. Teach you how to use magic without exhausting or killing yourself. Point you in a direction, hopefully the right direction."

"But why would you do that?"

"What else would I do? I have a gift that can only be effectively used in two ways. I don't want to bend anyone to my will, but I love to teach. So I teach. It's as simple as that."

"You'll teach me?"

"All I can," Kelvich said.

Zollin nodded, thinking. His first impulse was to leap at the chance. Here was what he had been hoping to find, someone who could teach him about his power. But he knew he couldn't take anyone at their word, not anymore. Kelvich had admitted that Sorcerers often took advantage of other magic users. In fact, he had demonstrated that he could manipulate Zollin's own power. It was a tempting offer, but he was afraid to trust the stranger.

"I'm not really sure that's a good idea," Zollin said, unwilling to totally close the door. In fact, he was hoping the Sorcerer would try to convince him.

"That's wise," said Kelvich. "You can't be too careful. I take it you've run into Wizards from the Torr?"

"How did you know that?"

"Well, there is a story floating around about a young boy who caused a lot of grief in Tranaugh Shire. Some have said he was a Sorcerer, causing several of the townspeople to run away with him. Of course, that was total nonsense to me. It sounds more like the young man was running for his life from the Torr."

"Who are they?" Zollin asked.

"Honestly? I don't know who they are, just what they are. They've held power in Osla for a long time. They're led by a man they call the Master, but his name is Offendorl. He's ancient, probably several hundred years old. He wants to control all the Wizards in the Five Kingdoms. They've recruited or killed all that I know about. They would have done the same to me, but I guess my power is too weak to be noticed here in the mountains."

"What do they want?"

"What does every mad man want?" Kelvich answered. "Power, money, control... basically anything and everything they see. Some people say that the Torr is the only safe place for Wizards. It's no secret that every King covets a Wizard, but since the Torr began, no kingdom has been favored with one. They'll reveal their plans in time, but for now it's enough to know that they don't operate with the same morals as most people. Murder is not a problem for them, and they don't care who gets in their way."

"Three Wizards from the Torr showed up in my village. They demanded that I go with them, but my father and I resisted," Zollin said. "My best friend was killed."

"I'm sorry," Kelvich said sincerely. "Our gifts do not always bring us happiness. I take it the others aren't your brother and sister."

Zollin shook his head.

"Well, that makes more sense, then. I think we have a lot to discuss, but it seems you should probably talk it over with your companions. And by the way, I think she's upset because you are showing young Miss Ellianna a little too much attention. Trust an old man, women aren't my specialty, but I've known a few.

"If you choose to visit me I'll be in my cottage on the edge of the woods, just follow the tree line west from the road," he said. Then, veering off the trail, he urged his horse into a canter and rode away.

Zollin's horse sat and watched him go, and then Zollin clucked his tongue and urged his own horse to move on. As he rode he pondered what Kelvich had said. The world of magic was much larger than he had imagined. He wondered what he could learn, what kinds of things he could do. But try as he might, he couldn't keep his mind from drifting back to Brianna. Why did she have to complicate his life so much? He wanted to hate her. She was annoying enough to drive anyone crazy, he thought. Why was she so drawn to him?

Was it his power? Did she hope that if she was with him, he would give her riches and glory? It was preposterous that she would care for him – she had never even given him so much as a passing glance before. He remembered that day in Tranaugh Shire, walking her to inspect her new home – she had seemed so spoiled, so typically fixated on girlish dreams. But she had been strong and confident as they made their escape from the village and faced the dangers of the road. He would have liked nothing more than to take her into his arms and kiss her soft, pink lips, but he could never do that.

Soon he could see her, waiting at the tree line of the forest for him. She had sense enough not to ride through the heavily wooded slopes of the valley alone, he thought. She was beautiful, even from a distance, so regal, sitting on her horse, gazing back down the valley as if she were a princess inspecting her kingdom. But there was none of the girlish pride or condescension on her features now. They were soft and warm, making his temperature rise despite the winter weather. He knew he could love her, but he also knew he couldn't. He had to push her away, to make it clear that they could never be together. He would not disgrace his friend's memory by stealing Todrek's wife.

He hardened his features as he approached. "At least you had the common sense to wait for me instead of riding into the forest all alone," he snapped at her.

She had been about to say something, perhaps apologize, but the words died on her lips. Her countenance faltered for just a moment, but then she regained her composure and turned her horse back toward the road.

"It took you long enough," she said icily.

The words were like salt in a wound to Zollin, but he was glad to hear them. Glad that she would not tempt him by being nice.

"There's no need to go further, we can watch the road from here," Zollin said.

She stopped her horse and turned it back to him. "Well, what did you have in mind, fearless leader?"

"Let's find a place off the road and wait," he said. "That's what we came to do."

"I don't know what your problem is but –"

He didn't let her finish.

"I don't have a problem," he said.

"Oh, acting like a jerk just comes naturally, does it."

"Just giving as good as I get," he replied.

Her face hardened even more, the color disappearing from her lips, which were pulled into a tight line.

"What is that supposed to mean?" she snapped.

"I'm just saying, if you treat me like the hired help, I'll treat you like a brainless wench."

"Ooohh!" she shouted and leaned toward him, swinging her hand in a wide arch to slap him, but Zollin leaned out of the way. Unfortunately, she leaned too far, and although she tried to grab the saddle, her sudden movement caused Lilly to shift away from Zollin's horse, throwing her even further off balance. She fell, and Zollin tried to catch her before she hit the ground. He lifted with his magic, but it was useless, the ring he'd given her repelled his effort.

She landed with a crunch but the thick snow had cushioned her fall. She cried out from the cold and surprise, but Zollin merely watched her.

"I hate you," she screamed.

"That's your right," he said, as if the remark hadn't felt like a knife being thrust into his heart.

She grabbed Lilly's reins and pulled herself back into the saddle. "I hope you freeze out here," she said.

"Not likely," he smirked.

She kicked her horse and headed back to the village, and only when she was out of sight did he let his shoulders slump in despair. He hated treating her so unfairly, but it was the only way to keep his vow.

He led his horse off the road and found a good spot to wait out the day. After a while, he wished he had been a little easier on her just so that he could have had some company. Instead he ate her share of the lunch Ellie had packed for them. The food was good, soft bread and cheese, although the cold air made the cheese hard.

He noticed that Ellie hadn't packed any apple tart in Brianna's rations. He didn't blame her.

Chapter 17

Early that afternoon, the storm began. Snow fell lightly at first, big, beautiful flakes that seemed to dance on the air. As he finished off Ellie's delicious apple tart, the snowfall increased. The air seemed to fill with millions of white snowflakes until everything seemed to be white, or at least a shade of white. Zollin quickly made his way back to the village, following the trail in the snow the horses had made earlier that morning. When he stepped out of the stable after rubbing down his horse and noticing that Brianna had tended to Lilly, he couldn't see the Inn. He knew it was only thirty or so feet from the stable, but all he could see was snow. It was everywhere. He had seen snowstorms like this a few times in his life, had heard stories of people being lost out in the open, unable to make their way back to their village and freezing to death. He was confident that wouldn't happen, but he wasn't sure he could make his way to the other side of the Inn without staggering around like a blind man. He walked as straight as possible until he was only a few feet away from the Inn and suddenly the low-roofed structure loomed up out of the whiteness ahead of him. He could vaguely make out a door. He didn't knock but pulled open the door and stumbled in.

The room he was in was full of wine barrels and kegs of ale. There was a commotion, and the Inn Keeper hurried in looking worried.

"Oh, it's you," he said. "I warned you about the weather."

"Yes, and I'm glad you did. I got back just in time. Thank you."

"Ah," the Inn Keeper's smile returned. "It's my pleasure. Right this way, and I'll show you to the common room."

Zollin followed the plump man through the maze of rooms, some used as pantries, others kitchen and laundry rooms. He had never thought of the amount of work it took to keep up an Inn. It made him feel bad for Ellie. They bumped into her as she hurried around the corner with empty ale mugs.

"Oh, Zollin, when did you get back?" she said, looking a little embarrassed.

"Just now, and just in time I'd say," said her father. "The white out is coming on strong – we'll be busy. Make sure there's extra food being prepared, hurry along."

She nodded and hurried off.

"She's a hard worker, that one. I couldn't have asked for a better daughter. Be looking to find her a good match soon," he said.

Zollin didn't miss the hint in the Inn Keeper's voice. He wondered why a man with an Inn would be so quick to want to marry his daughter to a stranger. He didn't have much time to ponder the thought. When he stepped into the common room, he found it half full of town's folk already.

"What about the weather?" he asked the Inn Keeper. "How will these people find their way home?"

"They won't, they'll stay here."

"Oh," Zollin said. It made sense; there was plenty of food and space for everyone. It would make for a lively evening. Zollin scanned the room for Brianna. She wasn't there, which didn't surprise him, but he was both relieved and disappointed at the same time. He knew she was close since Lilly had been safe and warm in the stable. He found a place near the wall that separated the sleeping rooms from the common room and settled in. He leaned back against the wall and watched the people. They were laughing and joking. There was a festive air, and it reminded Zollin of the Harvest Festival. He had always hated being snowed in. He loved his father, but being cooped up in their little house with a man who couldn't sit still was nerve-wracking. At least here there was plenty of ale and mulled cider. He was planning to ask for a cup when he noticed something strange. Every time the door from the kitchens opened, the laughter and talking stopped. It was only for a moment, but it happened repeatedly. People would look up toward the door, then go right back to their conversations. It was odd, Zollin thought.

He was thinking of asking Ellie about it, but Quinn and Mansel showed up and began describing the Gateway Inn. It had caught fire and most of the kitchen and storage rooms had burned.

The fire had been extinguished before spreading upstairs, but the owner wanted the second story floor to be replaced. It would take at least two months to complete all the work.

"And that's only if we can get the lumber milled," Quinn said.

"And that's not likely with weather like this," Mansel added.

"Oh, I'm sure people here have learned to cope," Zollin said.

"Looks like their way of coping agrees with me," Quinn said, taking a mug of ale from Ellie.

"Any chance I can get some of that mulled cider?" Zollin asked.

"Of course," she said, beaming.

"I've always liked this town," Quinn said. "I would have settled here, but your mother couldn't deal with the cold."

"You've been here before?" Zollin asked. "Was it with the army?"

"Yup, seems like a long time ago. The Skellmarians are savage people. But living in weather like this year-round would make you crazy."

"What are they like?" Mansel asked.

"Well, I only ever saw one or two," Quinn explained. "We came up the coast from Isos city by boat and entered the Great Valley on the western end. I was stationed here, or actually to the north of the river. We were never raided – Brighton's Gate rarely is. But some of the other villages along the valley, especially those that harbor miners that work the northern mountains, get raided all year long."

"And the Skellmarians?" Mansel urged.

"They wore big, thick coats and close fitting hats made of some kind of animal fur. They had long hair and dark skin. They had what looked like really large bear claws threaded into necklaces, but what I remember most was the smell. They stank worse than your father's tannery."

Zollin snickered at that comment, and Mansel looked pained. It was a common joke in Tranaugh Shire – the tannery was a smelly place and Mansel's family was constantly teased but took it good naturedly.

Soon food was being served, and everyone was talking and laughing. Brianna appeared but never looked at Zollin. Even when Ellie came by to chat, Zollin noticed that she stared at the fire and seemed not to hear or care about their conversation.

Mansel was soon too into his cups to be much fun – his ale made him melancholy. Zollin suspected he was a bit homesick and didn't blame him. If his mother were alive, no amount of stench or teasing could keep him away.

As the evening wore on, people began to sing. Ellie, Ollie, and Buck the Inn Keeper set out large pitchers of drink so that people could help themselves. It was a merry evening until the kitchen door banged open and three large men came in, shaking the snow off their clothes and demanding ale.

Ollie and Buck hurried to serve them, and the room grew quiet.

"Don't stop singing on our account," said one of the men in a gruff voice. "Sing dammit!" he shouted. Everyone obeyed, but there wasn't merriment in the room any longer. Ellie hurried in with a platter of mugs and two pitchers of ale. She began setting the drinks on the table when one of the men pinched her. She flinched but continued working.

Zollin started to rise from his seat, his hand clutching his staff, but his father laid a hand on his arm. Zollin looked at his father, who shook his head discreetly but never took his eyes off the three men.

"Don't be a fool, Zollin," Brianna hissed. "You try and be the hero with magic, and the town will know who we are. They'll run us out in this weather and we'll all freeze to death. Your little girlfriend isn't worth it."

Zollin didn't know what made him angrier, the three men abusing the Inn Keeper's daughter or Brianna rubbing his nose in what she didn't understand. But she had a point; if he blasted the men, they could very well be thrown out into the cold.

"Well, we can't just sit here and do nothing," Zollin said.

Another of the burly men grabbed Ellie and pulled her onto his lap. She wailed and he laughed. Ollie came charging over, shouting for the men to let her go, but one of the others stood in her way.

"You better let her go," Quinn said in an easy voice.

The laughter stopped, and even Ellie was quiet. The man holding her turned slowly to see Quinn standing a few feet away. Zollin noticed that Quinn's dagger was stuck into his belt at the small of his back. He wanted to stand up and help, but he would be no match for the big men in a fight unless he used magic, and that could only be a last resort.

"I don't know you," said the gruff man.

"I'm new in town," Quinn said. "Let the girl go and let's have a drink together. I'll tell you all about me."

The man didn't move and he didn't let Ellie go either.

"You had better sit down," said the third man. He had a big woolly beard and greasy hair that hung down around his shoulders.

"Not until you let the girl go and mind your manners."

The three men laughed. Then suddenly the one with the big beard lunged at Quinn, but the Master Carpenter darted away. Zollin leapt to his feet and swung his staff at the man who had lost his balance. The thick wood smashed into the man's face and snapped his head back violently. His feet flew up and he dropped to the floor in a heap. The man who had blocked Ollie's approach started to draw his sword, but Quinn drew and threw his dagger so fast his hand was a blur. The knife buried itself up to the hilt in the man's stomach just under his rib cage. The man's legs went rubbery and he fell to floor, moaning in pain.

"That was a mistake," said the man who still held Ellie on his lap. He suddenly shoved her at Quinn, who grabbed her. The man was instantly on his feet with a long, heavy-looking knife in his hand. "I'm going to carve you up and then start on your pup over there," he said, thrusting the knife in Zollin's direction.

Quinn never said a word, just stepped in front of Ellie, who quickly hurried back to her mother, and waited. The man looked him up and down, probably trying to see if Quinn had another weapon.

Zollin felt a lump rising in his throat. He had never seen his father fight before the confrontation in Tranaugh Shire. Now he stood unarmed and seemingly helpless before a much larger man with a deadly looking knife.

No one had noticed Mansel rise from his bench. The boy was swaying a little, his head swimming from too much ale, but he bellowed at the big man and stumbled toward him. The big man never looked away from Quinn, but his left fist shot out and smashed into Mansel's face, sending the boy reeling backward.

Suddenly, the man swung the big knife in a long arc that was aimed for Quinn's head. Quinn leaned back out of reach of the vicious swipe and then stepped forward, brought his leg up and kicked straight down onto the man's knee. There was a loud pop and the man howled, dropping the knife and falling to the floor clutching his knee. Quinn picked up the big knife in his slow, methodical way, looked at it, and then, holding the blade, he slammed the handle down on the back of the man's head.

The man slumped to the floor, unconscious. No one moved. The entire room full of people just stared at the Master Carpenter. Quinn laid the big knife on the nearest table and walked over to the man he had stabbed with his dagger. The man had fallen back and was only faintly breathing. He removed the knife and wiped it on the man's shirt.

"Oh, my," said the Inn Keeper. He hurried over and looked down. "Did you kill them?"

"Only one," he said. "The other two are just unconscious. I'd lock them up somewhere and lose the key." Quinn sat back down at the table with Zollin and the others and took a long drink of his ale. Mansel was slow getting back to his feet, but soon he was drowning his pain and humiliation with more ale.

The townspeople finally came to life. Some gathered around Ollie and her daughter, who was sobbing quietly. Some of the others began dragging the three men out. A few even came over to congratulate Quinn and Zollin.

"Never seen the like," one man said.

"Where did you learn to fight like that?" another asked.

"I thought you were a dead man," said yet another man, which was followed by a chorus of agreement and laughter. The ale was flowing again, and the room was filled with cheerful voices. Buck the Inn Keeper came and took a seat beside Quinn.

"Those men all work with Trollic in the mines," said the Inn Keeper. He refilled Zollin's mug and continued. "These three run supplies back and forth. They were in town earlier today, and I figured they'd be back. They run up big tabs and never pay, they terrorize everyone, and we've had no way to stop them till now."

"Why didn't you band together and run them off?" Zollin asked.

"Trollic's got a large crew a hard day's ride from here."

"So where are the King's soldiers?" Quinn asked. "Shouldn't they be patrolling on the north side of the river?"

"We haven't had a patrol in several years," Buck explained. "We just don't get raided often enough."

"But there are raids," Quinn said. "Didn't you send a delegate to the King to request protection?"

"Of course, we sent one twice. The first one returned without aid, so the town Council sent the head Councilman. The King had him beaten for insolence, saying that his word was final and that we should know better than to ask twice."

"That doesn't sound like King Felix," Quinn said.

"It was the Prince who did it," said Buck. "King Felix's been ill for some time and the Prince has been governing in his absence."

"Prince Dewalt?" Quinn asked.

"No, his younger brother, Simmeron. Dewalt's the ambassador to Osla."

"Well, that explains your poor treatment."

"It doesn't solve the problem, though," Zollin said. "We may have put the town at risk if this Trollic decides to retaliate."

"I doubt he would do that," Quinn said. "Brighton's Gate is his only source of supplies. Besides, no one seems to think that what we did was wrong."

Quinn waved his cup and some of the men nearby gave a cheer, but Buck's face was pinched, as if he knew something he didn't want to say.

It had been enough excitement for one night, so Zollin took a slice of bread and returned to his room. He lay down on the soft mattress and thought about his day. He was excited about learning from Kelvich, but he knew it would be several days before the weather would allow him to travel back out to the Sorcerer's cottage. He would probably have to endure several days working with his father and Mansel. There were weighty topics to occupy his mind, but he couldn't stop his thoughts from drifting back to Brianna. He saw her in his mind, tall and regal, sitting on her horse with snow falling softy around her. His heart ached as he saw her face, shocked at his rudeness and filled with frustration, but he hadn't asked her to care about him. He replayed their conversation outside the stable. He wondered why he had given her the ring. Was he protecting Todrek by giving her the ring, or was he showing deeper feelings, things he hadn't been willing to admit even to himself?

The internal argument swung back in forth in his mind as he ate his supper. The bread was good, but his appetite was ruined. When Mansel finally stumbled into their room, Zollin pretended he was asleep. He didn't want to talk or pretend that everything was fine. He lay there in the dark, listening to the lonely wind blowing the snow against their window. The room was chilly, and he pulled his blankets around him and tried to sleep, but he couldn't. He was miserable, but it couldn't be helped. He had made his vow and he could never break it.

Chapter 18

It was snowing again. Branock was sick of the cold, sick of the wet snow that seemed to cling to him and chill him. He had fully restored his body and even managed to remove most of the scarring on his face, but had not been able to regrow his hair. And his left eye was a milky white color. He didn't care about the disfigurement, but his head was cold. And he was still walking. He knew that the passes into the mountains would be closed, and although he was certain he could make a way into the Great Valley, he had decided to wait for spring.

He was heading south, and in the distance, he could see the smoke of a farmhouse rising up into the sky. The smoke was a dirty gray color against the falling white snow. He was hungry and tired, but he needed to keep moving. He had wasted so much time already. He pondered his next moves as he walked through the fields toward the small home. Wytlethane was still a factor, although he doubted the elder Wizard would be trying very hard to accomplish his mission. It seemed to Branock that Wytlethane was content to let others do the work as long as he could take credit. Clearly the elder Wizard had expected Cassis to bring Zollin in, at which time Wytlethane could rejoin his colleague for their triumphant return.

But Cassis was dead, and Wytlethane was probably recalculating his next moves. Branock was also sure that his Master had felt the battle between Zollin and Cassis. Branock could vaguely remember a time when magic was abundant in the Five Kingdoms. The subtle pulses and currents of power were everywhere. A battle or magical birth would be hidden from those not close enough to witness the scene among the richness of power all around. But now that the landscape was barren of power, only the simplest users could exist undetected and therefore unmolested by the Torr's quest for ultimate power. His Master would know they had failed, and he would turn to other means to see that this new threat was eliminated, Branock was certain of that. He would have to turn the situation to his advantage.

He was almost at the farmhouse now. He saw the farmer emerge from the small barn, his arms full of supplies he was carrying toward his small home. When he saw Branock, he stopped and waited. Then a look of terror crossed his face and the farmer ran inside. It was to be expected, Branock thought. He wasn't a hideous sight, but his face was certainly damaged enough to strike fear in the heart of most people. He would take what he needed from the farm and leave – he had no wish to share their company. When he arrived at the home, he could smell food cooking. The door was sturdy and bolted from the inside. Branock could have blasted it to splinters, but he was in a generous mood. He visualized the thick beam used to lock the door and lifted it free of its place. He heard it clatter to the floor, the only warning he would give the farmer.

He swung the door open and entered the little home. He was in a common room, both kitchen and sitting area. A fire was crackling brightly, warming the room nicely. There were pots and pans hanging from a rack in the ceiling. A wash tub was full of water, and freshly baked bread was cooling on a small table in the corner. Over the fire was a kettle of stew. The simmering meat and vegetables made the Wizard's mouth water. He found a good-sized wooden bowl and ladled out a generous portion of the stew. He tore off a chunk of the bread and settled on a small wooden stool. The stew wasn't quite finished, some of the vegetables weren't cooked all the way through, the meat still tough, but Branock didn't care. The bread was soft and warm, the stew hot. It was the first civilized meal he had eaten in days. He wolfed it down, not noticing or caring about the taste. Once he had finished, he left the bowl on the table by the bread.

He went back outside to the barn. The snow was falling heavily, but Branock dismissed it. There would always be snow, and he couldn't let that keep him from his task. There was only a short farm horse in the stable, obviously more accustomed to the plow than to the saddle. But there was a saddle in the barn, and Branock used it on the horse. He still had his own saddle bags, and he laid them across the horse's rump behind the saddle and led the horse outside. He went back into the farmhouse and refilled the wooden bowl with stew. He took two whole loaves of bread and uncovered a mound of sharp smelling cheese. He cut the cheese in half and wrapped it in a threadbare towel. He stuck the cheese and bread into his saddle bags. There was a bottle of wine which the couple had obviously been saving. He took that too. He took the half eaten loaf and tore it into chunks which he dropped into the bowl of stew he was taking. There was a thick blanket folded neatly on one of the wooden chairs near the fire. He wrapped it around his shoulders and picked up the bowl of stew. He was about to walk out the door when a small flicker of pity fought for life somewhere in his conscience. He started to snuff it out, but something stopped him. It wouldn't hurt him any to help this poor family. He was leaving them destitute after all. He reached into the coin purse that was bulging under his tattered and singed robes. He pulled five gold coins out and stacked them neatly on the table where the bread had been. It was probably more money than the couple had ever seen, and it meant nothing to Branock. The Master would call this weakness, he thought to himself. But he didn't care. In fact, it made him happy to defy his overlord. It was the first smile to touch his scarred face in a long time.

***

The next day in Brighton's Gate, the snow continued to fall, although the blizzard was over. The people began to dig out from under the heavy snows which were as high as a grown man's chest, the drifts taller than most of the little cottages and shops around the town. Paths were formed leading to all the homes and shops. Despite the weather, people were genuinely happy. With more time on their hands, they would gather at the Valley Inn to drink and talk.

For three days, Zollin helped clear the Gateway Inn of debris so that it was finally ready for the restoration work to begin. There was a mill not far downriver, and they took another day to help clear the road. Finally, they took a day to rest and stayed around the Inn. Brianna was spending most of her time in her room, but with Quinn sleeping off a late night spent drinking with some of the other townsfolk, she was driven out of hiding by the Carpenter's snoring.

Zollin was sitting alone at one of the long tables when she entered the common room. It was early and there weren't many people around, but she joined Zollin anyway. It was awkward at first, but neither of them felt like keeping up pretenses. When Ollie, the Inn Keeper's wife, appeared with bowls of oatmeal, Brianna looked at Zollin questioningly.

"What?" he asked.

"Where's your friend?"

Zollin shrugged. "I'm assuming you're referring to Ellie, and the answer is I don't know. She hasn't been around much since the blizzard."

Brianna frowned. Zollin expected a cutting remark or even a rude suggestion, but Brianna seemed to be thinking. Finally she spoke her thoughts aloud, but in a hushed tone meant only for Zollin.

"Don't you find it strange that no one seems to be concerned about the Miner coming into town to see about his men?"

"I've wondered about that. Perhaps they've found their courage."

"Perhaps," Brianna said thoughtfully. "Or perhaps they've found their scapegoat."

"I doubt that," Zollin said.

"It's possible. If this Trollic shows up, they can claim we're responsible and hope that he directs all his retaliation on us."

"The people of this town are good people. They wouldn't do that to us."

"I agree, they're good people, but we're the outsiders. We don't have any ties here, any history. We're expendable."

"I just can't believe that."

"You're too trusting," she said, but there was kindness in her eyes.

She took a bite of her breakfast and Zollin watched her. His heart still beat faster when she paid him attention. She made him feel like a child with sweaty palms and weak knees. He decided to take a chance.

"I'm going to the hermit's house today," he said tentatively. "You want to join me?" he said as nonchalantly as possible.

She stopped chewing and looked at him. There was a question in her eyes, and Zollin plowed ahead before he lost his nerve.

"Look, Todrek was my best friend. I'm really glad you're here, and I want to be your friend. No strings, no agenda, just friends."

Brianna's look was both hopeful and hurting. Zollin couldn't believe she wanted to be with him. He told himself it was just a lack of options. Perhaps the trauma had tied them together in some way. But he knew he couldn't stand the thought of her hating him – he hated himself too much for that. She had shown mercy when she should have hated him. It was his fault that she didn't have the happy little family in the cozy little home his father had built for her. Still, she was here, and he didn't want them to be angry with each other. All he needed to do was control his emotions. He could do that, he told himself.

"Well, okay," she said.

He smiled. "Great, I'll get the horses. You leave a note for Quinn and Mansel."

Half an hour later, they were riding through the narrow pathways of snow that lead out of Brighton's Gate. Zollin hoped that the horses could plow through the snow until they were far enough out of town that he could use magic to clear the way before them. Before he felt that they had reached that safe distance, they came to a trail in the snow. It was only wide enough for one horse to pass at a time, but Zollin had an idea who had made the trail, so they followed it.

It took about twenty minutes to reach the tree line, but the trail led them farther into the forest. They crossed into the trees, and from there they could see a little cottage in a small clearing not far away. There was a neat stack of firewood and a small chicken coop at the rear of the cabin. Unlike the structures in town which were built mostly of stone, this little house was made of logs with a thick, white, muddy substance filling the gaps in the walls.

"Is this it?" Brianna asked.

"I think so," Zollin said. "I'll see if he's home."

"Of course I'm home," came a voice behind them. "What took you so long to get here?"

"I've been working," Zollin said as he turned to see Kelvich.

The Sorcerer was wrapped in animal skins with the fur on the inside. He was short with a thick stomach like most older men had. It was obvious he was fond of his ale. His face was ruddy with the cold and he wore thick mittens on his hands.

"Ah, well, we shan't waste any time then. Young lady, there is a pot of broth heating over the fire. Please slice the vegetables and keep it boiling."

Brianna looked at Zollin in surprise, but the young Wizard simply shrugged. He hadn't known what to expect, and perhaps bringing her here was a risk he shouldn't have taken, but he had done it impulsively. So she needed to go inside and cook. Zollin thought that was reasonable enough.

She sighed and threw her reins at Zollin before walking toward the cabin.

"I hope she doesn't poison us," Kelvich said.

"Oh, she would never do that," Zollin said defensively.

"A woman will do whatever she thinks is right, reason and loyalty be damned," Kelvich said in a merry voice as if he were talking about baiting trout with an old friend. "Let's walk a bit. You can tie your horses to that tree," he said, pointing to a towering pine whose branches, heavy with snow, were forming a natural shelter.

Zollin led the horses over, tied their reins to a tree limb, and rejoined the Sorcerer.

"Tell me what you can do," said Kelvich.

"Well..." Zollin was a little unsure. He had never thought of what he could do. "I can lift things. I can start fires. I can even cook things. I can blast people with my staff."

"Go on," said Kelvich.

"Well, that's about it. Oh, I can block spells, too."

Kelvich looked at Zollin thoughtfully, "Tell me what you know about magic."

"Only what I've told you about."

"No, what I mean is the history of magic, the classifications, basic lore, that sort of thing."

Zollin returned Kelvich's look as they walked through the trees with a blank stare.

"You're saying you know nothing?"

"Sorry," Zollin said, shrugging his shoulders.

"We've lost so much," Kelvich said, but he was merely speaking his thoughts aloud. "I'll start at the beginning. Do you know where magic comes from?"

"No..." Zollin said, thinking about the question. "But I can sense the different kinds. Like my staff seems to be filled with magic that I think it acquired when the tree was struck by lightning. I can tell that certain plants have properties that are healing. I've sensed magic that seemed dark or evil."

"That's good. It seems you are very sensitive. Most Wizards can sense magic in others but not usually the orientation. Magic is a mysterious thing. No one knows where it comes from or why some people can use it and others can't. It seems clear though that it is supernatural, yet a proper understanding of the natural world only enhances it. I'll explain that more later. Magic in most people, as well as things, resides in them. Religious people talk about humans having a soul, an immortal part of who they are that resides unseen within them. If this is true, then I would say that Wizards and Sorcerers, Warlocks and the like have an invisible part of who they are, a sort of magical reservoir. But the magic itself is not a part of us, not like a person's soul. It only dwells within us, empowering us with certain skills and abilities. Do you follow me?"

Zollin was a little overwhelmed, but he understood that magic was an abstract thing. He could feel it, but he knew it was separate from him too. It was like water – he couldn't grasp it like a sword, but he could contain it like the banks of a river. He felt he could shape it too, and he could even direct it.

"Yeah, I think so."

"Good," said Kelvich. "Now only on the rarest occasions can an object bestow magic on a person without the guidance of a skilled practitioner, such as a Wizard like yourself."

They had come into a small clearing in the forest. They were probably three hundred paces from Kelvich's cabin. The snow was thick on the ground here, unbroken by any activity. The boyish part of Zollin wanted to run and jump right into the snow, but another part admired the beauty of it.

"Do you sense anything here?" Kelvich asked.

At first Zollin didn't. He looked at the trees around the clearing, but he sensed nothing in them. The snow-covered clearing didn't feel like anything, until he focused his mind on the ground beneath the snow. He felt it then, like tiny whispers of life, hundreds of little sparks of magic cocooned in the snow.

"I don't know what it is," Zollin said. "It feels like tiny bits of magic. It's life-giving magic."

"Impressive," Kelvich said. "Most people can't sense the Augmire weed in its frozen state. Certain plants and herbs contain magic and can be used for healing, like the weed in this clearing. It's used to treat upset stomachs and digestive diseases."

"Di – what?"

"Digestion is the function of your body to break down food into nutrients, and the rest as waste."

"What do you mean?"

"You can study anatomy later," Kelvich said. "Digestion is what happens to the food you eat as it passes through your body and crap it out. Okay?"

"Oh, yeah, sure. Digestion. I got it."

"Okay, so some plants and herbs heal, others kill and are used in poisons. There are also some minerals that contain magic. Most magical objects are made from these types of minerals."

"What exactly is a mineral again?"

"A mineral is a naturally occurring substance such as copper or tin or even gold. Now, not all minerals have magic – you can have magic in one gold ring and not in another. Take your friend's ring for example. Do you sense magic in the ring?"

"Yes," Zollin said. "That's why I bought it."

Kelvich merely raised his eyes at Zollin, which made the young Wizard reconsider his answer. He knew the ring contained magic, so why wasn't that the right answer, he wondered. The Sorcerer waited patiently as Zollin puzzled it out. Finally he realized that the magic wasn't actually in the ring, just in the milky white stone.

"Oh, of course. The magic's in the stone, not the ring."

"Correct. Now a skilled Alchemist could have combined the stone's power with other materials that enhanced that power, making an extremely powerful magical object. You understand?"

"Yes, but what's an Alchemist?"

"All in due time, my boy, all in due time."

Chapter 19

"There are several levels of magical users," Kelvich explained as they sampled the soup that Brianna had made. It was fine soup, not fantastic but certainly warm and filling after tramping around in the forest. Zollin and Kelvich had located several types of wild flowers and naturally growing herbs. Zollin described their power, Kelvich named the plant and its uses.

"Not everyone who has magic is a Wizard. The simplest level of magical ability is Illusionists. They can perform simple tricks and often work to con people out of their money or possessions."

"Yeah, I think I met a guy like that," Zollin said.

"Who?" Brianna asked.

"The performer at the Harvest Festival. He definitely didn't agree with you, Kelvich. He was pretty set that magic didn't exist."

"That's not surprising, really," said the Sorcerer. "Their illusions are the only power they have. If they tried other things, they would fail. For Illusionists, magic manifests itself in their abilities. So it's natural that they would try more, fail, and then become convinced that magic doesn't exist. Take yourself, for example. Do you create the magic?"

"No," Zollin said. "I just sort of channel it."

"And that is why an Illusionist would fail. He has no real power other than an ability to make others see what he wants them to. An Herbalist is the next step. Their magic often takes the form of knowledge about plants and herbs. There are Herbalists and Apothecaries that have no magical ability. They simply have the knowledge of what plants and herbs to use in making medicines and salves, but others have an innate sense of what those plants can do. They are drawn to plants with magical properties, the same way you are, only they can't sense the magic, they just know which plants are helpful. They often create new medicines just by feel without much experimentation."

"Wow," Zollin said. "That's impressive. Do they know they're magic users?"

"No," Kelvich explained after he had chewed the vegetables in his mouth. "They can't sense magic, and without guidance, they may never fully develop their abilities. In a similar way, Alchemists have an innate knowledge of minerals. Alchemists can even transform some objects into completely different materials all together. Again, most Alchemists today don't realize they have power. They just experiment and try things. In ages past, Alchemists were highly sought after by Kings and those in power, but as the Torr gained strength and many Alchemists were killed or driven into hiding, much of their lore has been lost.

"Alchemists can create powerful magical objects, such as the famed Sword of Inosis. It was unbreakable, just as the legends say, but it was just a normal sword made from magical iron that an Alchemist had forged. Some Alchemists specialize in working with certain materials, but the most powerful can work with them all with such incredible skill that the most gifted craftsmen could never compete with.

"The next level is a Sorcerer," he said with a little bow. "We have several unique abilities. The first is a powerful sense of magic in all things. Unfortunately, we can't usually control that magic. Like an Herbalist or an Alchemist, I can sense the power in plants and minerals, but I can't manipulate them skillfully. I can also recognize magical objects, from those imbued with power, such an ambulate or say the Sword of Inosis, to objects that are themselves a source of magical power, like Zollin's staff and willow belt."

"What belt?" Brianna said, looking at Zollin's trousers.

"He keeps a belt woven from willow branches around his waist, under his shirt," said Kelvich with a twinkle in his eye.

Zollin turned a little red before saying, "There's a reason I wear it under my shirt."

"No doubt, no doubt, but friends shouldn't have secrets," the Sorcerer said matter-of-factly. "Now, Sorcerers have another power, one that is easily abused. We cannot control magical objects ourselves, but we can manipulate and even control other magic users. Shall I demonstrate?" he said, speaking directly to Brianna.

"No," Zollin said loudly.

"Yes, please," she said, her smile melting Zollin's heart.

"Of course, now let me see. What is it that our young Wizard here would never do?"

"I've never seen him dance," Brianna said with enthusiasm.

"Yes, excellent. And is he a singer?"

"No, please," Zollin begged.

"I would love to hear him sing," she said, pretending to be serious. "How about the 'Absent Farmer's Daughter'?"

"Excellent choice, my lady. If our performer will please stand," he said to Zollin.

"No way, this isn't fair."

"It's part of my lesson," Kelvich said, sounding hurt.

"Then change it."

"But where's the fun in that? Now, as I said, Sorcerers can manipulate magic users."

Suddenly Zollin sprang up from his seat. He had an overwhelming urge to dance and sing. It was irresistible. He cleared his throat and began to dance and sing, clapping his hands in time. Some small part of his brain was screaming that he should stop, but the desire to sing and dance was just too strong. He shouted out the words to the popular tune, hopping and spinning as he clapped his hands. Brianna and Kelvich clapped along and joined him on the chorus. When he was finally done, the desire suddenly disappeared and he realized what he had done. Brianna was laughing and telling him what a good job he had done, but the embarrassment was too much. He grabbed his staff, resisting the urge to blast Kelvich into a glowing ember, and ran from the cabin.

"Oh, no, we've embarrassed him," Brianna said, a little distressed.

"He'll come around," Kelvich said. "But you'd better be getting back to the Inn. It won't do for a brother and sister to be gone so long together. People might begin to talk."

Brianna blushed and hurried to the door, but just before she opened it, she turned back.

"Can a Sorcerer read a man's thoughts?" she asked.

"No, but when you've been around as long as I have you learn a thing or two about people."

"What do you know about me?" she asked.

"Ah, well, that is a discussion for another time, but I think what you are referring to is your attraction to Zollin. And that, my girl, is plain and clear, but dangerous at this point in the game. Be sure to hold your feelings close."

"Why? Do you think he feels the same way?"

"I think Zollin is a very conflicted young man. Give him time, he'll see what matters most before long."

Brianna smiled a shy but beautiful smile and darted out the door. Zollin was across the small yard, untying his horse.

"Wait for me," she called.

He didn't look up, but he didn't immediately ride away either. He stood waiting by Lilly as Brianna hurried over.

"I'm sorry, Zollin," she said.

"I don't want to talk about it."

She untied Lilly's reins and they pulled themselves into their saddles as Kelvich walked out onto his little porch. He had a long tube made from stiffened leather in his hands. He waved it to them.

"Take this with you," he called. "Tell anyone who asks that I'm tutoring you in preparation for a career in law."

Zollin wanted to ignore the old man, but he sawed at the reins until his horse was standing close enough for him to take the strange container. There was a strap sewn onto the tube, and Zollin slung it over his shoulder.

"What's in it?" Zollin asked.

"Lots of legal jargon," Kelvich said. "I'm sure Ollie will have gone through every paper soon enough. She'll confirm your story, and in the future I can give you things you'll want to study."

"What makes you think I'll ever come back here again?" Zollin challenged.

"Ah, well first of all, curiosity, but also because I promise never to do that to you again."

"You said that the last time we met," Zollin said.

"No, I said I would never use your magic without your permission again. This time I'm promising to never make you sing and dance before a lovely young lady again."

"Promise you'll never control me like that," said Zollin harshly. "Give me your word, Sorcerer, or you'll never see me again."

Kelvich sighed. "Alright, alright. I promise. But the next time you come, bring me a cut of pork from the butcher. I grow tired of chicken."

Zollin nodded, his anger still simmering just beneath the surface. He could feel the heat from his magic swirling inside him. He pulled hard on the reins and galloped out of the forest. Brianna followed, feeling bad for having joined in with Kelvich. She had thought the song and dance adorable, and would have told Zollin so. She hated to see him wounded, but she was carefully pondering what Kelvich had told her. She wondered if she had made things unnecessarily hard for Zollin. She liked him. He had cast a spell on her that day in the alley at Tranaugh Shire when he had revealed his newfound skill to her. She hadn't admitted it at first. It wasn't proper to fall in love with your betrothed's best friend. And she hadn't wanted to hurt Todrek any more than Zollin. He was just a big, tenderhearted boy and she regretted greatly that he had been slain, but she couldn't stand the thought of Zollin leaving without her. She had chased after him that day without a thought for anyone else, not even her husband.

Now she needed to comfort Zollin, but she realized that he was still smarting from embarrassment. She needed to proceed with finesse. She kept all these things to herself, of course, choosing to remain silent until they reached the wider access of the village roads. The cold was wicked as the afternoon waned. The wind was blowing, and it managed to find every crease in her cloak. Her hands were aching as they finally reached the village.

"Would you take my reins?" she asked him.

He turned and looked at her, surprised. She could see the hurt there and longed to wipe it away, but she kept her distance.

"My hands are nearly frozen," she explained.

He reached over and took her reins and then hesitated.

"Give me your hands," he said. "And take off the ring."

Her heart fluttered, but she tried not to let her excitement show. Zollin felt a lump rising in his throat. He probably should just lead her horse back to the Inn, but he hated to see her freezing hands. She had long delicate fingers that were turning blue from the cold. She pulled the ring off her finger and dropped it into the pocket of her cloak, then held her hands out to him. He put his own around them and projected heat with his mind. Her hands grew warm and he was careful to control the magic as it flowed through him. He didn't want to burn her.

"That feels so good," she said. "Better than a fire."

He nodded and, after a minute or so, let go of her and handed back her reins. They rode the rest of the way back without speaking. When they got to the stable behind the Inn, she finally said what was on her mind.

"I'm sorry if I've made this trip hard on you," she said.

Zollin stiffened. He wasn't sure what to say. He didn't want her to be sorry. He was glad she was here, but he couldn't give her what she needed. Nor could he stand the thought of her with anyone else. It was a terrible feeling, and it showed on his features.

"It's okay," she said. "I've been out of line, but I do want to be your friend."

He nodded, the lump seeming to choke off any possible words.

"I really appreciate you inviting me along today."

"No problem," he managed to say, although his voice was strained.

"Do you mind if I go on in?" she asked, pointing over her shoulder to the Inn.

"No, go ahead," he said. He watched her walk away, and although he tried, he couldn't tear his eyes off of her. Finally, when she was out of sight around the corner, he led the horses into the stable. He took his time rubbing them down and ensuring that they had fresh water and plenty of oats. Then he went back to the Inn. The common room was filling quickly. Ollie and Ellie were busy serving food and drinks. Mansel was in the corner looking green and unhappy. Quinn was sitting with a man about his own age but wearing elegant-looking garments. Brianna was not in the common room, so Zollin joined Mansel.

"You okay?" he asked the young apprentice.

"No, I drank too much last night," he said in a voice that was little more than a moan. "I'll never touch mulled wine again as long as I live."

Despite being angry with Kelvich and confused by Brianna, Zollin laughed. He laughed at himself and his predicament with Brianna and his good fortune in meeting Kelvich and the rankling way the old Sorcerer had. He laughed because even though his heart ached with the loss of his best friend, and the life-long absence of his mother, he was happy.

Chapter 20

Two days passed before Zollin made it back out to Kelvich's cabin. The weather was unseasonably warm, which translated into the temperature rising slightly above freezing. Most of the snow insulated itself, so very little melting took place, but any rise in the temperature was welcome. Zollin remembered to bring the Sorcerer a bit of pork. In fact, he bought some pork ribs and several pork chops.

They spent the morning sitting at the little table sharing information while Kelvich prepared the ribs to be cooked in a small smoker he had built.

"So, did Ollie find your papers?" Kelvich asked.

"I believe so. I left them easily accessible, and she straightened our room herself."

"And where is your sister this morning?"

"She's actually helping the Tailor. Her father is a Tailor, and she's trading some labor for warmer gear for all of us. It's really quite nice of her," Zollin said, feeling the thick wool tunic she had bartered for him. "My father set it up, but she's been working hard. Not really apprentice work, but odds and ends, whatever the Tailor needs. I have to admit she has skills."

Kelvich changed the line of conversation.

"Alright, so we discussed Sorcerers but not Warlocks, and it's really not fair to talk about one apart from the other. Warlocks have incredible power, more than all but the strongest Wizards, but they can't control it. In fact, have you noticed that your magic has a mind of its own?"

Zollin thought for a moment. There were certainly times when he felt he had to control himself. It was like riding a powerful horse which you had to constantly remind that you were in control. And there were other times when he had reacted without thought, the magic responding to need rather than command. He nodded and Kelvich continued.

"Often that power will drive a Warlock insane, but if a Sorcerer finds a Warlock, he can tap into that power. In the past, Sorcerers collected Warlocks like a Carpenter collects tools. They would control the Warlocks, use them up and then discard them like trash. It's the temptation of our power, to control and dominate. Hence the stories you've probably heard, which are mostly all lies and exaggerations. And while a majority of Sorcerers were cruel and evil men, grasping for power that was not theirs to have, some became teachers."

He bowed low to the ground and Zollin laughed. He was beginning to trust the old man, but he wasn't quite ready to let his guard down completely.

"We have the ability to help young Wizards understand their powers, to demonstrate techniques and improve their skills. But it isn't easy. To see others so full of power and potential without any real desire for it, to see them waver like autumn leaves with every breath of wind, knowing that I have the answers, that I know right from wrong, that I could do so much good with their gifts is very difficult indeed. I've spent most of my life secluded. It's just easier that way, not to mention the Torr would rather see me dead than let my power be wasted teaching others rather than controlling them."

"How long have you lived here?" Zollin asked.

"I don't know, fifteen or twenty years. I was living in a separatist community in the Rejee desert before that. But I got so sick of the heat I moved here. The winters can be hard, but I love the snow and the cool climate the rest of the time. And now I have a student, if only for a short time. It feels good to be useful again. That is your gift to me, that and these succulent pork ribs. I shall enjoy them thoroughly."

"Good," Zollin said with a smile, "they weren't cheep."

"Ah, well, when you learn to transform lead into gold, you won't care so much about money," Kelvich said.

"You can do that?"

"If you know enough, magic is all about what you know. If you know how something works, you can fix it. If you know enough about the properties of two objects, you can transform one to other. We'll get to all that."

"Today?" Zollin asked. He couldn't help but think of what he could do with limitless gold.

"No, not today, and wipe that silly grin off your face. That kind of power takes years to hone. Just knowing you can do it doesn't make it happen. You have to have a lot of control. Now I won't lie, you've got power. Your raw potential is amazing, but you've got to apply yourself. It's like finding a gold vein in the mountains. You wouldn't take the flakes that have fallen to the ground and just leave the rest buried in the rock. You'd dig and buy equipment and work that vein until you had unearthed every last fragment. That's what you've got to do."

"Why?" asked Zollin. He didn't disagree, although the thought of that much work didn't sound appealing. But he wondered why Kelvich was passionate about him learning.

"You just do. It's your destiny."

"I don't believe in destiny," Zollin said.

"You were destined to have that power and you're destined to use it. You just don't know it yet," Kelvich said. He threw up his hands. "Wait, wait, I see your questions, and trust me, you'll get the answers, but we have to start at the beginning. Now, the most powerful magic user is a Wizard," he said with a flourish. He had finished working on the pork ribs and took a seat at the table.

"Wizards can have the powers of every other magic user, but they don't all come naturally. Some begin with a bent toward one discipline or another, but with study and practice they can become proficient in all the disciplines. Beyond that, a Wizard is himself a source of magic. And some have more power than others, but just like a muscle, it must be developed. What I see in you is a person of incredible power, but most of that power has yet to be tapped. I'm sure that's why the Torr was pursuing you – it wouldn't do to have a Wizard who can challenge their power roaming around."

Zollin was shaking his head. "I'm no challenge to anyone."

"Don't sell yourself short," Kelvich said. "But let's not worry about that right now. I want to take a look at some basic skills you need to master."

They worked all afternoon on simple spells, like discerning direction, levitation, projecting light, and binding things together. Kelvich refused to let Zollin borrow power from his willow belt or staff, and even though the spells were fairly simple, he was soon soaked with sweat and trembling with fatigue. Kelvich fed him sparingly, forcing Zollin to strain and work harder than he ever had. Even with his father, Zollin had always been able to stop and take a break when he needed it.

When the ribs were finished cooking, Zollin ate more than his share, then rode back to the Inn and had supper again. He fell into his bed exhausted, going to sleep almost instantly. He heard Mansel stirring around in the predawn light and groaned. He knew he needed to get up and rarely had trouble rising in the mornings, but he felt as if he had just closed his eyes a moment ago. He was seriously considering just rolling over and going back to sleep, but then his stomach growled. He couldn't believe how hungry he was. He rose slowly and dressed quickly, then joined his father and Mansel in the common room. When Ellie brought them a bowl of fresh milk with bread crumbled in it, he ate without tasting the sweet breakfast. He was about to head out when Ellie returned with a roll of parchment sealed with a strange wax seal. He looked up wonderingly.

"Master Kelvich," she said politely, before turning away. She was still a jolly girl, but she seemed to have lost all interest in Zollin. Mansel certainly noticed the fact and made a snide comment, but Zollin didn't hear him. His attention was on the roll of parchment. It was tiny, hardly big enough for one line of print. It said, "Come on foot."

It was a curious request, one that Zollin couldn't quite understand, but he guessed he could walk out to the Sorcerer's cabin.

"What's the note say?" Quinn asked.

"He wants me to walk instead of ride out today."

Mansel laughed, but Quinn frowned.

"Are you sure that old man is right in the head?" Quinn asked.

"I think so."

"Well, you better get going if you're walking all that way."

Zollin rose quickly from the table and grabbed his staff. He stepped out into the yard of the Inn as the sun was just peeking over the mountain tops. He set out at a brisk walk. The snow was packed hard along the streets, and he didn't have much trouble making his way, but the cold from the snow made his breath sting in his lungs. He kept up a brisk pace, but still it took over an hour to reach the cabin in the woods.

"You're late," Kelvich said.

"You told me to walk," Zollin said.

"I told you to come on foot, I never said walk."

"What... you want me to run all this way?"

"That's right," Kelvich nodded. "For you to be all that you should be, you need to strengthen your body as well as your mind.

That morning they practiced defensive spells. Kelvich tied Zollin to a post so that he couldn't move. His hands were secured behind the post as the Sorcerer threw small, bean-filled sacks at Zollin, who practiced catching the sacks in the air before he was hit. He was exhausted by mid-morning from his long walk and the constant practice.

"I need to rest," Zollin complained.

"Push yourself," Kelvich said, throwing another bag, which made it past Zollin's defenses and hit the helpless Wizard on the shoulder.

"Why? I'm too weak to stop anything. Please let me eat something. I'm about to pass out from hunger."

"Hunger is weakness. Don't let it control you."

"Everyone has to eat," Zollin cried.

"Not you – you're not like everyone else."

Another bean bag made it through his defenses and hit Zollin on the head. He was getting angry, but he felt so weak, so tired. He was trembling despite the bonds that were holding him to the post. He focused on the ropes, imagining them snapping and setting him free. He pushed the thought out, but the ropes were too strong without the aid of his staff and willow belt. He slumped, getting hit with another bean bag.

"Come on, you're not even trying," Kelvich complained.

"I'm too exhausted."

"No, you're not. You only think you can't do it."

"Do what?"

"Whatever you can imagine," Kelvich said, hurling another bag.

Zollin pushed the projectile off course and it flew wide. He was straining at his bonds again, trying to break them, but he was too weak.

"You can do this. You haven't even begun to tap into the reservoir of power inside you."

"I'm using all I've got," Zollin said.

"No, you're only using the overflow."

"I don't understand."

"And I can't explain it to you," Kelvich said. "You have to discover it. And you need to find it soon if you're going to survive."

"What do you mean?"

"You'll see," Kelvich said. Then he turned and walked into the cabin.

Zollin was relieved at first. He expected the lesson to be over, for Kelvich to come out and untie him. His mouth watered as he thought about the food they would share over lunch, perhaps the rest of the pork he had purchased from the butcher in the village. But the Sorcerer never came out of the cabin. Zollin yelled at the old man, begged him to help, but he was alone.

Snow began falling shortly after midday, and a cold wind seemed to rush down from the northern mountains. Soon Zollin was aching with cold, his hands stinging, and the wooden post felt like ice to his back. His arms and legs grew stiff from the lack of movement. The snow soaked his clothing until he was shivering uncontrollably. He tried again and again to break the bonds, but he just couldn't do it. Finally, as the afternoon waned, he fainted from exhaustion.

When he woke up, he was in the cabin, wrapped in warm blankets, his clothing drying near the fire. He was so tired that he could hardly move. He looked around the room and saw Kelvich sitting in a rocking chair, his feet near the fire, dozing. He wanted to be angry, but he was just too weak.

"Food," he managed to croak.

Kelvich stirred, "Ah, you're awake. Good, I've got some broth here for you."

Zollin wanted meat, not broth, but he was so weak that Kelvich had to help to a sitting position. The warm liquid was the most delicious broth Zollin had ever tasted. He spooned the broth down and looked up. He felt better, stronger, but not well. His arms and legs still felt heavy, his stomach was full, but he was still hungry.

"It's best not to rush things," Kelvich said.

"It's best not to leave me tied to a post in the freezing cold," Zollin said bitterly, his anger returning with his strength. "I don't know what you're trying to do, but I don't like it. Don't ever leave like that again. And another thing, I'm not practicing without my staff and my belt again."

"I understand your anger," Kelvich said, his tone as mundane as if he were discussing the weather.

"No, I don't think you do," Zollin said, standing on shaky legs. "Until you've been left helpless in a snow storm you don't know how I feel."

"You weren't helpless."

"Let me explain how this magic thing works," Zollin said, his voice getting loud. "I can only do so much without rest. Every time I use magic, it drains me. I need time to rest and recover. I trusted you, but I won't make that mistake again."

"Good, you shouldn't trust me. I would have thought that was clear from our last lesson."

Zollin was confused, but he was too angry to ask questions. He was tired of all the cryptic threats and hints about greatness. He was just a regular Wizard, as if there was anything regular about being a Wizard. He stood on shaky legs.

"I'm through," he said, even as he closed his eyes to stop the room from spinning. "Give me some dry clothes and your horse. You can pick it up from the Inn the next time you walk all the way into the village."

"You're in no condition to go anywhere," Kelvich said. "Besides, the snow is still falling and the trails will be filled by now. You can stay here until it clears."

"No, I've had enough. I'm leaving."

"Sure, if that's your decision I respect that. I've got some clothes in that cubby in the back room that you can wear. Help yourself."

Zollin made it about halfway across the room before the dizziness and his shaky legs got the better of him. He fell to the floor and lay still. Kelvich closed his eyes and waited for the Wizard to stir.

When Zollin finally felt like moving, he managed to roll over. The Sorcerer's indifference to his plight infuriated him. He wanted to scream and shout at the man, but he didn't have the strength to back up his threats. Besides, his anger obviously didn't faze Kelvich. He struggled back to his feet and managed to sit at the table. There was bread and cheese laid out, and Zollin helped himself. He ate ravenously and waited for Kelvich to object, but the Sorcerer seemed to be asleep in his chair.

The dull grey light that managed to pass through the thick clouds was fading quickly, and the snow was falling heavily. It wasn't quite blizzard conditions, but the amount of snow falling was substantial. Zollin knew that, as weak as he felt, he would never be able to make it back to the Inn that evening. When he felt strong enough, he walked slowly back to the room at the rear of the little cabin. He stayed close to the rough-hewn log walls so that he could steady himself when he felt dizzy. He found a bed in the back room and fell across it. He wrapped the blankets tightly around his fragile body and fell asleep.

Chapter 21

"He should have returned by now," Brianna argued.

"He left on foot, remember?" Mansel said. "I don't think you'd want to walk home in all this snow."

"He might have gotten caught out in the storm. We should at least go make sure he's alright."

"If we go out we'll be the ones getting caught in the snow," Quinn said. "The paths are filling back up and it'll be a while before we can make our way to the forest again."

"So we're just going to sit here and do nothing?" she asked.

"No, of course not," Quinn said. "We're going to drink ale and tell stories and stay warm by the fire."

Brianna leaned down close to the Master Carpenter, her voice strained but quiet.

"He's your son. Don't you even care about him?"

"I raised him to know better than to go wandering around in a snow storm."

Brianna wanted to scream at him, but Quinn seemed unfazed by her. She didn't want the whole town to know that she was worried about Zollin, and the Inn was still full of people who had come in to ride out the storm. She tried to act like a typical little sister, but she couldn't stop worrying when he hadn't returned the night before. She had waited in the common room all day, but he still hadn't arrived. She wanted to go to her room, but she was afraid he would return and she wouldn't know it. It made her angry to see the common room full of people without a care in the world. She wanted to pace but made herself sit at the table next to Mansel.

Quinn was worried too, but he knew he couldn't help Zollin now. His son had changed so much in the last year. He had never been fond of Wizards, not that he had ever known any, but magic was just too strange for his simple mind to grasp. He liked things he could see and feel. He had been a good soldier, and was a good Carpenter, but those were things he could see and touch. He understood how wood worked, how it was strong with the grain, weak against it. He knew how to frame a house, or build a table, but magic couldn't be seen or held in your hands. He had seen Zollin do things that boggled his mind. The constant danger they had been in and their need to reach a safe place was the only thing that had kept him sane during the last few weeks.

He thought back to the summer and fall in Tranaugh Shire. He wondered if he should have spent more time with his son. As Zollin had grown and matured, Quinn had treated him more like a hired hand than a son. The boy had so little skill with his hands that it had seemed natural to let him take on the chores around their cottage that Quinn detested. He had thought that Zollin was spending time in the woods around their village playing, as he had as a young boy. It was obvious now that something had been different, but at the time he just hadn't seen it. He wondered how he would have felt if Zollin had come right out and told Quinn that he was a Wizard. Would he have been supportive? Could he have helped somehow? Those questions nagged at his mind as he drank his ale and laughed at the exaggerated tales being told around the room.

Still, even though he hated that Zollin had changed, that he would never be a Carpenter like himself, that he would never see his son settle down and marry, have children, and enjoy a peaceful life, he had to admit that his son had skill. He doubted very much, after what he had seen Zollin do, that a snowstorm would get the best of him. He was sure that Zollin was in the woods with the old man named Kelvich. At least that's what he told himself, over and over as he smiled and laughed and tried to pretend that his son wasn't on his mind at all.

As the night wore on, the crowd at the Inn grew rowdy. Brianna wanted to leave but forced herself to stay. She noticed the thin man that entered from the kitchens. He was tall and thin, dark cloak dusted white with melting snow. He had thick gloves and tall, heavy-looking boots, but he seemed to move like a shadow and made no noise, at least none that could be heard over the drunken townsfolk. He saw Brianna watching him but ignored her and caught hold of Buck the Inn Keeper's arm as the man was moving back toward the kitchen to refill his pitcher of mulled wine. The two spoke in whispers, and Brianna saw that Buck was nodding in her direction. The man moved back against the far wall and seemed to melt into the shadows. There were lamps in the big meeting room of the Inn, but the fire was so bright in the fireplace that none had been lit. Some light spilled from the kitchens but not enough to see the man clearly. He stayed in shadows as the night wore on. At one point, Buck brought the man a pint of ale and a bowl of stew, but Brianna noticed that no one else went near the man. She wondered if anyone else even knew he was there, but at one point she saw Ollie, the Inn Keeper's wife, dart a scornful glance in the stranger's direction.

When Quinn finally decided to retire for the night, Brianna got up and helped stretch Mansel on the floor near the fire. The apprentice Carpenter just didn't know when to stop drinking. She had planned to stay in the main room of the Inn all night as the other townspeople did, just in case Zollin returned, but the stranger made her uneasy. She hadn't been able to stop herself from looking into the shadows. So she followed Quinn back to their room.

"There's a stranger at the Inn tonight," she whispered slowly.

"I saw him," said Quinn.

"You did? Didn't you think he looked..." she wasn't sure how to describe the man. "Dangerous or something? He looked dangerous to me."

"Why should we care," Quinn asked as he opened the door to their tiny room.

There were two beds and an accordion screen that could be folded against the wall or straightened to provide privacy. She didn't have a nightgown and was used to sleeping in her clothes. There was a small woodstove in the room, but it did little to keep the cold at bay. Brianna wrapped her blanket around her shoulder and sat on the tiny bed as she watched Quinn in the light of the single candle he had lit.

"It doesn't bother you that a potentially dangerous man is now in the Inn?"

"Should it?"

"Of course, what if he kills us?"

Quinn took a deep breath before explaining himself. "Yes, I saw the man, and yes, I'm a little more wary to see a stranger that sits in the shadows all night. I noticed that no one spoke to him and that only the Inn Keeper himself served the man. But I don't know that he's any more dangerous than the Tailor who sat across the room and nursed his cups without speaking to anyone."

"He's harmless."

"You think that because you know him," Quinn said. "You suspect the other man because you don't. It's good to be wary of strangers, especially now, but until the man makes his intentions known, I can do nothing."

"What if his intention is to kill you?"

Quinn smiled. He liked Brianna's straightforward approach and protective manner. She was perceptive, too. She would get by in this world just fine, Quinn thought.

"If he intends to kill me, I'll just have to stop him."

"Oh, well, never mind then," she said, falling back on her bed. "I don't know what I was worrying about. You'll just stop him."

"I meant that I can't worry about it. It won't help me and it would only make me miserable," Quinn said, then changed his tone. "Look at you, worried sick over Zollin. He's probably cuddled up to a warm fire with some nice mulled wine without a care in the world."

"Who said anything about Zollin?" Brianna snapped as she rolled over and faced the wall beside her bed.

"I did," Quinn said under his breath.

***

Zollin slept through the night and late into the morning. He woke up famished again and found his clothes laid out on a small wooden chair beside the bed. There was the smell of eggs and bacon being fried coming from the main room of the cabin. He was still shaky and weak, but he managed to get dressed without the nagging dizziness he had battled the day before.

"Ah, you're up," said Kelvich as Zollin slowly entered the room. "Here, have some breakfast."

The Sorcerer sat a plate heaped high with eggs and bacon, bread and cheese on the table. Zollin ate ravenously, tearing the bread with his teeth and biting into the cheese without slicing it first. The Sorcerer chuckled and rubbed his stomach.

"Ah, the appetite of youth is wasted on the young," he said.

Zollin ignored him and continued eating until his plate was empty. He was beginning to feel his strength returning but had no desire to practice magic again.

"I'm not doing anything else today," Zollin said in a sulky tone.

Kelvich just raised an eyebrow and stared at the young Wizard. Zollin felt a little embarrassed at his behavior, but he remembered being tied to the post and being left out in the snow. He stood up and went back to the little room, where he promptly fell asleep again.

When Zollin woke up, it was late afternoon. The snow was still falling, big, soft flakes that were covering everything in a beautiful blanket of white. He was hungry once again and wished that he were back at the Inn. He missed Brianna, but he tried desperately to keep the girl from his mind. She was still a subject of sticky feelings and desires. He knew nothing could ever happen between them, and he constantly reaffirmed his pledge to Todrek, but he still couldn't keep his mind from returning to her every few minutes. It was frustrating and exhilarating at the same time. There was a nagging thought that kept returning to his mind though: would she care about him if he were just a simple Carpenter like his father? Was she drawn to him or to his power? He told himself that it didn't matter because they were just friends, but the possibility that she cared for him simply because of the excitement, because he was different, nagged at his resolve. He tried to push her out of his mind and think about something else, but suddenly he was worried. What if more rough men, like the miners, showed up at the Inn? What if they were mistreating Brianna? Worse yet, what if she had forgotten about him? Perhaps she was content there without a thought for him at all? Or what if some other boy had caught her attention? The thoughts made him feel queasy and he tried once again to think of something else.

He walked into the main room of the little cabin and found Kelvich in his chair, dozing by the fire. He decide to cook something. He was hungry and needed something to keep his mind occupied. He found onions and potatoes in the pantry, along with the remnants of the pork tenderloin that Kelvich had apparently eaten the night before. Zollin took the kettle from the fireplace and stepped outside to fill it with snow. The snow was thick, having built up past Zollin's knees, and it was still snowing. He sighed as he wondered how long it would take before he was able to return to the village and see Brianna.

He cursed himself for letting the girl slip back into his thoughts and scooped up snow with his hands. He went back inside and hung the kettle over the fire, which was snapping and popping from moisture in the wood. While the snow melted and began to boil, Zollin cut up the potatoes. When he was finished, he dropped them in the water and let them boil while he cut up the onions into small pieces and searched for butter. He found a crock of soft butter and put a thick glob into a large pan. He removed the kettle and carefully situated the pan on a small metal frame above the fire. He fished the potatoes out of the water and dropped them into the pan, along with the diced onions. He sprinkled salt into the pan as the butter crackled and popped. He stirred the potatoes and onions, letting them cook down and get soft before he added the pork tenderloin he had chopped up.

A rich, homey aroma filled the cabin and woke Kelvich up.

"I see you're not totally helpless," the Sorcerer said.

"Not completely," Zollin replied. "Thanks for sharing the pork with me, by the way."

"I was sharing my bed," Kelvich said. "My generosity only goes so far. Tonight you can sleep in the rocking chair."

Zollin felt a stab of guilt but ignored it as he found two plates. He scooped out the food and handed a plate to Kelvich. They sat at the little table and stared at each other until Zollin felt like he would scream if he didn't say something. Kelvich seemed unfazed by the lack of conversation.

"Don't you ever talk?" Zollin asked.

"I didn't think you wanted me to," Kelvich said. "As I recall, you said you were finished with me."

"Well, I was angry," Zollin said in frustration. "You left me outside in a snowstorm tied to a post."

"It was for your own good," the Sorcerer said.

"How could that possibly be good for me?"

"If I don't push you, who will?"

"Why do I need to be pushed?"

"If you don't, you'll spoil," Kelvich said. "You have a gift, Zollin. You must learn to develop it."

"Why? Why must I learn to develop it? It's my gift and I like it just the way it is."

"But don't you see," Kelvich pleaded, "your power was meant for something more than just entertainment."

"You think that's what I want, to do tricks and entertain people? In case you forgot, I didn't come here for a winter holiday. I was pursued by Wizards and mercenaries."

"Isn't that enough for you to want to develop your skills?"

"Sure, I want to develop my skills, but I don't want to be your target dummy that you leave outside tied to a post when you get bored."

"Oh, poor Zollin, tied to a post. Don't you understand that you could have gotten loose if you had just tried?"

"I did try. I was exhausted," Zollin was almost shouting now. "I needed my staff and belt to do more."

"Those are just crutches."

"No they're not," Zollin said. He felt like Kelvich was insulting him somehow. It was odd, he thought, to take offense for his staff and belt, but he had come to rely on them so much they were like friends to him.

"I can only do so much," Zollin insisted.

"That is where you are mistaken. You have a depth of power you haven't imagined yet, but you have to find that place inside of you, the source of it all. That's what I'm pushing you to find."

"I think you're crazy," Zollin said, stuffing his mouth full of fried potatoes.

"One day you'll thank me."

"I doubt it."

"Does that mean you are resuming your studies?" Kelvich asked with his eyebrows raised.

"Only because I'm bored out of my mind," Zollin said.

Kelvich grunted and continued eating.

***

The thin man was back in the main room of the Inn when Brianna arrived the next morning. She had left Quinn snoring in his bed and gone back to the dining hall to see what the weather had done in the night. Many of the townsfolk were still asleep, rolled in their cloaks by the fire. Some were stretched out, others huddled together. Mansel was still where she had left him the night before, but the thin man was now in a chair next to the door. There was the sound of bustling work in the kitchens, but no one was eating yet. Brianna made a show of checking on Mansel and then returned to her room. Zollin had not returned, and a wave of panic ran up and down her spine. What if the man is another Wizard? she wondered. What if he's here to kill Zollin when he returns, she thought. She paced in her room, wishing Quinn would wake up so that she could tell him what she had discovered. Although it was only a theory, she was sure it was right. Would Zollin know the man was there waiting for him or would he walk in the door totally unaware and be killed before she could tell him how she felt?

She sat swiftly on the bed, shocked at the thoughts in her head. She had felt drawn to Zollin, knew she cared about him. But thinking about declaring her feelings made her heart race and her knees feel shaky. She lay back on the bed and thought about his face, sweet and honest. A pain pierced her heart and she felt tears stinging her eyes. He carried his power so lightly, never burdening anyone with the weight of it, never throwing it around to show off. Perhaps he knew the man was at the Inn, she wondered. That would explain why he hadn't returned. He could sense the man was waiting to kill him – and suddenly she felt relieved. Of course he hadn't come back – he was probably planning to rescue her even now. She closed her eyes and thought of him as she drifted back to sleep.

She dozed through the morning until she heard Quinn stirring. She got up and checked her appearance in the polished brass the Inn used for a mirror. After some minor adjustments, she felt better about herself. She was hungry and glad they would soon be getting some food. She looked at Quinn, who seemed older. He sat on the edge of his bed, his hair sticking up in odd directions. His shirt was untucked and his eyes were bloodshot. His face was lined with gray stubble, his skin pale. He wasn't looking forward to breakfast, Brianna thought. Why did men have to drink so much? It was ridiculous to drink all night when you knew perfectly well that it would leave you feeling so terrible in the morning.

"Are you going to sit there forever?" she asked him. "Or are we going to breakfast?"

He covered his face with his hands and shook his head.

"The man from last night is still here," she said.

"Of course he is," Quinn croaked, his voice ragged and scratchy. "Where else is going to go in this weather? Stop worrying about him."

"I can't..." she paused as he looked at her. "Well, what if he's a Wizard here to kill Zollin? What if –"

"Stop," Quinn said, holding up his hand and rising slowly to his feet. "If we go and get you some breakfast, will you just stop talking?"

Brianna frowned, but she knew Quinn was just sick from too much drink the night before, his head probably throbbing with her every word. She walked past him and opened the door, motioning with her arm for him to go before her. He moved slowly out the door. It was hard to match his slow, careful pace, but she remained behind him. When they reached the main room, they found most of the townsfolk stirring. They looked just as miserable as Quinn did, most holding their heads and keeping their eyes closed. Quinn sat at the first table and was consequently straight across the room from the thin man, whose chair was still propped against the wall beside the door.

Mansel was still asleep, but no one seemed to mind stepping over him. Ollie came out of the kitchen with a tray of steaming mugs. She set one before Quinn and spoke quietly.

"Best remedy for a night of too much fun," she said, smiling. "Drink it slow and it'll stay down, guaranteed." Quinn nodded but looked doubtful. "I'll send Ellie out with your breakfast in just a moment dear."

Brianna started to say thank you, but before she could speak, a man sat down opposite Quinn without an invitation. It was the man from the night before, and he laid a knife on the table in front of him.

"I hear that some men started some trouble in here a while back," said the man in a low voice that seemed too deep to come from such a thin person.

"That so," said Quinn. He was staring hard at the man, the look of sickness gone completely.

"Word is it was you that they ran into," said the man. "Seeing how you aren't beat to death or full of wounds in your back, I'd say you're ex-army, King's Guard maybe."

Quinn didn't speak. He just stared at the man.

"Personally, I didn't care for that bunch. We're all better off without them. But the boss pays me to ensure that nothing disrupts his business. And while for the most part those three were worthless, they were in charge of bringing supplies back to our camp."

"What is it you want?" Brianna said, her voice shaking. She wasn't sure if it was from fear or anger. How dare this man come to them and defend those barbaric miners!

"I just want to hear what happened," said the man.

"I expect you've heard enough," Quinn said.

"I've heard quite a bit, and I know my boss will want to meet you when he comes to town, but I've also heard about a group of people that were run out of a small village called Tranaugh Shire. I heard a lot about Wizards and mercenaries and battles. Of course, you can't believe everything you hear. But then again, we've been

180

getting our supplies from this little village for a while and no one ever made a play before."

Brianna looked at Quinn, but the Master Carpenter was still staring straight at the man across from him. Brianna looked at the knife on the table. It was the length of a man's hand, from palm to finger tips. It was forged entirely from one piece of metal, the handle merely wrapped with leather. It was exactly like Quinn's dagger, the one he had thrown and killed the miner with.

"I'm also wondering if there might be a more lucrative reward for a group that's being chased by so many," said the man. "I could report to my boss, tell him I found the man responsible. He'd be glad to hear it, but something tells me that I could do a lot better if I just took you south."

"We aren't who you think," Quinn said. "I'm just a Carpenter. We're from a village called Winsel. Don't want no trouble."

"Most people don't, but trouble has a way of coming around, don't it."

"Don't think because I don't want it that I'm not prepared for it," Quinn said.

The man smiled. "That's what I figured," said the man. "My name's Dex. Be seeing you around."

The man stood up and walked away, leaving the knife on the table.

Chapter 22

Branock rode through the falling snow and pondered his future. He knew that he could not return to the Torr without Zollin, but even if he managed to capture the boy, he had no desire to remain subservient to his Master. His battle with Zollin and the resulting wounds had changed him. He wanted to enjoy the life his power provided him before he was too old to enjoy anything except cruelty. He wanted to rule, but he could never truly do that while his Master lived. Still, he wasn't strong enough alone to challenge the Torr. His Master was much too powerful for him to overcome alone. He also needed to deal with Wytlethane. The elder Wizard did not rival Branock in strength, but he could not allow his foe to rejoin their Master, and a prolonged battle would severely weaken him in his attempt to gain Zollin's allegiance.

He closed his eyes and let the cold seep into his body. He could feel the ragged toughness of his scar tissue just below the surface of his skin. He had full movement, but the damage was still there – he had merely been able to bypass it. He knew that he needed to move quickly, but he also desperately needed an ally. Wytlethane would be in Isos City, but Branock had turned his farm horse south and headed toward Orrock. He knew there was no turning back now. If he failed in his attempt at freedom, he would be hunted down. The best he could hope for would be a quick death. If his Master captured him, he would die slowly.

Still, he knew there was no reward where there was no risk. He had always felt that he could sense opportunities. Some people saw the unexpected as setbacks, but Zollin's escape seemed to Branock to be a blessing in disguise. Wytlethane was alone and vulnerable. Their Master was certainly aware that Cassis had been defeated, but he could not foresee Branock's plan. That was the just the edge that Branock needed.

It took nearly a week of travel before he approached the city. He passed the outlying villages that sprang up around any great city. There were venders under colorful awnings stretched tight like sails from a ship. They spread their wares on blankets and quilts laid on the snow-covered ground. The snow had not been as heavy out of the mountains, and the constant traffic of men and animals had churned the pure white flakes into muddy heaps that clung to everything. The road was a sucking mud-path that coated his mount's hooves and legs.

The houses here were hovels, most made from mud and thatch, but some of scrap wood. The walls of the city loomed ahead, and the people lived here in the shadow of safety, many tending to the less savory demands a large city imposed. On the far side of the city were the riverside docks where goods were shipped downriver and loaded onto ships fit for sailing up and down the coast. But not in winter, when the seas were too stormy to risk, and so local trade thrived during this short season. There were people everywhere, some herding sheep and goats, others butchering animals. The merchants were calling loudly to any who passed by, most of whom were on foot. Branock's appearance caused people to stop and stare. His hairless, slightly scarred head, his disfigured ear and milky white eye set him apart. He saw people making gestures with their hands to ward off evil. He chuckled to himself, as if they could stop anything he desired to do.

As he approached the city, he saw the guards talking as they leaned on their heavy pikes. Had Prince Dewalt been in the city, the soldiers would have taken their duties much more seriously. The first prince was bright and cared deeply for his people, demanding the best from those entrusted with their governance and safety. He would have made a fine king, but that would never happen now. King Elwane had sent his eldest son to Osla as an ambassador. In his absence, the city had grown soft and ripe like a plum. When Branock had been to see the King with Wytlethane and Cassis, they had been greeted by the King's second son, Prince Simmeron. He was a grasping, devious young man, impulsive and overly fond of his power and position. He was also probably behind his father's illness and would likely have his brother assassinated so that he could be king.

The streets of the city were paved with cobblestones and had been swept clean of snow. There were merchants here, and Branock planned to visit one soon, but first he needed to make his presence known. The Prince would make him wait, and he did not wish to sit in a cold room with sycophants and minor dignitaries hoping for an audience. He needed a more direct approach. He rode through the winding streets and finally came to the walls of the castle which rose like cliffs in the middle of the city. The gate was guarded more carefully than the city, but this was the King's own guard.

"Hold," said the guard who stepped up into the road before Branock. "State your business in the castle."

"I'm here to see Prince Simmeron's steward," said Branock.

"His steward," said the solider. "Why are you here to see the steward?"

"Royal business," said Branock, pushing a sense of trust and acceptance toward the guard. He felt the magic flow out and saw a change in the guard's appearance. "Is it possible that you could run ahead and bring him out to me? It's urgent."

"Of course," said the soldier, spinning on his heel. He called for one of the older soldiers to take his place at the gate while he jogged inside.

Branock rode forward. He was tired and cold and hungry. He looked forward to sitting near a fire and eating warm food again, not to mention lying in a bed rather than on the cold, hard ground. Not that Branock needed much sleep, since his magic could keep him going for days without rest, but eventually he needed to sleep and regain his full strength. He would sleep soon, but first one last task kept him in the saddle.

He waited in a side courtyard while the soldier ran in and herded the steward out into the cold. It took several minutes, but finally the guard returned. He was practically dragging the steward along by his collar, the official sputtering in rage. Branock smiled as the steward caught sight of him. His sputtering protest died as a look of revulsion swept over him.

"You are the Prince's steward?"

"Yes," he said.

"Good," Branock smiled. "I will see the Prince in the morning. Meet me here after sunup and escort me to him. Is that clear?"

"Yes, lord," said the steward.

Branock did not even have to use his power – the man's fear would be motivation enough. He turned his horse and rode back out of the castle. He made his way to the finest Inn. There was a young serving boy, shivering in the cold, who took his horse as Branock dismounted. His body ached from the cold and from days spent riding. He felt pain in his wounded side that flared from time to time and now seemed to spasm with every step. The young servant stared openly at Branock's ruined eye. It didn't bother the Wizard to be gawked at, and the boy's fear would cause him to treat the horse well. Not that Branock intended to keep the small farm horse. He would sell the horse and buy a proper animal before leaving the city, but the horse had seen him this far and deserved a warm night in a proper stable with plenty of oats to fill his belly.

Branock strode into the Inn and was greeted by a short woman with a hooked nose and pinched expression. He could tell she was practiced at hiding her reactions to what she saw and heard. Business secrets were often discussed in her rooms, and she was probably good at listening quietly before entering to bring food and drink. She had obviously prospered by exploiting what she had seen and heard. Branock admired those traits, even if they were underhanded in nature.

"I need a room, a hot bath, a hot meal, and your best wine," he said.

"I'll have the water heated immediately," said the Inn Keeper. "Would you care to dine in the common room?"

"No."

"I see, right this way, my lord."

She led him down a wide hallway to the room at the end. It was large, with a fine wooden table, a couch with embroidered cushions and a padded chair with a foot rest near the fireplace. A crackling fire was already burning brightly in the room. There was a large bed at the far end of the room, with heavy curtains hanging from a frame around it.

"Is this room acceptable?" asked the woman with a false sense of modesty.

"It is, now send a servant with the wine who can do my bidding," Branock said as he dropped gold coins into the woman's outstretched palm.

She bowed, the coins disappearing into a hidden fold of her gown. Then she turned and left the room, closing the door as she went. Branock walked to the fire. He was wearing dirty, tattered clothes. The boot on his wounded side was misshapen from the fire attack and he struggled to pull it off. Once both boots were removed, he dropped into the padded chair and extended his cold feet toward the fire. A servant entered carrying a decorated glass bottle of wine and a large crystal goblet. Branock took the goblet as the servant removed the cork from the bottle and poured the dark liquid into his cup. The man sat the bottle on the table as Branock tasted the drink. It was smooth and rich, warming him as it flowed down his throat and into his stomach.

Branock turned to the servant, who was about the age of the young Wizard he was pursuing. Zollin had never been far from Branock's thoughts, but having focused on this part of his plan for the last several days, he had let the boy fall further and further from his mind. Now he was reminded of the task and consequently the dangers involved. He pushed those thoughts from his mind.

"Run and fetch me the finest tailor in town," he ordered. "Tell him he is to meet me here with all haste. This should motivate him," he held up a gold coin. "Then take this boot," he said, holding out his one good boot, "to the best cobbler in the city. Tell him I need two pairs of his finest work before sunup. There will be more of these if he can please me," said the Wizard, holding up another gold coin. "I'll need food for a week's ride, wine in skins but not watered down, fresh but hardy bread, and smoked cheese. I want salted meat and be sure it's good quality. And I'll need the best horse money can buy here in the morning. If you please me, there will be a few of these for you as well, boy."

The servant nodded, taking the gold coins and smiling. He hurried from the room, and Branock closed his eyes. He would be busy soon, eating, bathing, being measured and fit with the finest clothes. His body showed no visible scars, but the unnaturally white skin on his left side was different enough. His bald head, ruined ear, and milky eye would make him stand out among the city. There would be rumors and gossip even now among the servants and city guard. Soon it would include the merchants and nobles, and by morning even Prince Simmeron would have heard of the stranger whose frightening appearance was as intriguing as his rich purse. That was as it should be. He was tired of lurking in shadows, blending in with the crowd. People should know his power and fear him.

***

The next morning, Branock was well rested and well fed. He was wearing leather breeches over linen undergarments. He had a thick wool shirt and leather vest, with a short, fur-lined cape over his shoulders that hung down just below his waist. Tall boots came up just below his knees and he had matching gloves tucked into a belt that was lined with silver studs. As he stepped out into the weak winter sunlight, he was met by a man with a thick beard holding a short rawhide whip.

"You the man looking for a good horse?" the man said.

"I am," said Branock.

"My name's Henrick, got the best in Orrock."

"Did you bring your best?" Branock questioned.

"Brought two, just depends on what you want. You looking for speed or reliability?"

"I take it the faster horse is spirited?"

"Spirited is a good way of putting it," Henrick said. "He's a young stallion, very fast and strong, just needs a strong hand to guide him."

"I'll take him. What's your price?"

The man offered a good price and Branock paid him in gold, then sent the young servant who had run his errands the day before to buy a good blanket and saddle for the horse. He gave the young boy a small purse of coins and told him to bring the horse to the castle and to wait for him. Then Branock set off for the castle himself, walking on the cobblestone street with long strides to stretch the stiff muscles in his leg and back. The boots felt good and he was warm in his new clothing despite the temperature. There was ice in spots on the street, and water barrels had to have the layer of ice broken to get to the clean water underneath. With the rest of his body so warm, Branock noticed just how cold his head was now without any hair. He made a mental note to purchase a hat of some kind before leaving Orrock later.

At the castle gate, he was met by the same guard as the day before, who escorted him back to the small courtyard.

"You're looking better today, if I may say so, lord," said the guard.

Branock ignored him. They were met at the courtyard by the steward who looked visibly relieved that the Wizard's appearance wasn't as frightening as the day before.

"Ah, right this way, sir," said the steward. "I'll take you right up the Prince. You may have to wait a while, as the Prince is a slow riser."

"You can wake him, my business won't wait," Branock said.

"I'll not be waking his majesty, sir," said the steward with some measure of resolve. "All courtiers must wait –"

Branock cut him off before he could finish. "I'm not a courtier, and if you don't wake your master immediately, I'll see to it personally that he has you hanged from the castle walls by your feet."

"Sir, I protest your foul treatment and I'll have you know – arggghh –"

Branock slammed the man into the wall with a wave of his hand. The steward's feet were far from the floor, his face red, eyes bulging in pain.

"Do you now understand the measure of my resolve or do you still need to be convinced?" Branock said, his voice harsh in the quiet corridor.

The steward shook his head and Branock released the spell. The man fell in a heap on the floor. He moaned and rubbed his throat as he gasped for breath. Branock gave the man what he felt was a reasonable amount of time to recover, then he kicked the man.

"Now wake the Prince," he growled.

"Yes, sir, right away."

The steward hurried to a flight of stairs, and they made their way up two flights until they were at a large wooden door with horses carved into surface. There were guards standing like statues on either side of the door. The steward produced a key and opened the door. Branock followed him inside.

The room was large with lavish furniture scattered about and thick rugs overlapping each other and covering most of the floor. On one wall was a large fireplace that was full of smoking ashes. Opposite the fireplace, on the far side of the room, was a large desk, littered with parchments and slate tablets. There were candles and jars of inks. A large peacock quill lay atop the heap, and Branock was reminded of Simmeron's vanity.

There was a door on the far wall and the steward opened it slowly and shut it behind him. Branock waited in the large outer chamber. After several minutes, the steward stuck his head out from the door and spoke.

"He'll only be another minute." Then he ducked back into the bedroom without waiting for a reply from the Wizard.

When finally the door opened again, Prince Simmeron walked into the room. His hair had been combed hurriedly, his clothes were regal, but his face was swollen from sleep. His eyes were puffy and red-rimmed. His checks were red and his weak chin was spotted with stubble.

"Who are you?" the Prince demanded.

"My name," Branock said, "is not as important as you think."

"This realm pays the Torr for protection. You've come to the wrong place if you think you can bully me."

"I am not here to threaten you, lord," said Branock in a somber tone. "I wish to be of service."

The Prince's eyes narrowed. It was no mystery that every king wished to have a Wizard in his service. But the Wizards of the Torr had overcome any who resisted them, and they claimed to serve the Five Kingdoms equally. Branock's master had grown wealthy and powerful over the years and had provided a measure of equality among the kingdoms. But Branock was sick of waiting in the shadows, oppressed by his master. It was his time to rule, and all he needed to succeed was Zollin. But to get Zollin, he had to remove Wytlethane and whoever else his Master might have sent against the boy. Prince Simmeron's vanity and lust for power would provide Branock the resources he needed to bring the boy under his control.

"Service how?" the Prince asked.

"The time of the Torr is passing. Two of the Wizards who visited you a month ago are now dead."

"That's impossible."

"Is it? I suppose they told you they were here for a boy. They did not know that the boy was my apprentice for they do not know me. I was born here in Yelsia, and I've come now to break the power of the Torr and see that the Five Kingdoms are united under Yelsian rule."

"You'll forgive me a little skepticism," said the Prince. "I've never met you before. And if there were a Wizard living here in my kingdom, I would have known it. Nothing happens in my lands that passes my knowledge."

Branock bit his tongue. The fledgling Prince was already claiming sovereignty over the kingdom, despite the fact that the King still lived, as did his older brother Prince Dewalt, who was the rightful heir to the throne.

"I've been away for many years, honing my craft, my liege, but I assure you I have the power to save the kingdom. The Master of the Torr is planning to subdue you – surely you are aware of it. Why else would your father have sent your brother to Osla?"

"He was sent away because he displeased my father. King Felix intended for me to rule, not my arrogant brother. He shall be dealt with at the proper time."

"You have plans. Well, perhaps my services are not needed," Branock said, bluffing. "I shall not take up any more of your time."

"Hold," Prince Simmeron said, the tension in his voice evident. "I have many plans but I also have a nose for opportunity. You say you are a Wizard and that you have killed two Wizards of the Torr. How can I be sure of your strength?"

"I'm sure a man of your quality can devise something."

"Indeed," said the Prince. He walked over to where a velvet rope hung and pulled it.

From the corridor outside came the sound of running feet. Suddenly the door burst open and ten elite soldiers came in, weapons drawn. They were men of the King's Guard and they rushed toward Branock. He pushed against them with his magic and it was as if they had crashed headlong into an invisible wall. They all staggered back. Then Branock lifted them, cracking their heads against the wooden support beams in the ceiling and then dropping them in a heap of clattering weapons and armor. The men were dazed and slow to move. Branock had seen no reason to kill them, and so he turned to the Prince, who was smiling deviously. There was an evil gleam in his eye that reminded Branock of Cassis. The elder Wizard was forced to suppress a sudden urge to choke the life from his royal body.

"Convinced?" Branock asked.

"Party tricks," said the Prince lazily, as if single-handedly defeating ten of Yelsia's most accomplished and deadly warriors was child's play. "Show me some real power."

Branock's eyes narrowed. He had thought the Prince to be somewhat reasonable, but it was apparent that he cared nothing for his people. Not that Branock cared about the soldier's lives, but he appreciated their value. He let the magic build in him for a moment, the raw power scorching his wounded arm, side and leg. He endured the pain for a moment and then released a surge of blinding, white-hot flame that engulfed the royal guard. The heat was so intense that Prince Simmeron staggered back, but Branock's work was quickly done. He let the flame dissipate, leaving only the charred remains of the men's armor and bones in a heap on the floor. The thick rug beneath them had been burned away, but the floor was solid stone and was only blackened from the heat. Some of the furniture around the room was burning, but Branock extinguished it with a wave of his hand. His side was aching and felt raw – obviously his work to heal himself was incomplete, but he would deal with it later. He had plans to make, and now that he had pacified the Prince, he intended to see his plans move forward.

Chapter 23

The snow finally stopped, and the village of Brighton's Gate began to dig itself out again. Brianna was troubled by the thin stranger who had disappeared shortly after his confrontation with Quinn, but nothing else had happened. Mansel was sick, but Quinn's cure for too much ale was to work hard. He cleared a path through the snow with the other townsfolk while Brianna stayed busy bringing warm cider, bread, and cheese to the working men. The day passed quickly and Quinn ate a quick supper before retiring early for the night. Brianna also went to bed, but she couldn't sleep. Zollin was never far from her thoughts. She wondered what he could possibly be doing and battled the fearful thoughts that he was perhaps hurt or even dead, buried beneath the snow.

Her thoughts also never strayed far from the stranger whose threats she had dissected a hundred times in her mind. She was positive that people at least guessed the truth of where they were from. How news of the battle at Tranaugh Shire had reached into the mountains ahead of them, she could not guess, but apparently it had. If the stranger knew who they were, then surely the people of Brighton's Gate had their suspicions, and it was only a matter of time before it became an issue. She realized Quinn's rescue of the Inn Keeper's daughter Ellie had been all the confirmation most people would need. It was obvious that Quinn was no stranger to violence, and only an experienced man such as he could have escaped into the mountains from the armed mercenaries that had attacked them at Tranaugh Shire. She wasn't sure how much information about the Wizards had been spread. It was likely that most people wouldn't believe it even if they heard it.

Of course, she had heard of Wizards and knew about the Torr, but other than the occasional traveling showman, like the one from the Harvest Festival, magic was as far away from her as the moon was. She had never given it much thought, not since as a little girl when she had sat in her father's lap, listening to him tell stories before bedtime. She smiled at the memory. Her father had always been kind, doting on her and her sisters. He had no sons but didn't seem to mind. He loved to create beautiful clothing from the bolts of cloth he ordered from Isos City and Orrock. He could have been a king's tailor but was content in Tranaugh Shire, raising his girls and somehow living with her mother. She didn't miss her mother, who was always prattling on about how to do this or how to do that. She and her sisters had done all the work while her mother stood back and criticized. A pang of guilt sprang up, but she pushed it away. She didn't miss her mother and would not feel bad for thinking the truth. Her mother used her and her sisters, and she would be very unhappy when the last of them was married and moved out, when she would have to actually do something for herself.

Quinn was snoring again, and it brought her mind back to Zollin. She saw the outline of his face as she had seen it the morning they had awoken before the others, sitting under a canvas and collecting wood for the fire in the predawn light. He had seemed so close one moment, so distant the next. She knew he grieved for Todrek. They had been friends for as long as she had known either of them. It must have been terrible for him to see his friend cut down so ruthlessly. She felt another pang of guilt, but she had not known Todrek that well. He was big and strong but as clumsy around her as a newborn calf. He had staggered around their house on their wedding night, drinking strong wine while she prepared herself in the bedroom. She had taken her time, and when she had called to him, he hadn't come. She had assumed he was nervous like she was, but in fact he had fallen into a drunken stupor by the fireplace. When she'd finally come out and found him asleep in a chair, she had felt relieved. She had covered him with a blanket and gone to bed. The next day he had been slain, and she had left her life forever behind to go with Zollin and his father.

Sleep was finally overtaking her. She swam in the wonderful darkness, with vague images of Zollin drifting past her, as if she were floating down a slow-moving river. Then the darkness turned cold and she felt scared. Someone was coming, his face familiar yet unrecognizable. She couldn't see details, only vague perceptions.

There were daggers being slowly drawn from silent scabbards while the sound of marching soldiers filled her ears – then shouting and screams and fire, the lurid yellow and orange light casting shadows in the darkness.

Brianna awoke to darkness and the grinding sound of Quinn's snores. She was cold and pulled her blankets tightly around her. She was worried. She remembered her dreams of Zollin riding off from her, the dreams she had had before the events in Tranaugh Shire. This dream had the same eerie realness that frightened her so much. At least she hadn't woken up screaming.

***

Zollin's lessons began slowly. He was searching for the source of his power. It was hard to keep his mind from wandering. He could feel the magic flowing around inside his body, feel his heart beating and lungs moving back and forth as he breathed. There were other organs too, but he was less familiar with them. He tried to stay away from his stomach, which always seemed to be hungry. He tried to keep his mind from thinking about Brianna. He was looking for something, but he wasn't quite sure what it was. A reservoir of power, the source of his magic, as Kelvich had described it, like a well brimming to the top with power. As it began to run over the top and spill into him, he had discovered it – the day they were framing out the new Inn in Tranaugh Shire, the day he had lifted his tool bag. That power, according to his mentor, was much deeper than he had imagined, but since he had not found it, he could not use it. That was why he was so weak without the staff and willow belt. He could tap into their power when in direct contact with those objects, but his own was still hidden. When he used up the overflow of his own power, his magic came from his physical body, his strength, his mental and emotional energy. If pushed too far, that draining effect could cripple or even kill him. He needed to find the source of his power so that he would not be dependent on other things, but so far he had failed.

"Let's take a different approach," said Kelvich. "To perform more complicated spells, you must understand what you are doing. You can cast a spell just by thinking it, but you have to know what you are doing."

The Sorcerer held up a hunk of rotted wood. "Let me show you. I want you to transform this wood into a knife."

"How do I do that?" Zollin asked.

"Just imagine the wood becoming a knife, and push with your magic as you do so. You need to see the picture of the knife clearly in your mind or what you are left with won't be complete."

Zollin imagined a simple knife: a short, slender blade of gray steel and a handle of polished wood. Slowly he pushed the thought forward, and the magic inside him churned. He had to concentrate to keep his mind from wondering why he could feel the magic but not find its source.

The wood began to tremble, then it seemed to blur. Suddenly it was moving, like mercury, liquid and solid at the same time. Then it took shape, the exact shape of the knife Zollin had imagined. He focused his power and gave a final push, and the knife was finished. It rested on the table, just where the wood had been.

"That's unbelievable!" Zollin exclaimed.

"Yes, now pick it up," Kelvich instructed.

The knife was incredibly light, but solid and real. The steel felt cool to the touch. He ran his thumb gently down the edge of the blade. It was sharp.

"Now, shave off a sliver of wood from the table," said Kelvich.

"Are you sure?" Zollin asked.

The Sorcerer nodded, and Zollin placed the knife blade at an angle to the edge of the table and began to push. The knife began to slice a thin sliver from the table and then suddenly, the blade snapped clean off.

"What happened?"

"Let me see the knife," Kelvich said, holding out his hand.

Zollin gave it to him and the Sorcerer took the handle in both hands and snapped them in half. Then he showed Zollin the inside of the handle. It was still the rotted wood he had begun with.

"You see, you transformed the shape, but you didn't change the basic components of the wood."

"What are the basic components?" Zollin asked.

"Ah, the secret of the ages," Kelvich said smiling. He stepped outside and came back in with a handful of snow. He sat across the table from Zollin and shaped the snow into a goose. "Is this a goose?" he asked.

"No, it's snow."

"Yes, you know this because you see the snow fall. You see thousands of tiny flakes falling from the sky, but when they are lumped together you get what seems like a solid object. You see we are all made up of tiny little particles, smaller than dust. These tiny things are so small you can't see them, but you can feel them with your power. It takes intense concentration, but as you move farther and farther into an object, you can feel each part, how it fits with the others to make the whole. Move deeper and you come to find what each part is made of. So, to transform a piece of wood into a piece of steel, you would need to go deep into the object and transform the smallest parts, those basic components. Take a look at this."

He pulled what looked like a rock from a wooden box near the fireplace. The rock was red- colored and tiny, dust-like flakes seeming to fall from it where Kelvich handled it.

"Do you know what this is?" he asked.

"It's iron ore, right?"

"That's correct. Now, you can transform an object just like a blacksmith. He takes this raw iron, heats it in his forge, and creates steel. Then he fashions and shapes it with hammers and tongs and molds until it is exactly what he wants, a sword, a hammer, a pot or kettle. We do the same thing, only we don't need the forge, and we don't have to use excessive heat or force to transform an object. We use magic."

"That makes sense. Could I turn that iron ore into a knife?"

"You could, but it would be brittle and weak just like the ore is. You would need to transform the ore into steel to get what you really wanted."

"But how do I do that?" Zollin asked.

"Time, concentration, practice, those are the traits of a true Wizard. It is simpler to use your strength to take what you want. But that makes you no more than a bully or a tyrant. You must learn to tap the strength deep within yourself and take the time to see things the way they truly are. So here is your lesson for day." He handed Zollin a thick book titled "Anatomy" and smiled.

"This book shows you how your body is made, the bones, the muscles, the organs and so on. I want you to study the book and then search yourself to find what you have learned. Look deeply until you can feel the blood moving through your body. Practice when you eat, feeling the food as it enters the stomach, what happens to it, how it moves through your body. As you go back to town today, practice feeling each flake of snow. See if you can fine a quicker way to move through the snowbound land than simply digging a trail."

"It'll be dark soon, shouldn't I wait until tomorrow?" Zollin asked.

"No, you need to work through these lessons before we can move on. Some things you learn through study and others through experience. Each has its own virtue. Take your time – winters are long here in the Great Valley."

"Great," Zollin said standing. He started to pick up his staff and willow belt.

"You won't need those," Kelvich said. He reached out and took them from Zollin.

He frowned at the Sorcerer as he wrapped his cloak around him and opened the door. The snow was thick and the light was fading. It would take all night to dig his way back to Brighton's Gate in this, he thought. Not that he would have the strength to do it. He had no tools, and although he could plow a furrow through the snow with his magic, without the belt and staff he wouldn't be able to sustain himself very long.

See if you can find a quicker way to move through the snowbound land... What did the old man mean by that? He heard the door shut and lock behind him. Alright, thousands of flakes floating gently down, he thought as he took a step into the snow. His foot buried down almost to the top of his boot. This was not going to be easy. He started to take another step but then he thought about the flakes, hundreds of individual flakes just lying gently down on top of one another. He pushed gently with his magic, and the snow packed down in front of him. He took a tentative step, expecting the snow to buckle under his weight. But the snow held firm and he stood on top of it, several feet above the ground. Before him lay a pristine path out of the trees and through to the open fields that ran down toward Brighton's Gate.

He moved quickly along, even after nightfall. He could see the lights of the village like a beacon at sea, and he no longer worried about tripping or falling into a ditch. Packing the snow before him was easy enough, although when he reached the edge of the village, he was exhausted, starving, and so cold he felt the moisture of his breath freezing into tiny icicles in his nose. He made his way quickly through the paths made by the townsfolk that day and entered the Inn. There was little activity in the common room. Most people had turned in for the night already, but there was a warm hash made of the leftovers from the night before. Zollin ate three bowls full and nearly a whole loaf of bread. He was sipping some sweet cider and thinking of going to bed himself when he remembered his studies. He sat the book on the table before him – he was near the fire which gave plenty of light for reading. He could have been in his room with a candle, but the common room was warmer.

Before long, engrossed in his study, he found himself alone in the room when a tall, thin man walked quietly into the room. The man came and warmed himself by the fire. After a few moments, he spoke quietly.

"Looks like everyone's made an early night of it."

"Yes, I believe so," Zollin said, trying to be polite.

"You're one of the newcomers, studying law or something with that old hermit?"

"That's right," Zollin said.

The man nodded his head and looked around the darkened room again.

"You mind if I have a seat?" the stranger asked.

"Not at all, but I'm not much company, I'm afraid."

"That's no trouble. I've seen your father around. He's a handy man, alright. Moves more like a fighter than a Carpenter, though. I guess he's seen service in the King's forces?"

"Yeah, he was in the army before he met my mother," Zollin said.

"King's Guard?"

"I don't know. He doesn't talk about it much."

"Aye, well, I don't mean to pry, just have an inquisitive nature, I do. I've always wanted to know things, how they work, what makes them tick, that sort of thing."

Zollin nodded but didn't really know what to say.

"For instance," the man continued. "I'd wonder how a Carpenter, even one army trained, could take out three grown men the way your father did. That must have really been something to see."

Zollin, still looking at his book, was suddenly very still.

"I mean, two men, maybe, but three? That takes some rare skill, I'd say."

"I took out one of them," Zollin said as he looked up at the man. "He was bothering the Inn Keeper's daughter and he deserved it."

"Is that right? I guess I heard that too. Hit him with a stick didn't you? I wonder what would make a lad like you do something like that?"

"It's hard to just sit back and see people mistreating others," Zollin said. He was scared but his voice didn't shake. He looked directly at the man, who was staring right back. The stranger had a strange glint in his eyes that gave Zollin a chill that was unrelated to the cold night air.

"I know those three," said the man. "They are an unsavory bunch, but my boss isn't too happy that the town would hold up his supplies. He's looking to make a statement before he comes down to make things right. I reckon you'd make a good messenger."

"I won't help you," Zollin said, wishing he had his staff more than ever. He could feel his power rolling within him. He just wasn't sure he had the strength to really hurt the man.

"Ah, well, no need to actually do anything," said the man

with a smile. Then he whipped his hand toward Zollin and the young Wizard felt as if he'd been hit in the stomach. He doubled over and dropped from his seat onto his knees, but then he swung his arm as if he were swatting a fly and the stranger flew into the stone chimney, cracking his head and falling unconscious by the fire.

Zollin looked down and saw the handle of a knife sticking out of his stomach. He fell backward in shock and surprise. Then the pain erupted in his body like a torrential rain storm. His hand was shaking as he took hold of the handle. He knew he needed to act fast or he was going to die. The room was beginning to spin. He closed his mind and allowed his magic to flow around the knife blade inside him. He could tell that his stomach had been pierced, could feel the severed abdomen muscles and the blood seeping into the space between his organs.

He needed to remove the knife, to bind his body back together, but he couldn't just heal the surface as he had done with Todrek. He needed to heal each wounded area, bit by bit. Only he wasn't sure he was strong enough to stay conscious that long. He pulled slightly on the knife, and his agony intensified. The blade was still an inch or so into his stomach, which was still stuffed with his supper. Luckily the digestive fluids hadn't leaked out, nor had too much blood gotten into his stomach. The blade was acting much like a cork in a bottle, but he knew he needed to get the knife out and heal his body. If he could pull the knife out bit by bit and mend each part as he did it, perhaps he could make it. But he had to pull the knife out several inches just to get the blade clear of his stomach. He pulled a bit more, but the pain was over whelming. His hands were shaking and he knew he needed help, but there was no one around. His mind began to drift and he savagely focused on the task at hand. He had to do something. He reached for the knife again, but his hands were shaking too much and felt so weak.

"Ooohhhh!" said the stranger who had attacked Zollin. The man staggered to his feet and Zollin pretended to be unconscious. He heard the unsteady footsteps of the man as he approached. It took all of Zollin's strength and concentration not to breathe. He didn't want the man to stab him again, but he was hopeful that the man would pull the knife out and allow Zollin the chance to heal himself.

"Guess it was handy I finished you quick," the man said. "You might have caused some problems and that's a fact."

Zollin braced himself for the pain of having the knife ripped free, but the man moved away, leaving the young Wizard alone on the floor of the common room. He heard the kitchen door swing on its hinges as the stranger left. It was now or never, Zollin thought to himself. He rolled onto his side and vomited on the floor. Then he reached up and grabbed the table, pulling himself to his knees. His instinct was to bend over double, but leaning forward at all sent waves of excruciating pain through his whole body. He stayed rigidly straight even as he felt the muscles in his back threatening to cramp. He managed to get to his feet, but his legs felt incredibly heavy. He felt like he was carrying heavy timber for his father as he staggered along the wall. If he could just get far enough down the hallway, his father would help him. He wanted nothing more than to lie down and close his eyes. Even lying down on the rough and dirty hallway floor would be heaven. The pain was so intense and every step was a monumental task. The hallway seemed to stretch on forever, and he was bleeding freely now – he could feel the blood running down his waist and legs.

Finally, he reached his father's room. He pushed on the simple lever handle, but the door was locked. No, he thought, it can't be locked. Then a truly terrifying thought crossed his mind. He had been absent from the Inn for three days. Perhaps his father and Brianna and Mansel had left. Perhaps they had gone out looking for him and were away. He could die here, alone, in the hall of the Inn. He rattled the lever, but it held fast. His knees buckled and he dropped to the floor. His back cramped and he fell back, the agony in his stomach too much to bear. The world went black.

Chapter 24

Brianna woke with a start. The door lever was shaking. Someone was trying to get into the room! She started to cry out in fear but bit her tongue. She rose and moved quietly over to Quinn to wake him.

"I hear it," he whispered. He rolled out of bed and approached the door with something in his hand. It was dark and Brianna couldn't make out what it was. "Get ready to light that lamp, but keep it covered. I don't want them to know we're awake."

Brianna's hands were shaking, but she managed to get a red-hot fuse from the stove, its tip glowing red. She covered the lamp as she lit it, then nodded to Quinn. There was a thump outside the door and then all was quiet.

Quinn removed the locking bar and slowly opened the door. He waited for a moment, but the hallway was dark. There was a form lying on the floor. Quinn knew there was nothing else to do but reveal the lamp. If there were assassins in the shadows, uncovering the lamp would only make him vulnerable, but he couldn't sit locked in his room either.

"Uncover the lamp," he said.

Brianna pulled up the shade and the pale light seemed bright in the darkness.

"Oh my God!" Quinn said loudly. He dropped what was in his hand and jumped into the hallway. "Get that light over here," he shouted.

Brianna hurried forward and almost dropped the lamp when she saw Zollin. His face was pale and wet with sweat. There were dark stains on his stomach and down his pants, not to mention the handle of the knife that was protruding from his stomach.

"What do we do?" she asked, her voice shrill with fear.

"I'm not sure," Quinn said.

"Dad?" Zollin said. His voice was weak, and Quinn bent over him. "Pull out the knife, I can fix it."

"What? Are you insane?" Quinn responded.

"I can heal myself, so pull it out slow. Don't let me black out again."

"Alright, hold on," Quinn said after Zollin had insisted.

"What?" Brianna asked. "What did he say?"

"He says he wants to heal the wound, but he needs me to pull the knife out. Come on, let's get him in the room first."

When Quinn pulled Zollin across the rough Inn floor into the room, Zollin thought he would pass out again. But the pain had sharpened his senses, and as his father knelt over him again, he was able to concentrate on the tip of the blade.

"Go ahead," Zollin whispered.

The blade started to move and Zollin clenched his jaw and dug his fingernails into the wooden floor to keep from screaming. Finally, the knife blade eased out of his stomach. Immediately he pulled at the edges of the punctured stomach and focused on healing.

"Wait a second," he muttered as he imagined the flesh mending together again.

Immediately the pain lessened. It was still agonizing, but he could tell it was working. Once he felt sure his stomach was whole again, he nodded at his father. Quinn pulled the knife as slowly as possible, and Zollin used his power to heal anything that felt out of place. Finally, the blade passed through the muscles of his stomach. Zollin felt the fibers of the muscle and imagined each piece pulling toward the others and finding its mate. He healed the wound, and when the blade pulled free, he laid his shaking hands on the torn skin and healed it as well. Then he looked inward, searching for anything he had missed. The pain was only a memory now, but still too fresh in his mind. There was blood in his guts, but the organs were working and everything felt whole. He would need to consult the anatomy book or speak to Kelvich about the blood, but he felt that everything would be alright.

He opened his eyes. Quinn was bent down over him, his eyes full of worry and doubt. Standing over him was Brianna, her blond hair falling in beautiful spirals all around her face. There were tears on her cheeks and nose.

"I did it," he said. "I'm okay."

"Are you sure?" his father asked, the worry still clearly evident in his voice. "Gut wounds are almost always fatal."

Zollin lifted his hands and wiped away the blood from his stomach.

"Look," he said. "It's finished."

There wasn't even a scar where the knife had cut him.

"That's unbelievable," his father murmured.

"Oh, Zollin," Brianna said, a sob catching in her throat. "Are you sure you're okay?"

She dropped to her knees beside Quinn and took one of Zollin's hands. Then, without waiting for him to answer, she bent down and laid her forehead against his neck. She shook as she cried, but she was quiet, and Zollin patted her head with his free hand until she calmed down. When at last she sat up, it was Quinn who spoke.

"Damn," he said. He was holding the knife that he had pulled free of Zollin.

Brianna looked up and saw that it was exactly like the knife the strange man had laid on the table before then them that morning. She cringed at the thought of that man with his cruel eyes hurting Zollin, and then the realization that she was right popped into her mind.

"I told you-"

Quinn raised his hand. "I don't want to hear it," he said. "Zollin, did this man say anything to you?"

Zollin was still on the floor.

"He was a stranger. Tall and thin." Quinn nodded his head so Zollin continued. "He said his boss was angry, and then after he threw the knife at me I slammed his head into the fireplace."

"You killed him?" Quinn asked.

"No, I didn't have my staff and I wasn't strong enough. He was only out for a few minutes. Then he said it was good he had taken care of me, that I could cause some problems. Then he left the Inn through the kitchens."

Quinn swore for a minute, and then he picked up what he had dropped – it was a knife just like the one the man had thrown at

Zollin. He tucked it into his pants and told them to wait for him before slipping out the door.

"Help me up," Zollin told Brianna.

He was afraid the pain would return when he moved, but it didn't. He stood up and walked a bit, then sat on his father's bed. He was tired, but the relief from the pain was so great that a sense of euphoria swept through him. He smiled.

"Quite an evening, huh?" he joked.

Brianna looked at him aghast and slowly she smiled. Then a giggle, and then they both laughed. Zollin, his clothes ruined, looked sickly and weak. Brianna's face was puffy and red from crying and lack of sleep. They stared at each other and laughed.

Quinn silently crept through the common room and into the kitchen. He checked every room, closet and pantry, but the assassin was gone. He checked the back door and found it unlocked. There was a fresh trail in the thigh-deep snow, but Quinn knew it was the wrong time to track down the assailant. The man was returning to the mining camp, and then the miners would return to the town. It wouldn't be pretty, but at least he knew what to expect. His first priority was to keep his family safe. To this point, he had done a poor job of it, but he would remedy that soon enough. First he had to erase the evidence that Zollin had been attacked. It wouldn't help him convince the town that standing against the miners was a good idea if they were terrified of Zollin. He returned to his room.

"Well, he's gone," Quinn said as he closed the door. "We need to get you and this place cleaned up."

"I'm afraid I won't be much help," Zollin said. "It's all I can do to keep my eyes open right now."

"I understand. Let's get you to your room."

Quinn pulled Zollin to his feet and walked him out of the room. He opened the door to the room he shared with Mansel and they were hit with the stench of stale vomit.

Quinn swore again and Zollin smiled. He didn't care about the smell, he just felt so happy to be alive.

"It's okay, I'll be fine, Dad."

"Well, get out of those clothes. I'll need to burn them. If the

206

Inn Keeper tries to clean them we'll never hear the end of it. Besides, we don't want the whole town to know what happened."

Zollin pulled off his clothes and handed them all to Quinn, even his boots. Then he walked over to his bed. The room was cold, and Mansel had helped himself to one of Zollin's blankets, but from the smell of things, he needed it. Zollin wrapped up in what was left of the bedclothes and fell asleep.

Quinn took the boots back to his room, and then he and Brianna went to the common room. There was blood on the fireplace and tracking up the hallway. Quinn threw the ruined clothes onto the embers of the fire and watched for a second as they flamed up. Then he got some water and two brushes from one of the closets in the maze of rooms beyond the kitchen. They spent the next two hours scrubbing the floor. The Inn floor wasn't spotless to begin with, so they hoped the blood stains would blend with the marks on the rough wooden planks. When they finally got back to their rooms, Brianna fell into bed, exhausted. Quinn sat up for a while and cleaned Zollin's boots. Then with only a couple of hours left until dawn, he couldn't resist the urge to check in on his son one more time. He took the lamp to the room Zollin shared with Mansel. He held his nose as he pushed open the door. Zollin was sound asleep, his breathing steady and deep. In fact, he looked healthier than Mansel, who was still pale amid the ragged bed he had obviously been confined to since drinking himself into a stupor two nights past.

At last he lay back down on his own bed. His body ached, his back sore from shoveling snow, his joints aching from the cold night air, his mind numb from lack of sleep. But when he closed his eyes, he saw the thin stranger. The knife he laid down on the table was evidence enough. The man had been King's Guard, the same as Quinn. He might have hoped the miners were led by an overconfident man inexperienced at organizing an assault, but the stranger wasn't. The tall, thin, assassin would tell the miners just how to come against the town. Their only hope was Zollin. And the stranger thought he had dealt with Quinn's son. How wrong you are, Quinn thought. And as he fell asleep, he thought that just might be enough to save them.

***

The next morning, Quinn gathered everyone together in the common room of the Gateway Inn to talk about what had happened.

"We can't pretend anymore," said Quinn. "That man who attacked Zollin was sending me a message. The miners are coming, sooner or later. And when they get here, if the town doesn't give us up, they'll destroy the town."

"I can't believe I missed everything," Mansel said. He was still pale, but at least he was out of his bed.

"So we should leave," Brianna said.

"We can't leave," Zollin argued. "I've got too much to learn, and I've only just started."

"But we can't risk the town," Brianna said.

"We can fight," said Mansel.

"Not all by ourselves," said Brianna. "We don't even know how many miners there are."

"There'll be quite a few," Quinn said. "You don't send three men for supplies if it's a small operation. Plus, there's the possibility that the town could turn on us."

"What'll happen if we just leave?" Zollin asked. "To the town, I mean."

"Can't say for sure," Quinn said. "The miners could ignore the town and come after us, or they could destroy the town. It's hard to say."

"I don't feel right about leaving these people to fend for themselves," Zollin said. "They were terrified of the three we already dealt with. If the miners come in a large group, there could be a lot of people hurt or killed."

"At what point do we stop worrying about everyone else and start looking after our own interests?" Brianna asked. "I mean, we've got Wizards chasing us, and now miners. Even if they don't come until spring, what are we going to do then?"

"That's another good question," Quinn said.

"Is it possible to stay here?" Zollin asked. "Isn't this place as good as any to make a stand?"

"That depends on who's coming," said Mansel.

"What do we hope to gain by moving on?" Brianna said. "Is there a place beyond the reach of these people where we might live some kind of normal lives? Or is fighting our only option?"

They all looked at Quinn. He sighed and shook his head.

"I don't think there is anywhere in the Five Kingdoms where we won't be hunted down eventually."

"That means we either fight or try to cross the Wilderlands," said Zollin.

"If we fight," asked Brianna, "what do we hope to gain? Won't whoever is chasing us eventually regroup and come for us again?"

"Probably," said Quinn. "But I don't like the idea of running."

"I certainly don't want to cross the Wilderlands," said Mansel.

"All the magic in the Five Kingdoms is based at the Torr," said Zollin. "What if I go there? The rest of you would be safe then."

"That's a bad idea," said Brianna.

"I don't have much experience with Wizards, son, but I have a bad feeling about you going there."

"So, we're right back to where we started," said Zollin.

"True," said Quinn, "we don't have a lot of options. But my father once told me, wherever you go, whatever you're doing, try to leave the places you travel and the people you meet better than you found them. Brighton's Gate is a good town, but they're vulnerable, either to miners like now or to Skellmarian raiders. The army has pulled back, leaving them exposed. We could help these people learn to defend themselves and at least leave them more prepared than when we found them."

They all thought about this for a while, and one by one they nodded.

"I guess we brought this trouble on them," Zollin said. "The least we can do is help them now."

"I agree," said Quinn. "So, learn as much as you can. You're our secret weapon. That assassin thinks he killed you, so they won't be expecting you. That's the only advantage we've got."

"We've got you," Mansel said to Quinn. "You were King's Army. You know strategy and how to fight."

"But so do they," said Quinn. "The assassin was Royal Guard. That's what he was saying when he put that knife on the table. Only the Guard are trained with that weapon."

"So he'll know what you know?" Brianna asked.

The realization hit Zollin for the first time. His father hadn't just been in the Army, he had been in the King's Royal Guard. He felt a little betrayed that he had never known before. He saw the realization dawning on Mansel's rugged features. There was a gleam of pride in the bigger boy's eyes.

"It's really a matter of experience," Quinn said. "I only served a few years. When I met Zollin's mother, I left all that behind."

"Do you think the miners will be trained men, like this assassin?" Zollin asked.

"It's possible, but I doubt it. Mining is difficult work, not the kind of the thing people with other options normally do. But you can bet they'll be violent men, the kind that won't hesitate to slice your throat."

"Okay, so what do we do?" Brianna asked.

"The first thing is to convince the town that they have a problem that won't be solved by handing us over to the miners. Then, we'll need to start planning for some sort of defense."

"How do we convince the town?" Zollin asked.

"Well, we'll have to tell them the truth. You feel like putting on a little show?"

***

That afternoon, Brianna went around the village inviting everyone to the Inn for a special night of entertainment. Zollin wasn't convinced that this was the best idea, but they didn't have much choice. If the people ran them out of town, they'd be no worse off. Zollin's main concern was to ensure that Kelvich was not mentioned or his secret revealed. Zollin thought the best way to ensure that was to invite the old Sorcerer to the show. He could act surprised, just like everyone else, and defend himself if accusations came his way. Besides, Zollin would need his willow belt and staff to do some really amazing magic that would convince the town that they had an upper hand against the miners.

He saddled a horse and rode through the thick snow. The horse tired quickly, but Zollin helped as much as he could. He found Kelvich wrapped in a thick blanket reading a book on his porch.

"Shouldn't you be studying?" Kelvich asked.

"Yes, but unfortunately I was stabbed last night."

"Hilarious, what are you doing here now? I don't suppose you've memorized a whole book on anatomy already?"

"No, but I really was attacked last night."

Zollin spend the next half hour explaining how Quinn had fought the miners and how the tall man had accused Quinn and then stabbed Zollin with the throwing knife. He described how he had managed to heal the wounds as his father drew out the knife.

"That is fascinating," said Kelvich. "Unbelievable, really, to think that you could have such control in the midst of that kind of shock and pain."

"Well, that leaves us in a bit of an awkward situation. We know the miners are coming, probably with enough men to take the town. So..."

"You're leaving?" Kelvich asked. "But it's too soon. You're not ready. I need more time."

"That was an option, but we decided it would be better for everyone if we stayed."

"But if you stay, you'll have to fight. The townspeople won't like that. They've grown soft with the King's Army patrolling the northern mountains."

"Now you see why I'm here. I have to reveal myself tonight to the town. Father thinks it may be the only thing that convinces them to stand against the miners."

"Could be... of course, that would cast a lot of suspicion on the old hermit Kelvich," the Sorcerer said.

"That was my thought too," Zollin replied.

"Well, I'll just have to show up tonight, act surprised, perhaps even offended that my new student is actually a Wizard, ha!"

Kelvich laughed at the thought of it. "It might even be fun."

"Good, I was hoping you'd be okay with our plan."

"If it were me, I'd find an excuse to move on, although you'd have to be insane to leave the Gate while the snows are still thick. Still, I'm not sure I'd risk my neck for these people. You know they blamed your father, and by association you, when the assassin came to see what had become of his associates. Now, they may run you out of town and take their chances with the miners."

Zollin nodded. He was aware that their future hung on the tenuous thread of the townsfolk's good will.

"If they do, circle wide, then make your way back here," Kelvich said. "I'd rather be cramped for a season than lose a good student."

Zollin smiled. "You won't lose me. Just be at the Inn at sundown."

"Oh, I wouldn't miss it. I love dinner and a show. I just hope I have something to wear."

Chapter 25

The Inn was full. No one knew what to expect, but the dull winter months often passed with nothing to break up the monotony of day after gray day. The prospect of unexpected entertainment had brought the townspeople out in droves. It was standing room only when Zollin finally took his place near the roaring fireplace. The lamps around the room were all lit and burning brightly. Zollin looked to where his father and Mansel stood on either side of Brianna. There was always the possibility that the town would turn against the little group, perhaps even getting violent. Quinn was prepared for any outcome. Their belongings were packed, along with rations for several days. Mansel had seen to the horses – they were saddled and waiting in the barn. If things turned ugly, they would flee. Zollin had no desire to see anyone hurt on his account, but he didn't relish the winter cooped up in Kelvich's little cabin.

He raised his hands and the room grew quiet. Then he spent the next half hour making small objects fly around the room. His staff was behind him, but his willow belt was under his shirt, next to his skin. He could feel the power of the supple tree branches mingling with his own. Kelvich stood in the back of the room next to the Inn Keeper. He was pretending to be amazed, but his talkative manner and overreaction to Zollin's tricks was so out of character for the old hermit that Zollin doubted if he would be believed.

The townsfolk were shocked at first and then delighted. They all assumed Zollin was performing tricks, not unlike the illusionist that Zollin had seen at the Harvest Festival in Tranaugh Shire. Zollin ended his short performance by making all the ale cups hop and dance along the tables. They ended up in a tall stack in front of the Inn Keeper.

"What?" he cried. "You can't make them clean themselves? What good are you?"

The townspeople laughed and clapped. Many who were seated at the long tables stood. Zollin moved back from the firelight as Quinn stepped forward. He cleared his throat and the room grew quiet.

"We're new to Brighton's Gate," Quinn said. "And while I've always regarded this town and its people highly, I need to bring some things to your attention." There was murmuring among the crowd but Quinn pressed on. "I was here over twenty years ago, not as a carpenter, but as a King's soldier, guarding your village from the threat of Skellmarian invasion. I remember Brighton's Gate from that time being a lovely place, full of happy, forward-thinking people. But I also remember the constant readiness of the town for attack. We've only been here a short while, but it is obvious that you are not ready for the threats against your city. The King's Army has withdrawn, and yet you have no plan of defense, nor any defensive works to keep enemies out of your town.

"And when you allow miners to run roughshod over you, it is obvious that you've lost all fight. I know that it was convenient for you to blame us for what happened. We chose not to sit by and allow brigands to do whatever they pleased. We are not angry, but we are concerned. The miners will come now. They've sent their spy to see what condition the town is in. What will they find when they return? Will you stand against them, or cower in your homes as they rob and plunder, murder and rape?"

"Who are you to speak this way to us," shouted one man. "No one asked you to kill that miner or accost his companions. If the miners come, it's you they'll be wanting, not us."

"Do you really believe they'll just go away once they kill us?" Quinn asked. "Don't be naïve. They won't leave their mines and livelihood without taking whatever they want from you." Quinn pointed his finger at the man. "Will you try and stop them?"

"How can we?" said another man. "We're not warriors. We have no one to fight them."

"You can fight," said Quinn.

"Better to be alive and penniless than dead with fat purses," said the first man.

"You have the advantage," Quinn said. "We can secure the town. Let the miners see that you're not going to roll over and give

214

up everything you've worked so hard for. That'll make them think twice before rushing in to attack."

"Perhaps," said Buck, the Inn Keeper. "But what if we just give them you?"

There was an outburst of loud talking at the Inn Keeper's comment. Zollin was pleased to see that many people were shocked at the thought of turning them over to the miners. Quinn raised his hands again and waited for the room to calm back down.

"That is an option, although I have to say we would not go quietly. Or we could leave the Gate, but that would leave you exposed. I doubt this miner, Trollic, would be pleased to find that his quarry has flown the nest. We would not leave you without help."

"How much help could one small family make?" asked Kelvich. There was murmured approval at the question.

"Yes, well, let me see if we can show you. Please try to remain calm."

Without moving, Zollin began to work. He had allowed his senses to reach out through the room as Quinn had begun talking. He could feel every person, distinguish the men from the women, sense the heat from their bodies and almost hear the beating of their hearts. Slowly he lifted them into the air. Now he could hear their panic, sense the terror in their helplessness. The room seemed to shake from the screams and shouts. Some people were outraged, others terrified. As Zollin slowly lowered the people down to the ground, he was afraid they might mob him.

"Who's doing that?" Kelvich shouted.

"The boy, he's a Sorcerer!" shouted another man.

"Kill them," shouted a woman holding a small baby to her chest. "Burn them or they'll curse us all."

"Please," Quinn shouted over the noise. "Please listen to us."

Slowly the room quieted, but not before several townspeople had left the Inn.

"Zollin is not a Sorcerer, he's a Wizard," Brianna said. She had come to stand next to Quinn and now she had the entire room's attention. "I know it doesn't seem like much of a difference but there is. He is good and he would never hurt you. But he can help us. He

215

can help you defend your village."

"I can't believe this," Kelvich shouted. "You betrayed me, boy." There was such conviction in his outrage that Zollin was startled. "All this time tutoring you in law, and you're a Wizard."

"A Wizard is still a person," Zollin said. "I'm sorry, Master Kelvich, but I did not harm you, nor did I take advantage of you."

"That's beside the point," Kelvich snarled. "How do you expect us to trust you if you aren't honest with us?"

"We are being honest now," Quinn said. "We didn't tell you everything up front because we didn't expect you to ever need to know. But now you do. Now you need us and we'll help. We'll also answer any questions you have."

"Where are you from?" asked one man.

"Tranaugh Shire," Quinn said.

There was whispering around the room before Kelvich asked, "Didn't we hear something about trouble in Tranaugh Shire?"

"Yes," Quinn replied. "A band of Wizards from the Torr arrived in our village with hired soldiers. They wanted to take Zollin away, and we fled."

"How do we know the Torr won't follow you here?" said another man.

"They will, but not until spring," Quinn explained. "The winter snows hold them back, just like the rest of the world. When the snows start to melt, we can move on if you like."

"You could move on now," said a burly looking man in a dirty coat.

"Yes, we could, but that won't help you. Can't you see we're trying to help?"

"Well, what do you propose?" the Inn Keeper asked.

"I propose that we plan for your defense and train you to handle whatever or whoever might threaten you," Quinn said.

"When are we supposed to do that?" said another man. "We work, you know."

"Yes, and so do we. But we have time to learn some basic skills and ensure that everyone knows what to do in case the town is attacked."

"And you'll help us?" Kelvich asked.

"Yes, of course. We'll do all we can."

"And the Wizard?" said one man. "What's he going to do?"

"He's actually our greatest advantage," Quinn said.

"Don't you think the miners will have guessed that you all are the people from Tranaugh Shire?" said the man in the dirty coat. "I talked to that man they sent. He asked if we had seen anything out of the ordinary. He suspects your boy is a Sorcerer, and I'll bet they're ready for him."

"Actually," said Brianna, staring at the man with a cold look. "He thinks that Zollin is dead. The man attacked him and left him for dead, right here on this floor." She pointed down at the rough wooden planks. "If you don't think these men are serious, then think again. They'll kill you without a thought. They have no qualms about spilling your blood and taking everything you own, including your wives and daughters."

"You've brought this on us," said a woman in the back.

"No," Quinn said quietly. "Your lack of preparation and failure to stand against the miners brought this on you. We may have been the spark that started the fire, but it was coming. The only difference is that now we're here to help you. Please take some time to consider what we've said. Tomorrow you can let us know what you would like us to."

The group went back to Quinn and Brianna's room. They tried to remain positive, but they couldn't help but listen to see if a mob had formed to storm their room. An hour passed, and they all began to relax. Eventually, there was a short knock on their door. Quinn answered it. The Inn Keeper looked relieved. Quinn had talked to him earlier in the day and the man had agreed to start the questioning. He had been afraid the room would break out into a colossal brawl, but the townsfolk had taken the news much better than expected. In fact, people had been wondering what to do for some time about the miners. Quinn and Zollin had given them something to focus their attention on, and for the most part it was positive.

"Most people are on board with your plan," said Buck.

"There are a few that would rather run you out of town or just turn you over to Trollic if he comes, but not many. Your teacher was very convincing," Buck said to Zollin. "I can see why you'd want him schooling you."

"You think most of the town's on board then?" Quinn asked.

"I can't speak for those who left, but there aren't many of them either. The rest of us are convinced. We'll stand with you if the miners come. We should have done it all long ago."

"No need to worry about that now," Quinn said. "We can clear the common room of the Gateway Inn to teach some basic combat skills. Is there a place where we might train archers?"

"We could mark out a range behind the Inn here," said Buck. "It'll take several men most of the day to do that, though."

"I'll handle that," Zollin said. "If that's okay?"

Buck nodded and Quinn smiled.

"Good, we'll get started tomorrow," Quinn said. "Let's meet with the village leaders tomorrow evening. Can you arrange that?"

Buck nodded and then said good night.

Zollin and Mansel went back to their own room.

"You were pretty impressive out there," Mansel said.

Zollin smiled, a little embarrassed at the older boy's praise.

"Too bad you can't make our room smell better, mighty Wizard."

And just like that, the world was back to normal.

Chapter 26

The next day was busy, with people going from place to place despite the cold weather. Zollin spent about half an hour moving the snow in a long rectangular space behind the Inn. There was plenty of room, and Zollin piled most of the snow up around the sides to block the icy wind. In the Gateway Inn, Quinn had almost finished the common room. It had really only needed the ceiling reinforced and some of the molding redone. There were no benches or tables, just a long open room. All day, men came by and pledged their support. The kitchens of the Inn were still unusable, so Ollie and Buck made lunches for the men coming in to practice their sword work. Quinn drilled the men on the most basic maneuvers with both sword and shield.

Once the archery range was finished, Mansel built a simple frame and attached straw-filled dummies to the wooden posts as targets. Men and women began arriving and practicing with their bows. Zollin had gone back to his room to study the anatomy text when he saw Brianna walk past with a bow in her hand. Her face was flushed with cold and excitement, and Zollin thought she was beautiful. He pushed those thoughts away and tried to focus on the diagram of blood flow through the body, but his mind just wasn't in it. He kept seeing her face, the ruddy cheeks, her smile, the way her hair was tied back and the wispy ends that had escaped the ribbon she had tied it with. He tried to wait until supper time, but finally he slammed the book closed and went out to find her.

She was in the common room sitting by the fire. There were several other women sitting there, all with cups of steaming drink. Zollin thought of returning to his room – he didn't want to interrupt their conversation. But before he could go, Brianna caught sight of him and hurried to where he was standing.

"Guess what?" she said, her eyes twinkling in the orange light from the fire.

"What?"

"I'm being trained as an archer," she proclaimed, and the other girls giggled.

"An archer?"

"That's right. Tobin the Brickmaker was an archer in the King's Army. That was years ago, of course, but he's a good teacher. He rounded up several of the ladies like myself and is teaching us to shoot."

"Really?" Zollin asked. "That's great, I guess." Actually he was a little appalled at the idea of women being trained for war. He certainly didn't want Brianna anywhere near the fighting. His mind flashed back to the mercenary racing toward her in the forest, his sword raised for a killing stroke. He shook the memory away.

"You guess," Brianna said frowning. "You don't think I can do it?"

"No, of course you can. It's just the idea of it..." He let the words die on his tongue. Brianna looked at him, and now her eyes were ablaze with fury.

"What idea do you have of me, Zollin? Perhaps in a kitchen, fixing your supper? Or maybe bathing children? Is that more of what you had in mind for me?"

"No, nothing like that, it's just-"

"Just what?" she demanded. "You say you think I can do it, but you don't think I should. Let me tell you something, I didn't come with you so that I could hide in your shadows. I can take care of myself."

"I'm sure that's true," Zollin stammered, wondering how the conversation had taken such an abrupt turn. "I'm not saying that you can't learn to shoot, or that you shouldn't. It just took me by surprise, that's all."

"It didn't surprise Mansel," she said in a superior tone. "In fact, he thought it was great idea."

Anger, white-hot, sprang to life in Zollin's chest. He knew that his father's apprentice was glad that Brianna had come with them. He probably hoped to win her affections, but Zollin would die before he saw Todreck's bride with that overgrown ox.

"Did he?" Zollin asked a little too angrily.

"That's right. He said he was going to give me a present soon. He even offered to give me some pointers if I wanted."

"I'll bet he did," Zollin said.

Just then, Quinn came into the Inn. He stomped his feet on the floor, knocking the snow off his boots. He looked up and saw them, then made his way over.

"Town Elders should be here soon. You two want to join the conversation?" he asked.

"No," Zollin said.

"Yes," Brianna said.

Neither one looked at the other as Quinn looked first at Zollin, then at Brianna.

"What's going on with you two?" he asked.

"Zollin was just telling me how he thought it a bad idea that I learn archery."

"That's not what I said," the young Wizard argued.

"No, it's what you didn't say," Brianna snapped.

"What's that supposed to mean? How can you be mad for something I didn't say?"

"If you're too thick to figure it out, just forget it."

"Is this making any sense to you?" Zollin asked his father.

Quinn had taken a step back, and he looked startled to be dragged back into the conversation.

"I'll need ale to understand either one of you," he said. "A lot of ale."

"See, your father knows how to keep his mouth shut."

"You asked me a question. All I tried to do was answer it."

"Well, your answer was as selfish and insensitive as you," she said.

"Give me a break, I said I was happy for you."

"You suppose you're happy, that's what you said."

"I know what I said," he snarled, his voice rising.

"You're such an idiot," she said as tears sprang up in her eyes.

Zollin didn't reply, and she turned away. He started to walk back to his room, but then he noticed that everyone was watching him. He wasn't sure what to do, but his pride got hold of his tongue before he could think of what he was saying.

"I wish I'd never had a sister," he said quietly.

Brianna gave him a look like he had just slapped her, then she ran down the hallway toward her room. He could hear her crying and then heard the door slam shut. He felt terrible. He hadn't really meant it, but he couldn't take it back now. He settled onto the nearest bench and stared at the table top. He was angry at himself for letting his surprise show, but that's all it was, surprise. He didn't want her in danger, that's all. Wasn't that noble? Didn't that show how much he cared about her? But then he had gone and let himself speak without thinking. How often had his father warned him about that? Now he understood, but she had pushed him into it. She just kept biting and snarling when she knew he didn't mean what she was accusing him of.

"Looks like you and your sister are getting along just as people would expect," Quinn said, handing Zollin a mug of ale.

Zollin didn't really like ale – it was strong and pungent. He preferred sweeter drinks like cider or watered wine. But he didn't complain, just took a long drink of the frothy liquid and then wiped his mouth on his sleeve.

"She's overreacting," Zollin said.

"You act surprised," Quinn said.

"I am surprised. She announces that she's learning archery, and I didn't know what to say. Is that so wrong? I mean, give a guy a chance to think about something before you throw him to the wolves."

Quinn laughed and clapped his son on the shoulder.

"You've got to have quick wit to please a girl like that," his father said.

Zollin looked stunned, but then he noticed that the group of young girls was still sitting near the fire. They were glancing his way and then talking quietly, their conversation laced with giggles.

"I wouldn't worry about it too much," Quinn said. "Looks like your show last night caught the attention of some of the young maidens hereabouts."

Quinn stood and walked over to a group of men who had just come in the door. Zollin guessed that they were the town Council or town Elders or whoever was going to work through the plan of defense with his father. Zollin thought of going back to his room, but he'd been cooped up in the tiny, windowless space all day and he had a longing for fresh air. He turned and was about to stand up when Ellie appeared with a plate of food. She hadn't spoken more than a few words to him since the miners had accosted her, but now she looked in the mood for conversation.

"I brought your supper," she said sweetly.

"Thanks," Zollin said, taking the plate of steaming food.

"It's braised lamb with stewed vegetables and fresh barley bread. There's some soft cheese and fresh churned butter. I can get you some mustard too, if you like that on your lamb."

"Wow," he said, surprised. "It looks fantastic. Thank you."

"It's no problem. Mother likes to cook something fancy for the city Elders, but I made the bread."

"It's wonderful," Zollin said, pinching off a bite.

Ellie seemed pleased, and as she walked away, Zollin glanced back at the group of girls by the fire. They were watching Ellie with looks of loathing that they didn't try to conceal. Zollin wasn't all that hungry, but the food looked wonderful and he started to eat. After only a few bites, one of the girls from the fireside group came over and spoke.

"Hello, Zollin," she said. Her cheeks turned pink with embarrassment.

"Hi," he said around a mouthful of food.

"Would you mind if we joined you?" the girl asked.

She looked so hopeful that Zollin didn't have the heart to say no. All he wanted was to get out of the common room and perhaps stretch his legs. But now he would have to finish his supper and probably make conversation with the group of girls.

"Sure, that would be great," he said, trying to smile and not look distressed.

The girls flocked over, all chatting and giggling. Luckily Zollin didn't have to say much. The girls seemed satisfied to do all the talking. He listened, eating his dinner, and when the time was right, excused himself. The girls seemed a little disappointed that he was leaving, but he steeled his resolve and beat a hasty retreat to the kitchens. He intended to escape out the rear door, but as he entered the labyrinth of rooms, he came face to face with an excited Ellie.

"Oh, I was just coming to rescue you from that bunch of gossips out there," she said.

She took his plate and set it aside and then grabbed his hand and led him back toward a dark room that was full of barrels, some filled with wine and others with ale. There was a large barrel to one side with a white cloth draped over it. On the barrel were a candle, a pie, two plates, and two cups of wine. Zollin felt ambushed. He had gone from one uncomfortable situation right into another. It looked like Ellie had something planned, and while he didn't want to hurt her feelings, all he really wanted was to get out of the Inn.

"I thought you might like some dessert," she said, stepping close to him. She moved her hand until her fingers were entwined with his. Despite his desire to leave, he felt his heart beating faster and his breath coming in shallow gasps. "Or we could do something else."

She was looking up into his eyes, and Zollin noticed how the light danced in her large, dark eyes. She had a pleasant face and her lips seemed to shimmer in the light of the candle.

"I, uh, already ate," he managed to say.

"That's okay," she said. "I'm not really hungry either."

Then she was standing on her tiptoes, her face only inches from his own. Zollin smelled apples and cinnamon on her breath. Then she kissed him. Her lips were soft and warm on his, and he felt his whole body trembling and the magic inside of him tingling.

When he pulled away, she was smiling. There was a look of satisfaction on her face, almost like triumph. He felt a flicker of warning, like things were not all they seemed to be, but he pushed the thought aside. He was about to lean down to kiss her again when Brianna's face appeared in his mind. He suddenly felt guilty.

"I have to go," he said. He didn't wait for a reply but pulled his hand free from hers. He practically ran through the maze of

224

laundry and storage rooms until he found the rear door. He burst out into the snow-filled yard, the cold night air stinging his exposed skin. He wasn't dressed for the weather and knew that he couldn't stay out long, but he needed to get free of the Inn and all the confusing people inside. He moved along the shoveled path toward the stable when he heard voices.

"It's not finished yet," said one voice that Zollin immediately recognized as Mansel.

"I can't wait," said Brianna.

Zollin could see them now, walking slowly toward the front of the Inn. They were close together, but both had their hands shoved into deep pockets. Zollin couldn't tell if they were standing close because they wanted to, or if it was just because the trail through the waist-deep snow was narrow.

"It's not much, really," Mansel was saying. "It should be done in a few more days."

"I can't imagine what it could be."

"Well, you'll just have to wait to find out," Mansel said.

Zollin thought the older boy sounded goofy. Brianna didn't seem to notice. She was leaning toward Mansel now.

"It's so cold," she said.

"Would you like to go in?" Mansel offered.

"No," Brianna said rather suddenly. "I just want to enjoy the moonlight a little longer. It's so beautiful reflecting off the snow. Do you mind?"

"No, of course not," Mansel said.

They stood quietly for a minute, and Zollin knew what she was doing. She was just like the girls in the common room, just like Ellie. She was letting Mansel know that she liked him, and an icy shard of disappointment lanced through Zollin's heart. His eyes watered as he watched them.

"Do you miss Tranaugh Shire?" she asked.

"No," Mansel replied. "I was only ever happy there when I was working with Quinn."

"Do you miss your parents?"

"Well, I guess I should, but they were always so busy. I rarely saw them. I had chores in the mornings and evenings too. I saw them at breakfast and sometimes at supper time, but usually we ate when we could and fell asleep exhausted every night. So, no, I don't really miss them. Do you?"

"I miss my father," she said. "He always saw things the way they were. You know, without the emotional clutter of your feelings mixing things up in your mind. I could always talk to him and feel better afterward. My mother, on the other hand, I don't miss at all. She's a good person I suppose, but I outgrew her. It's strange to realize your parents aren't perfect."

Mansel nodded but didn't say anything. Zollin was shivering but didn't even think of moving away. He was too engrossed in their conversation.

"I miss my sisters some," Brianna continued, "but I doubt they miss me, except for the chores I would have done had I been there. I miss the house that you all built – it was so quaint. I wonder who is living there now."

"Yeah, that's a wild thought, huh? I wonder which one of my brothers took my stuff the moment they realized I was gone."

"Do you think you'll ever go back?" she asked.

"Maybe," he said, slowly putting his arm around her.

At first she seemed surprised, but then she didn't move away from him. Zollin bit his lip to hold in the wail of pain at seeing them together. Part of him was outraged for Todrek. How could Mansel care so little for the vows Brianna had made? She had hardly grieved, and now here was the overgrown apprentice selfishly moving in to steal her affections. But another part, a lonely part that was buried deep inside of him, a part of himself that until now had been reserved solely for his mother, now longed also for the pretty Tailor's daughter. He did not consider the possibility that Brianna didn't like Mansel. He was strong and tall, his smile contagious, his easygoing manner pleasant to be around. He was everything Zollin was not. The young Wizard was thin and his movements awkward, he stumbled over his words and was constantly second guessing every decision he made. Now, he felt truly alone.

"I think I'm ready to go in now," Brianna said.

They turned and walked away, and Zollin stumbled into the barn. It was warmer inside the little shelter. The floor was dry and the body heat of the animals kept the space above freezing. Zollin dropped into a pile of hay and shivered. He needed to go back inside the Inn, but all the excitement of his first kiss with Ellie had evaporated and he was left with bitter despair over Brianna. He told himself again that he could never have loved her, as it was an affront to his best friend's memory. But the excuse was too thin to be of any comfort. He had wanted Brianna's affection, he had secretly hoped that she would love him, but now that thought was like bile in this throat.

He tried to tell himself he was better off. He was a Wizard after all, and being pursued by other Wizards. That was no life for a man in love. His father's words floated into his mind. He thought back to the Harvest Festival, when Todrek had won Brianna's hand in marriage. Zollin had asked his father why he had left home and joined the King's Army. It was over a girl, his father had told him. And so perhaps it was time he left too. He had planned to leave anyway, planned to leave his father in Tranaugh Shire. Now he could leave, and his father could make a home here in Brighton's Gate. Brianna could marry Mansel, but he didn't have to stick around and watch.

The miners would come and he would need to help his father defeat them, but after that, once the winter snows were thawing and he had learned enough from Kelvich, he would leave. Perhaps the Wizards pursing him would leave his father and friends alone. It was no more dangerous for them than traveling with him. He made up his mind and then quietly made his way back to the Inn. He moved like a shadow through the winding set of rooms in the back, then moved swiftly down the hallway to his room. He would spend as much time as he could in the hermit's cottage from here on out, he thought to himself. Then he dropped onto his bed, wrapped the blankets around his shivering body, and fell asleep.

Chapter 27

The next three weeks passed in a blur of work and routine. Zollin spent most of his time at the little cottage at the edge of the woods. He studied and practiced, exercised and meditated. He occasionally returned to the Inn and met with his father. A plan of defense was devised for the town and the morale of the townsfolk improved. Many of the women had taken up archery and spent time every day on the practice range. Mansel had crafted for Brianna a beautiful bow with a snake-like curve. Although the bow was small and the draw weight relatively light, it shot with amazing power and accuracy.

Zollin often saw the two of them together, but did his best to avoid them both. Mansel didn't seem to notice, but Brianna often watched him when he came into town, her face set into a mask that revealed nothing of how she felt. Zollin didn't know whether she cared for him or hated him. And although he tried not to let it bother him, the loss of her friendship was like an open wound that refused to heal. He could bind the fabric of his body, transform objects into almost anything he desired, but he could not mend the constant ache that he felt for her.

Ellie continued to work for Zollin's affection, but he had lost all interest in the Inn Keeper's daughter. He was polite and often ate his meals in the storeroom with her, but he never kissed her again, always keeping her at arm's length.

Quinn and Mansel trained the men with swords each day, drilling over and over in the empty common room of the Gateway Inn. Mansel was showing excellent skill with the blade, his strength and quickness making him a dangerous opponent. And although the he was still learning his trade, it was obvious that the sword was his true passion. He often stayed at the Gateway Inn practicing after a full day of work.

The snows came and went, but no more storms. The sun was making regular appearances in the dull, gray sky. The river that ran through the Great Valley continued to run under several feet of thick ice. The trails through the town remained mostly clear, and the people moved freely through the short winter days. The nights were spent around crackling fires with mugs of mulled wine that warmed them from the inside out.

Scouts had been posted at several outposts beyond the river to watch for the miners. Everyone knew it was only a matter of time before the rough men led by Trollic would arrive. Zollin happened to be at the Inn when a scout came running into town. It was quickly growing dark outside, but the man charged into the Inn calling for Quinn and the city Elders.

"What's happened?" asked Buck.

"I've seen the miners," said the man, his clothes wet with snow. He was shaking, but Zollin couldn't tell if it was from fear or from the cold.

"I'll get Quinn," Zollin said.

"I'll see about the Elders," said Ellie, who had been showing Zollin a gown she was sewing.

She was industrious, much like her mother. And although their relationship had settled into a solid friendship, Zollin was constantly aware of the deep feelings the girl had for him. She kept them hidden just beneath the surface, but they were there. Zollin wasn't sure if he was being fair to her, but he didn't have the heart to tell her he would never feel the same way. Her parents were not pleased that their daughter was giving the Wizard so much of her attention, and Zollin was counting on their disapproval to help keep the girl from forcing his hand.

Zollin moved quickly to the Gateway Inn where his father and Mansel were busy rebuilding the storerooms. He found them and relayed the information the scout had given. Mansel and Zollin stayed to put away the tools and ensure that everything was squared away before they returned to the Valley Inn. When they arrived, they found the common room full of people waiting to hear the report from the scout and the city Elders. Zollin and Mansel found Quinn still speaking with the Elders. Soon Brianna joined them, but no one was talking. The consensus was that the miners would arrive by noon tomorrow, but scouts were posted to ensure that the miners didn't attack that night. Winter battles were rare, as were night raids, but they occasionally did happen, and the Elders were taking no chances.

Many of the townsfolk spent that night at the Inn, with weapons sharpened and ready. Brianna spent the evening inspecting her arrows, ensuring the shafts were true, the heads sharpened and the feathers securely glued.

Ellie was busy serving a full house, which made Zollin and her parents happy. She didn't have time to flirt with him and he could relax, as much as that was possible seeing Brianna and Mansel sitting close and talking in hushed tones. He knew his part in the defensive plan, so he sat back in the shadows and nursed a mug of mulled wine.

The night passed slowly, but uneventfully. After a hearty breakfast, Quinn, Zollin, Mansel, and Brianna made their way to the river. There was a large snow bank just outside of town that had been built up for the women who had been practicing archery. The river was about two hundred yards away and the trail through the waist-deep snow was only wide enough for one man to walk at a time. It was a bottleneck that would give the defenders a great advantage. If the miners broke through the defensive force at the river, they would be forced to come down the trail single file or struggle through the snow. Either way, they would be easy targets for the women on the snow banks.

Although Brianna had trained with the women, she followed Quinn and the others to the riverbank. The river had cut a channel through the valley until there was the height of a tall man from the surface of the water to the top of the bank. The river's frozen surface was covered with snow that was compacted at one place into a circle. The village side of the river had been cleared of snow so that a man with a sword had plenty of room to fight against an invader trying to make his way up the riverbank. Several yards back from the riverbank was a long line of compacted snow for more archers. This would allow the archers to shoot over the heads of the swordsmen without being exposed on the front line.

It was a good place to fight – the snow was working for the villagers. If it had been summer when the miners came, the city would have been much more exposed. They were inspecting everything again with the city Elders when a scout came running up the path toward the river bridge. The river bridge was a permanent structure, unlike the bridges further downriver which could be raised to allow trade boats to travel up and down the river. The Gateway Bridge was an ancient stone and wood structure that had been built ages before, when the mountain pass was first discovered and Brighton's Gate first settled. It was wide enough for two fully loaded wagons to pass side by side. All the snow had been cleared from the bridge and the wooden walkway was being soaked in lamp oil now. If the miners tried to cross the bridge in force, it would be set on fire.

The scout was breathing hard in the cold air, his breath puffing in little clouds around his head. He ran straight for the group of Elders.

"Are they coming?" said one of the Elders.

"The Skellmarians," said the boy as he gasped for breath. "The biggest... raiding party... I've ever seen."

"Skellmarians!" exclaimed another Elder. "We're not ready."

"No," said Quinn in a firm voice. "We are ready. The plan stays the same, only we'll need the miners to help us."

"The miners?" said the first Elder, a tall man with gray hair and stooped shoulders.

"That's right," said Quinn. "In fact, I'll bet they're fleeing from the Skellmarians and that's why they're headed here."

"So what do we do?" asked Mansel.

"First we need someone to warn the town of what's happening," said the stooped Elder.

"I can do that," said Brianna, and she jogged back down the path toward the town.

"We'll need to burn the bridge," said one of the other Elders, a short, fat man with a jolly face.

"We need to let the miners cross first," said Quinn.

"What if the Skellmarians overtake them? We won't have time to destroy the bridge."

231

"I will," Zollin said. That didn't earn him any looks of admiration. Fear was running through the Elders at the thought of the barbaric Skellmarians. Their eyes darted about nervously and they looked as though a strong wind would knock them over.

"We can't take that chance," said the stooped Elder.

"We won't leave the miners stranded on the other side of the river," said Quinn.

"Why not? They would do it to us," said one of the townsmen who had joined the group near the river bridge.

"Perhaps," said Quinn. "But we are still men of honor. We will still be standing tall when all this is over. Don't you want to be able to look your wives in the eye, to tell your children the story without feeling the shame and guilt of innocent lives that were lost because of your fear?"

"You brought this on us," said the stooped Elder. "Where do you get off calling us cowards?"

"I brought the Skellmarians from the mountains, did I?"

"You've done nothing but trouble us since you arrived," the Elder snarled. "You and your demon spawn son."

Zollin's anger erupted inside of him. The city Elder was saying his mother was a devil, and it took all his strength to control the power raging inside of him. He wanted to blast the man into a smoking heap of dust. Blue energy crackled up and down his staff, but Quinn stepped in front of his son.

"Calm yourself, Zollin," Quinn said. "His insult comes from fear. He doesn't mean it."

"He is a coward!" Zollin said through clenched teeth.

"The Skellmarians have taken note of the miners," Quinn said. "They feel that mining weakens the mountains, and since their religion ties them to the mountains, allowing the miners to burrow into their sacred hills weakens them. Once they found out the King's Army isn't guarding Brighton's Gate, they were tempted to take the city. If they control the pass, then they can raid into Yelsia, perhaps even destroy every settlement in the Great Valley. They'll be like rats in the storehouse – you'll never get rid of them. But seeing us ready and waiting for them here will make them pause, make them think we aren't the ripe plums waiting to be picked that they've observed these last few months."

"You think they've been spying on us?" asked the fat Elder.

"Absolutely," Quinn said. "They may look like savages, but they're men, and they're intelligent."

"Do you plan to challenge them?" asked another Elder.

"Yes, if I can. If I defeat their chieftain they might return to the mountains without a fight."

"And the miners?" asked the stooped-shouldered Elder.

"We'll deal with them afterward," Quinn said, with a knowing look.

***

The miners arrived at the river a short time later. They were moving as fast as their weary feet would carry them. Trollic and his assassin spy rode horses. The rest of the miners, about twenty-five men all told, followed behind. They were exhausted, their eyes wide with fear. They seemed relieved to have reached the river, but stopped just short of the bridge.

Quinn stepped up to bridge and stood waiting. Zollin was well back from the front lines, waiting and watching with the archers. He saw the assassin, tall and thin, his wispy hair covered with a thick, fur-lined hat. The man pointed at Quinn and leaned close to speak to his master. Then Trollic nudged his horse forward and began to cross the bridge alone.

Quinn walked forward and met the man on the center of the bridge. They talked for a moment, and then Quinn turned and started back toward the village. Trollic waved to his men and followed Quinn across. There was murmuring and even a few shouts, but Quinn waved his hands for everyone to be quiet.

"Trollic has given me his word that his men will be no trouble," shouted Quinn. "They'll fight alongside us against the Skellmarians if it comes to that. For now, they need food and rest."

A young boy was sent to the Valley Inn to gather food. Soon the miners were sprawled on the ground along the river. They had weapons, mostly long, heavy knives, but they were so tired that they wouldn't last long if the Skellmarians attacked.

Zollin could see movement inside the tree line on the far side of the river. The Skellmarians were taking stock of the town's new defenses. Quinn walked back across the bridge and waited. Before long, a man in heavy armor came out of the trees. He was a big man, with what looked like a hat made from bone and fur. He carried a long-handled ax and a curved knife. There were ribbons and threaded beads tied around his arms and neck. Zollin could see long hair, smeared with thick brown grease, hanging like oily ropes from the helmet he wore.

They spoke for a moment and then Quinn turned back toward the town while the Skellmarian turned back toward the trees. When Quinn was safely back across the bridge, Zollin joined the group clustered around his father.

"His name is Borrak," Quinn said. "He's offered us terms of surrender, claiming they'll let everyone but the city Elders leave the city safely."

"The city Elders?" said the stooped-shouldered man. "What does he want with us?"

"He says that the Elders are responsible for sending the miners into the mountains."

"That's nonsense," said the stooped Elder in a shaky voice. "We had nothing to do with it."

"In their culture, the Elders are responsible for everything that goes on in their villages. Because the miners got their supplies from here and fled here, they assume they're from here. He proposes to sacrifice the Elders to strengthen the mountain god they worship and take over the town."

"That's insane," said the stooped Elder. "They don't even live in houses. They're animals."

"Should we take their offer?" said one of the men from the town. He was young, and Zollin seemed to remember he had a new baby back in the village. He didn't blame the man for thinking of the safety of his wife and child.

"You should consider it," said Trollic.

"Consider it?" said the stooped Elder. "It's your fault they're here in the first place."

Trollic's hand fell to the heavy knife in his belt, but Quinn raised his hand and spoke.

"Let's all calm down. We'll stick to the plan. Trollic, make sure your men are ready to fight. I'm going to challenge their chieftain."

"What plan is he talking about?" Trollic snarled. "Why should we stay here to be slaughtered? I'm taking my men and leaving this pathetic little mud hole of a village."

Quinn turned back to the miner. "You'll stay here and fight, or you'll find yourself on the other side of the river with the Skellmarians."

"I doubt that," Trollic smirked.

He was in the middle of an arrogant smile when Quinn's hand shot out and slammed into the miner's jaw. Trollic fell to the ground, his arms and legs stiff, his eyes rolling back in the sockets. The assassin was instantly over his boss with a knife in each hand. Quinn's hands were empty, but he looked into the tall assassin's eyes. "I'll deal with you when this is over," he said.

"I look forward to it," said the pale-skinned assassin.

Quinn walked back to the bridge and called out to the Skellmarians.

"My name is Quinn, son of Delmar, son of Salick. I challenge Borrak to single combat for the right to Brighton's Gate."

The voice that replied from the trees was heavily accented but plain enough to be understood.

"When I kill you, Quinn Delmarson, I will burn the village and kill everyone who does not flee before me."

Quinn took a torch and threw it onto the bridge. The fire spread rapidly and soon the entire bridge was in flames. Steam from melting snow rose up and joined the black smoke of the fire. A group of warriors, about fifty in all, moved as a group from the trees. Zollin could see Borrak in the middle of them. They walked to the river's edge. Quinn had already moved down to the space Zollin had created for the duel. He had a short, two-edged sword and a wooden shield reinforced with bands of steel. In his belt at the small of his back he had the two throwing knives Trollic's assassin had left behind, one of which he had stabbed Zollin with. Quinn's own knife was inside his right boot.

The group of Skellmarians parted, and Borrak made his way down onto the frozen river. He was still wearing his armor and strange helmet, but he had traded his battle ax for a curved sword and small hand shield that looked about as big as a large pie. He also had a curved knife in his belt, and on a thin belt which was slung over his head and one shoulder was a small climbing ax or pick.

The two men circled each other on the hard packed snow. Because Zollin had used magic to pack the snow down, it hadn't melted and become slick, but the longer the fight progressed, the more treacherous the snow would become. As if on cue, snow began to fall. It was a soft snowfall, the big flakes seeming to float down, and to Zollin it made the fight about to take place seem like a dream. His father was risking his life for the village of Brighton's Gate. Perhaps he should have been used to the grip of fear on his heart as he watched his father face an opponent intent on killing him, but it was like being on a wild horse. He felt totally out of control, and even though he knew his father was a skilled warrior, it still made him uneasy to see the only family he had ever known within reach of an enemy blade.

The Skellmarian attacked first, slashing his curved sword at Quinn's head. It was easily evaded and the two men continued circling. Borrak continued to test Quinn with feints and looping attacks that were just barely within range of the barbarian's longer sword. Quinn was content to bide his time. In fact, even though he could feel the cold air and the snow melting into his clothes, he knew his opponent's heavy armor would be wearing on him. So the duel continued, around and around the circle of hardened snow. The villagers watched in silence, and Zollin knew that if his father was slain, the townsfolk would break and run. They would flee into the winter mountains and probably die there.

Finally the Skellmarian swung his sword in an overhead strike that would have split Quinn's skull, but the wily carpenter raised his shield over his head and blocked the blow. Then with the speed of a much younger man, he thrust his sword at the

Skellmarian's chest. Borrak swung his small shield down to deflect the blow, but the sword found the barbarian's thigh. It wasn't a deep gash, certainly not life threatening, but Quinn had drawn first blood and it infuriated the Skellmarian. His warriors on the far riverbank roared in protest, shouting at their chief in their native tongue. It sounded like gibberish to Zollin.

Quinn had been waiting for just such an opportunity. The curved swords of the Skellmarians were perfect for hacking and slashing, but a straight thrust was foreign to them. Quinn had proven he was more than just an average warrior. Now the Skellmarian rushed forward, his sword swinging in a horizontal slash aimed for Quinn's shield. Quinn braced for the impact, but the larger man's power rocked him. Just as quickly, Borrak spun around and put his full weight into an arcing slash toward Quinn's exposed side. Quinn raised his sword to deflect the blow but the force of the impact sent the Carpenter sprawling. The Skellmarians cheered wildly and Borrak rushed forward, his sword swinging down like a man chopping wood. Quinn rolled to the side and Borrak's sword plunged into the snow. Quinn scrambled to one knee and slammed the edge of his shield into Borrak's leg. The Skellmarian howled in pain and hopped away. Quinn quickly regained his feet and charged forward. He swung his sword first at Borrak's shoulder, which the man caught on his shield. Then he batted away a feeble counter by the Skellmarian and thrust his sword at the man's chest again. This time the sword was deflected up and it caught the warrior chief's helm. Borrak's head was thrown back as the helmet was knocked away. Borrak snarled in rage and dropped the long sword to grab the climbing ax from the belt around his shoulder. He pulled it free and blocked Quinn's next cut on his shield, then swung the small ax at Quinn's face. Quinn raised his shield, but the pointed steel tip cut through the wood and gouged deeply into his arm. Now it was Quinn's turn to stagger back. The ax was stuck fast into the shield and the Skellmarian let it go, but Quinn couldn't pull his arm out of the shield's leather thongs while the ax point was piercing his arm. He slid his sword under the ax head, but Borrak was charging forward with the curved knife. Quinn swung his sword out to keep the barbarian at bay, but it was only a matter of time before Borrak broke through the feeble defense and ended the fight.

The Skellmarians were screaming in a blood frenzy now, but Borrak was the first to slip on the hardening snow. Quinn dropped to his knee and used his sword as a lever to loosen the climbing ax from his shield. The Carpenter wailed in pain as the serrated edge of the pick sawed loose from his forearm, but he was able to pull his hand from the shield just as the Skellmarian slashed at his face with the knife. Quinn threw himself back, but not quickly enough. The blade sliced into his cheek and scraped against the bone. Quinn could feel the snow beneath him, could feel the cold seeping into his body. His left arm was numb and useless even though it was free of the shield. He struggled to rise to his feet before his enemy was on top of him, but then he too slipped and fell onto his wounded arm. Pain throbbed though him and his vision dimmed, but he stayed conscious.

Borrak flung himself on top of Quinn, knocking the breath from the smaller man's lungs. He raised the knife for the killing stroke, but Quinn grabbed the barbarian's wrist and held fast. Borrak raised his upper body to punch down at the Carpenter's head, but at that same moment Quinn bucked, arching his back and throwing the Skellmarian forward. It was a desperate move, but Borrak hadn't expected it. He lost his balance and Quinn swung the bigger man around. Now Quinn was on top, but he couldn't let go of the Skellmarian's wrist for fear that he would be killed by the wicked knife. Instead, Quinn slammed his forehead into the bigger man's face. The Skellmarian's nose shattered in a sickening crunch of cartilage and bone. Blood sprayed out and the barbarian screamed in pain.

Quinn struggled back to his feet which seemed too weak to hold him up. He managed to scramble back without falling as Borrak rose slowly, wiping the blood from his eyes. The Skellmarian was covered in blood by the time he got his feet. But his eyes were focused and he bellowed as he raised the curved knife and charged forward. Like a flash, Quinn's hand shot out. Suddenly a knife appeared in Borrak's throat. The big Skellmarian chief fell dead and slid along the now bloody snow at Quinn's feet.

Instantly the Skellmarian warriors jumped down into the snow that had collected on the frozen river and charged toward Quinn. The Carpenter was running back toward the village side of the river, but his legs were too weak. Zollin stood and thrust his staff toward the river. He could feel the ice, several feet thick and as solid as an oak tree. He unleashed all the pent up fear and anger within him and felt the ice on the river bend. He strained, and the ice gave a little more. He could feel the tiny cracks growing, but it wasn't enough. He felt his heart racing and his head hurt. Then there was a crack that sounded like a broken twig, only the sound carried to the mountains and echoed back. The ice on the river suddenly broke apart, the solid pieces pitching up and tossing the Skellmarians into the icy depths below. Zollin slumped to the ground in exhaustion and managed to look up in time to see his father slip from the ice and disappear into the dark depths of the river.

Chapter 28

When Quinn's body hit the icy water, his muscles contracted, pushing the air from his lungs and curling him into a ball. He struggled to move his arms to catch hold of the ice above him, but the river current had already pulled him past the opening. His fingers brushed against the ice that was above him now. He kicked out, trying to swim back upstream, but he was too weak. He knew he couldn't make it. Still, there was a part of his mind that refused to give up. His lungs were on fire, his skin felt like it was made of stone, and every movement was agony, but still he thrashed and fought the current, struggling for life. Then he was hit by another thrashing man, one of the Skellmarian warriors. And Quinn's body locked up. His mind was screaming to fight, but his body rose gently in the swift water, bumping against the ice.

Zollin had seen his father fall, and his first impulse was to leap up and save him, but when he tried, the world spun around and he fell onto the hard packed snow. The villagers and miners were cheering even as more Skellmarians ran toward the riverbank. Most of the warriors who had jumped onto the frozen river had fallen in and had been swept away, but a few had managed to climb back to the opposite bank.

Zollin closed his mind and reached out with the power inside of him. It felt weak and feeble, but still he reached. He could feel the men in the river, moving farther and farther away. He could feel some fighting and kicking, others drifting lifelessly. He searched each one, trying to find his father. Finally he found him, but Quinn wasn't moving. Zollin pulled, but it felt like Quinn was just beyond his grasp. With one hand Zollin gripped his staff, and with the other he took hold of the willow belt around his waist, but the power wasn't enough. He felt his father slipping away.

He stretched his entire body, the men around him stepping back, not knowing what was happening to the young Wizard. He demanded the magic go farther, but it was no use. There was nothing left of the magic he controlled. His father was too far away.

Then he felt a tremble from deep inside, at first a whisper, then a rumble, and then he felt power flood through his body. He jumped to his feet, his eyes blazing. The archers around him stumbled back. He could feel his father again, and this time he pulled him easily through the water, like a child landing a tiny fish. He pulled Quinn until he was under the gaping hole in the ice, and then he lifted the man. Quinn shot into the air and came rushing toward Zollin. Quinn's wet clothes hardened into ice almost instantly in the frosty air, but Zollin poured heat into his father's body. He felt the lungs deflated and struggling to open to the air the body desperately needed. The heart was beating sluggishly, the mind pulled so far into itself it seemly like only a tiny spark. Zollin could feel power rushing through his body as if he were standing in the flames of magical power, but he was not consumed. He willed the lungs to open and they did. He massaged the weak heart, imagining strength and vitality. Quinn's mind opened like a flower toward the sun. Zollin sent radiating heat down onto his father until the older man's clothes were dry and he lay on the brittle grass in a circle of melted snow.

Quinn opened his eyes. "What happened?" he asked.

"It's not over," was all Zollin said.

Zollin pulled Quinn to his feet and they walked toward the river. The Skellmarians, over a hundred strong, were shouting and gesturing at the villagers. Quinn turned to the archers and signaled for them to fire a volley at the barbarians. The arrows arced over the river and fell on the Skellmarians, who screamed in outrage but retreated back toward the trees.

"Will they attack again?" said the stooped-shouldered Elder who had come up behind Quinn.

"I don't know."

"Let me see your arm," Zollin said.

He could feel the throbbing pain pulsing out from the jagged wound, but it would take time to mend the flesh and muscle the pick ax had torn.

"Where's Trollic?" Quinn asked.

The city Elders had gathered all around Quinn and Zollin now, but none could answer where the miner had gone to. Quinn turned to see Mansel and Brianna approaching, along with most of the miners and townsfolk who had witnessed the duel and resulting magic.

"We need to find the miner," Quinn said to the Elders. "Leave a guard along the river and send everyone else to their homes."

Orders were given as Zollin and the others returned to the Valley Inn. The power inside of Zollin had always felt like a small flame, a candle illuminating a world that most could not see. Now he felt the raging fire burn low, but it was still kindled inside of him, not a neat little flame, but a radiating current that spread through his body. While the others shivered in the cold, heat poured off of Zollin. He couldn't keep from smiling either – he had found the power inside that Kelvich had talked of and he knew that things would never be the same.

When they reached the Valley Inn, they found everyone outside, including the Inn Keeper, his wife and daughter. Ellie lit up when she saw Zollin and ran toward him, but he lifted his hand to stop her. Just before she reached him, he saw her face turn pale and she looked frightened. He stalked past her and followed Quinn to speak to her father.

"What's going on?" Quinn said.

"Trollic's man carried him here and left him by the fire. Then he ordered us all out."

"That's all?" Quinn asked.

"No," Buck said, talking to Quinn but looking at Zollin. "Several of the other miners followed him. There's probably a dozen of them in there now, all armed."

"We need to gather a few more men," Quinn said. "We can come at them from both entrances."

"No," Zollin said. "I'll go."

"You can't go in there alone, son," Quinn said.

"I think he can," Brianna said, laying her hand on Quinn's arm.

Quinn looked at her, then followed her gaze to Zollin. His son looked the same, only there was something about him that radiated strength. Quinn was both drawn to him and frightened. He stared at his son and nodded.

Zollin stepped up to the doorway, and they all heard a crash inside, then the sound of two bodies flopping onto the floor.

"Try not to tear things up too bad," the Inn Keeper's wife said as Zollin opened the door. He ignored her and walked inside, stepping over the unconscious bodies of the two men guarding the door.

There were men standing along both sides of the room. Near the large stone fireplace, Trollic sat, and the pale assassin stood beside him. Trollic looked frightened, but the assassin just looked frustrated.

"Thought I'd killed you already," said the man.

"You came close," Zollin replied.

Three men came at Zollin from behind, but they ran headlong into an invisible wall. They bounced backward and fell to the floor dazed. One sat up, but Zollin swung his staff in a whirling circle and slammed it into the man's head.

"I'm here for him," Zollin said, pointing to the pale assassin standing beside Trollic. "The rest of you can leave, just drop your weapons and go out this door with your hands on your heads."

One man started to move, and the assassin's hand shot out, the throwing knife burying itself into the man's chest. He gave a startled cry and slumped to the floor.

"You're a handy man to have around," said Trollic from his seat by the fire. "You can work for me if you like. I've decided to take over this crummy town. It's better than they deserve, but for now it'll do. All I need you to do is bring you father in here and have him beg me for his life. Then I'll spare the town and make sure the Skellmarians don't invade and kill us all. What do you say?"

Zollin didn't answer, just gave a little push with his mind, and Trollic's chair tipped backward and fell into the fireplace. The miner screamed, and his assassin scrambled to pull his boss from the flames. The other men either hurried to help or dropped their knives and ran for the door. There were five men left, counting Trollic who only had some minor burns and smoldering clothes.

"I think you will either drop your weapons and lie face down on the floor," Zollin said, "or I'll kill you all."

"Who do you think you are?" Trollic screamed.

"My name is Zollin, son of Quinn, son of Delmar, son of Salick. I'm the Wizard of Brighton's Gate, and I will suffer your arrogance no longer."

Three of the men ran at Zollin, but he raised his staff and blasted them with blue energy. The blast knocked them off their feet and slammed them into the back wall, the magic crackling over their twitching bodies. Trollic stood and held his hands out in front of him. He was babbling something, but Zollin couldn't hear him. The magic inside of him was churning and swirling like a tornado. He felt his emotions rising on the wind of its power. He wanted to kill these men, to blast them into dust. As he entertained the thought, he imagined laying Brighton's Gate to waste, blasting apart the buildings and homes like toys beneath the feet of a toddler. He smiled and felt laughter rising up inside of him. All he had to do was let the magic take over, to give in and let himself feel this sense of giddy power always.

And then Brianna's face appeared in his mind. He saw her hair falling softy around her shoulders. Her eyes were bright with excitement, her lips smiling, her laughter touching his heart. And then everything came back into focus. The fire inside him slipped back into the invisible reservoir that he could not feel or find. He felt his body sag with fatigue, his stomach churning with hunger. He no longer wanted to kill anyone. He didn't want to blast anything or fight the men in front of him. He only wanted to rest, and to see Brianna again.

He felt stupid for having denied his feelings. There was a sharp prick of fear at the thought that perhaps it was too late. Perhaps she had given herself to Mansel. But he didn't want to think about that now. He looked at the men in front of him. Trollic was still begging for his life, but the assassin had noticed the change. Zollin saw his hand sneak around his back, and then the knife was coming.

It was as if time had slowed, and he could see the firelight glinting on the blade as it raced toward his heart. The assassin was taking no chances this time – the knife would kill him instantly. There was a flutter in Zollin's mind and he saw the knife tumble to the floor. He looked up, but the man was already in motion, a short sword just like Quinn's coming up to plunge into his stomach.

Zollin jumped aside and the assassin slid past. He sent a blast of energy toward the man, but he jumped out of the way. Zollin was about to finish the man when he sensed movement behind him. He thrust the butt of his staff up and out behind him and felt it ram home in the man's chest. There was a gasp of air, and Zollin swung around and slammed his fist into the side of the man's head. Trollic fell in a heap against the wall, but Zollin knew he was too slow. His mind was screaming a warning about the assassin who was now behind him. Zollin spun, but the sword sliced through the skin of his hip, grating against the bone, severing the willow belt. Zollin felt the willow branches' power rush out of the supple limbs and he fell, dropping his staff. He was so weak, the pain on his hip like fire searing into his side. The assassin stood over him.

"Well, all good things must come to an end," the pale man said.

"What's your name?" Zollin asked.

"Is that important?" the man said.

"It is to me," Zollin said. He knew he could rekindle the magic deep within him, but he was afraid he couldn't control it. He was powerless, and that was okay. This way, he knew the people of Brighton's Gate, and his family, would live. That was the most important thing.

"Stop!" came a voice from the kitchens.

Then Mansel was standing over Zollin, his sword longer than the assassin's, double-edged and the steel a dark blue color. The assassin flicked his sword toward Mansel's throat, but the boy batted it harmlessly aside and brought his blade whistling toward the man's elbow. The assassin darted back. His tall, pale body was agile and fast. Zollin watched as the man darted back in, their swords flashing above him. Mansel countered every attack the man tried. Then he tried throwing his last knife, but Zollin rallied enough power to stop the blade in midair. He had a flashback of Kelvich throwing beanbags at him while he was tied to the post in front of the old Sorcerer's cottage.

Mansel stepped forward and swung his sword into the hovering knife. It flew back at the assassin who tried to dodge out of the way, but it slashed into the side of his neck. The man screamed and jumped toward Mansel, but the boy held his ground. The blades swung in a blinding fury, but Mansel held his defense, position after position, just as he had been taught. Blood was leeching through the man's fingers as he held the wound in his neck, and soon his left side was drenched with blood. Mansel parried every strike but refused to fight back. The assassin's blows slowed as he lost strength, and eventually he sagged to the floor.

Then Quinn was beside his son. "Are you hurt, Zollin?"

"Not too bad," the young Wizard said.

Quinn helped Zollin to stand. The Inn was filling with people. Mansel still stood over the dying man, his sword raised and ready, but he had no interest in slaying the wounded assassin. Brianna stepped up and supported Zollin on his wounded side. He was in pain, the room filling with people and noise, his body aching for sleep, but all he could think about was how close Brianna was. He could feel her fingers on his arm, sense her body close to his. He wanted to turn and declare his love, but before he could speak, he heard the dying man.

"Allistair," he rasped. "My name is Allistair. Forgive me, I made so many bad choices and I just could not stop."

"Your maker will have to forgive you," Quinn said. "That is not in our power. But we'll put a marker on your grave. It shall say, Allistair, Royal Guard."

The man smiled weakly and nodded his head. Then he slumped back, his breath rasped one last time, and he died.

"Why did you promise that?" cried the stooped-shouldered Elder. "I say we throw him out for the wild animals."

"That's because you've never been given a second chance," Quinn said. "Now, if you'll excuse us, we have some wounds to see

246

to."

Quinn and Brianna led Zollin back to their rooms. Zollin was asleep before his head touched the pillow.

***

It was snowing in Isos City, which was a busy port town built around the edges of a natural harbor. There were lots of Inns, mostly catering to merchants and seafarers, but Wytlethane had managed to find a quiet place among the hustle and bustle of city commerce and far away from the petty criminals and rowdy seamen. He was alone in a common room with a bright fire, eating a rich soup and drinking wine. He had felt Branock approaching for some time. His fellow Wizard felt as familiar to him as a favorite chair. He was certain the other Wizard would find him, not because their tastes were similar, but because he knew Branock could feel him as well and would not stop searching until he found his fellow member of the Torr.

Branock had ridden quickly across the country side, his new horse seeming only too happy to be out of the city and into the open land beyond. In Isos City, Branock had searched through three stuffy Inns for Wytlethane. He knew that the older Wizard would want a quiet place, far from any signs of life. Branock, on the other hand, would have enjoyed some company. He didn't mind using his power to satisfy those around him, and it reminded him of his childhood so many years ago. But he had work to do. He needed to restore his relationship with Wytlethane. He was certain that the older Wizard knew his plan was to get to Zollin before Cassis and Wytlethane – their striving for power within the Torr was not a secret, and creating alliances to strengthen their standing was standard practice among the Wizards. Still, he needed help if his plan was to work.

He stopped at an ancient looking structure. The sign over the door said Serenity Inn. Not an inviting place in a city full of merchants and sailors, all looking to make a profit and have a good time. Still, it was exactly the kind of place that Wytlethane would find appealing. He wrapped the horse's reins around a low post and walked inside. He stomped his feet and brushed the snow from his shoulders. He had purchased a thick scarf at Orrock that he kept wrapped around his bald head. He took the garment off and shook the snow out of it. It took some time for his eyes to adjust to the dim room. There was only one patron, and the man was sitting beside the fire, his features hidden by the glare of the bright flames. Branock could only see a silhouette, but he could tell the patron was Wytlethane – the old Wizard's posture and proximity to the fire were all the clues he needed.

He walked boldly up to his rival and stood staring down at the Wizard. Wytlethane was slowly eating his soup and had yet to look up. Finally Branock cleared his throat to get the other man's attention.

"What do you want?" Wytlethane said.

Branock realized the other Wizard hadn't recognized him. He smiled. He forgot that he looked so different. For an instant he considered attacking Wytlethane, but he quickly discarded the idea. He still needed the older Wizard as part of his plan, and even though he might not have recognized Branock, another Wizard this close was enough to ensure Wytlethane's defenses were up.

"It's me, brother," Branock said.

Wytlethane looked up and peered into Branock's eyes. After a moment, he waved at the seat across the table. Branock sat just as an elderly maid waddled over and set a crystal goblet down on the table.

"Food, sir? Lodging?"

"Yes," Branock said, producing a gold coin from his robe and handing it to the woman. "And we'll need more wine."

"Of course, sir."

When the maid was out of hearing, Wytlethane asked the obvious question.

"What happened to you?"

"Almost the same thing that happened to your apprentice," Branock said as he poured wine into his glass.

Wytlethane's eye twitched, but otherwise he took the verbal jab without any outward sign of his anger. He knew Cassis was rash and not as talented as the boy imagined, but he should have been a match for the new Wizard. Now, things were more difficult. Still, he had expected the insult, but he hadn't expected Branock to admit that he too had been bested.

"The boy?" Wytlethane asked.

"Yes," Branock said, taking a long drink of wine. He hated admitting that he had almost been killed, but he needed Wytlethane to believe that Branock needed his help. "I came upon the group and underestimated the boy. He escaped me."

"It looks as though he did more than escape."

"Indeed, I'm not as handsome as I once was."

"I think the outside is starting to match the inside," Wytlethane jeered.

Branock swallowed the insult with another mouthful of wine. He wished he could destroy his rival, but that would only invite the wrath of their Master, and Branock was not yet strong enough to defeat the head of their order. He smiled and did his best to sound believable.

"I thought I could take him by myself," he said in a humble tone. "I was wrong. I should have listened to the Master."

"Yes, and I should have insisted that we stay together."

"We will need all our resources to bring the boy in."

"I'm sure that other methods have been employed," Wytlethane said.

"What do you mean?" Branock asked, not having to pretend to sound surprised.

"I believe the Master has employed the Mezzlyn."

The statement hung in the air like a thick cloud of noxious fumes. Branock hated the Mezzlyn. They were assassins, extremely skilled assassins, but without a trace of human feeling and utterly vicious. If the Master had hired the Mezzlyn, it could only mean that Branock and Wytlethane's lives were forfeit. Even if they did manage to bring in the boy, would the Master trust them again? He felt a deep bitterness erupt inside him. He couldn't believe that after years of service, he was suddenly being replaced like an old broom.

"How do you know?" Branock asked.

"I have seen them in this town," Wytlethane said.

"That doesn't mean they are after the boy. The Mezzlyn have agents in every major city."

"Agents yes, but this is a mass gathering."

"Perhaps they are meeting to discuss leadership or something," Branock suggested, but he sounded desperate and he knew it.

"Don't be naïve," Wytlethane snapped. "The Master felt Cassis' death the same as you and I. We have failed, they have been employed, and our only chance now is to bring in the boy."

"Will that be enough?" Branock wondered aloud.

"It will have to be. Dead or alive, we must not return empty-handed."

"I agree, but perhaps we can use this situation to our advantage."

"What do you mean?"

"If we can get to the boy before the Mezzlyn, somehow begin to earn his trust, if we rescue him from the assassins – perhaps we can bring him back alive."

"That is a farfetched scheme," Wytlethane sneered. "I don't think the boy would trust us, not after Cassis' attack on him."

"What if, instead, we ally ourselves with the Mezzlyn?" Branock proposed. "That would allow us to keep track of the assassins, and at the right moment, steal away with the boy."

"He would be dead."

"True, but at least we would be alive."

"I don't trust the Mezzlyn," Wytlethane said.

"Neither do I, but our options are limited. We do not even know what the Master's orders were. They may be here for us as well."

"How can we possibly infiltrate their ranks?"

"Just look at me. If I turn up with information about the boy, I can offer to lead them to him. They won't recognize me – you didn't. You can stay at distance, and I'll contact you when the time is right. What do you think?"

"It might work," Wytlethane said slowly. "Or you might get killed."

"I'm not that easy to kill," Branock scoffed. "Besides, I doubt you'd lose much sleep if that happened."

"True enough," Wytlethane conceded. He actually thought the idea of not having to put up with Branock was divine, but he was also afraid. If they failed, that would mean Branock's death and, by proxy, his own. Still, he could think of no better plan.

"Alright," said the elder Wizard. "Infiltrate them and report their plans to me."

"Of course," Branock said. Inside he was bristling at Wytlethane's superior tone, but he held himself in check. If things worked out, carrying out his master plan might be easier than he anticipated. "I should go," he said, standing.

Wytlethane merely waved his hand as a platter of food was set before him by the elderly maid. Branock helped himself to a small loaf of warm bread and the full bottle of wine the maid had brought.

"I'll not be needing that room after all," he said as he strode out of the common room. At the door, he was met by an icy blast of wind. He wrapped his scarf around his head and smiled, then stepped out into the cold twilight. He couldn't help but smile. Things were finally working out in his favor. He had bet his future on his alliance with Prince Simmeron, and now it looked as if that gamble would pan out. He recalled a sailor's song he had learned as a boy and began whistling as he rode off through the snow toward the harbor, where he expected to find the Mezzlyn and his future.

Epilogue

The Master paced back and forth in his tower. He had felt the surge and sent all his evil intent toward the boy, but he had been rejected. Sentimental fool, the ancient Wizard thought to himself. It was a shame such power had to be destroyed. The boy had already disrupted his plans. Cassis was dead, and now he would have to send his most secret and powerful weapon to intercept the boy if he moved south. Still, the assassins might succeed. He had little faith in the tottering old fool Wytlethane, nor in the scheming Branock. But there was still a chance.

He remembered the days when he had been young. He had traveled the Five Kingdoms and battled his way to supremacy. He had no desire to do that now. He would send the twins. He could count on their combined power and absolute loyalty. He had given the girls everything they wanted and kept them from the other Wizards. When the spring thaws came, he would send them north. Until then, he would have to wait. He could feel the world powers moving, propelling him forward, toward his destiny – to rule the Five Kingdoms and be the sole source of magical power in all the land. To do that, he would have to kill, but he had no qualms about shedding innocent blood. When the time came, and it would be soon, he would come down from his tower and let the world tremble at his feet. He was Offendorl, Master of the Torr, and all would know his name and fear him.

***

Zollin opened his eyes. Brianna was there, sitting on a stool beside his bed. His stomach growled loudly, and she smiled. Her eyes were blue around the edges, and turned a rich, green color toward the dark pupil. It reminded Zollin of autumn leaves.

"How long have I been asleep?" he asked. His voice was raspy from his parched throat.

"Almost a day and half," Brianna said. "But Master Kelvich says that's normal. Here, have some water."

She raised a cup to his lips and let the cool water trickle in. It tasted better than any drink he had ever had. He sucked greedily at it until the cup ran dry. She poured more water from a pitcher near the head of Zollin's bed. He drank that down too, feeling the cold liquid run down his throat and into his empty stomach.

"Master Kelvich said you would be hungry too," she said, helping him sit up.

His head was a little dizzy, but otherwise he felt okay. She settled a tray with soup and bread onto his lap, and he smiled. The warm soup smelled so delicious, he couldn't help himself and started eating right away.

"You are hungry," she said, smiling.

He nodded, and after a few more mouthfuls, he managed to ask a question.

"How's my father?"

"He's fine. Working, of course. He and Mansel are next door, but they should be here soon."

At the mention of Mansel, a dark cloud appeared over Zollin. He wanted to tell Brianna how he felt about her, that she was constantly in his thoughts, that she was the most beautiful girl he had ever seen, that he would do anything for her. But what if that caused more problems? He thought about his dilemma as he spooned more soup into his mouth. If she and Mansel were together, declaring his love could drive them all apart. But he wasn't sure if he could hold back his feelings. She was watching him, her autumn eyes peering deeply into his soul.

"Is there something on your mind?" she asked.

"No," he said with his mouth full.

"I'm glad you're okay," she said softly. "I was worried about you."

"Worried?" he said bashfully. "Why?"

"It's just, when I saw you lying on the floor, bleeding..." she let the thought trail off.

"I don't know what I would have done if Mansel hadn't saved you," she said.

Saved me, he thought to himself. Mansel didn't save me, I

saved him, he wanted to say, but he knew that Mansel had stepped in right as the assassin Allistair was about to kill him. I guess Mansel hadn't mentioned the fact that I saved him from the assassin's knife, he thought bitterly. But now he knew he couldn't say anything. He owed Mansel that much. Brianna obviously loved him and he would not divide her heart.

"Yeah," he said. "Mansel was terrific."

She smiled, and it felt like a knife in Zollin's heart. He wished he had died. He closed his eyes and yawned. He knew it was rude, but he couldn't help it. Besides, Brianna being this close only made him yearn for her, and that was a longing he could never fulfill.

"I'll let you sleep," she said.

She took the tray, and Zollin lay back on his pillows. He closed his eyes and saw Todrek's face. His friend, Brianna's slain husband, smiled at him. It was the first time he had remembered his friend without seeing Todrek's angry glare, or his face contorted with pain and fear as he bled to death outside Zollin's home in Tranaugh Shire. I've got to let go of her, he thought as if he were speaking to his friend. He heard the door close as Brianna left and heard voices in the hallway outside. He recognized Mansel's somber tones although he could not hear what the older boy said. Tears sprang from his eyes and he felt the aching loneliness he had always felt for his mother springing up again, swallowing his hope and happiness. Then sleep came, and he floated away into the bliss of nothingness where his wounded heart no longer ached.

***

"Is he awake?" Mansel asked.

"Yes, he ate and drank a little, then went back to sleep."

She made her way down the hallway of the Valley Inn toward the large common room.

"Did you tell him how you feel?" Mansel asked.

"No, I..." she wasn't sure why she hadn't said anything. "I didn't think the time was right," she lied. She knew why she hadn't said anything – it was because she would have sworn Zollin was about to say something. Not that she knew what he would say, probably that he wished she had never come with him, but she had hoped he might say that he cared for her. She had realized that she loved him, but she didn't know how to show it. Sometimes she thought he felt the same way, and sometimes he acted like he hated her. She knew he blamed her for Todrek's death. She blamed herself too, but she knew she was supposed to leave Tranaugh Shire with Zollin. She had dreamed it, and even if he rejected her, she would never regret it. Her dream had almost come true, she had almost been left behind, and the thought of it had filled her with dread. Now a new fear was rising. She was still seeing the evil man with the ruined eye in her dreams. She always awoke to the sound of marching feet and screams of horror. She didn't know why she needed to be here, with Zollin, but she did and that was enough for now.

We're glad you've enjoyed this adventure. You can follow Toby Neighbors on Facebook:

http://www.facebook.com/pages/Toby-Neighbors-Author/210621225652500

Read on for samples from Toby's other great novels.

Third Prince Sample

Prologue

Outside the tower where queen Mirahain lay gripped by the rigors of child birth, the wind was howling a lonely tune. Mirahain herself was howling occasionally, as the contractions grew more intense and more frequent. In a small room, down a dimly lit corridor, sat the High King of Belanda, Realm of the West. He was a large man, with weathered skin and thick, brown hair that covered his head and cheeks and chin. He sat before a fire, kindled more to gaze upon than to warm the room. In fact, King Belhain was fond of the cold, and often wore summer trappings all through winter. Between the chilly temperature of the room, the hypnotic light from the fire, and the howls from without and within the castle, no one was comfortable. This was Graeson Tower, the place where royalty was born. It was a single tower, four sided, built on a cliff that stood over the sea. There were no battlements, no moat, just the tower. And no one could remember how long it had stood, nor how long kings and queens had been born there.

Inside the room with King Belhain were two men, one was tall and thick through the chest, the other was smaller, slimmer and stooped just slightly. The tall man wore a tight fitting leather vest and breeches. He had black boots with fur spilling out of the tops and his arms were bare except for his left forearm which was wrapped in long leather strap. He stood leaning against the wall and watching the door. The other man was wrapped in a plain brown cloak. His hair and beard were streaked with gray, and he leaned on a tall wooden staff. His gaze was fixed on the fire.

No one spoke in the room, there was little to be said. King Belhain had two sons, his legacy was insured. The only anxiousness this night was for a healthy child and a safe delivery. The king's nurse claimed the child would come in spring, but it was barely midwinter, and the pains had begun two days ago. The journey to Graeson Tower had been short, but now the minutes shuffled slowly. The nurse had said they should wait as long as possible to have the

257

child, but Belhain knew better. He believed the body of his wife knew best, and now was the time. Still, there was something in the air, like a current of cold water running through a warm creek in the summer sun. Everyone knew something was wrong. The man in the gray cloak had spoken of omens, but the king had rebuked him. There would be no talk in his presence of the old ways, of superstitions, of religions that had once been the central beliefs of the Western Realm. Belhain believed in the Way of the One God, to him all else was blasphemy.

Then, without warning, there was a third cry rising above the wind outside and the sounds of labor from the queen's apartment. It was a strong cry, and it brought a twinkle to the eyes of the king, and a smile to the face of the warrior. It wasn't long until a knock was heard at the wooden door and Belhain nodded to the man watching it.

Outside was a small girl, no more than fifteen years old, she bowed low before the king and waited for him to acknowledge her.

"Well, what is it?" He asked kindly.

The girl never looked up. "Boy," she replied.

"Another boy, you are blessed by the One God," said the warrior.

"Is he healthy?" rasped the man in the cloak.

The girl did not speak, she did not look up.

"Well," inquired the king, "is there something wrong?"

"He is healthy, my lord, but he is marked."

The girl's voice trembled as she spoke. The smile disappeared from the face of the warrior. A hiss, barely audible, escaped from the cloaked man. The King's face hardened, but did not change. He waved a hand at the girl and she backed out of the room.

"Lord, I must go and see this child," said the man with the staff.

"Why? A mark means nothing."

"But Lord?"

Then another knock at the door. The warrior moved to the door, his right hand drawing a curved dagger from a sheath hidden at his waist.

Outside was a woman, her hair was long and gray and her hands were wringing a dirty clothe between them. It was the king's nurse, the one who had taken care of him as a child and the only person the king trusted with his own children. She had delivered all the King's children.

"Sire, there are two," she said softly.

"And?"

"One is a boy, he is marked. The second is a girl. They are both small but healthy."

"Where is the mark?" asked the king.

"It is over the child's heart."

Another hiss escaped the cloaked man before the king could reply.

"It means nothing, Tooles!" he shouted. "Marks, stars, animals, the weather, they are all meaningless. Our choices make us who we are."

"And what is your choice for this child?" said Tooles, his voice as grating as metal on stone. "Will he eat at your table? Will you be able to hide the fact that he is marked? Will you-"

"Enough!" said the king.

An awkward silence fell over the room. No one moved except Tooles, whose hands fumbled under his cloak. Finally, the nurse spoke again.

"I am having the third Prince cleaned, then I shall send him to you. You should see him before you make a decision."

The nurse backed out of the room and the warrior closed the door after her. The king stood and reached for the ceiling, stretching the stiff muscles in his back and arms. So there had been something in the air after all. As much as King Belhain hated to admit it there were things he couldn't explain away. In fact that wasn't the problem, after all, the One God could never fully be understood. The problem lay with the perceptions of others. What would people think of a birth mark, especially on the boy's heart? Tooles would certainly make the worst of it. Others, like Fairan, the king's personal guard, would overlook it completely in time. Still, he had to make a decision. The third Prince would undoubtedly effect his entire family, perhaps even the kingdom. The king prayed for wisdom as they waited for the baby.

It wasn't long before a third knock on the door was heard and the young girl was back. She held a bundle in her arms that whimpered softly. The king held out his large hands and took the baby. Fairan and Tooles stepped in closely to see the child. Belhain unwrapped the soft birthing clothes and beckoned for light. The young girl lifted a torch from its place at the wall and held it close to the baby. The mark covered the boy's left breast and was a dark red color.

Tooles gasped as he saw it, "Lord, it is the falcon."

The king looked intensely at the birthmark. It did indeed look like a perched falcon, it's wings enfolding it like royal robes.

"It is unquestionable that this child shall rule Belanda." said Tooles.

"Shut your mouth!" snarled the king. "There is only one way that will happen and I will not allow it. He is a prince but only a third prince. His brothers shall not die prematurely just so that this one may rule."

"Lord," said Fairan, "What is your wish for this boy?"

"No one knows of him but the six of us here." replied the High King. "Fairan, you must take him to the monastery at Aquista, in the mountains of Keldar. There he shall live his days in meditation and reflection of the One God. We shall announce only the birth of his sister. And we shall record his birth, and his fate, only in the Royal Chronicles."

"And his name, my lord?" croaked Tooles.

"He shall be Elkain, but you are to call him Kain when you take him to the brothers at Aquista."

"I understand," said the guard.

"Girl, take this one back to his mother and tell her I shall be in shortly." ordered the King. "Fairan, be ready to leave in one hour."

"Aye, Lord."

Chapter 1

Kain opened his eyes. He had been sleeping under the shade of an enormous tree. The weather was uncommonly warm for the Keldar mountain region. From where Kain lay, he could see the stone walls of the Monastery that had been his home for the last 26 years, rising above the ridge. He had hiked out to this spot for a bit of reading, which was really an excuse to stretch his legs and use the muscles that were never used as he spent day after day in the scriptorium hand copying the manuscripts that were brought to the Monastery from all over Belanda. Today he had gotten away, but there was a strange sound, an odd rumbling. In fact, he felt the sound more than heard it, but he was still groggy from his nap and it took a moment for him recognize what he was hearing. Horses, and from the sound of it they were in a hurry.

Kain got to his feet and brushed off the grass that was clinging to him. He felt anxious, exposed, but he wasn't sure why. He had never really felt fear before, not like this. There had been fear of punishment as he grew up, but never this unknown, life threatening kind of fear, and he wondered at the sensation. He felt his skin begin to tingle as the hair on his arms and the back of his neck stood up. He shook the feeling off, he had no reason to fear anyone or anything. He was a monk, a scribe. He had read of raiders, of thieves who maimed and killed others for money and valuables, but he had no money, nothing of value except the book he carried.

All further thought and fear vanished as the sight of two riders appeared over the ridge. One was the High Prefect of Kain's order, the other was dressed in armor and carried a flag with a dark red falcon on a gold background. Kain held back the smile that appeared as he watched the High Prefect bouncing along on the back of the horse. The monastery kept no horses, preferring to travel on foot. Something must be happening for the High Prefect to ride with this stranger.

As the two men approached they reined in their horses. The High Prefect quickly dismounted, and said, "Ah, Kain, there you are. I had no idea this ridge was so far away. But no matter, we have important news and this is as good a place as any for you to hear it."

The man in armor stayed on his horse, but removed his helmet. His hair was grey, what was left of it anyway. He had strong, sharp features, especially a scar that ran across his left check, from ear to nose.

"This is General Fairan, of the king's personal guard," continued the High Prefect. "In fact, the General was one of the King's closest advisers. He has news that you need to hear."

Kain looked from the High Prefect to the soldier and waited.

"This may be difficult for you to hear, but you must," Fairan said, his voice was deep but soft. "Many years ago, I brought you here, to this Monastery. It was your father's wish that you live out your days here in peace. Unfortunately, that cannot be."

Kain frowned at this but said nothing.

"Your name is not Kain, but Elkain. You are a prince of Belanda. You had two older brothers, but they and your father, High King Belhain, were murdered."

At this last statement the old soldier's voice broke. His face was as hard as stone, but his eyes watered as he spoke of his king, "They were on pilgrimage to the church in Hollist, and were attacked. You and your sister are all that is left of the royal family. You because no one knows you exist, and your sister, because she is part of the plan Derrick of Westfold has for becoming king of Belanda."

Kain wasn't sure what to think. He had always been told that his family had dedicated him to the service of the One God, but he knew nothing of them. He certainly had never been told he was a prince.

"I don't... I mean... I think you have the wrong person," said Kain.

"I have met General Fairan only once before," said the High Prefect. "I cared for his horse while he met with the High Prefect Alton, years ago. I never knew his name, or why he came, but he did bring you here."

"I can prove that you are the Third Prince." stated the warrior. "You have a mark on your left breast. It looks rather like a falcon."

"That doesn't prove anything. If you brought me here as a baby then you would know I have that mark."

"Your birth was recorded in the royal chronicles. You shall come with me to the Royal City, and there we shall prove your birthright. And you shall be made king."

"This is the craziest thing I have ever heard. I'm not leaving Aquista. I'm no king."

"Your father thought that you would respond this way. He wrote this shortly after you were born, in case our worst fears came true. I will leave you with your priest to read it, then we must set out for Royal City." Fairan wheeled his mount around and trotted some distance away.

"Prefect Mantos, is this some kind of a joke?"

"I am not sure what it is, but I do remember the General bringing you here. We were all told that your family had dedicated you to God, but that was all we ever knew. The General came with a letter from the King's councilor Vestpin Tooles, verifying what you have just heard. It has the royal seal and I am afraid I have no choice but to send you with him."

Kain looked at the High Prefect with astonishment. "But if I leave I can never return, or have you forgotten the statutes of our order?"

"I have not forgotten. Nor have I forgotten that we are to obey the High King, and I cannot find any reason to doubt that General Fairan is a legitimate member of King Belhain's council. Now if what he says is true, and the High King has been killed along with his sons, who is to rule us? Belanda will almost certainly be divided by civil war. Perhaps this is the hand of God?"

Kain was boiling with emotions. He was so unsure of what to do he looked at the only thing available, the letter Fairan had given him. It was a stiff parchment, sealed with wax, then bound by purple ribbon and stamped with the High King's seal.

Kain turned it over and over in his hands.

"You should read it," said the High Prefect.

Kain broke the seals and unfolded the parchment.

Dear Elkain,

Please forgive me for keeping your birthright a secret. The rigors of ruling the Western Realm have not been easy. We have made great progress in shinning the light of the One God in Belanda, but there are many, including our enemies, who still hold to the old ways. You were born with a mark, many still believe such physical signs come from the spiritual realms. Your mark being what it was, I feared for the life of your brothers, although I have prayed often for strength and forgiveness. Likewise, I feared the implication that our enemies would make about the mark being a curse, or weakness, thereby thrusting us into unnecessary violence. And so I sent you to my old friend Alton, High Prefect of the order of Aquista, in the hopes that you could live out your life in peace and reflection of the goodness of the One God. But as you are now reading this letter, it is certain that I am dead, and your brothers also. I ask two things, one that you will attempt to understand my actions, I did what I did out of love for you and for our family. Second, that you will be strong in the character that comes with your royal blood, and put the needs of the kingdom above your own. I need not remind you that the One God is always with you, but your mother's thoughts and love, as well as mine, were ever on you as well.

Belhain, High King of Belanda,

Realm of the West

Kain handed the letter to the Prefect Mantos and after the older man had read it, they looked at each other.

"I don't know what to say?" stammered the High Prefect.

"Nor do I, but I guess I will go with Fairan. If nothing else, I must find out who my parents really were. I'll never be happy until I do."

"I understand. We will all be in prayer for you."

"Thanks." Kain said as he waved to General Fairan.

The warrior again brought his horse under the shade of the tree near the High Prefect and Kain.

"I'll go," Kain said.

"Good, we leave at once."

Chapter 2

Kain rode back to the Monastery with Fairan and began to pack his things. There wasn't much really, he lived in a small room, with a bed, table and 2 chairs. He did have books, but he would send for them later. He packed his new set of robes and a few other personal items in a bag, rolled up his blankets and tied them, then walked out into the sunshine of the courtyard. There were the monks and prefects of the Monastery, assembled to say their good-byes. He hadn't realized until that moment how much he would miss them. He thought that this should be an amazing time of excitement, he had often dreamed of life outside the serenity of Aquista, but now that his departure was imminent, a dark cloud of unspeakable sadness enveloped him. He looked at the faces around him and realized that he did not want to leave.

One of the monks approached Kain with a bag full of bread, cheese, fruit and some dried meat.

"It isn't much, but it will keep you full until you reach Royal City," said the man.

Kain nodded and took the bag, but did not speak. He felt as if the sadness within him was welling up, threatening to spill out if he opened his mouth.

Just then the bell tower began to ring out the call to afternoon prayers. Kain heard the High Prefect's voice shouting above the bells.

"Wait, do not go inside yet. Today, we honor one of our own." The portly prefect was waddling through the crowd. He held a long, slender object wrapped in a crimson cloth. He approached Kain and motioned for the crowd to gather in close.

"It has been a long time since Saint Onnasus brought the good news of the One God to the Realm of the West. It is said that he sailed across the oceans for two months before landing on our beautiful shores. Most men of Belanda know that Onnasus was a man of great learning, and of greater compassion. But, he was also a warrior. And understandably so, this land was once, and in many ways still is, a pagan land, hostile to the truth we cling to and cherish. Many of you have seen and even copied the Scrolls of Truth which he brought us. But that was not the only token that has survived the many years. I have here the Sword of Onnasus."

With a flourish the High Prefect pulled the cloth from the sword. It shone brilliant in the afternoon sunlight. The scabbard was emerald green, with foreign characters inscribed in crimson down its length. It was a straight sword, not curved like the Oddolan weapons from the East, and it was narrow, unlike the broad swords of Belanda. The handle was long enough to be grasped by two hands and wrapped in leather that was once dyed red, but was now faded into a dark brown. The hand guard was small and square, and looked to be made of a black metal.

"Onnasus, it is said," continued the High Prefect, "won many converts with his skill as a swordsman. His movements were precise and overcame the brute strength of the native Belandians. And although this weapon is slight, it is as strong as any sword, as strong as the heart that wields it. For countless years it has been kept by the High Prefect of our order. It has been passed down from generation to generation with this admonition, that one day a hand will take this sword. And that day has come. I can think of no better use for the sword of Onnasus, than in the hands of our future king."

There was much murmuring among the crowd, and then, as the High Prefect placed the sword in Kain's shaking hands, a great shout went up with applause from the throng. And at that moment the weeping came. But Kain was no longer sad, in fact a wave of love and support like he had never felt in his life, lifted him on it's crest. The crowd began to put their hands on him. Familiar faces flowed past him with hugs, admonitions, and prayers. It felt like a dream, but tangible.

Kain had never known the close love of parents, but now he saw the pride and joy on the faces of the older monks. There were tears of joy on many faces, but one face in particular stood out - it was Tellis, a monk the same age as Kain, and a close friend. While Kain had studied and mastered the art of the scriptorium, Tellis had chosen the path of the priesthood. Both had known that one day soon Tellis would leave the Monastery to travel through Belanda, teaching the ways of the One God. Now Kain was leaving, it was strangely sad.

"This was not how I imagined our parting," said Tellis.

"Nor I, but you can come to me, in Royal City. I will need a good friend."

"I will, I promise."

Kain continued his goodbyes, and soon Fairan was waiting with the horses. With the monks and prefects watching, Kain mounted the horse Fairan held for him. They rode out through the gate, and as Kain looked back over his shoulder, he was surprised to see the men he had lived with all his life, moving off to different chores as if nothing had happened. He watched them, some walking to the chapel, others to the scriptorium, some gathering tools for the garden.

"Life goes on."

Kain turned, surprised to see that Fairan was watching him.

"They act as if nothing has happened."

"Isn't that the life they chose. To live in a world set apart, dedicating themselves to their god."

"Yes, but... but I thought this moment would be different. If feels normal, like any other day, and yet I am leaving all I have known behind."

"Sometimes momentous occasions only feel that way when remembered," Fairan had a distant look in his eye. "The day I brought you here, that was a normal day, but now I look back on it with sadness. It is unfortunate that your family was denied you, and now the life you were promised is denied. And the road ahead will not be an easy one. Are you familiar with the sword?"

Kain looked down at the gleaming weapon that lay across his thighs, "I did not know it existed before today."

"Not that sword," Fairan exclaimed. "Do you know how to use one?"

Kain shook his head, "This is the first one I have ever touched."

The big man grunted, but said nothing else. In fact, they road for over an hour without speaking. Kain was lost in his thoughts, trying to get his bearings and trying to stay on the horse.

Finally, Fairan broke the silence.

"I don't suppose you've done much riding?"

"No. We don't keep horses at the Monastery."

"I see, well, we'll stop under that tree up ahead and take a look at that new sword of yours. We have a lot to do and not much time to do it in. Are you familiar with the law of Kingship in Belanda?"

"No."

"Well, I am no teacher, but I do know that the King rules with the Council of Nobles. Together they make decisions on the governance of the people of Belanda. In the last few years, Derrick of Westfold has slowly increased his position on the Council. Now he charges that with your family dead, he should be named King. He has secured the loyalty of the priest at Royal City, and together they are trying to force your sister into marrying Derrick."

"How can they do that?" Kain asked.

"She has no family left to speak for her. The priest has claimed that right in the name of your father and has pledged her to marry the man who is responsible for the deaths of your parents and brothers."

"Surely not, a priest of the One God would never stoop to such low handed and sinful practices. If he has pledged my sister to this man then it must have been her father's wish."

"Don't be a fool! You have lived your life in a place of innocence. All at the Monastery are pledged to the same god, the same way of life. They have the accountability of one another. It is different for the rest of us, we live for different purposes. We do not have the accountability that you have lived with. The priest at Royal City has grown in power due to the influence of your father and his dedication to that religion. And as often happens to people who taste power, the priest longs for more of it. He has brokered a deal with Derrick, I am sure of it."

"What proof do you have?" Kain asked. He was growing angry, both with the callous and cynical claims of the warrior, and the despicable ways of the people he was going to lead. "How do I know who to trust? You could be setting me against them for your own purposes. I don't know you any better than them."

Fairan reined in his horse. They had reached the tree and the big man stepped down from his mount and tied the animal securely to a low branch.

"You don't, but you will in time. I was pledged to your father, much the same as you were to your god. We grew up together, fought together. I promised him my sword, but I was not there to die with him." A hardness touched the features in Fairan's face. "But we can discuss that later. For now, come down and take a rest."

"I'm not tired." Kain said.

"But you will be sore tomorrow. We will take our time until you become used to riding. I knew a priest once, your father made him ride from the lake in Sulhain all the way to Royal City, a hard day's ride. The priest was bed ridden for week afterward. He never walked the same after that. He complained of the pain until he died. I do not want to push you too hard."

Kain nodded and stepped down from the horse.

"Now, take off your robes."

"What?"

Fairan grinned. "You'll need to wear different clothes than those of the Monastery." He reached up into the shaded branches of the tree and pulled down a large knap sack. "Here," he said, "try this on. It may be a little tight. I wasn't expecting you to be quite so thick in the belly."

Kain's face burned with embarrassment. It was true that he was a little pudgy, but when a person spends all their time at a desk copying manuscripts there just isn't much time for exercise. He pulled off the robe and pulled on a stiff leather vest.

Kain laced the vest together tightly with a brown cord.

"You have the build of your father, and don't worry, we'll work off that baby fat soon."

Again Kain burned with shame. He was beginning to not like the warrior at all. He had never paid much attention to his appearance before. Mirrors were frowned upon as a vanity at Aquista. He had a little hand held mirror to shave with, he had packed it in his bed roll.

"Here is your mail," Fairan said, pulling a shirt of metal ringlets over Kain's head. "This is why the leather is so stiff. The metal can stop an arrow, even some blades, but not the impact. So be careful, and always wear the leather vest. It will take a while to get used to, but since you'll be riding and sleeping in it, I imagine you'll take to it soon."

Fairan then slipped a dark blue tunic over the mail, the sleeves were loose, but had straps attached to the cuffs. Fairan proceed to tie these around Kain's wrists, over the ends of the mail shirt.

"This keeps your sleeves from sliding up and down your arms when you raise your sword." Fairan explained. Finally, he placed a dull gray, metal helmet on Kain's head. The inside was leather and although it was heavy, it fit rather comfortably. It was an open face helmet, reaching from mid-forehead down to the top of his neck with slight curves for the ears.

"That's called a skull cap. It was your dad's, and your oldest brother Fairhain's too."

"My brother Fairhain? Am I really a prince?"

"Of course."

"It seems so hard to believe. I have seen the royal family, but only from a distance. The queen commissioned several books from the Monastery. I had the privilege of working on most of them. She even came and watched me work once. I was so distracted by her presence I had to throw out that day's work."

"She was your mother and although you were sent away at birth, they never stopped loving you. In fact, your father gave you the life he had longed for. He was very devoted to your god."

"But you aren't?"

"I don't..." there was a pause as Fairan searched for the words. "My beliefs," the last word was spoken awkwardly, "are personal."

"Now," said the warrior firmly changing the subject, "step into these."

He held out a pair of leather leggings, like pants with an open seat and fly, held together with a thick belt which was wider at the back than the front. Kain pulled them over his breeches which were lightly woven wool. Fairan buckled the belt rather snugly and with all that Kain was wearing he felt as if he could barely move.

"You are beginning to look like a man." said Fairan.

"I feel as stiff as a scarcrow in all this. How do you ever fight in it all?"

"You'll get used to it. Now you need weapons. Let's see that sword."

Kain withdrew the sword from it's scabbard. The metal rang and the blade gleamed. It was edged razor sharp on only one side. The blade was long and did not taper as the broadswords of Belanda did. The end was angular with the sharpened side ending a mere inch before the other and turning stiffly to the sharpened point. The non lethal edge was polished to a mirror shine which gradually faded to a cold gray hinting at the danger of the blade.

"How does it feel to you?" Fairan asked.

Kain swung the sword, slashing awkwardly and thrusting.

"It feels good, I guess." Kain said.

"A sword must feel better than good. A sword must feel like it is part of you, an extension of the deadliness of who you are."

"I'm not very deadly," Kain interrupted.

"Not yet, but you will be. I think that blade suits you. A king's sword must be special, it is the symbol of his power. Yours is unique and if it is as good a sword as the High Prefect claimed, it will suit you well. We will stop at a place I know and be sure that it is good. Now, here are the weapons you will keep on your body.

For the next half hour Fair displayed and demonstrated various weapons for Kain. The first was a dagger, as long as Kain's hands end to end and kept in a leather sheath. The blade was an inch wide at the hilt and narrowed steadily into a dangerous point. There was a loop in the leather belt for it. Next was a set of three knives, each about half as long as the dagger and sharpened on only one side. One was strapped onto each calf of Kain's legs and one tucked into the belt at his back. Fairan demonstrated the usefulness of stabbing with the knives or throwing them. Then there was a belt of black canvas, like the sail of a ship. It fastened in the back and hung low on Kain's hips, over the scabbard of his sword and the sheath of his dagger. In the front were small, wedge shaped pockets. Into each pocket fit a steel lump, shaped like an egg with one end slightly larger than the other, Fairan called them Mogs. The sides of the Mogs were smooth. Fairan said they could fracture a man's skull if thrown hard enough.

Then, with Kain fully armed, they added the weapons that he would carry on horseback. First was a quiver of arrows hung at the back left hand edge of the saddle. The bow was shorter than normal, Fairan explained the need for its size.

"A long bow would get hung up on your saddle and gear as your aim moved from one side of your horse to another. With this shorter bow, you have the freedom to aim in any direction. The arrows are shorter too, but you'll not be needing much distance if you are fighting from your horse.

"The next weapon is an extra sword, that is hung on your horse's left shoulder. Should something happen to your sword, perhaps wedging in bone and being wrenched from your hand, then you draw this one. On your horse's right shoulder is a battle axe."

The axe was as tall as Kain's forearm from elbow to fingertip. The blade was as wide as a big man's hand, with the edge curving around until the points almost touched the handle. Opposite the axe head was a thick metal spike.

"Now the axe will give weight to your attack, but it will lodge in a person easily. Finally, you'll have a lance." Fairan held out a staff that was as tall as Kain was. One end narrowed to a point and was covered with metal rather than having the tip attached onto a head of its own. "The lance will kill a man using the momentum of your horse. Most mounted knights carry a lance of some sort.

The lance is deadly but takes an exacting amount of skill. Most knights train with lances from the time they are very young boys. The danger of using the lance is that it can easily unseat you, leaving you vulnerable to attack. If you ever have to use your lance, hold it loosely. It would be better to lose the lance than your horse. And we also attach our colors to the lance."

At that, Fairan tied a purple flag with the red falcon onto the lance. Then he slid the butt end of the lance through a set of hoops on the right side of Kain's saddle. The flag hung down neatly from the end under the horse's head.

"I'm armed for war it appears," said Kain. "Is all this really necessary?"

"Yes!" Fairan's rely was heated. "Do you not understand that you are the last remaining heir to the throne of Belanda? That alone makes you are target. One man is a seemingly small obstacle to a throne. Your enemies have already shown that they will not hesitate to murder you. They murdered your mother. They killed every servant, every soldier that rode with them that day. And that is no small fact considering that your family rode with ten Royal soldiers, your father was a master with the sword, and your brothers were raised with weapons. A troop of thirteen, seasoned warriors could only be overcome by a sizeable force. No raiding party is that big. No gang of killers would have risked it. The only people with the men and motive are nobles. And the only one with the audacity to do it is Derrick of Westfold. He is a dangerous man as you will learn soon enough."

They mounted their horses then and began to ride.

"We'll ride for another hour and then make camp. I want to get off this road as soon as possible. I know the river path, we'll take it soon."

"This is really too much. You said earlier that no one knows about me. They all think the royal family is dead. How do you propose that I become King?"

"That is a good question. One we will have to deal with soon enough, but we shall not have to deal with it alone. I am taking you to a man named Tooles, he was your father's chief advisor at one time. He has returned to his ancestral home… and religion." At the last word Fairan eyed Kain nervously.

"He does not worship the One True God?"

"No. And you are going to find that there are many of our people who only follow your god in name. Their lives are still lived according to an older standard. That is why you were sent away."

"What do you mean?"

Fairan grimaced. "This is difficult to explain. Not everyone was raised by priests."

"Monks and Prefects," Kain corrected.

"Yes, well, most people live in two worlds, sometimes even more. You will find that people will behave in the way they think you expect. And most people will worship the One God at church and follow the old gods at home."

"What does any of that have to do with me?"

"I'm getting to that," Fairan said irritably. "I told you I was no teacher. I fumble with the words and have no patience with students."

"Sorry," Kain said.

"No. You do not have to be sorry to me. You are the Third Prince of Belanda. I am nothing. I am a man without honor. A warrior who was absent during the battle. Never be sorry to me."

Kain nodded. It saddened him to see the big warrior dealing himself so lowly. It was obvious that Fairan was a man of honor, but also obvious that he blamed himself for the king's death.

"Well, you have the mark." Fairan continued. "And not just any mark, but a falcon, over your heart. Many people would say you are marked by the gods to rule Belanda, or perhaps cursed by your birthright. Either way, if you had stayed with your family, people would have talked. Whether your father and mother believed it or not, surely you can see the strain it would have put on your family. Your brothers would have resented you, perhaps feared you."

"Why?"

"Because people would say that you were destined to be king. The only way for that to happen would be if your brothers were dead. And not only your family. Rumors of that sort would reach the ears of your enemies. They would see you as a weakness to exploit, either by superstition or through your father's love."

Kain was silent for moment. There was simply too much to comprehend. He had grown up in a place of utter security. There was never talk of war or fighting, never talk of fear. In fact, Kain could not remember a grievance among the brothers of Aquista ever. It seemed naïve to think that way, but it was the world he knew. Now he was being called on to rule a world he knew nothing about.

"Here is where we leave the road," Fairan said.

"Is it really necessary?" Kain asked.

"I do not believe we would survive if we stayed on the road."

"But you said no one knows about me."

"That is true, but Derrick knows me. He knows I will avenge the death of King Belhain. He knows I will not rest until those that raised arms against the royal family lay cold and dead, food for the crows."

"But, do they know you are here?"

"Yes, I have been watched for many days. I believe Derrick seeks to know what I know. We will stop soon and make ourselves ready."

"Ready for what?" Kain asked.

"You shall see."

At that they fell into another silence, but this one was different. Kain wanted to talk, to know more. But the cold hand of fear was pressing down on him so that conversation would not come. He felt a tingle in the air as fear crept back into his heart. And there was a heightening of his senses. The air felt cooler on his skin and he felt it on his hands, on his neck, even on his eyelashes although the breeze was light. He could hear the sounds of the horses hooves on the dirt path, every creak of their saddles, every clink of the metal. And he could hear the sounds of the wilderness around him, the river in the distance, the breeze as it swayed the leaves, the animals scurrying through the underbrush. He could smell the dampness of the forest where the sun could not shine through the canopy of leaves overhead to dry the nightly dew. He could see everything so clearly, the colors were so vivid. He could not remember ever seeing leaves or grass or anything as green as those of the forest. He began to notice things, the texture of the bark on the trees, the way certain places in the grass looked trodden down, even the size of the horses they were riding, and the way the muscles flexed and rolled under their sleek hides.

Soon they came to a rise in the path they were following. The terrain rolled for some distance until finally they came to the top of a small hill. Here the trees thinned out and they could see far into the forest. To one side of the path a rocky cliff face jutted out of the earth and rose as high as the trees around them.

"This is it," said Fairan. "We'll make camp here tonight."

"So soon? I mean, I know you want to take things slow, but there is probably an hour of daylight left. Are you sure you want to stop?"

"Yes, now let me take your horse."

Fairan took his own horse down one side of the hill, right next to the cliff face. Then he led Kain's down the other.

"What are you doing with the horses?" Kain asked.

"It is very likely that we will be attacked tonight. Luckily for us we have a few things in our favor. First, we are expecting them, so if they are counting on surprise being an advantage for them, it won't be. Secondly, we have chosen the place for the fight, and this is a good place. We'll be able to see them coming and if they try to flank us from either side, the horses should alert us."

"I've heard of guard dogs, but not guard horses," Kain said somewhat in jest.

"It is a trick I learned from your father. Finally, I don't believe that they will risk killing you. They do not know who you are yet. They will come to capture you and kill me, thinking that you can tell them my plans."

"And that is an advantage?"

"Yes, considering you've never held a sword. Now let me show you a few things."

Fairan drew his sword and demonstrated as he talked.

"If a man comes at you with his sword raised above his head, which is a foolish thing to do, wait for him to strike at you with your own sword held low, like this." Fairan demonstrated. "Then simply step aside and slash your blade across his body. Leave your sword in its scabbard and practice it a few times."

Kain stepped in front of Fairan and the older man raised his sword above his head. They practiced the move in slow motion first and then gradually sped it up.

"Now you'll be tempted to watch your enemy's sword."

"That makes sense," Kain said.

"But don't do it. Always watch your opponent's eyes. If you follow his sword you'll be fooled by it. A man's eyes will reveal his plan. Now if he comes at you with his sword held low, but pointed at the sky," again Fairan demonstrated, "his attack will be obvious, he'll have to draw it back to strike with any power. So set your feet like this, with your right foot a little farther forward than your left."

Kain stood as Fairan instructed.

"Now always keep your sword low. A swordsman always attacks low first, it is much harder to avoid a low blow and it will force your enemy to parry with his own weapon. Now I am going to show you a very basic strike that will work against most fighters. Hopefully you'll live long enough to realize that most men are given a sword and expected to use it with no training. Your nobles will have grown up with military training. But most others have not. So block with your sword only when you have to. If you can avoid the blow, then your sword is free to strike. If you have to block the strike of your opponent, then it is wiser to wait for a particular moment to switch from defensive combat to offensive. Now the strike you are waiting for is from high to low, again, just like before, if you can avoid it do so and slash across the body. If you have to defect it, then swing from the side. If your parry is over handed then you can swing over his sword as soon as his momentum carries his sword away from your body. If for some reason you end up blocking his sword above your head in an underhanded move," once again Fairan demonstrated, "then allow his sword to continue down, but push it away from your body. Then as his sword slides down your blade, step forward and slash as soon as your weapon is cleared of his."

And so they practiced. The sound of metal on metal rang through the forest. The Sword of Onnasus very quickly became comfortable in Kain's hands. He began to understand what Fairan was saying about the sword being an extension of a person, and as he put his mind to the task of learning, the fear that had crept into his mind was forgotten. He was amazed at how fast, agile and strong the warrior was. Fairan drilled Kain until the moves were sure and then he began to speed up his attack. He moved faster and faster, striking hard. And as the light began to fail, Kain was sweating but effectively defending himself.

So they put away their weapons and gathered wood for a fire. They talked lightly as they prepared their meal, Fairan asking questions about growing up in the Monastery. The time passed quickly and although Kain had never been outside of the walls of the compound at Aquista after dark before, the fire and Fairan's presence keep the fear at bay. They were almost ready to eat when Kain heard the clink of metal far to his left. At once all the hair on his body stood straight up.

"Put on that skull cap." Fairan said, just as they heard a twig break somewhere in the darkness. "Pull that sword slowly, they can see us in the light of the fire. There's no need to let them know we're ready."

Kain, did as he was told. His heart was pumping as if he had run a race; it felt like it could break through his ribs. His skin felt cold and the urge to relieve his bladder was suddenly overwhelming.

Then it happened; there was a shout from down the hillside and four men rushed into the light from the campfire.

The Other Side Sample

Chapter 1

The hospital room was finally quiet. The only sounds were soft sniffles. Alex lay in the bed too weak to move. Leukemia had robbed him of his strength; the chemo therapy and radiation had stolen his hair and made the last year of his life miserable. He knew the end was coming soon. The doctors had stopped coming by several times a day. Now even the nurses had finally stopped coming in at all hours, they only made their appearance to administer medication. They had even removed most of the monitors and wires that had for so long been like shackles that held him in place. He hurt all over, but the pain medication made everything numb so that he only felt a dull sense of the agony the cancer was causing. He was fully awake and his mind was clear of the narcotic fog that usually made everything seem miles away. He couldn't remember the last time he was able to see and think so well.

"Mom," he said, his voice a horse whisper.

"Yes, sweetheart," said his mother.

She had been the one sniffling. She was doing a great job holding back the tidal wave of grief that she felt over losing Alex. She raised her head from the bedside where she had been leaning over in prayer. She was giving him a beautiful smile. Alex had always loved his mom. It had just been the two of them for most of his life. His father had been killed in the Iraqi war when Alex was just a little baby. Now she would be alone and that thought made Alex's hope that his death was near a little less welcome. But the suffering had gone on too long for any escape from the pain, nausea and constant poking and prodding by doctors, to be anything but a relief. His mom was being brave for him and it made him love her even more.

"I love you, Mom," he said.

"I love you too honey," she said as tears ran silently down her cheeks. "I love you so, so much my brave little man."

"I think it's almost time, Mom. I'm ready and then you can go home. You won't have to worry about me."

"Oh, Alex," she said and the sob caught in her throat.

"Do you have anything you want me to tell Dad when I see him?"

Alex's mother felt like her heart would stop from the pain. She couldn't speak for a moment. She had to hold back the gut wrenching sobs that she knew was coming. She didn't want to ruin this moment with her little boy. It might be her last.

"Oh, baby. Tell him that I love him. Tell him to take good care of you or else."

She tried to joke but it fell flat.

"Don't be sad for me, Mom. I'm so happy that it's finally going to be over."

"You aren't afraid?" she asked.

"No, I'll be in heaven and I'll be happy. No more tears, no more sickness, right?"

"That's right baby."

Alex felt sleep coming. He could no longer fight to stay awake or keep his mind clear. He didn't mind though, soon it would all be over and he would be free again. He had total faith that he would go to heaven, even though there was a little voice somewhere far back in his mind that said. . . what if? It *was* possible that there was no heaven, no God, no eternal life. He had to admit that his life could be ending forever. It didn't seem fair. He was only 12 years old after all. And four of his years had been spent battling leukemia. The last six months he had been confined to this hospital bed. So even if there was nothing after death, it would at least be a release from this pain.

"Hold my hand, Mom," he said. Then he fell asleep.

It took about two hours for his breathing to become labored. He fought for each breath and his mother thought it must be like trying to breathe through wet fabric. There was a gurgle in his rattling chest and his arms and legs twitched with the effort.

Fortunately Alex experienced none of the death pains his body was going through. His mind had pulled far into itself to escape the agony. He was in a deep coma only minutes before death, when he heard the sounds of a frantic battle around him. He tried to open his eyes and see what was happening but his eyes no longer seemed to obey him. He was sure he could hear it; there were growls and shouts and the clash of swords and shields. The shouting seemed to be in a foreign language that was almost musical. His death came now, right as the fighting seemed most intense. It was sudden, even though his mother would have said that she thought each of his desperate breaths for the past hour would have been his last. She had been praying frantically, begging for God to spare her only son, but her mind was constantly listening for the next breath to be sure her baby was still with her.

When Alex died he felt a snap and suddenly the pain and the fog of morphine was gone. He opened his eyes and sat up on the bed. The room was dim and although he could have looked at his ruined body or at his mother who was still holding his lifeless hand and praying silently as she shook from sobs of grief, his attention was riveted by two beings standing at the foot of his bed. He thought of them as beings, not creatures, because it was obvious that they were not made of flesh and blood. Both were glowing, one much brighter than the other, but both luminous. The brighter of the two was smiling, his face the size of an adult but clear and bright, almost anxious; like a child on his way to the park. There were no worry lines, no age or defect in what Alex thought of as skin. His teeth were perfectly uniform, his hair was thick and full, falling to his shoulders but not a strand was out of place. He stood at least six feet tall and looked in every way like a man except for the hint of wings at his back. He wore a cloak open at the chest revealing the angular lines of muscle. His arms were bare and his hands were folded on the foot rail of Alex's bed.

The other being looked tired. His face was smooth like his companion but his jaw was set hard and his eyes pierced into Alex. This being had only a garment around his waist. His upper body seemed to be covered with armor of some type that flowed over each shoulder and angled down across his stomach so that it formed an X across his body. His arms though, were bare and muscular.

"Greetings mighty warrior!" spoke the dimmer of the two beings.

"Alex Napleton," said the brighter being. "It is my pleasure to greet you. I am Felix and this is Mirdoc. We're here to help you."

"Help with what?" Alex asked.

"Your transition," said Felix.

"It's time to make a decision, Alex," said Mirdoc. "Your mortal life is over."

"So I'm dead," Alex said, a little afraid to hear the words spoken out loud but confident that he knew the answer already.

"Yes, we lost the battle for your life," said Mirdoc.

"The battle?" Alex asked. "You mean the fighting I heard was real?"

Mirdoc nodded.

"I thought I heard singing or something," Alex said.

"That is the language of the Bright Ones," said Felix. "You are speaking it now."

"I am? It sounds like English to me."

"That's because English is all you have known. But now you shall see things as they truly are. However, you must make a choice. It is time for you to leave your mortal life and move into eternity."

"We could use a brave warrior like you," Mirdoc said. "I know this is a lot to ask of a twelve year old, but we need you."

"Need me for what?"

"In the battle of course," Mirdoc said passionately. "The Dark Ones have grown strong again in recent years. There are fewer and fewer of us left to hold back the tide of evil that threatens to engulf Earth."

"You see, Alex Napleton," said Felix soothingly. "When a mortal dies he must make a choice between moving into eternity or staying to fight alongside the armies of heaven. It is an important choice because once it is made it cannot be unmade. If you choose to stay and fight, then you will remain here in the universe until the end of time when the King of Light and Laughter comes and reclaims all that he has made. Likewise, if you choose to step now into eternity, you cannot return to this existence until all is remade. So, now you must choose."

284

"I'm not sure I understand," Alex said. "You're saying that when people die they have to decide whether they go to heaven or stay on earth?"

"Well, not everyone has a choice of heaven, but essentially that is correct. Those, like yourself, who believe in the Great Truth, Father of All Life, the Singer of the Universe, can choose at their death to join him immediately. That is their right as his son or daughter. Likewise those who have hardened their hearts and clung to the lie of the Great Deceiver, their choice is to move immediately into the place of the dead."

"Who would choose that?"

"There are some," said Felix sadly. "Some people who do not savor the evil of their lives or despise the goodness of the Great Truth. They do not wish to spread their vile influence on the innocent and so step into the eternity that awaits them."

"But most don't," said Mirdoc. "Most of them are insane or driven mad by the realization of their deaths. They are turned loose by the Dark Ones to wreak havoc on the world. That's why we need you. It seems that as their power grows, now their forces swell and ours dwindle."

"But what can I do? I'm just a kid."

"No, you are much more than that," said Mirdoc, his face glowing more brightly as he talked. "You are a great strategist, a strong, creative, man of valor."

"No, I'm just a kid," Alex argued.

"You used to be a child," Felix said. "Now you are an eternal being like us, with no age and no limits. But you are right in one respect. You have only the experience of a twelve year old mortal. Your life was tragically cut short, so you must continue to become the person you were created to be in eternity or in the great war. It is your choice."

Alex thought for a minute. He didn't quite understand what was being offered to him. It wasn't exactly as neat and orderly as he had learned in church or as his mom talked with him toward the end of his life in the hospital. He had had real questions, the kind that made the volunteers at his church a little nervous. He had wanted to know about what happened when a person died. His mother had taught him as much as she knew, even though it varied from what their priest had taught. What the hospital Chaplin said was even more different. Still, that was all moot now. Alex's mind was weighing his options. He wanted to see God, even though the he had always been frightened at the prospect of standing before his Maker knowing that God knows everything about him, every bad thought, every lie he ever told. But there was something about staying and fighting that appealed to him too. He couldn't put his finger on what it was, the thought was terrifying and exciting at the same time.

"Can you tell me more about staying here?" Alex asked.

"Of course," Felix said. "There is still time."

"We've been in a war," said Mirdoc, "ever since the Great Usurper turned against the Truth."

"I remember that from church," Alex said. "Didn't he take a third of the angels of heaven with him? If there are twice as many good angels as bad ones, why do you need my help?"

"It's not as cut and dry as that sounds," Mirdoc said. "Yes, the numbers add up as you say, but most of the Light Ones are messengers carrying the words of Truth to the faithful throughout the world. And there are those who stay and worship the Great King of Light and Laughter, serving around his throne and in his Holy Temple. Then there are others that are artists, great singers and composers, painters and creators, story tellers and more."

"The great warriors of the Light are few and many have been imprisoned," explained Felix.

"Imprisoned?" Alex asked. "What did they do wrong?"

"They did nothing wrong," said Felix. "But the enemy is actively opposing them and their defeat leads to imprisonment in chains of darkness. Now, it is time for you to choose."

"But I have more questions."

"I'm sorry, Alex Napleton, but this not a safe place."

"And time's short, kid," said Mirdoc.

"Well, can you answer one last question, just one?" Alex asked.

Felix and Mirdoc looked at each other and nodded.

"Can you tell me where I can find my dad?

Made in the USA
San Bernardino, CA
05 July 2015